"WHY TH[ ] DIDN'T YOU TELL ME YOU CAN'T SWIM?"

Pierce ground out as he drilled a look at Molly.

Molly's cheeks puffed up with unspoken epithets. "You ... you almost drowned me!"

"Drowned you? I probably just wrecked a good pair of boots tryin' to save you!"

"Save me? How dare you take credit for saving me when it was you who threw me into that water!" She raised herself onto her forearm, recoiling as Pierce's dog deposited a stout stick by her hand. "Why does he keep shoving this piece of wood at me?"

"He's a Newfoundland Retriever. He wants you to throw it."

She obliged.

Pierce threw his arm up to deflect the missile. "Not at me dammit!" It bounced off his wrist and fell to the ground. Pierce hurled the wood into the river and when he looked back at Molly she saw something so dangerous in his eyes that she boosted herself on her knees to run. He got to her first, dragging her backward against his chest.

His hand was cold against her cheek, but his mouth was hot. "Now," he said in a whisper that frightened as well as excited her, "show me how an 'Englishwoman' kisses ..."

The Irish Bride

The Irish Bride

Mary Mayer Holmes

Not for resale, for loan only

Copyright © 19__ by Mary Mayer Holmes
All Rights Reserved.

Popular Library® is a Registered Trademark of
Warner Books, Inc.

Cover art by Morgan Kane

Original Murder license was published by
Popular Library, a
unit of Warner Books.

Popular Library Edition/Original Edition

Printed in the United States of America
First Printing:

POPULAR LIBRARY

An Imprint of Warner Books, Inc.

A Warner Communications Company

POPULAR LIBRARY EDITION

Copyright © 1986 by Mary Mayer Holmes
All rights reserved.

Popular Library® is a registered trademark of
Warner Books, Inc.

Cover art by Morgan Kane

Popular Library books are published by
Warner Books, Inc.
666 Fifth Avenue
New York, N.Y. 10103

 A Warner Communications Company

Printed in the United States of America

First Printing: December, 1986

10 9 8 7 6 5 4 3 2 1

To the memory of Nana, Papa,
and Charlotte Lindemann—
who touched my life...
and left footprints on my heart

"There stands the City of Bangor, fifty miles up the Penobscot, at the head of navigation for vessels of the larger class, the principal lumber depot on this continent, with a population of twelve thousand, like a star on the edge of the night, still hewing at the forest of which it is built, already overflowing with the luxuries and refinements of Europe, and sending vessels to Spain, to England, and to the West Indies for its groceries—and yet only a few axe-men have gone 'up river' into the howling wilderness which feeds it."

—Henry David Thoreau

Prologue

In 1805 while other boys in the town of Bangor, Ireland, dreamed of becoming men, sixteen-year-old Duncan Blackledge dreamed of adventure on the high seas and excursions into lands that ripened with something other than the potato. The bond tethering him to Ireland was a weak one. His family had died in a cholera epidemic in 1795. He called no one kin other than the Deacons, the family who raised him as their own after the death of his parents. He called no one brother other than Michael Deacon, the only Deacon child who lived past the age of two.

For ten years the two boys shared the same room, ate from the same pot, and dreamed the same dreams. But then a restlessness began to grow within Duncan, and he saw that his life would follow a path different from that of his friend Michael.

In July of 1805 Duncan Blackledge signed on as cook's boy on a ship bound for Boston Harbor. He bade farewell to Michael Deacon and promised to find some way to keep in touch with him—no easy task since neither boy could read or write.

Duncan found another Bangor in the Maine District of Massachusetts and began to ply his trade as a cook for the axemen who worked the forests there. In 1811 he married Sara Pierce and four years later, on Christmas day, celebrated the birth of his first son, Conor. He found a missionary father to pen a birth announcement to Michael for him, complete with a brotherly suggestion: "If you could find your tongue and ask Annie Nelligan to marry you, we might even arrange something between the children. There's nothing can bind a friendship like a betrothal in the family."

Duncan fathered a second son before Michael found the courage to ask Annie Nelligan to marry him. In 1825 Michael wrote with the news that he and Annie were proud parents of a baby daughter: "We've named her Molly. She has the disposition and face of an angel and I'm thinking she'd make your Conor a fine wife."

Duncan Blackledge, who by this time had learned to read and write, penned his own response: "When the tyme is rite, mye Conor will send for your Molly. Molly Blackledge. Has a nice ring, don't it?"

In March of 1840 Michael Deacon's body was found floating facedown in a reflecting pond on the estate of

Lord Clevedon Berryhill. Fifteen-year-old Molly wrote to inform Duncan Blackledge of her father's death, but, for reasons known only to Blackledge himself, he never wrote again.

Chapter One

On this twenty-ninth day of April in 1845 the street that bordered the steamboat landing in Bangor, Maine, was clogged with four-oxen tote teams, delivery wagons, and one buckboard-for-hire that was bouncing in and out of every pit and pothole the street had to offer.

"What'd you say that man's name is, ma'am?"

Molly Deacon clung two-handed to the armrest of her seat. The flesh on her face was quivering so violently that she thought it about to part company with her skull. "Blackledge. Duncan Blackledge." She was not surprised to find her voice vibrating worse than her face. "He lives on Hancock Street. Number forty-seven."

The driver nodded and with a growled command to

his horse, rounded the corner of Washington Street onto Exchange.

From the river Bangor looked like a city that had been built on top of itself—a waterfall of houses and roofs clinging to numerous hillsides. But on closer examination, Molly realized her first impression had been wrong. Exchange Street was ordered with fine clapboard buildings and raised plank sidewalks. To her left was a flouring mill and tea company, and outside the East India store there were a dozen advertising bills nailed onto barrels: BOOT CALKS ONE CENT EACH. SANTA CRUZ RUM ONE DOLLAR A GALLON. ABSOLUTELY NO CREDIT! She eyed the sign for Collett's File Manufactury and by some trick of her imagination saw the letters transpose themselves into the words: LADIES' FINE APPAREL, Proprietress—Molly Deacon. She frowned at the name Deacon. Her imagination did some quick readjustment. Proprietress—Molly Blackledge.

As the wagon approached a narrow building on the right, the doors of the establishment burst open. Out shot a man who hurtled down the stairs and sluiced through the April muck like a log in a flume—and landed directly in the path of the advancing wagon. The driver pulled back on the brake lever. The buckboard pitched forward, then back, causing Molly to flinch as every bone in her body popped in and out of joint.

"Outta the road!" yelled the driver, but the man didn't move. The driver grumbled under his breath, looped the reins around the brake lever, and hopped to the ground. "S'cuse me for a minute, ma'am." As he slopped through the mud, Molly read the sign above the establishment that had ejected the man: SILVER DOLLAR SA-

LOON. She had no sooner raised her eyebrows in disapproval than the doors flew open again.

The barroom emptied. Men spilled into the street like river water. The air crackled with the sound of flesh smacking flesh. Grunts. Yells. Then, close by, a full-bodied thud that combined flesh, bone, and muscle. The buckboard pitched sideways as a man vaulted over the side, crashing to the floor at Molly's feet.

"Oh, dear." She didn't know whether to give a cry of alarm or pain. He'd landed on her right foot, and she could feel his hipbone welding her toes to the leather of her new hightop boots. "Could you—" Her voice came in a rush as the pain increased. "You're crushing my foot."

The man lifted his hip, then rolled backward, propping his head against the dash. "Jeesuz." He swallowed great gulps of air as he braced his forearm across the top of his head. "Sorry. I just need to . . . catch my breath."

It was then that Molly was afforded her first good look at the man, and what she saw made her stare, her smarting toes quite forgotten.

He wore not one, but two flannel shirts that were red as boiled lobsters and open at the throat to expose barn-red long johns and a neck that was rugged and smooth. Wide suspenders held up his black wool trousers, though his brawling had pulled one strap askew. Molly sensed power in his movement as he reached to readjust his suspender. His was not a gentle hand. Cords swelled beneath his flesh and his bruised knuckles looked as if they were practiced in felling men and breaking jaws. She saw the reflexive stretch of his shoulder as he hauled the suspender into place, and she resisted a sudden urge to shape her palm around that shoulder to see if it was as thick with sinew as it looked. And wide! From shoulder to shoulder she guessed he was wide as an ox cart.

Her eyes shifted upward. His face surprised her, for it was not wild and stubbled, but lean, and defined with long, shapely bones. His eyes were a vivid green, his hair thick and black and glossy. Two depressions, as delicately shaped as the curve of her fingernail, graced either side of his mouth. To Molly it seemed that they must have been etched with a feather quill, so fine were the strokes.

He was lean and strong and splendid. And she thought, *Why, he's beautiful.*

With his knuckle he wiped blood from a cracked lip. Seeing this, Molly removed a froth of lace from her reticule and pressed it to the corner of his mouth. "You've a nasty cut," she whispered. The small square of lace reddened with his blood.

The man held the hanky to his mouth. Molly saw him smile as an edge of the lace brushed his cheek. The creases on either side of his mouth deepened with that smile, and she found herself resisting an impulse to trace her fingertip along the curve of his mouth. She wanted to smile in return, but Molly Deacon had not yet learned the art of levity.

The deep brim of her bonnet prevented her from seeing the giant who stood at the side of the wagon. But she saw the arm that whiplashed toward the green-eyed man and leaned back in her seat as the giant yanked the man back into the street.

"Aye bane looking for you, mick."

The buckboard wobbled again as the driver hopped back aboard. "We're outta here, ma'am." He unlooped the reins and shook them out with a rousing "Hiyahhh" that set his piebald mare in motion. Molly reached for the armrest of her seat again, and as she did so, sneaked a look over her shoulder. She searched for a red shirt and black trousers and discovered that every man in the street was red-shirted and black-trousered.

"You all right, ma'am? The waterfront's an unsafe place for ladies when the rivermen end their drive, what with all the boozin' and brawlin'."

Molly gave up her search and turned back to the driver. "Were those men all rivermen?"

"River drivers. Axemen. Woodsmen. They don't mean no harm, but they're kinda rowdy when they're fresh outta the woods."

Molly wondered if Conor Blackledge was a woodsman. She'd been betrothed to him for twenty years, but she had no idea what he looked like or how he made his living. But she would know soon enough. If he'd received her letter, he should be anticipating the arrival of his Irish bride. She wondered what he would think if he knew the main reason why she'd left Ireland. She swallowed her nervousness and tried to enjoy her first ride through Bangor.

It would be nice if his eyes were green.

Duncan Blackledge's house sat at the base of an impossibly steep hill. It was a two-story structure with mustard-yellow clapboards, black shutters, and a wide veranda that boasted a wooden porch swing. It occupied a high bank and was surrounded by a tidy stretch of lawn that rambled in lazy swells to the waters of the Penobscot River. A solid, practical house, its one concession to frivolity was the elongated oval of glass embedded in the wooden frame of the front door. Crocheted lace curtains dressed the three windows that overlooked the porch, and balanced on the upper sash of one window, in letters big enough to be seen from the street, was a sign that read, MILK.

Molly stood on the porch beside her solitary traveling chest. Her eyes roved the house with quiet awe. It had none of the majesty of Lord Berryhill's manor, but it was sturdy and respectable and she wondered what her father would have thought of this grand home built by his friend Duncan. She wondered, too, how different her own life would have been had her father displayed some of Duncan Blackledge's courage and followed his friend to America. Maybe then there would be seven fewer grave markers in the cemetery of St. Bridget's parish.

In the center of her brow four tiny creases appeared. She smoothed them with a gloved finger and tried to think of something else, but thoughts she had long ago buried intruded upon her consciousness.

For years her father's only lasting joy had been to boast of the fine match he'd made for his Molly with Duncan Blackledge's son. She could hear his voice now: "Have I told you about my Molly and Conor Blackledge? She'll be joining him in America one day." For fifteen years he deluged the village men with talk of the betrothal, prideful that his daughter would have something that no other man in the village of Bangor could offer her—a life and home away from Ireland. Molly thought it unimaginable that she would one day have to leave her parents to marry a man she'd never seen. But as she learned, time and circumstance can reshape emotion.

She'd worked their three-acre potato field with her father. There were years when the harvest was hard and black as pebbles. They had lived with hunger those years. Hunger had bred disease, and disease had bred death. Five Deacon babies had succumbed to the sickness wrought by famine. In Molly's lifetime famine became as powerful a religion as Catholicism, and the desire to escape the pangs of hunger became as great as the desire to escape the fires of hell. People began fleeing the country, and for the first time Molly saw that marrying Conor would be far less frightening than staying in Ireland, waiting to die.

She buried her mother in '39 and realized then that if you're poor and Irish, you can be robbed of everything. Everything. Unable to pay the rent on their land and cottage, Molly and her father lost the lease on their farm. With no place to live, they sought employment on the estate of Lord Clevedon Berryhill, the gentleman to whom they had paid their rent.

They had been there only three weeks when someone found her father in the reflecting pond. Drunk, they said. Fell into the pond at night and drowned. Molly had cried then—cried enough tears to fill a hundred lifetimes. At age fifteen she had already divined the lesson of being poor in Ireland: whatever you love can and will be taken from you. So she cried for her father, but it was the last time she permitted herself the luxury of tears.

At Lord Berryhill's she learned to depend on no one but herself. She learned not to form attachments or friendships because people died and left you with nothing but empty memories. She also learned something about herself.

She had an extraordinary talent for stitchery. And this was something that no one could take away from her.

For five years she worked as the estate's seamstress, not only altering and mending garments, but cutting the cloth for new garments as well. She even began to experiment with women's clothing. Late at night, in the manor house's sewing room, leftover muslin became flounces. Shot taffeta became ruching. Bits of lace became tuckers. Merino wool became bodices and overskirts. Her creations were a montage of remnant fabrics, but what they lacked in visual appeal, they made up for in design and detail.

So what began as an experiment became her grandest obsession. She substituted work for friendship and found delight in her creative solitude. Her work was something she could control, something that couldn't disappoint her. It became her life, her dream. She perfected her craft to such an extent that she imagined herself fashioning clothes for the grand ladies of society. Perhaps she could rent a modest shop where she could display her designs. But that kind of dream wouldn't be feasible here in Ireland mid the stink of rotting potato vines. No. There was only one place where dreams of that magnitude could be realized. And she would never get there if Conor Blackledge didn't send for her.

She'd heard nothing from Conor in the five years after her father's death. It seemed that he, too, was going to disappoint her. But she would not be disappointed again. She would not be robbed of her dream. She would have her dressmaker's shop in America. She would prove her talent was worthy of notice and respect. And if Conor didn't send for her soon, she would find some way of getting to Bangor herself.

She stepped to the door of Duncan Blackledge's house and gave a loud rap on the wood.

Through the curtain that veiled the oval of glass in the door, Duncan Blackledge saw the shadow of a wide, bell-shaped skirt. When he opened the door, his expression turned wistful, for it seemed his spectacles were allowing him to look forty years into the past.

The girl was small and spare and stood as straight as a whalebone busk. Her hair was concealed beneath a deep-brimmed bonnet, but what little he could see of it was parted down the middle, flat against her head, and the same color as her father's had been—a deep charcoal-brown. Her skin was fair and unblemished and bore the tightness of youth. She'd inherited the fine bones of Michael Deacon's nose and chin. And her eyes . . . Duncan removed the briar pipe from his mouth. Her eyes were the same blue-gray as Annie Nelligan's.

"Molly Deacon." He shook his head in disbelief. "Annie Nelligan did your father proud. Been expectin' you."

"You received my letter, then?"

"Eayh. Last week."

She looked beyond him, as if expecting someone else to join in the greetings. Duncan shifted uneasily. "I'm not gonna chew the fat off your ear right here 'n' now, though. Let's get you inside. You're probably feelin' all used up after your trip."

"A little, maybe." Her first impression of Duncan Blackledge was that he seemed exceedingly vigorous for a man of his fifty-six years. She was glad the passing decades had treated him with such kindness.

Duncan dragged her traveling chest across the threshold and stowed it against the wall next to the hall tree. He motioned her into the front room.

It was a room whose use New Englanders set aside for the observation of births, deaths, weddings, an occasional visit from the preacher, and the unannounced arrival of guests "from away." It was carpeted in gray wool with bright splashes of pink and mauve that took the form of roses in various stages of bloom. Over-stuffed furniture in shades of rose and puce crouched around the fireplace, the backs and arms of each chair protected by crocheted pineapple antimacassars.

Molly sat down in one of the chairs and reached up to untie her bonnet. "I suppose I should explain about my sudden decision to come here."

Duncan relit his pipe and took a few nervous puffs. "Don't have to on my account."

"But I should, because I was supposed to wait for you to send for me . . . and I didn't."

"Said in your letter that some woman was comin' this way and needed a travelin' companion."

Molly nodded. "Lord Berryhill's spinster cousin. I left her in Boston and took the side-wheeler to Bangor by myself." She peered toward the hall door. If she was going to marry Conor Blackledge, it would be nice to know what he looked like. You'd think he might even be curious about what *she* looked like.

Duncan took a deep breath. He seemed to be growing more and more uncomfortable. "And I s'pose I should explain to you why I never wrote after your Da died. Guess I just didn't know what to say. Hard on a man when his best friend passes on. Draws the sap clean through you."

She'd been disappointed that Duncan had never acknowledged her father's death, but her own acquaintance with death had taught her that grief sometimes put your tongue in irons. "My Da never let a day pass without mentioning your name at least once. He saved all your letters. In fact, after he learned to read, he recited from them so often that I learned each letter by heart."

"Hope you didn't memorize my bad spellin' too."

Molly glanced toward the door again. Maybe Conor was working. She wondered at what. "Duncan, on my way here, I was caught in the middle of a terrible brawl on the waterfront. My driver said that most of the participants were woodsmen. Conor isn't a woodsman, is he?"

"Conor a woodsman?" It seemed he couldn't suck enough air into his lungs. His voice was strained and brittle. "Nope. He's not a woodsman. He's a priest."

Chapter Two

Molly stared at Duncan as if unsure of what he'd just said.

"And that's the other reason I never wrote you again. Didn't have the courage to tell you the Almighty took first dibs on the man you were s'posed to marry."

She couldn't move. She couldn't think. But she knew it was happening again, and she felt betrayed. "A priest." A tightness formed in her throat. She averted her eyes from Duncan and searched the room for solace, but there was none. She couldn't stay here if she wasn't married to Conor. Duncan would send her back to Ireland, and for the rest of her life she would remain nothing more than a servant who could work a fancy stitch.

Damn you, Conor Blackledge. And she didn't care if she *did* go to hell for cursing a priest. He'd been betrothed to her and had no right deserting her like this. It was his duty to recite marriage vows, not religious vows.

"You're about the color of almond paste, Molly. Should I be diggin' out the spirits of ammonia?"

"No, I . . . When did all this happen?"

"Took his vows 'bout five years ago. Same year your Da passed away. He's assistant pastor of St. Michael's Church on the other side the city now."

Her father had betrothed her to a priest. It was unthinkable. She tried to mask her disappointment with civility. "You must be very proud of him."

"Woulda been just as proud if he'd decided to make me a grandfather instead. But as the feller says, that's neither hay nor grass. You about ready for me to take you up the spare room? T'ain't fancy. No heat up there, but come winter we'll put a couple a flannel bricks in your bed to keep you warm."

"Winter?"

"Eayh. In these parts it sets in round the Fourth of July and stays till April. You never heard a winter?"

"Yes but—you sound as though you expect me to stay."

"Course I expect you to stay."

"But how can I if I don't marry Conor?"

"That's got nothin' to do with nothin'. You're here where your Da would want you to be and I aim to keep you here. Your Da's folks opened their home to me when I had nowhere else to go. Kinda tickles me to think I can do the same for you. So it's settled. You'll sleep in the yellow room."

"But—"

Duncan stood up and nodded toward the hall. "I'll leave your chest to sit for a spell. Pierce can carry it up later."

Instinctually she stood to follow him while in her mind one thought kept repeating itself: *He's not going to send me back to Ireland. He's going to let me stay. And I don't have to devote myself to the care of a stranger who would become my husband. I can find work, and earn money, and open my dress shop. It's possible. I know it is.*

She'd felt a twinge of guilt that the only reason she'd been willing to marry Conor was to secure herself a healthy environment for her dressmaking. It was not a motive she was proud of, but some dreams were more important than pride. This one was. To be someone in her own right, to create something that could not be taken from her—these things were more dear to her than friendship, or laughter, or love. One day, perhaps, she would allow herself the time to pursue these other things. One day, when there was a sign hanging over a shop that read: LADIES' FINE APPAREL: Proprietress—Molly Deacon. But there would be no rest for her until then. She wouldn't waste one precious moment. She would work as she had never worked before, and she would earn for herself a reputation that would be hers to keep . . . forever. There would be no husband making demands of her time, no friends to bother her with gossipy chatter. She could work without restraint or limitations, and in such an environment, dreams could be realized.

She inhaled a deep, cleansing breath. It felt as if a massive weight had been lifted from her shoulders. Perhaps it was not so terrible a thing that Conor was a priest. She would say a firm act of contrition tonight as penance for having cussed him.

As she passed the mantel, she saw a painted miniature nested among the curios and stopped to peruse it. "Is this Sara?"

The miniature depicted a plain-faced woman with sad, dark eyes and lips as thin as the cutting edge of a knife. Her most attractive feature was the circle of polished brass that framed her face.

Duncan turned at the doorway. "Eayh. That's my Sara. Homely enough to bite a nail in two, but they didn't come any nicer."

Molly jerked her head around, shocked by his candor. For some unknown reason she felt compelled to defend the woman. "I . . . I don't think she's homely at all."

Duncan laughed. "Didn't marry Sara for her looks. Married her for her disposition. The roof coulda collapsed atop her and she'd-a found somethin' good to say about it. Conor, he favors me. But Pierce, he favors his mother."

Molly recalled the letter in which Duncan had made reference to Pierce: "He's a puny little thing, but Lord willing, he'll catch up to Conor one day." She took a closer look at the painting and imagined what the male counterpart of Sara Blackledge would look like. She shook her head. *Poor man.* Perhaps she would say a prayer for him tonight too.

* * *

It was past nine that evening when they were finally able to hang up the wet dish towels and drag the Boston rockers before the stove in the kitchen. Molly eyed the black leviathan with awe. Not even Lord Berryhill with his great wealth had owned a cookstove with an oven. An ominous-looking thing it was too with all its pot-black lids and shiny dampers.

Duncan tamped tobacco into his pipe. "Figured I deserved one a these considerin' what I'd been cookin' on for the past forty years. Wish I'd had one when I worked the swamps up north. So, does your room suit you?"

"It's lovely. Thank you. Which reminds me. How much should I set aside to pay you for my board and room?"

Duncan cast a sidelong look at her as she dug an embroidery frame out of her carpetbag. "Pay me?"

"I certainly don't expect to take advantage of your hospitality. If I'm going to eat your food and occupy one of your bedrooms, I intend to pay you some kind of recompense."

"Don't need your money."

"Well, you might as well name some figure because I'm going to pay you anyway."

Duncan rocked peaceably back and forth. He watched Molly slant a needle into a square of white muslin and draw a strand of sewing silk through the material. Calm as a clock he finally said, "Ten dollars."

Her hand froze. She pivoted her head to look at him. "A month?"

"A week. And I want all or nothin'."

In her five years at Lord Berryhill's she had saved a total of twenty-four dollars, and she'd spent most of that on fabric and shoes for her trip to America. Ten dollars was a staggering amount. "Ten dollars a week?" Hopelessness weighted each of her words.

"Too steep for you? Good. If you can't pay me all of it, don't want any of it. But if you still feel like you have to give me somethin', make me one of those hankies like you're embroiderin' there. Initials 'id be DB 'stead a MD, and you can leave off the frilly border."

She would have continued the argument had she not heard a thump on the backstairs and a crash that shook the whole side of the house, followed by an angry "Kee-reist."

She shot a worried look at Duncan, who merely shrugged in return. "Too late for the milkman. Gotta be Pierce." He walked into the back hall and opened the outside door. "Thought it was you. C'mon, boy, unlace those boots. You'll not tear up my floors with those cussid spikes."

Molly sat back in her rocker and made a stitch in the Old English D that was traced on her handkerchief. She could understand now why her father's friendship with Duncan had lasted for more than forty years. It was difficult not to like the man.

She heard the outside door bang shut and looked across the room as Duncan steered his son into the kitchen. Her eyes grew wide as she took in the massive shoulders and the shock of black hair.

Oh . . . my . . . God. This was Duncan's son? No, this couldn't be Pierce Blackledge. This man was a riverman. This was the same man who had landed in her wagon this morning!

" 'Fraid he's over the bay some," Duncan apologized.

"Am not," said Pierce.

Duncan took firm hold of his son's elbow and navigated him to the kitchen table. He pulled out a chair. "Si'down, boy," then to Molly, "This here's my youngest."

Pierce Blackledge landed hard on the chair and swayed sideways against the edge of the table. Molly eyed him from the feet up—the red wool socks with his big toe poking through, the black trousers, the red flannel shirt that was encrusted with Exchange Street muck. His face was black with grime, but somewhere beneath that smear of dirt and blood Molly knew there lay long, shapely bones and eyes as green as sliced limes. And to think that out of a sense of pity for his homeliness she'd been going to waste valuable time praying for him!

She set her embroidery on her rocker and joined Duncan at the table. "You said he looked like Sara."

"Said he favored Sara. Disposition-wise. Looks like no one I know. Used to say he came in a flour barrel."

Her eyes darted from his bruised knuckles to the weal on his lip. "He's a riverman, isn't he?"

"Am not," Pierce slurred, his head bobbing up and down as if it were connected to his neck by a spring. "I'm a wood . . . bitcher."

Molly fired a questioning look at Duncan. The old man shook his head. "Wood butcher's what he means. Mind your tongue, boy. There's a lady present."

Pierce tilted his head horizontally and observed the two people before him with one green eye. Duncan

headed for the cellar door. "I'm goin' down-cellar see if
I can find a bottle a Jamaica Ginger. Come mornin', the
boy's gonna need it to kill the pain. Wouldn't mind if
you washed some a that muck off his face, Molly. He
gives you any gaff, just cuff 'im the side his head."

She could feel Pierce's eyes on her as she removed
the basin from its nail over the dry sink and poured a
dipperful of tepid water into it. She whisked a mesh
soap-saver through the water to make it sudsy, removed
a clean flannel cloth from the towel rack, and headed
back across the floor.

He was still staring at her. It made her wonder if her
hair was parted in a straight line, if the collar of her
gown was high enough to hide the mole on the back of
her neck.

"Don't get too many ladies at forty-seven Hancock
Street."

Molly stepped around his long legs and held the wet
flannel above his head. "If you greet them all like this, I
can see why. Tilt your head back."

Back went his head. "Greet 'em like what?"

"Drunk."

He closed his eyes. His lashes were so spiky and long
that they flirted with the high slope of his cheekbone.
She envied him those eyelashes. "Am not drunk. Just
. . . happy."

Molly remembered what had happened to her father
when he'd been "happy," and it suddenly galled her that
Pierce Blackledge could treat his condition so blithely.
Anger stiffened her arm. When she set the flannel to his
face, she began scrubbing as if the cloth was a soiled
shirt and his jaw a washboard.

"Jeesuz-God!" Pierce thrust her hand away. His head shot up. "You mind leavin' me enough skin to shave in the mornin'?"

Contrite for having vented her anger so childishly, Molly relented. "Sorry."

"Goddamn." He rubbed his jaw and sat there looking injured.

"Tilt your head again," she said, but she wasn't any too pleased about his use of profanity. So she began a second time, more gently. "I hope your vocabulary changes when you're sober."

"Does."

"Thank God for that."

"Gets worse."

She frowned into the one green eye that was squinting at her. "Close your eye before I get soap in it."

Down went his eyelid. And for some odd reason she felt like smiling, but suppressed the urge. She would not treat his drunkenness lightly.

The grime came off in sticky little balls and flakes. She cleansed the rise of his cheekbone to the tail of his eye and found the underlying flesh to be soft and milky and smooth as a woman's hand. She washed the dark silken hairs that ridged his brow, and in her chest felt an unfamiliar giddiness rise and expand. Shifting her gaze, she followed the span of bare flesh that flowed from the underside of his jawline to the collar of his shirt. His heartbeat duplicated itself in a tiny throbbing tic in his neck, and when Molly saw the flesh at his throat lift with the quiet strength of that pulse, she felt a pulse within her respond in kind and a mist of sensation float through her veins to her fingertips.

His eyelids suddenly flew up. He grabbed her hand and held it away from his face. "That was you."

She felt as if she'd just been caught performing an unnatural act in public. "What—what was me?"

"In the wagon. With the feet." He placed her hand back on his face. "Hope I didn't hurt you."

She hadn't expected an apology. She hadn't even expected him to remember her. But it somehow pleased her that he did. "No. You didn't hurt me."

She rinsed out the flannel and changed the water in the basin. With his face partially clean she turned her attention to the gash on his lower lip. He let out a yelp when she touched it.

"I'm sorry."

"Jeez-zuz."

She dabbed at the gash, brushing away dried blood. "You're awfully squeamish for someone who's as big as you are." She looked down the length of him. He probably stood two or three inches over six feet and was certainly not the scrawny thing that Duncan's letter had suggested. "I read somewhere that you were puny."

"I grew. Ouch!"

"Don't move your mouth so much. You'll start bleeding again. Here. Hold this on your lip while I get a dry cloth."

He watched her cross the room, and despite the throbbing pain in his lip, he grinned, eyes mischievous. When she returned, she removed the flannel from his mouth and bent her head to examine her handiwork. "How does that feel?"

He shrugged his big shoulders. "Don't know. Have to test it."

His hands went around her head. The next thing she knew her mouth was pressed to his and she was feeling with her lips the curve that she had earlier wanted to trace with her fingertips. His jaw was scratchy, his lips were firm, and he tasted of things that stung her senses —soap and spirits, with an aftertaste of moist earth.

"Mmmh!" She pushed against him, but when her palms were flat against his chest the only thought that filled her mind was, *He's hard like a stone wall is hard*.

She felt the warmth of his breath mingling with her own, then as quickly as he had grabbed her, he released her, and she stood back, breathless and indignant.

Pierce tested his gash with a finger. He nodded his head. "Feels pretty good. Thanks."

"You . . . I . . . *Oh!*" She threw the dry cloth at his chest and would have dumped the basin of dirty water over his head had she not been concerned about getting the floor wet. Instead she emptied the contents of the basin into the sink and met Duncan at the top of the cellar stairs. "His face is clean. Do you need me to do anything else?"

He didn't, so she gathered up her embroidery and carpetbag and left the room without a backward glance at Pierce Blackledge.

Pierce slid his arm onto the kitchen table and cradled his head against his bicep. "Don't know who she is, Da, but do you s'pose we could keep her?"

The house was quiet now save for the snores trumpeting from Duncan's room. Molly sat up in her bed, too excited to sleep. She had never slept in so grand a room. The floor was wide-planked, the ceiling high, and the windows hung with starched curtains in yellow-and-white checked gingham. Rag rugs sat like palettes of color on the floor. Against the south wall stood a bureau with a tilted lacework mirror and drawer pulls that were not simple brass rings or china knobs, but fruit and leaves hand-carved with painstaking detail. Her bed was plainly fashioned, with high block posts that were capped with wooden cannonballs, though one ball tended toward the oblong and looked more like a lemon. She slept on not one but two bed pillows stuffed so full of feathers they were hard as bricks. As she punched and fluffed them for the fifth time, she remembered the years when a pillow to her meant a sack filled with straw. She wished her father had come to America. Their lives might have been so different then.

She lay back in her pillows and dragged her hair out from beneath the covers. The braid that she wore at night was long as a horse's tail and twice as thick, the loose ends soft as a man's shaving brush. She bent the end hairs back and forth in the candlelight, then touched them to her face—down her right cheek, above her top lip, down her chin. Pierce had touched all these places with his kiss, with his breath, and the intimacy had seemed to change the texture of her skin. Her cheek felt softer, her lips more full.

She rolled her eyes at her own fancifulness and put Pierce Blackledge out of her mind. She couldn't allow the man to distract her. She was here to work, and work was what she would do. First, she would have to convince someone in the city to hire her as a dressmaker. If she charged fifty cents a week, she might earn enough money in two or three years to rent a shop. *Two or three years?* Too long. She would charge a dollar a week and earn the money in half the time. A year and a half sounded more manageable. But a dollar a week was an outrageous sum for a woman to earn. Could she convince anyone she was worth it?

Yes, I can, she decided. *I'll make myself sound so indispensable that women will be pleading to pay me a dollar a week.* She gave her head a determined nod. Life on the Berryhill estate had taught her one thing about women, especially wealthy women. If they wanted something badly enough, they were willing to pay anything for it. She would have to find out the name of the city's wealthiest woman then, and convince her that she could not possibly live without gowns fashioned from the needle of Molly Deacon.

That settled, she also decided to set money aside each week for Duncan, whether he accepted it or not. She couldn't allow herself to depend wholly on his generosity for her welfare. If she regularly set money aside for room and board, she would have resources to draw from if something happened to Duncan and she had to move. That seemed the sensible thing to do. She had to prepare herself for every circumstance.

With the end of her braid she ticked off points on her fingers—employment, room and board, ask Duncan about potential customers, have Pierce carry her travel chest up to her room in the morning . . . if he was sober by morning. Her mind drifted again. She slanted her hand away from the candlelight so that her palm was in shadow. Like a Renaissance painter she stroked her palm and fingers with the tips of her hair, dusting the places that would forever remember the feel of solid flesh overlaid by red flannel. She wondered what his flesh would feel like without the red flannel, and just as quickly scolded herself for entertaining such indecent thoughts. She'd lost one man today and had no intention of finding herself another, no matter how broad his shoulders or green his eyes. Her needlework was everything. She couldn't forget that. And she couldn't jeopardize her good fortune by wasting time mooning over a drunken wood butcher.

She doused the candle at the side of her bed and snugged the patchwork counterpane around her neck. She fought off fragments of conversation that continued to float through her head.

"I read somewhere that you were puny."

"I grew."

Indeed he had. And despite her conviction that there was little in this world to smile about, she did.

Chapter Three

In the kitchen the next morning the smell of burning wood mixed with savory breakfast smells—griddle-cakes, maple syrup, black China tea, and oven-baked biscuits. Morning sun inched along the floor like spilled honey. Molly was watching Duncan add more edgings to the firebox when the hallway door creaked open and a squinty-eyed Pierce Blackledge slid a shoulder around the doorjamb. His shirt was open and untucked. His suspenders were unhitched so that his trousers rode low on his hips. He made a fist over his eyes as he yawned, and his long johns pulled back and forth as his right hand rubbed and scratched its way down his chest. He coaxed one eye open, but finding the light too bright, he opened his fist and used it as a blindfold.

"Unhhh."

"Jamaica Ginger's on the table," said Duncan. "And button yourself up proper so's you don't embarrass yourself in front a our guest."

Pierce flipped his hand up like a visor. His green eyes looked pained and glassy as he squinted at the girl who was standing beside his father. "Jeesuz, Da, you could've warned me."

Pulling up the waist of his droopy trousers, he turned in the opposite direction. He thrust his buttons through the buttonholes, tucked the flaps of his shirt into his trousers, and pulled his suspenders over his shoulders. But he couldn't turn around to face the girl. He thought the creature in the kitchen last night had been only a dream. But she was no dream if she was still here this morning, which she was. And there was something else. In his dream he'd kissed her. But he couldn't have done that to a lady guest in his father's house. Could he?

Buttoned, tucked, and hitched, he turned around. His eyes drifted to Molly's face. Oh, Jeesuz, he *had* kissed her. And his body was quick to remind him how much he had enjoyed it.

Duncan made the introductions. "This here's Molly. Michael Deacon's daughter. Woulda told you who she was last night, but last night you weren't fit to meet Job's turkey."

Pierce combed his fingers through his shaggy hair and stepped into the kitchen. He nodded his head at Molly. "Ma'am."

"Your eyes could pass for two cane holes in a cow

flap this mornin', boy. Get some a that tonic down you 'fore you decide you feel bad's you look."

Pierce looked from Molly to the table before he decided to move. Bare feet slapped bare wood. There was a swagger and bounce to his step as he crossed the floor. A jaunty swing to his shoulders. He slid into a chair.

Duncan removed a plate of griddlecakes from the stove's warming trivet and handed them to Molly. "You and Pierce can start on these."

Molly set the plate on the table and seated herself opposite Pierce, who had just swallowed a spoonful of painkiller and looked in no mood to eat anything. She'd decided to forgive him his indiscretion last night, so there was no reason that she shouldn't be civil this morning. "Would you like some?" she asked, indicating the griddlecakes.

He waved his hand to take them away. "End result wouldn't be pretty if I ate griddlecakes this morning. I'll spare you the sight."

"Tea, then?"

He watched her smooth her fingers along the handle of the tea pitcher and was struck by how very pretty her nails were—short, yet formed into fine ovals that were a pale, blushing pink. "No tea, thanks." When he looked into her face, he saw that she had a shallow dimple in her left cheek that curved from her cheekbone all the way to her jaw. It was the lookingest thing he'd ever seen. He wondered if it deepened when she smiled. And her eyes. They were a pewter-gray underlaid with a soft misting of blue. *Pretty eyes,* he thought. *Almost as big as her face.* "When did you arrive?"

"Yesterday afternoon."

"Oh, yah." *Remember?* he asked himself. *You almost broke her foot.* "You're the daughter of that buttonhole relation of Da's, aren't you? The one that Conor was supposed to marry. Came all the way from Ireland, didn't you? Awful long way to come to find out your husband-to-be's recited his vows without you. So when are you goin' back?"

She held the maple syrup over her plate, hesitating before she began to drizzle it over her griddlecakes. "Your father has been kind enough to invite me to stay here indefinitely."

An uneasy look crept into Pierce's eyes. He'd heard tales of what it was like living with a woman in the house. No belching at the table and no cussing. Jeesuz. Well, no creature was gonna change the way he lived. He was a Bangor Tiger and a Bangor Tiger lived by certain rules. He was too hardfisted to need the company of women, except of course when he got back from the drive. He was too smart to be led around with his head in a bucket, which is what most creatures wanted to do to men. And until he quit the woods, he never, ever, thought about getting married, which is what most females thought about *all* the time. This female was probably no different. Since she couldn't marry Conor, she'd probably want to marry *him*. His head began to throb as he considered how much energy he'd have to waste fighting her off. *Nice goin', Da.* "You're gonna stay indefinitely, huh? Awful goddamn generous of Da, wasn't it?"

Across the table, he saw Molly cringe and bow her head.

Duncan took his place at the table. He took in the size

and color of Pierce's lip and shook his head. "Someone sure got you between the face and eyes."

"Yah, and the only thing I remember about the god-damn jeezer was that he was big." From the periphery of his vision he saw Molly bless herself. He wondered if the Irish from away always preceded each sip of tea or bite of food with some religious gesture. *Must take them forever to finish a meal.* "You should see Exchange Street, Da. It's crawlin' with Canucks."

"Canucks?" asked Molly.

"Canucks," repeated Pierce. "That's what we call the goddamn French-Canadians." He saw her hand fly into another sign of the cross. He frowned. "So if you're from Ireland, how come you don't sound Irish? Sound English to me. She sound English to you, Da?"

"Eayh."

Molly shrugged. "I spent five years in a room with several English seamstresses on Lord Berryhill's estate. I probably picked up more of their accent than I realized. I really sound English?"

"Sure as hell don't sound Irish."

"Well, neither do you," she snapped back.

"Yah, but I wasn't born and raised in Ireland."

"And speakin' a that," interrupted Duncan, "I wanna apologize again for havin' you make a special trip here to marry Conor and—"

"—findin' out that Conor married himself to the Church," Pierce finished for him. "But I dunno, Da. Maybe when Father Blackledge gets a look at her, he'll decide that a girl with gray eyes and one dimple has more to offer him than a life of celibacy."

A vertical crease split Molly's brow as she took exception to his comment. "I beg your pardon?"

Pierce unstoppered the Jamaica Ginger and wolfed down three more spoonfuls. "All I'm sayin' is that after spendin' five years with nothing but a goddamn flannel brick to warm his bed, he might be in the market to try something more hot-blooded."

Her hand made its circuit again. Pierce bowed his head and scratched the corner of his mouth. These Irish from away were certainly a queer lot.

"That's sacrilegious," she said.

Pierce rolled his eyes. It was startin' already. "So if Conor decides to stay a priest, and you decide to stay here, what do you intend to do with yourself?"

Molly broke a biscuit and slapped a pad of butter between the two halves. "It had crossed my mind that I'd like to open a dress shop."

Pierce howled with laughter, then grabbed his head as pain shot through it. He raised the medicine bottle to his lips and downed half its contents before slamming it to the table with his fist. "Well, you'd better uncross it from your mind. An Irishwoman? Open a dress shop? Not very goddamn likely."

Molly's hand went to her forehead, then froze at her breastbone as Pierce bellowed, "Why in the hell do you keep blessing yourself? Jeesuz-God, you keep whacking your forehead like that you'll end up crazier than Gideon's geese."

Color poured into her cheeks. Anger stiffened her spine. "I am praying, *Mr.* Blackledge, for the salvation of your immortal soul, though considering your limited and extremely *foul* vocabulary, I expect the effort will be a complete waste of my time."

Pierce scowled. Molly glared. Duncan raised a calming hand. "Don't see anything funny 'bout wantin' to open a dress shop. Sounds like a fair idea to me."

"It does?" Molly was thankful for Duncan's approval in light of Pierce's cynicism.

"Eayh, it does. Now you just go on with what you were sayin'."

Pierce shot his father a betrayed look. Molly continued.

"I wouldn't be able to open it right away, of course. I'd have to hire myself out as a dressmaker first."

More laughter from across the table. "Good luck to you if you think you can find someone in Bangor who'll hire an Irish dressmaker," said Pierce. "Irish are foreigners, and foreigners aren't welcome here."

Molly looked to Duncan for confirmation. "'Fraid the boy's right, Molly. Don't pay to be Irish in Bangor."

This was something she hadn't counted on. "There has to be someone who'd be willing to hire me. Who are the wealthy women in the city?"

"Celia Dwinel," said Duncan.

Pierce shook his head, negating the choice.

"What's wrong with Celia Dwinel?" asked Molly.

"Old maid. No style. And Celia and her brother don't hire Irish."

"Then there's Olympia Thatcher," Duncan offered.

Pierce was still shaking his head. "Humorless. Twice as cold as zero. And Thatchers don't hire Irish."

Molly compressed her lips. She fired an irritated look

at Pierce. "Perhaps you'd like to suggest a name that would meet with your approval."

He shook his head. "None of my goddamn business who you work for."

The man was impossible! She stabbed her fork into a piece of griddlecake. "If *you* can find a job in this city, I can find one too."

"Are you comparin' the two of us? I'm a man, for crissakes!"

"So? You're still Irish, aren't you?"

He looked exasperated with her feminine logic. "Some people don't know more than a goose knows God."

"We'll see who knows what," she challenged, his pessimism sparking her confidence. And this was the man with the good disposition? Huh! "Tomorrow I'm going to convince Olympia Thatcher that she needs a new dressmaker."

"No way in hell you'll convince her to do anything except maybe have you thrown out on your bonnet. Like I said, Thatchers don't hire Irish."

"We'll see."

"I won't. But you sure as hell will."

Her eyebrow flew up in an angry arch. Duncan cleared his throat, attempting to make peace. "Read in yesterday's *Whig and Courier* where the Misses Macromber are havin' a musicale tonight at City Hall. Might be nice if you got dressed in your other ones and took the girl, Pierce. Bet she'd enjoy some music."

Pierce sidled another betrayed look at his father. No way was he gonna be thrown together with any female to attend any musicale. But just as he was about to offer an excuse, he heard Molly provide her own.

"I'm sorry, but I still have some needlework to complete before I can make my presentation at Thatcher's tomorrow. That really needs to be my first priority."

And because no woman had ever turned down the rare offer of his company before, Pierce looked at Molly Deacon in some bewilderment. She had needlework to do? That was some lame excuse. He wondered what the real reason for her not wanting to go with him was. In a quick reversal of thinking, it suddenly became a point of pride for him to convince her to accompany him tonight. "You have all day to do your needlework."

She leveled a cool look at him. "No, I don't. I have laundry to do today."

"We don't do laundry till Monday."

"And then I'll have to start my ironing."

"Do it tomorrow."

"And I'd like to take a bath. I haven't had a sit-down bath for a month."

"We don't take baths around here till Saturday night. So there you are. You don't have anything to do. What time does the musicale start, Da?"

"I told you." She emphasized the words slowly, as if she were addressing a dim-witted child. "I have too much to do."

"Well, what the hell else do you think you have to do?"

"With the leftover wash-water from the laundry, I want to scrub the front porch."

"You wanna what? Jeesuz God." He rolled his eyes.

"It's sinful to waste all that soapy water." But she

didn't expect him to understand about waste. He hadn't grown up in Ireland. He hadn't eaten what she'd been forced to eat in years when the potato crop had failed.

"So you're gonna work like a lackey all day," he taunted. "Don't you ever make time to kick up your heels a little?"

She thought of what she was trying to accomplish, and why, and it peeved her that he would criticize her practicality. "Some people have more pressing things to do than kick up their heels. Some people don't have time to squander precious hours at musicales. Some people are more dedicated to their work than drunken wood butchers!"

"Drunken wood butcher?" His chest expanded with rage. His suspenders looked like they might snap.

"Now don't be gettin' yourself all humped up like a hog goin' to war, boy," Duncan cautioned.

"Don't get humped up? Don't get humped up! I'll say I'll get humped up! Did you tell her what I am?" He whipped his head around to face Molly. "Do you know what I am?"

"You mean besides rude and intemperate? I can't imagine."

Pierce braced his forearms on the table and impaled her with a look that would like to have made her disappear. "I'm a Bangor Tiger," he said, pride in his voice, challenge in his eyes.

Molly braced her own forearms on the table and matched him stare for stare. "Is that supposed to mean something?"

A flicker of incredulity passed over his face. "A Bangor Tiger, *Miss* Deacon, is only the finest kind of

ten about that. Jeesuz, he'd been pretty despizable to her this mornin' after she'd been so obligin' to him yesterday. *Nice goin', Pierce.*

He refolded the hanky into a wrinkled square, and before returning it to his pocket, skimmed a clean edge down his cheek and brought it to his nostrils. Its scent was light and fresh and so different from the smell of wet woolens and wood smoke that he frowned at the absence of anything feminine in his life. Nice-smellin' females had certain advantages that even Bangor Tigers couldn't fault.

He stuffed the hanky into his pocket. He'd have to wash that hanky and return it to her. He imagined her smiling her thanks, and he wondered again what she'd look like with her face all lit up. She hadn't smiled once during breakfast. Odd thing about that. But he wagered he could get her to smile, with her eyes as well as her mouth. She sure had pretty eyes. He liked gray eyes and long dimples and women who could give as good as they got. And there was somethin' exciting about a woman who sounded English but wasn't, who should've married his brother but couldn't, who might've let him bleed all over himself yesterday but didn't. And she had spunk. Damned if he didn't like spunk.

He headed out the door and across the flatform. *Maybe confession once a week wouldn't be so terrible.* By the time he hit the yard, he was whistling.

Chapter Four

The laundry was drying by noon and the porch scrubbed by one. At 1:15 Pierce heard a timid knock on his workshop door. He looked up from his workbench to find Molly brandishing an ancient flatiron in her hand.

She delighted his eye as she stood in the doorway. The hem of her gown was saturated with so much water that it clung to her ankles like flypaper. Her skirt was streaked with bluing. Skeins of runaway hair had wrapped themselves around her bare throat. The top four buttons of her bodice were unlooped, but these did not tease his imagination as much as the lower ones that were still fastened.

"I'm sorry to bother you," said Molly, "but is this the only iron your father owns?" It galled her to have to ask him anything, but she had no choice. He was the only one at home.

Thinking to make amends for his earlier behavior, Pierce smiled at her. "Something wrong with that one?"

"Only the fact that I could use three more of them. You don't have any sleeve or goffering irons?"

"Any *what?*"

"Goffer—" She looked disheartened at the blank expression on his face. "Any irons for crimping." But his face remained blank. "How does your father get up frills and ruffles?"

"We usually have our shirts and long johns made without 'em."

"Oh." A pause. "That's right, isn't it. You haven't had a woman living in the house for a while."

"Twenty years now."

She grew quiet at that. Twenty years was a long time to be without a parent. She softened at the thought of the child who had lost his mother, and she felt her ire starting to dissipate. "You were very young when she died."

"Two. How old were you when your Ma passed away?" He could see both pain and hesitancy in her eyes as she answered him.

"I was fourteen."

"You had your Ma a lot longer than I had mine. You're lucky. I wish I'd gotten to know mine. Da says she was really somethin'. And maybe if I'd had a mother around to box my ears when I needed it, I'd know better than to be so despizable at breakfast. I'm surprised you're even talkin' to me."

His openheartedness seemed at odds with his earlier behavior. And he was smiling. It confused her. "I'm surprised I'm talking to you too, but you were my only option."

"'Fraid so. Da won't be back till supper."

"Does he always spend so much time at the rectory?"

"Yah, he spends a good part've the week cookin' and cleanin' for Conor. Conor sees to everyone's spiritual needs, and Da sees to Conor's domestic needs. Works out pretty well." He nodded toward the window. "I see you got all your dimities hung out." In fact, in all his life he had never seen so much feminine frippery gathered in one place.

"I got everything hung out, but it'll take me a month to press everything with only one iron."

He shrugged his big shoulders and looked genuinely sympathetic. "Sorry I can't help you."

"Me, too." For a moment her eyes wandered. She was struck by the orderliness of the workshop, for she hadn't expected a man who drank and cussed to be orderly. Long and short planks were stacked on the floor and against the west wall. Along the south wall were barrels stamped with the words "Tremont Nail Company." From nails driven into the overhead rafters there hung wooden-handled implements with iron heads, metal tools shaped like elongated spoons, and wooden blocks of varying lengths and design. "I suppose you know what all those tools are for?" She nodded toward the ceiling.

He followed her gaze. "Yah, I'd better. Can't build furniture without 'em."

"Is that what you do in here?"

"For five months of the year that's what I do in here. And you don't have to stand in the doorway like that. You can come in. My head doesn't hurt as much as it did this mornin' so I guarantee I won't be as grouchy."

She thought that she should be putting the iron on the stove to heat, but perhaps she could spare him a minute or two. She stepped into the room.

"Like I was sayin', my specialty is cabinets and commodes and bureaus. I made the head- and footboards in your room. Course that was my first attempt at anything big, so that's why one of the cannonballs looks like a lemon."

This unexpected display of modesty touched her. She suddenly felt compelled to defend the bedstead. "It doesn't look that much like a lemon."

"If you squeezed it, you could probably make lemonade. Anyway, the other seven months of the year I work in the woods."

"Seven months. That's a long time."

"That's why most Bangor Tigers don't get married till they quit the woods. It's too hard on the women."

"I imagine." She wondered what the fabric of her life would be like if she were married to a man who spent seven months of the year away. She decided if she truly loved the man, she wouldn't like it much. "So do you work in the woods as a Bangor Tiger?"

"Kinda. I work mostly as a wood butcher."

"And what does a wood butcher do?"

It pleased him that she'd be interested enough to ask. "A wood butcher builds the cabins for the boss and crew and all its fittin's—dinner tables, sinks, cupboards. He can make a deacon's seat usin' nothing but a broadaxe and have it come out smooth as a smelt. He can build a sled from runner to pole to bunk and can cut a skylight that fits tighter than bark to a tree. If it weren't for wood butchers, there'd be no lumber camps."

He was sitting on a high stool with his right knee bent in such a way as to draw his trousers taut along his thigh. Molly looked away from the sight, for there were mysteries surrounding the shape of that thigh that she had no business thinking about. She turned her attention to the slew of papers that were scattered before him on the workbench. "Are you drawing up plans for a new lumber camp?"

"Nope. Just lookin' over some furniture sketches I made."

Molly set the iron on the workbench and took a few steps closer to peruse the drawings. Calculations and measurements accompanied each drawing, and again she was impressed by the orderliness of his work. "I make sketches before I begin any project too," she said, surprised by the similarity of their work styles.

"You do? Hell, I thought a dressmaker just took a pair of cutting shears to a bolt of cloth and went at it."

"I suppose she could, but the result might not be what she expected. I think it's better to know where you're going."

Pierce gave her an astonished look. "Yah. Me, too." He'd never known a woman to do anything the same way he did. It kinda tickled him. "This is a sideboard

I'm gonna build for Mrs. Constable up on Broadway."
He pushed the drawing at her. "Gonna be made of walnut. Seven and a half feet tall so it can do her fifteen-
foot ceilings justice."

Molly held the drawing up. "It's quite lovely."

"Yah?" He cocked his head to view it from a different
angle. It didn't look any too special to him, but he
warmed to the idea that she liked it. He threw a long
finger out to indicate its primary features. "It'll have
oval door centers, a crotch-grain top, and three shelves
round an oval mirror. I wanna connect the shelves either
with spindled rails or fretwork S scrolls, but I can't decide which. You have any ideas?"

"Me?"

"Yah, you. You're a woman. Which would you
prefer, the spindles or scrolls?"

Her brow lifted with surprise that he should want her
opinion. "Well, I'm certainly no expert but—" She
studied the sketch with a serious eye. "I think you
should choose the S scrolls. They're easier to dust."

"Yah," he said again in that astonished way of his.
"That's exactly what I was thinkin'." Their eyes touched
for a moment over the sheet of parchment, then quickly
sought safer territory. Pierce made a notation on the
drawing. "Funny how we'd both say the same thing."

She didn't know if it was funny, but she thought it
pleasant that they were no longer fighting. Leaning her
back against the workbench, she looked out across the
room. He built lumber camps and she built wardrobes.
He made furniture and she made clothing. He had lost
his mother and so had she. Perhaps the two of them

weren't so different from each other as she had imagined.

"Did you notice that the sky is cloudin' up?"

Molly spun round and angled a look through the window. Gray had replaced blue. "It can't rain. I have a thousand things drying on the line."

"It's April. April has no mercy on man or dimities. Here it comes."

And come it did, in one of those quirky surprises of Maine weather.

"Oh, no." She raced out the door, across the flatform, down the stairs, and around the back of the house. Pierce gave chase behind her.

The rain was cold and hard and fell like thorns. Pierce tossed aside the bamboo poles that elevated the lines. Molly set the clothes basket at her feet. She began pitching line pegs into the basket and throwing petticoats and chemises over her arm. The rain was soaking through everything. She shot a quick look at Pierce. He had removed her corset from the line and was studying it as if it were the eighth wonder of the ancient world. He turned it upside down, right-side up, and finally bridged it between his hands like an accordion at full extension. "Which way are you supposed to wear this thing?"

She marched toward him, plucked the corset from his hands, and flung it across the clothes weighting her left arm. "A real gentleman would never ask a question like that."

"Nope. But a common wood butcher might." He grinned at the next item on the line and hauled it down. "I suppose you want these too?"

She twitched her lips as she snatched her soggy drawers from his grasp. Spine stiff, she returned to the task at hand.

Lightning flashed overhead. Molly bowed her head and slatted her eyes against the driving rain. A roll of thunder boomed in the distance. "Bring the clothes basket!" she yelled to Pierce as she dashed toward the house.

"There's nothin' in it!"

"Line pegs!"

"But they're already wet!"

"Just bring it!"

Around the back of the house she ran, past the well-house, up the dooryard stairs, across the flatform, and into the back hall. She leaned panting against the wall as Pierce charged in after her.

"Why in the hell did . . . you want the . . . clothes basket?"

The ceiling seemed too low to accommodate Pierce's height, the hallway too narrow to contain the bulk of the clothes basket *and* his shoulders. She motioned for him to set the basket down, and when he did, she dumped what was in her arms on top of the masses of line pegs. Shrugging, Pierce did the same. Molly looked at the floor where she was standing.

"I'm making a puddle."

"Yah, but if we head upstairs to change, we'll leave puddles through the whole house. And that's one helluva lot've water to mop up." He nodded toward his workshop. "Better dry off in there."

She followed him inside and cupped her hands over her mouth to warm them with her breath.

Pierce removed a long sheet of flannel from a peg on the wall. "Cold?"

She bobbed her head erratically. Her teeth were starting to chatter. "I feel like winter just crept into my bones and set up housekeeping."

"Here. Put this around you."

The rain had flattened her gown against her thighs. As she reached up to help him with the flannel, he saw that there was a hint of suppleness in the curve of her thigh and the bend of her back, and he was given to wonder how her body would conform to the angles and curves of a man's body. He saw that the slender V of flesh at her throat was peppered with needle points of cold, that the wet muslin covering her breast revealed more of her femininity than it hid. With a keen eye he traced the hollows and rises whose presence the wet muslin had outlined, and he felt a sudden warmth set his long johns to prickle against his skin.

As a man knows a woman, he knew desire. It stamped itself in the pit of his stomach like a branding iron. It took its man's shape, and as nature had its way with him, slowly thickened. He fanned shaky fingers through his hair and grabbed a comb-backed chair for her. "Why don't you sit down? You're gonna break every tooth in your head if you don't stop shakin' so hard."

Gratefully, she sat and tented the sheeting around her. "Is Maine w-weather always this unpre-d-dictable?"

"Only when Irish girls are hangin' out their dimities." Marshaling his composure, he turned away from her and unlooped his suspenders from around his shoulders. His red flannel shirt was soaked through, but despite the wetness Molly could see where his suspenders had left their permanent imprint. Sunlight had faded the rest of the shirt, but where his suspender formed a Y down his back, the material was still a vivid red.

He peeled off one shirt, draped it over his barrel of Tremont nails, then started on the next one. Hoping to distract herself from six feet three inches of lean, wet male disrobing in front of her, Molly leaned over and began unlacing her boots.

"You wasted your time scrubbin' the porch. If you'd waited a little longer, the storm would've done it for you."

"Does the s-storm come equipped with lye s-soap?"

He laughed at her comment, a sound that seemed to start at his knees and work its way up from there, gathering depth and volume and spark. His was a deep laugh. A wonderful laugh.

As she had envied him his long eyelashes, she now envied him that laugh.

She slid her foot out from her boot, and after she made sure Pierce wasn't looking, she rolled her stocking and garter down her leg. She wiggled her toes to get some feeling back into them, but to no avail. She started on her other boot, sneaking a look at Pierce as she worked. His back was toward her as he ruffled water from his hair. His suspenders were still unhitched and dangling around his knees.

Tugging her left boot off, she set it aside and reached beneath her petticoat for her garter. From the periphery of her vision she saw Pierce hauling his suspenders back into place. Off came the stocking

from her leg in a frenzy of motion. She stuffed it
inside her boot, then curled her toes around the bottom rung of the chair and blanketed her skirt around
her feet. She was ashamed of the feet that had gone
shoeless for so many years. The soles were tough as
shoe leather and puckered with ugly scars. She didn't
want Pierce to see them.

"Getting any warmer?" A crack of thunder rattled the
windows and made her seem all the more cold.

"N-No."

Pierce carried a low rush stool over to her and set it
on the floor. She heard his joints crack as he sat down.
"Have to see what we can do about warmin' you up."
He parted his feet to balance himself and she felt a
strange sensation prick her as she marked the inviting
gap that appeared between his legs. "Where are you
hidin' your feet?"

"No! Please don't—"

He dug her right foot out from its shroud of wet muslin and wrapped his big logger's hands around it. Molly
sucked her bottom lip between her teeth as she anticipated his reaction to the ugly appendage.

"Is this the foot I landed on yesterday?"

She nodded.

He lowered it into the space between his legs to better
observe it. "Doesn't look any the worse for wear. But
it's cold as a well digger's elbows." He cradled it in his
left hand, and with the heel of his right began massaging the flesh from her toes to her ankle. He could feel
the pull of unyielding muscle in her leg but he ignored
her nervousness.

Quietly she watched the sure motion of his hand,

and she wondered how yesterday she could have thought that hand ungentle. She watched the calm set of his features and gradually felt her nervousness dissolve. Her eyes strayed after a time, dwelling on his chest as it expanded and contracted. He was so broad that each time he inhaled, his woolen underwear stretched taut and his placket buttons worried their buttonholes. On most people, long-handled underwear hung long and shapeless. But not so on Pierce Blackledge. He filled his underwear the way six stone of potatoes would fill a sack. But unlike a sack of potatoes, his bulges were longer and flatter and wondrously symmetrical.

She looked away before he caught her staring.

He shifted her foot in his hand. Folding his fingers over her toes, he began kneading them with his fingertips and thumb. He seemed at ease with the labor. His motions were efficient yet unhurried, and he suddenly didn't seem like a man who would be concerned with jumping higher and running faster than his fellow Bangor Tigers. She could feel the strength of his fingers and could imagine his hands crushing stone and leaving nothing but powder, wielding the tools that hung overhead and bending the metal with little effort. The roughness of his skin chafed her toes. She began to take shallow breaths as provocative currents began crawling up her leg, but he seemed unaware of the effect he was having on her.

"You getting any warmer?"

She nodded vigorously, not trusting herself to speak.

He was doing something different with her foot now. His thumbs were stroking the length of her sole; hard,

powerful strokes that made the skin tingle at the back of
her neck as well as the bottom of her foot. He angled
the flat of his thumb against her instep and after a moment began pressing, kneading, stroking, until her head
grew light with unimagined sensation.

"What's this on the bottom of your foot, Molly?"

Before she could pull back on her leg, he set her heel
on his knee and touched his forefinger to the multi-
branched scar puckering her skin. "Jeesuz, how did you
do that?" She tried to yank her foot from his grasp, but
his grasp would not be broken. "I'm not makin' fun of
it. Stop squirmin'. You should see some've my scars.
They make this look pretty."

She lowered her eyes. Pierce knew nothing of the
life she had lived in Ireland. He knew nothing of the
hunger or the way her mother had died. Her father
had been too proud to tell Duncan Blackledge the
truth, and she discovered she was too ashamed to do
any differently. How could she tell Pierce what she
had been digging out of the field that day when she'd
cut her foot? No. She couldn't subject herself to his
pity, or disgust. "I got that when I was digging in the
potato field one year. There was broken glass in the
field and I stepped on it."

"How come you weren't wearin' shoes?"

He said it as if he didn't realize what a luxury shoes
were. *I wasn't wearing shoes because my father
couldn't afford to buy shoes.* "I guess I forgot to put
them on that day."

"Looks like it was pretty deep."

She nodded. "I still don't have all the feeling back in
it. I probably never will."

Pierce outlined the scar with his thumb, then leaned forward and pressed his mouth to it. Molly's eyelids flew back into her head.

"Pierce!"

He motioned her to silence with his hand and continued what he was doing. It seemed to her that her foot was a lump of wood that he was planing with his mouth, erasing the ugliness, reshaping it into a thing of beauty. She felt his breath dance upon her flesh, his tongue play over the thick ridge of knotted tissue. His lips were soft as morning dew is soft. His lips anointed, and blessed, and elevated her spirit with the gentleness of their touch. She held her breath as the down that softened the inside of her calf and thigh suddenly sprang to life.

"Can you feel that?" he whispered against her foot.

"Yes, I . . ." She could feel in a way she had never felt before. Fullness. And thirst. And pulses that yearned to be tamed. "I can feel a little."

"Good. Maybe now we should do the other foot." He didn't set her right foot down immediately. Instead he began to unbutton his placket buttons, blithely, casually, as if he expected her to be accustomed to seeing a man's naked chest. "You can keep your foot warm in here."

"I can't put my foot in—"

"Says who?" When his woolens were unbuttoned to his waist, he opened the placket wide, startling Molly with more nakedness than she had ever seen. His was an axeman's chest—forged by lugging timber, hardened by lifting and prying it. It was dark with hair and thick with young muscle.

He scooted forward on his stool and snugged her foot

against the hard sinew of his stomach. He gave her toes a playful rub. "You're warmer already. Let me have your other foot."

Beneath her toes she felt the soft spring of his hair and the incredible warmth of his skin. He closed the placket over her foot. The wet wool was scratchy against her ankle. Its earthy scent filled her nostrils. She could feel his heartbeat vibrating through her leg, his thumbs massaging her left foot, and within her, she felt dampness where before she had felt only a kindling of warmth.

"Are you disappointed that you can't marry Conor?"

She moistened her lips, for they were suddenly dry. She was relieved, not disappointed, but she couldn't tell that to Pierce. "I'm surprised about Conor. I'd grown up thinking I'd be his wife, but now. . ." She shrugged. "I can't very well be angry with him for entering the priesthood, can I?"

He looked thoughtful as he rubbed her foot. "Was there anyone in Ireland you might've married if you hadn't been promised to Conor?"

"Are you asking me if I was unfaithful to my betrothal vows?"

"Jeesuz-God, no. Don't get all haired up on me. I was just inquirin' in a roundabout way if you had any notions of . . . well . . . marryin' anyone else right away."

"I don't know anyone else."

"You didn't know Conor."

"That was different."

"Was it?"

She opened her mouth, then closed it. She had no answer for that.

"So are you gonna be lookin' around for a husband to replace my brother?" He wanted her to say yes. He wanted her to say she had her eye on a green-eyed wood butcher. He'd been thinkin' that he wouldn't have minded if his Da had betrothed her to him instead've to Conor.

"I . . . I don't know. I mean, I suppose I'll marry one day, but I want to be someone first."

His fingers stroked her foot more slowly now. "Who do you wanna be?"

She locked eyes with him. His irises were so green it was almost painful for her to look at him. "I want people to respect me. I want them to say, 'There goes Molly Deacon. She's the finest dressmaker in all Bangor, maybe in all of Maine.' I want to earn a reputation for creating beautiful things, because that's something that will be mine forever, and no one will ever be able to take it away from me."

He saw in her eyes the fire of her determination and a few scattered threads of sadness. His voice grew soft. "Have you had so very much taken away from you?"

Her eyes starred with tears she refused to shed. It would be so easy to sit here and tell this man what was in her heart. Could she? Could she tell him of the memories that had imprinted themselves so vividly on her mind that she was still reacting to them? Was she able to share this part of herself with anyone?

She felt the gentle touch of his hand on her foot and wondered if he would treat her emotions with equal gentleness. She had no reason to believe he wouldn't, but in sharing, one formed bonds, and she had had so many bonds severed in her twenty years of life that she was hesitant to form new ones. A friendship with Pierce Blackledge could only complicate her life. Like brothers and parents and land leases, friendships could be taken away, and the resulting scar simply took too long to heal. Friendship would do nothing to help her establish her dress shop, and that, after all, was the primary objective in her life.

His question invited an intimacy she would welcome, but she could not admit him to the place in her heart that she had learned to guard with such caution.

Looking beyond him, she saw sunshine brightening the workshop window. "The rain's stopped. I'd better start rehanging my laundry or else nothing will ever dry. Thank you for the flannel"—she dropped it from her shoulders—"and for paying such kind attention to my cold feet." With reluctance she slid her right foot out from his woolens and wriggled the other one from his grasp. She stood up.

Gathering up her high-top boots, she headed for the door. Pierce followed close behind.

"You gonna put on your boots?"

"I don't want to get them muddy. I'll go barefoot."

"Watch out for glass."

She nodded obediently. "I will."

"Your feet'll probably get cold again."

She looked back at him—at the great width of his shoulders, the hard bulk of his chest, the size of his hands—and she thought, *I don't think my feet will ever be cold again.*

The storm had washed the air clean. Molly stood beneath the clothesline, listening to the coo of pigeons as they crowded atop Duncan's roof. But to her ear the cooing sounded like laughter, deep, wonderful laughter.

She pinned a flannel petticoat to the line. There clung to the material the strong smells of lye soap and starch and rainwater, but try as she might, Molly could smell nothing—except wet wool.

Chapter Five

At ten o'clock the next morning, Molly stood outside the wrought-iron fence that marched around the Thatcher property. Looking far up the granite stairs that led to the mansion, she wondered whatever had possessed a man to build so unconventional a house in a city that applauded clean right angles and symmetry.

The structure might have been the size of a city block. Neither rectangular nor square, it sported an array of peaks and angles whose placement seemed no more planned than those of a tree sending out shoots. The roof was sharply gabled in north-south sections and studded with chimneys and dormers that made it seem a skyline unto itself. A circular tower fronted the eastern corner and rose three stories where it was crowned by a dunce's cap of roof. Forest-green wood and gray stone formed contrasting surfaces. Arched windows and recessed balconies peeked out from stone. Rectangular windows and steepled porches peeked out from wood. It might have been an Irish manor house for all its dark wood and brooding stone.

Molly opened the gate, lifted her skirt, and stepped onto the first riser, recalling, as she climbed, Duncan's monologue of that morning concerning the patriarch of the Thatcher clan. "The old feller's name was Hastings Thatcher and he was monied 'fore he ever set foot in Bangor. Come from Newburyport. Began buyin' up timberland when Massachusetts started sellin' off parcels of Maine by lott'ry. Owned over a million acres of stumpage by the thirties. When we got hit by that big land speculation in 'thirty-five, he sold off a half million acres for ten dollars an acre. Heard tell he invested some of those millions in railroads and steamships, but Hastings was pretty closemouthed 'bout his finances. Built that house on State Street fifteen years ago, and there hasn't been a year go by that they haven't added on a room or a porch. Hastings passed on close to four years ago, but it's common talk that Olympia takes right after 'im. Has a twin brother, Evan, though the two a them look no more alike than Methuselah and his billy goat. She's always rippin' up something and doin' it over. I think she keeps half the cabinetmakers in Bangor in business, leastways all the ones who aren't Irish."

Molly took a deep breath as she reached the front door. *So, who has to know I'm Irish?* If she didn't sound Irish, why did she have to *be* Irish? Her nationality didn't have any bearing on how well she sewed. And what some people didn't know wouldn't hurt them. She straightened the pointed waist of her bodice jacket, threw her shoulders back, and lifted her chin, then pulled out the small brass knob on the right side of the doorjamb.

Within the house a bell jangled erratically. Molly experienced a sudden twinge of unease. Perhaps it had been folly to come here. Perhaps Pierce was right when he said she was wasting her time. Her stomach began to feel queasy. She clasped the leather handles of her carpetbag with two hands and took another deep breath. Her eyes wandered from the narrow windows on either side of the door to the fanlight above with its long ribbons of lead dividing the glass into wedges.

The door opened and a woman in a starched apron and ruffled mobcap stood before her. "Yes?"

"I'm here to see Miss Olympia Thatcher please."

The woman's face was coolly impassive as she dipped her eyes to observe Molly's carpetbag. "Are you expected?"

"No, but I'm sure she'll want to see me."

The maid was not so sure. She clasped her hands beneath her bosom and, looking as if she was about to recite a well-worn speech, addressed the speech above Molly's head. "Them that's seekin' work should use the back door. And we don't hire Irish. Good day."

As she started to close the door, Molly thrust her bag into the opening. Without skipping a beat she said, "I'm not Irish. I'm English." She skewered the woman with a look that could have withered the ruffles on her apron. "And now I'll thank you to tell Miss Thatcher that

Molly Deacon is here to discuss a business proposition with her. I shouldn't imagine your mistress would be overly pleased to learn that you had turned away a close friend of Lord Clevedon Berryhill."

A look of uncertainty crossed the woman's face. She hesitated for a long moment, then stepped aside. "I'll tell Miss Olympia you're here. Follow me."

She led Molly through a circular foyer whose floor was a checkerboard of black-and-white marble tiles. Arched doorways interrupted the dark wood paneling and radiated like spokes in six different directions. A massive hall stand, complete with wooden pegs, mirror, marble shelf, and umbrella rests, occupied the wall closest to the front door. Dark walnut hall chairs with steepled backs and Gothic crosses circled the foyer, and above each doorway, in frames of gilt, Thatcher ancestors perused each other and all who walked beneath them.

As Molly crossed the center of the room, she looked up. The staircase that curved along one wall to the second story spiraled upward to a third and fourth story. It was like being inside a giant nautilus. As they passed into a hallway to the right of the stairs, Molly heard a steady hammering echo out to her from the inner depths of the house. She wondered if Miss Thatcher was redecorating again.

"You can wait in here," the maid announced, indicating a room off the hall. "I'll see if Miss Olympia will see you."

Like the foyer the room was paneled in dark wood. Floor-to-ceiling bookshelves lined one wall and a flat-topped desk, long as a settee, presided at one end of the room. A sofa rested against the wall opposite the book-shelves, and it was to this that Molly directed her foot-steps. She sat down, removed her gloves, and smoothed her bare hand along the surface of the tufted burgundy leather, finding it soft as butter.

She settled her carpetbag atop her lap and looked toward the door. No one was coming. She tapped her fingers on the carpetbag and her heels on the floor. She looked toward the door again. Unable to sit still, she set her carpetbag aside, stood up, and wandered to the desk at the far end of the room.

Arranged at precise angles atop the desk were a hinged writing box, a cover for blotting-paper sheets, pen-wipe, and inkstand—all inlaid with cut brass and red tortoiseshell. A propelling pencil lay next to the pen-wipe. Lord Berryhill had owned one that was mounted in pewter. This one was mounted in gold.

Against the wall to Molly's right there stood a tall walnut bookcase with a glass front. Rather than books, however, it contained a collection of firearms from blunderbusses, to Forsyth sporting guns, to dueling pis-tols inlaid with silver. There were staghorn powder flasks, lead shot in velvet cases, and one pocket pistol with a bore so large that Molly had no doubt it could take off a man's head at close range. She shivered at the thought.

"Guns were my father's passion."

Molly saw the woman's reflection in the glass and turned round to face her.

"He always said that any man worth his mettle should learn all there is to know about horses, guns, and turning a profit. Mrs. Popham said you wished to speak to me. Do I know you?"

"My name is Molly Deacon, Miss Thatcher."

"So Mrs. Popham said. And?"

Molly hadn't expected Olympia Thatcher to be so abrupt, but having been exposed to the cream of society before, she was not about to be intimidated now. She felt the skin on her face tighten across her bones as she returned the woman's look measure for measure. "I have a business proposition to discuss with you, if you would have a few moments to spare me."

"As you can hear from the hammering, I'm having work done in another part of the house. If you can say what you have to say in two minutes, I'll listen. If not, I'm afraid I must ask you to leave. I don't trust these local carpenters. If I leave them unsupervised for five minutes, they're apt to knock out the wrong wall."

Olympia Thatcher looked to be a paragon of good sense. Not a pretty woman, Molly thought, but a handsome woman. She was tall, her shoulders wide, her bosom well defined and full, and she wore her pearl-gray satin day dress with aristocratic grace rather than affectation. Her hair was a soft red-gold, parted in the middle, draped over her ears, and caught at her nape in a fashionable knot. Her eyes were the color of hazelnuts, a muted green-brown threaded with strands of gold, and looked just as hard. Molly sensed that Olympia Thatcher was not a woman to be easily manipulated, but neither was Molly content to be shepherded out of the study like a stray lamb.

"I doubt I can make my presentation in two minutes,

Miss Thatcher, so perhaps I should go elsewhere. The only reason I came here first was because I thought it was your clothing that dictated fashion in Bangor, but I have the names of other women who might benefit from my services. I apologize for wasting as much of your time as I have."

"Other women?" Olympia inquired. As Molly walked back to the sofa to gather her gloves and carpetbag, the woman drew her shawl more tightly across her back. "Women like Celia Dwinel?"

Molly slid her left hand into her glove. "Why, yes, that was one of the names. Do you know her?"

"Yes, I know her, and she knows as much about fashion as the carpenters in my dining room know about transcendentalism."

"Then I would guess the lady is in dire need of a dressmaker from abroad." She pulled on her other glove and picked up her carpetbag. "Good day to you, Miss Thatcher."

Before she had taken two steps, Olympia asked, "Where from abroad?"

Molly slowed her pace but did not stop, as if she, too, were in a hurry. "Ireland. I was milliner to the family of Lord Clevedon Berryhill who owns estates in both England and Ireland, but for the past five years we've resided in Ireland."

"You were milliner for the entire estate?" Olympia looked skeptical. "I would guess you're rather young to have been given so much responsibility."

Molly stopped at the door and shrugged. "I was apprenticing with old Mrs. Barlow, who was the estate milliner. When she died, I replaced her. Mrs. Barlow said I had an uncanny knack for color and design, and Lord Berryhill didn't dispute her."

"So you're Irish."

"Oh, no, milady. I'm English. Lady Berryhill found me in the streets of London some fifteen years ago and put me to work in the scullery of their manor house."

"And your parents?"

"I'm an orphan." Never before had she told such outrageous lies, but never before had she wanted employment so badly. She hoped if she ever had to repeat the story, she'd have the good fortune to remember the details.

"An English orphan working as milliner to an Anglo-Irish lord. I could accuse you of reading too much Mr. Dickens, Miss Deacon." But Molly could tell from the expression on the woman's face that curiosity had triumphed over her earlier rigidity. "Very well, I'll see what you have in your bag, but if the carpenters destroy my dining room, you can expect a bill."

Molly spread the contents of her carpetbag atop the desk and watched as Olympia examined the lace bertha she'd completed last night. "You'll notice the horizontal puffings of muslin above the double row of flouncing. That's the latest style from France. I assume it will be quite the rage here this fall."

Olympia fixed the garment against her bodice. "It's rather busy, isn't it? Do you need eleven bows parading down the front?"

Molly compressed her lips. Here she was trying to impress the woman with her French puffings and all she could do was count bows. "Naturally we could remove as many bows as you'd like."

"Mmm." Olympia set the bertha down and went on to a muslin chemisette. Her face remained impassive. "Frankly, I think chemisettes are rather impractical. They belong in another century . . . with stomachers."

Molly shook her head. "The beauty of a chemisette is that it can be fashioned with materials that are much cooler than muslin, materials that would be quite fashionable for summer."

"The undersleeves are too puffy."

"They're detachable." Molly unbuttoned one sleeve at the shoulder and removed it from the lingerie bodice. "You can wear the bodice without sleeves, like so, or I could fashion a variety of undersleeves that you could wear beneath a variety of dress sleeves."

"I suppose so." But there was scant enthusiasm in Olympia's voice, and as Molly watched her skim the remaining articles of stitchery on the desk, she detected that the woman did so with polite disinterest. "Well, Miss Deacon, you're a talented young woman, but I fear your skill is of little use to me. I employ a private dressmaker in Boston who has given me no cause to be dissatisfied with her work."

Inwardly Molly sighed. This was more difficult than she had originally anticipated. "But every time you'd like a new gown, you have to make the long trek to Boston. I could save you several journeys a year."

"I look forward to my trips to Boston."

Molly hesitated, unsure what her recourse to this should be. "Even in the winter? You'd have to travel overland in the winter and I should think that would be most uncomfortable, not to mention cold."

"Well—"

"I work quickly." She raced on, deciding to overwhelm the woman with a list of her attributes. "Mrs. Barlow used to say that she'd never seen anyone's fingers move as quickly as mine." What she wouldn't tell Olympia was that Mrs. Barlow was the estate cook and had made the statement with reference to the time Molly had filched a dish of roly-poly pudding from the sideboard in the kitchen without anyone seeing her do it. "If you went to Boston, ordered two gowns, waited for them to be sewn, and returned again to Bangor, I'd wager I could have *four* gowns completed in the same amount of time."

Olympia's eyebrows lifted in a high arch. "A brash wager, wouldn't you say, Miss Deacon?"

"It's God's truth," Molly averred, though she wasn't quite as fast as she claimed. "And not only am I fleet of finger. I have a quick eye to gauge the cut of a sleeve or the shape of a bodice. I would challenge *Godey's Lady's Book* to provide an illustration of a gown I couldn't copy, and I can alter existing designs and create new ones that would be most complimentary to the feminine figure."

Olympia was clearly amused by Molly's harangue. "Should you decide to put aside your dressmaking needles one day, Miss Deacon, you should try your hand at public speaking in the Lyceum. I've heard people who have had messages of great import to deliver whose rhetoric has been far less convincing than yours. And now if you'll excuse me. I no longer hear the sounds of nail and hammer, which suggests that my carpenters are awaiting further instructions. I was forced into hiring a number of Irish this time, which isn't my normal practice, but they were apparently all that was available."

Molly didn't care what the woman thought about the Irish so long as she would give her a job, which, at the moment, seemed like an unlikely prospect. There was only one option left to try.

"I'll be on my way now," Molly said as she gathered her needlework into her carpetbag. "But next time you visit your dressmaker, perhaps you should ask her to select materials for your gowns that will enhance your coloring rather than dilute it. Pearl gray dulls your eyes and washes out your cheeks. But I suppose your dressmaker has her reasons for wanting to make you look ashen."

"Ashen?" Olympia's hand went to her cheek as if to hide it from view. Uncertainty reshaped every feature on her face. "She said pearl gray was the preferred color this year."

"Oh, I'm sure it is. What she failed to tell you is that pearl gray is not a color that looks particularly good on *you*. I would guess the fee you pay your dressmaker doesn't stipulate that she should be discriminating." She ripped a bottle-green bow off an undersleeve and handed it to Olympia. "You see how your skin tone assumes a golden hue against the green? That's the effect you're looking for. You should throttle your dressmaker for putting you in colors that reduce your complexion to the consistency of almond paste."

Olympia frowned as she made the comparison between the green of the ribbon and the gray of her gown. "The gray does make me look rather cadaverous, doesn't it?"

Beneath Molly's exterior reserve she was exuberant, for she could see that Olympia was starting to weaken.

"You're right, Miss Deacon. My milliner has done me a great disservice." She set the ribbon on the desk before riveting her attention on Molly. "I'm not in the habit of offering employment to people who walk in off the street, but you've made a persuasive case for yourself. I'll give you a month to prove that you're as good as you claim you are. If I like your work, you'll have a permanent position. If not, you'll be free to solicit Celia Dwinel or anyone else in the city. I'll expect you to work here at the house on Mondays, Wednesdays, and Fridays, and will allow you to work the rest of the time at your place of residence . . . which is—?"

"On Hancock Street."

"In the Irish section of town? You told me you were English."

"Oh, I am. I'm only staying on Hancock Street because"—she suddenly remembered the milk sign in Duncan's window— "I—uh saw a sign in the window of a house advertising a room to let and the family is Irish."

"Mmm. Well, then, I'll expect you at eight o'clock on Monday morning. There's probably a room on the third floor that we can convert into some kind of sewing room for you."

"About my wages, milady."

"Fifty cents a week plus your noon meal."

Molly hesitated. This was exactly what she'd expected, but she'd already made her mind up about the matter. She sucked in a nervous breath. "A dollar a week is my asking price."

"A dollar? Miss Deacon, my father bought prime timberland for less than a dollar an acre."

"I can't quote the price of trees, milady, but if you want me, it will cost you a dollar a week."

"I never paid my dressmaker in Boston more than fifty cents a week."

"Perhaps that's why she swaddled you in pearl-gray satin."

Olympia thought about this for a moment, then smiled. "Yes, I suppose that could be the reason. You make more sense than I would like to admit, Miss Deacon. A dollar a week it is."

As the two women returned to the foyer, the front door opened to admit a man who looked as much a part of Thatcher opulence as the gilt-framed portraits hanging over the doorways. Molly's first sight of him was from the back as he closed the door behind himself. His coattails ended just above the bend of his knees and swung freely against tight black trousers that strapped beneath his shoes. As he turned, he removed his top hat, tossed it into the air, and caught it on his walking stick.

"Someday you're going to spear your hat on that ridiculous cane, and then you won't consider yourself quite so clever."

"That, my dear Olympia, will never happen." He removed his hat from the cane, sighted it against one of the pegs on the hall rack, and with an agile flick of his wrist let it fly. The hat landed on its intended peg as neatly as a horseshoe around a stake. "A ringer," he boasted with a smile that seemed as spontaneous as Olympia's was forced. "And who have we here?"

"Molly Deacon," Olympia supplied without flourish. "My new dressmaker. And this, Miss Deacon, is my brother, Evan."

Molly dropped a proper curtsy and with one discreet pass of her eye assessed Evan Thatcher. He had the same hazel eyes as his sister, but unlike Olympia, there was an added softness about his eyes that lent his face an aura of openness and approachability. His hair was a similar red-gold, made dark, Molly suspected, by a liberal application of macassar oil. But that was where all comparisons ended. He was a tall man, lean of shoulder and hip, who wore his high-necked cravat and frilled shirt with subtle dignity. He did not look as old as thirty, but it was difficult for Molly to figure a man's age when he bore no lines of hardship on his countenance. As she stood before him, her vision was in a direct line with his chest, and she blinked in surprise when she focused on his shirt studs.

Their shape was that of small ovals. Their casing was gold filigree that surrounded painted portraits of ladies mounted behind glass. Each portrait was different, and Molly wondered if this was Evan Thatcher's way of paying tribute to the women he had conquered then tossed aside. Not even among the Berryhills had she met anyone so bold as to wear a portrait gallery of lost loves on his shirtfront.

"A new dressmaker?" Evan looked pleased. "Does this mean that you're going to rid yourself of old what's-her-name? Good. I never liked her to begin with." He leveled his eyes on Molly. "This is what a dressmaker should look like. And look at that dimple, Olympia."

Molly froze as he framed her face with his hand. His cream silk glove highlighted her cheek without touching it.

"Dressmakers of extraordinary ability always have dimples that curve all the way to their jawline."

Molly felt an embarrassing warmth seep beneath her flesh.

"You're making her blush, Evan. I think she's unaccustomed to rogues."

"I'll have to make sure she doesn't remain unaccustomed for long, won't I?" He grinned and gave her a lazy wink.

"Eight o'clock on Monday morning," said Olympia and herded Molly to the door.

"Eight o'clock," Molly repeated. "And thank you." She looked past Olympia and nodded politely when Evan tipped his head in farewell.

Olympia closed the door. She turned toward her brother. "Overdoing the flirtation somewhat, aren't you?"

He peered through the glass that flanked the door and watched the crown of Molly's bonnet disappear below the slope of the hillside stairs. "Pretty girl."

"Don't trifle with this one, Evan. If she's as good as she says she is, I'll want to keep her for a while."

From the east end of Hancock Street Molly spied the twin elms that shaded the entrance to Duncan's walkway. Her stomach growled as she walked, reminding her that she'd been too nervous to eat breakfast, but success rendered her hungry enough now to deplete Duncan's pantry of much of the food he had put up.

As she neared the house, she saw that Pierce was sitting on the front stairs. And even though she'd decided yesterday that she couldn't risk growing close to him, she felt her emotions conspiring to fill her with delight at the sight of him. She wondered if he had gone to the musicale last night without her, for he'd gone out early and not come back till late. She'd heard him climb the stairs sometime past midnight. He'd paused at the top of the stairs, then taken eight steps across the landing to his room. She had counted those steps, and she'd known when he reached his room, because she'd discovered that the floorboard abutting his threshold creaked, and she heard it creak on his eighth footfall. Eight steps from the head of the staircase to his threshold. She felt a secret pleasure that she had learned this detail about him—a detail that perhaps he didn't even know about himself.

Bypassing the dooryard walk in favor of the front walk, she promenaded straight down the gravel path toward him. After all, he did have to be told that she'd secured the job he swore she'd never get.

He sat with his axe riding his right thigh, the iron head perched on his knee, and she heard a *scrape scrape scrape* as he ground a rectangular stone against the metal. He looked up as she neared the house, and she saw his face mirror surprise as he regarded her. Then he did something that no man had ever done to her before.

He whistled.

She felt her neck turn redder than the silk lining of her bonnet, and she slowed her steps, suddenly self-conscious. She had worked for days on this gown before leaving Ireland. The bodice jacket, fashioned in black merino wool, formed a deep V at her waist and bore accents in bright red piping. Scarlet ruching hugged her neck. Her sleeves were tight and plain, the shoulder seams dropped low on her arm, and around the bottom of her bell-shaped skirt was a double row of flounces in black-and-red plaid taffeta. She felt pretty, but not pretty enough to be whistled at.

"Does this mean you've forgiven me?" She set her carpetbag on the bottom step.

"Forgiven you?"

"For not attending the musicale last night."

"Oh, that." He went back to grinding down the metal behind his axe bit. "Didn't bother me any."

His sleeves were rolled to his elbows, baring fine, brawny forearms that Molly knew would be the envy of many an Irish squire. In contrast to his chest his arms were practically devoid of hair except for a pale dusting that looked soft as floss silk. Sinew defined his flesh, and it was a stunning spectacle to watch the flow and slide of his muscles as he rasped away on his axe head. The sight of those corded forearms made something in the pit of her stomach go soft and dewy.

"So how'd they treat you at Thatcher's? Couldn't of been too rough on you. Your bonnet's still sittin' straight, so I guess no one threw you out on your head."

She felt like preening, but didn't. "Oh, they treated me fairly well. I start work Monday morning at eight o'clock."

His grindstone skidded to a halt. "You're pullin' my leg."

"An Irish-Catholic girl wouldn't discuss the existence

of your limbs, much less have the audacity to pull on one of them."

He grinned so deeply that the depressions appeared on either side of his mouth. "C'mon, Molly. Don't tease. Did the old bat really hire you?"

"Indeed, she did. But I'd hardly call her old, though she does look somewhat older than her brother even if they are twins."

"You mean Thatcher was there too? Jeesuz-God, no wonder you got hired." He jabbed the grindstone at her for emphasis. "He's populated half of Bangor with the bastards he's gotten on his maids. Toys with the ladies till he's had his fill, then drops 'em like millstones. You stay away from him. He'll chase anything in petticoats."

Her eyebrow shot up. "Olympia hired me before I met Evan. I impressed her with my stitchery, not my petticoats."

He bent his head and skated the grindstone across his axe. "Stay away from him anyway. Can't trust a man whose shirtfront has more frills than a doxy's backside."

Molly found his concern flattering, but misplaced. Men of Evan Thatcher's ilk did not associate with lowly dressmakers, be they English *or* Irish. Besides, she had no intention of lending her face to the man's already extensive collection of shirt studs. She would leave that to women who had less ambitious dreams than she. "I imagine Evan Thatcher has more pressing things to do than engage his sister's dressmaker in small talk."

But it wasn't the small talk that worried Pierce. "You just make sure he knows one thing—we Irish take care of our own. And it can upset us somethin' fierce to learn that our womenfolk are havin' to fend off improper advances."

Molly wondered if Pierce would define the kiss he'd given her two nights ago as an improper advance. Apparently not. *Improper* advances seemed to be the kind effected by other men. Pierce probably considered his own advances quite proper. His inconsistency tickled her.

He set his grindstone aside and brushed residue from the axe head with the side of his thumb. "Hung this myself," he said as he smoothed his hand down the long, curved helve. It was long as his thigh and slender as a woman's calf. "Made of hickory. Tough wood, but it's like elastic. If a man puts most've his force at the end of his stroke when he's makin' a cut, he gets almost no shock to his arms and shoulders."

He worked his big hand up and down the handle while he talked. His fingers were lean and well formed, and Molly watched them bend with a suppleness that seemed to belie their strength. Where his hands had excreted sweat and body oils, the wood was bleached and shiny from use. He looked comfortable with the feel of the wood as it glided beneath his palm, and Molly sensed his pride as he embraced his creation—the same kind of pride she experienced when she completed a gown.

Her eyes lingered on his hand. Up and down the hickory it went, up and down, with a slow, sensuous rhythm of its own. She thought back to yesterday when her foot had been the recipient of those same powerful strokes, and she grew uncomfortably warm at the memory. She turned her face to where the wind could cool her cheeks.

"With this axe a man can do a lot've things." Pierce stood up. He let the helve slide through his hand until his fingers and thumb were angled in a place where the balance was precise. "Only weighs three and a half pounds, but it can be a pretty deadly three and a half pounds. A good axeman can split a runnin' rat in half at twenty paces. He can do the same thing with the knot in that elm."

Molly squinted at the twin elms guarding the entrance to the front path. "Which tree has the knot?"

She felt movement at her side, then heard a great *whooshing* sound as his axe went hurtling end over end through the air. It thudded into the elm on the right and for long moments quivered like a spent arrow. Pierce nodded toward it. "That one."

Molly looked from the tree to Pierce, then without another word hiked down the path to the elm.

He laughed after her. "Somethin' wrong with your eyesight that you can't see it from here?"

She peered at the ugly knurl of wood. The axe blade lay buried deep within its center. Not to one side or the other. It was dead center. Amazement widened her eyes. How had he done that? She jumped as she heard his voice close by her ear.

"I ever hear of Thatcher botherin' you, I'll bury that blade in shirt frills 'stead've elm."

The implication of what he might do to Evan Thatcher turned the flesh beneath her ruffled collar to ice. She set her gloved hand on his forearm. "You wouldn't really hurt him?" But she saw something

within the depths of his green eyes that bespoke a tenac-
ity to match his extraordinary prowess. "Pierce?"

"He'd best watch himself, that's all I gotta say."

She pondered the reason for this sudden protective
streak of his and wondered if there was something in the
blood between her family and Pierce's that fostered such
feelings. Perhaps this was simply the way it would
always be between Blackledges and Deacons. But it
wouldn't do at all for Pierce to start threatening Evan
Thatcher with a poleaxe. For the sake of her future employment she would have to remember not to mention
Evan in Pierce's presence again.

Pierce lowered his gaze to the hand that Molly had
laid on his forearm. Seeing his expression she snatched
her hand away from him. It was considered improper
for a woman to take a man's arm unless the two people
were engaged. She might have touched Conor's arm,
but not Pierce's. And certainly not while it was bare!
Good Lord, what was she thinking of? "You, uh, you do
quite well throwing that thing."

Ridges of tendon strained against his flesh as he
wrenched the blade from the tree. "Ample. Not as good
as I'd like to be, but one day I'll be better."

"Better? I don't see how you could be any better."

He braced the axe atop his shoulder and motioned her
back toward the house. "Would you let me stick a sewing needle between your teeth, stand you against that
tree, and try to split the needle in half from twenty
paces?"

"I certainly would not."

"See? If I was better, you'd trust me to do that without any hesitation at all."

"I wouldn't trust Michael the Archangel to do something as crazy as that. What makes you think I should trust Pierce Blackledge?"

He flashed her one of those devilishly charming grins that could melt a miser's gold as easily as a spinster's heart. "I doubt that Michael the Archangel was a Bangor Tiger." He laughed at the face she made, and when she would have climbed the porch stairs, he stopped her. "It strikes me that we should find some way of celebrating this new job've yours even if you're gonna be in the same house as Evan Thatcher. What say I take you down to the Penobscot Exchange and treat you to some celebration victuals?"

Animation leapt into her eyes but dissolved quickly when she reminded herself how she had to spend the afternoon. She hated to do this to him again, but . . . "I'd love to, Pierce. I really would. But I still have more ironing to do."

"More? I thought you got it all done yesterday?"

"Only some of it."

"And I suppose it can't wait till tomorrow."

"Tomorrow's Sunday."

"So?"

She seemed surprised by the question. "You know it's a sin to perform servile work on Sunday."

He rolled his eyes at her. "Jeesuz-God, you can think've more excuses. I suppose you 'll even think of some excuse not to attend the bean supper at church tonight."

She lifted her carpetbag off the step and gave him a wary look. "Bean supper?"

"Yah. Da's makin' baked beans for some've the parishioners at church tonight. He's expectin' us over there round five."

"Oh?" She remembered Olympia saying she'd just hired some Irish carpenters, and she wondered if those men would be at the church tonight. Would Pierce know them? Would he introduce her as a buttonhole relation from Ireland? What would happen if she saw those same men at Thatcher's where she was supposed to be the new *English* dressmaker? She couldn't take the chance of being caught in her lie. "Actually, the more I think about it, the more I suspect that at five o'clock I'll still be slaving over a bosom board."

"So you're gonna stay home."

"Yes, I think I'd better."

He grabbed the grindstone off the porch, tossed it into the air, and caught it in his fist on its downward flight. "Tell me, you ever gonna leave the house again, or are you plannin' to keep yourself locked in the kitchen with Da's iron for the rest've your life?"

"One evening is not the rest of my life."

"Might as well be. You wouldn't attend the musicale because you had to iron. Won't go to lunch because you have to iron. Won't go to supper because you think you're still gonna be ironing. You're either queer for ironing or you just don't wanna be seen with me." And because rejection did not sit well with him, he drilled an accusing look at her. "Which is it?"

She wondered if he was so insensitive as to be blind to the emotions he aroused in her. He displayed no sensitivity at all if he could ask a question like that, and she resented the fact that he had. "I'm not going to dignify that with an answer." She marched up the stairs and threw open the front door. Pierce was right behind her.

"Seems to me if you're gonna be living here, you could make some kind've effort to fit in. Doesn't seem like it'd hurt you too much to set your work aside to meet some've our friends."

Up the hall stairs she went without a backward glance.

"And if Da's nice enough to put up with you, the least you could do is *smile* at him every once in a while! Jeesuz-God, you haven't cracked a smile since you've been here. Don't you know how?"

She stopped mid-stair and he knew by the straightness of her back that he'd struck a tender nerve.

"Wouldn't hurt if you tried smilin' at *me* once in a while, either!"

With that, she continued up the stairs. Pierce smacked his lips in exasperation and headed back out the front door.

At the top of the stairs Molly turned and stared into the emptiness of the lower hall. She touched her hand to her mouth, realizing that he had noticed this terrible inadequacy of hers. She'd hoped that she had masked it well, but he had noticed, and it made her feel ugly.

She didn't want to feel ugly. She wanted to feel pretty for him. She wanted something to take the ugliness away.

If only she could smile as easily as he.

Chapter Six

The steeple clock in the parlor was striking a quarter past the hour of nine that night when Molly set aside her lace bertha and gold-eyed Sharp and began tidying things in her bedchamber that didn't need to be tidied. She straightened her counterpane and fluffed her pillow, then walked to her bureau and mindlessly rearranged combs and hair needles. Duncan had given her a ball of lemon-balm soap for her bath last night. It sat in a porcelain dish atop the bureau's handkerchief drawer, and as she stared at it, she sniffed her wrist, amazed that the fragrance still lingered on her flesh. She touched the lacework that framed her mirror, then trailed the tip of her fingernail down the glass itself.

Her image, as reflected in the dark, hazy surface of the looking glass, seemed an oblique rendering of her actual being, so she moved nearer, until her nose was almost touching the glass. Her features seemed distorted and ugly, like the bottom of her foot, so she puffed up her cheeks and pulled a face at herself. But the image proved more sad than funny.

Straightening up, she backed away from the mirror. "Hahaha," she said to her reflection, but the result was mirthless. Laughter was a difficult quality to imitate. So she tried again. She tried with her voice high. She tried with her voice low. She tried with her mouth open. She tried with her mouth closed. She tried "hee's" instead of "ha's." But the result was the same. Laughter sounded unnatural coming from her mouth. She would never laugh like Pierce Blackledge.

Turning round, she eyed the lemon-shaped finial on her bedpost. Ever since Pierce had told her he'd built this piece of furniture, she couldn't help but see his face every time she looked at the thing. "What are you staring at?" she flung at it, for it seemed to have been spying on her all night, mocking her inability to laugh as he laughed, to smile as he smiled.

Whipping her bonnet off the bureau, she strode to the bedpost and plopped it none too gently over the intrusive finial. "Much better," she said, nodding in satisfaction at the transformation. She wandered to her window. The waterfront was alight with the glow from whale-oil lanterns. She wondered if Pierce was toasting a mug of ale in one of those lantern-lit grogshops. Maybe he'd stayed late at the bean supper. Or maybe he spent his Saturday nights with women who liked his attentions.

Not liking that idea, she spun round and shot the bonnet on her bedpost a disapproving look.

From the vicinity of the kitchen she heard a window sash shoot upward. Pierce had told her in a few clipped sentences earlier that afternoon that she could expect his father home fairly early from the bean supper. Well, one of the men had come home over an hour ago and she surmised it was Duncan. She wondered what he was doing downstairs all by himself.

With a listless step she ambled back to the bureau, suddenly brightening. She didn't know what time mass began tomorrow! She'd have to go downstairs and find out. And while she was down there, maybe she would spare a few minutes to cheer Duncan up. Poor man. Spending Saturday night all by hmself, in an empty house, with no one to talk to.

She threw a broadcloth shawl over her chemise and flannel petticoat and, after dousing her candles, headed downstairs.

The kitchen door swung open before her outthrust hand. Compared to the relative dimness of the hall, the kitchen exploded with lantern light, and Molly threw her hand up to shield her eyes from the brightness. She looked away from the glare, caught sight of the big tin hip bath by the stove, then saw a shape rise from behind it.

It wasn't Duncan who'd come home. It was Pierce. And he was wearing his wool trousers and nothing else.

"Jeesuz, Molly, I thought you'd be asleep by now." He pulled up the trousers that hung slack around his hips, and where the fly front lay open she saw a dark strip of hair arrow downward into shadow. She felt her neck go hot at the thought of what lay within that shadow.

"I . . . I thought you were Duncan." A hot, liquid pressure filled the cavity behind her eyes as she stared at him, for she had never seen a man more naked, or more beautiful. "I'm sorry, Pierce. I didn't mean to interrupt you." She bobbed her head toward the door and took a step backward. Her tongue felt suddenly lumpish and she didn't know if she could form words around it. "I'll just go back to my room and leave you to finish—"

"Don't go," he said. His eyes roved her flannel petticoat and long shawl. The idea of her standing before him in only one layer of clothing made the blood sing in his ears. "Is—uh, is there somethin' you wanted?"

From the gentleness of his tone it seemed to her that he'd forgotten his earlier irritation with her as quickly as he'd forgotten yesterday's anger at the breakfast table. An Irishman who didn't carry a grudge was an oddity to her. Perhaps he'd inherited his mother's good disposition after all. "I only came down to ask your father what time mass is tomorrow. But I can wait till he gets home to ask him." She took another step backward and clutched her shawl more tightly to herself, as if his nakedness made her more conscious of protecting her own.

"You could ask me, you know. I attend mass too."

But she couldn't ask him anything, not when the lantern light was casting so intricate a pattern across the long, naked slant of his ribs. *Flesh to be gentled*, she thought, and grew warm at the intimacy. She could not see the bright points of color on her cheeks, but Pierce did, so he turned his broad back to her and spoke over his shoulder as he buttoned his trousers.

"Mass is at eight, so we usually leave the house at seven-thirty. You want me to wake you when I get up tomorrow?" His back flexed with the purity of young muscle. His skin was tight and unblemished, and she wondered where he was hiding the scars he claimed to have. The shadow in the front of his trousers came to mind, and she felt her neck go hot all over again.

"No, I—uh, I'm usually up by five," she said. His shoulders were so massive that their outline seemed blurred by the light. He worked the straps of his suspenders over his arms, and she watched those shoulders dip right and left and his shoulder blades rise and fall like heavy mallets, stunning her with the athletic grace and exquisite beauty of a man's body.

"If you get up by five, then you can wake me. Why do you get up so early?" He turned round to face her.

"I like to get up early." The webbing of his suspenders lay flat against his chest in two-inch-wide strips, but rather than conceal his nakedness, the webbing seemed to enhance it. *Like gift wrapping*, she thought, suddenly wondering how many women had had the pleasure of unwrapping the gift.

His eyes ranged over her like a slow hand. "I like to sleep in," he whispered, making it sound more like an invitation than a pronouncement. He smoothed his fingers over the curve of his naked bicep, and Molly felt her knee joints unhitch as she sensed what it was he would like to be caressing with those long fingers of his. She imagined that the curve of that bicep would fill her hand from her fingertips to the heel of her palm, and her breathing quickened at the earthiness of his appeal. She bowed her head, embarrassed to look at him, reluctant to leave. Pierce watched her hair wing forward onto her temples like great dark blinders, and he stretched his fingers as if in imitation of smoothing the lustrous strands from her face.

"Da decided to stay later at the rectory than me," he said in a moment of awkwardness. And not knowing what else to do with himself, he lifted a bucket full of bathwater off the floor and headed toward the window with it. "Seems that someone mentioned somethin' about a poker game, and Da's not one to pass up a good game of five-card draw." He tossed the bathwater outside, then slammed his fist against either side of the sash to unstick the open window, but it wouldn't budge. "Thought I'd come home early. Had some work to catch up on." He pounded on the sash again, but still it wouldn't move. "Damn thing. Da painted it shut once, and it hasn't worked the same since."

Molly took slow steps around the kitchen table. He was pounding the sash with his axe-throwing arm, and she remembered the blade that had sliced through the air as she watched that arm—a limb so powerfully masculine that his veins strained against the smooth fit of his skin. "Can I help?" she asked as she neared him.

He turned round quickly and peered down at her as if questioning how she got there. 'Don't know what anyone the size of you can do, but you're welcome to try." Indeed, the stuck window gave him the perfect excuse to be near her. And he wanted to be near her, close to the slender hands that clutched her shawl, close to the fingers he could well imagine pleasuring a man.

"Why did you throw that water out the window?" she asked. She was trying to distract herself, for his upper body was still wet, and she could see that water had pooled in the shallow cleft at the base of his throat and was floating downward to mingle with the dark coils of hair on his chest.

He looked out into the night, away from the shawl that he knew was hiding something only a husband should see. "That's where we throw all the slop water. Into the flower beds. Asters just seem to eat it up." He looked back to her. "Da didn't tell you about the water?"

"No. No, he didn't." But she saw the water that caressed the ridges of tendon that patterned his flesh; saw it hug the contours of work-hardened muscle and dip into hollows where light had turned to shadow. Compared to this, all other talk of water was of little consequence. She inhaled a quick breath.

Feeling self-conscious with her perusal, Pierce cleared his throat and set the bucket on the floor. "Guess we'd better see about gettin' this thing down. Why don't you try pushin' down on the lower sash while I work on the upper one?"

She nodded in agreement. "Where do you want me?"

He thought she might not be down here in only one layer of clothing if she knew where he really wanted her, but he clamped patient hands around her shoulders and positioned her directly before the window. "Right about here is good." He stood behind her, legs parted and body so close to hers that she could feel his warmth on her back. He angled his torso over her head and, steeling his fingers around the wood of the upper sash, ground his teeth together and heaved downward.

"All right. Push!"

The cords in his neck strained. He pushed. She pushed. The window held.

"Harder!"

He grunted. She panted. He bowed his head with the effort, squinting at the girl below him, and then he saw that her shawl had come loose, and he stared.

Where her hair was drawn upward from her neck, he saw the pale translucence of her flesh, and he ached to feel its softness beneath his lips, to cup the fragile shape of her head within his hand. A feathering of hair dipped below her hairline, shading flesh he guessed had never been touched by the sun. A mole sat low on her neck, round as a peppercorn and smooth as a patch of velvet. He wondered at the taste of it and could almost feel lemon balm washing over his tongue. He was so near he could see the down that formed a silken glaze across her nape, and when she turned her head, he saw flesh and bone glide into a shape as sweet as anything he had ever turned on his lathe.

His breath hovered in suspension. His blood thickened in his veins. And he was overcome by such yearning that tears sprang into his eyes.

The window slammed shut with a bang. Pierce cursed at the unexpected jolt. Molly's shawl slid to the floor.

She scooched down to retrieve her shawl and found Pierce kneeling there beside her, the shawl already in his hands. He was near enough that she could see a spherical imperfection that marred his collarbone, but even though it was the size of a nickel and much whiter

than the rest of his skin, it did nothing to detract from
his beauty.

"You found my pockmark," he said when he realized
what she was staring at.

"You've had the pox?" She knew of no one who had
survived the dreaded pox. In her eyes Pierce Blackledge
assumed a kind of mystical aura.

He threw his head back in laughter, baring the elegant
curve of his neck to her greedy eyes. His laughter made
the air dance around her ears. His neck made her suffer
the sweet agony of wanting to touch it.

"I haven't had the pox, but I've been in a few saloon
brawls. That's where I got this. Battle scar from a Canuck who didn't bother takin' his spiked boots off before he hauled off and kicked me."

"Oh, Pierce." She bit her bottom lip as if imagining
the pain.

"Wasn't all that bad," he said softly. "Don't remember it bleedin' that much even." Her chemise was
square-necked and low, and he dropped his gaze almost
shyly to the place where her flesh was framed by white
muslin, then lower. There was a fullness beneath the
garment that he had not suspected, a fullness that lifted
the muslin into a shape that made him crave to feel it
beneath his palm. He felt a stirring of his flesh that he
could not control, and to mask his discomfiture he
draped the shawl over her shoulders. "Here. You'd better put this on." Fixing his hands around her waist he
lifted her to her feet.

Beneath his fingers he felt the yielding curve of her
body and he realized she'd taken off her stays. *Jeesuz,
she's so soft.* His hands lingered for seconds longer than

they should have. His thumbs rested vertically along her ribs, their tips pressed against the weight of her bosom as it rose and fell within the muslin. He could smell the starch and rainwater smells of her freshly laundered clothes, and he found himself responding to the feel and smell of her in the oldest way known to man.

He released his hold on her before he made a mockery of himself with his arousal. "I think the beans were kind've salty at supper tonight. I could use a drink of water. You want one too, Molly?" Grabbing the bucket, he headed toward the sink where she would not hear his heart pounding against his rib cage.

"Yes, please." She didn't move immediately, but when she did, it was to touch her hand to the underside of her breast where his thumbs had lain with such gentle warmth. She drew in a tentative breath, trying to dispel the sensations kindled by the feel of his hands around her, but it was impossible.

"You wanna get a couple've glasses?" he called from the sink.

On legs like india rubber she walked to the cupboard, removed two glasses, and placed them on the table. She could feel the floorboards deflect as Pierce crossed the room to her, and she looked up at him as he filled a glass to the brim and handed it to her. His hair was a glistening black in the lantern light, his eyes soft and green and smoldering. Her fingers brushed the tips of his as she accepted the glass, a fleeting touch of flesh that conjured unbidden images of him in the hip bath, scrubbing himself with that hand, with those fingers. She suffered a nervous twitch in her thumb when she considered where his fingers had been in the past hour, and what they had touched.

"Thank you." Water sloshed onto her thumb as she removed the glass from his hand, but he brushed it away with a slow glide of his fingers. She swallowed with difficulty. It was only the beginning of May yet his flesh was warm as the inside of a freshly baked biscuit. She could only wonder how warm the rest of him would be.

He watched her bring the tumbler to her mouth and, remembering his own thirst, a thirst that had little to do with salty pea beans, he poured himself a glass and quaffed it down in one long swallow. Finishing first, he wiped his mouth on his bare forearm, then watched Molly set her glass down. When she turned back to him, he saw that one pearl-drop of water still clung to her bottom lip, shimmering there like dew on a leaf. He would like to have bent down and licked that drop away with his tongue, kissed it away with his mouth, smoothed it away with his thumb, but she denied him all his likes. She parted her lips and with a flick of her tongue flattened the shimmering droplet against her flesh. He watched the tip of her tongue slide back into her mouth, and as he watched, he felt something wrench painfully in his loins and he thought he would go mad.

Molly glanced back at the table to find the sketch of Mrs. Constable's sideboard lying beneath the spill of light from the whale-oil lamp. "Is this the work you had to come home to finish?" She picked it up and found beneath it a pencil as lovely as the sketch it had rendered. "Oh, Pierce, how lovely." She replaced the sketch with the pencil and rotated it in her hand. It was a propelling pencil sheathed in a slender tube of cobalt-blue glass, and to her eye it seemed more appealing than either Lord Berryhill's pewter or Evan Thatcher's gold.

Pierce smiled at the delight on her face. "You like it?"

"It's beautiful. And so efficient. You don't have to waste time whittling the wood away with your pen-knife." She turned the end of the pencil to elongate the lead, then poised it in her hand and drew a series of cursive *n*'s in the air. "Are these terribly expensive? I mean, do you suppose I could find one somewhere for less than"—she calculated her financial situation— "four cents?"

"Don't know. I won that off a Canuck in a card game last year. But I think I know where you can get one for nothing."

"You do?" She flashed him a hopeful look.

He looked gently upon her face, touching her with eyes that communicated all the untaught, unintended erotic messages that a man can send a woman. "You can have that one."

Her lips parted as if to object, but she could no more speak than she could look away from the tenderness in his green eyes. She could not decide which astonished her more—the look on Pierce's face or his offer. But whatever the source, she was suddenly filled with such joy that, quite spontaneously, she did something that she had never done in his presence.

She smiled.

And not just a feeble smile. It was wide and unaffected and showed him the even line of her teeth. It lightened the blue-gray of her eyes and softened every angle of her face into an alluring curve. He had thought her only pretty. He realized now she wasn't pretty. She

was beautiful. And he had an uncommon desire to make
such beauty his own.

He tilted her chin upward with his forefinger.
"Where've you been hiding this?" he said of her smile.
With his thumb he traced the length of her dimple, finding that when she smiled, the depression became as long
and deep as his baby finger. "You can smile, Molly.
Jeesuz, can you ever." He imagined what it would be
like coming home to Molly Deacon after spending seven
months in the woods. Up north he shared one long bunk
with a dozen axemen in long-handled underwear. He
stirred at the thought of sharing a lone bed with Molly,
with nothing between them except naked flesh.

Within the depths of his eyes she saw emotions that
frightened her as much as his nakedness had shocked
her. Unable to hold his gaze she tried to bow her head,
but he slid his long fingers around the back of her neck
and stepped closer. He smelled so clean that she wanted
to rub her cheek against his hand to see if it would
squeak, but she had little nerve for such things. His
fingers were warm on her neck, his naked chest was
only inches away from her face, and she would liked to
have leaned into him to be cradled within the embrace
of his powerful axe arm, if only for a moment. But fear
was a strong deterrent against the stirrings of desire. It
was not right that she be down here with a half-dressed
man. What if Duncan came home? She closed her eyes.
What if—? And when she felt the touch of his lips on
her forehead, she lowered her face. "Please, Pierce,"
she whispered. "This isn't right."

"It is," he said, his voice low and hoarse against her
brow, his hands hungry to loose the pins from her hair.

"Your father—"

And that was all she had to say. He shot a look over his shoulder as if her words would send Duncan waltzing through the door, and it suddenly went through his mind how his father would react to his canoodlin' with their houseguest. With a curse delivered under his breath, he lifted his head and stepped back from her. He could bide his time, he told himself. Molly Deacon meant more to him than a quick toss with Fanny Bright on the waterfront.

He tamed his willful hands by hitching his thumbs around the leather fastenings of his suspenders. His fingers caressed the leather as they had caressed her neck. She touched her hand to the place on her neck that he had made warm and suffered an ache that his hand was no longer there.

An awkward silence lengthened between them. Pierce stood there with his weight on one leg and his hip shunted outward, the casual stance of a man who welcomes danger, the stance of a man who desires—but cannot have. Molly clung tightly to her shawl, then set the propelling pencil on the table.

"I can't keep this, Pierce. When I admired it, I didn't mean that you should give it to me. I'll buy one for myself someday. I'd feel guilty if I took yours." She looked up at him. His eyes were still dark with his passion, and she felt slightly wicked knowing that she was the cause. "I—uh, I suppose I should be getting to bed. I don't want to fall asleep during Conor's sermon tomorrow."

"So you'll give up your ironing for Conor but not for me." But he said it kindly, so she took no offense.

"I finished all my ironing earlier."

"Good thing, because I have it on good authority that it's a sin to perform servile work on Sunday."

She smiled again, shyly, and it took every ounce of fortitude he could muster to stop himself from reaching out for her and smothering her against him. Distraught and frustrated, he laced his fingers together, cracked his knuckles, then braced his interlinked hands behind his neck. For the space of a heartbeat he closed his eyes and tensed his muscles, and Molly felt a fluttering in her stomach as she watched the subtle flexing of his shoulder, the facile slide of sinew beneath his flesh. He was hard and soft, and he taunted her in ways that made her acutely aware that she was a woman.

"I'll see you at seven-thirty then," she said as she backed toward the door. She couldn't stay here any longer. It would be too dangerous. "Good night, Pierce." Her voice was breathless as she hurried into the hall.

"Night." And when he could no longer hear her footsteps, he leaned against the table and expelled a long, hot breath.

Water slashed through the city of Bangor in a giant Y; the Penobscot River forming the city's eastern boundary; Kenduskeag Stream angling through it from the west, cutting the business district in half. St. Michael's Catholic Church sat on Court Street on the opposite side of Kenduskeag Stream, though Molly thought calling the Kenduskeag a "stream" was pure understatement, for it looked to be every bit as wide as the Penobscot and just as deep. The church where Father Conor

Blackledge served as assistant pastor was wood-framed
and small, and as Molly entered its doors, she wondered
how many Irish carpenters would be present this morning. In Ireland, though the men followed the tenets of
the Catholic faith, many of them rarely attended mass,
claiming weekly services to be the bailiwick of womenfolk. She rather hoped this would be the philosophy of
the Irish carpenters who were working at Thatcher's,
and when she saw the great number of women in the
congregation, she breathed more easily. Perhaps her lie
would not be discovered after all.

Conor celebrated the mass, but it wasn't until he
stood in the pulpit to deliver his homily that Molly
chanced her first good look at him. He was short like
Duncan and nearly as wide as the pulpit that supported
him. He had the dark Blackledge hair, but it covered his
pate so sparsely that when he bent his head, Molly
could see patches of pink flesh shining through. His
multiple chins quivered as he preached. Once, as he
warned of the fires of eternal damnation, he made a fist
with a hand that was pale and untried, as delicate as
Pierce's was rugged. She questioned how she would
have reacted had Conor not been a priest. She supposed
if the marriage had taken place, she would have been a
loyal and devoted wife, but she wondered if she ever
would have been drawn to him in the same way that she
was drawn to Pierce.

Under cover of her bonnet she peeked at Pierce
Blackledge as he sat stiff as a church beside her, his
thighs compressed tightly and ; hands snugged between them. She remembered that only a few days ago
she had commended her father for having the good

sense not to have betrothed her to Pierce. She decided
now that she had spoken too quickly.

*It might not have been such a terrible mistake if you'd
betrothed me to Pierce, Da. I wouldn't have minded. I
wouldn't have minded at all.*

Chapter Seven

On Monday morning, while Molly was climbing the backstairs to the Thatcher mansion, Evan Thatcher was knocking on his sister's bedchamber door.

"Come in, Evan."

He entered his sister's sitting room and placed a kiss on her forehead. "I missed you yesterday. Did you have a pleasant time at the reception?" He seated himself in one of the dainty rosewood chairs that circled the fireplace.

Olympia got up from her chair and walked to a side table. "Would you like tea?"

He declined the offer with a gesture.

"I hope you don't mind if I pour myself a cup."

She walked back to her chair, teacup and saucer in hand. "Did I have a pleasant time away?" she repeated. "It was most interesting. That's why I asked to see you."

He laughed. "You make it sound ominous."

Olympia didn't return his laughter. She took a sip of her tea, then set cup and saucer down. "I heard some disturbing talk in Portland. At the reception I was even confronted by one irate father who wanted to know why my brother had ceased correspondence with his daughter. He told me the girl had already made several trips to her dressmaker to discuss her trousseau, and she was beside herself with your apparent rejection. He said he thought a man of your status would have nobler intentions than you demonstrate. He also mentioned something about informing his business associates in Boston of your tawdry nature."

"Tawdry?"

"His word, not mine."

"And you told him . . . what?"

"What could I tell him . . . except that it was not yet widely known, but you were planning to marry a local girl, and that's why you had ceased all correspondence with his daughter."

Evan laughed again. "What a brilliant liar you are."

"Brilliant, perhaps. But I'm not going to be proven a liar, Evan. I've given the matter much thought and I've concluded that it would be best if you did marry."

The smile stiffened on his lips. "You can't mean it."

"I'm afraid I do. We can't allow your dalliances to place our business dealings in an unfavorable light. A man with your social standing should leave no room for speculation about his moral attitudes. You need the trappings of a man of respectability. You need a wife."

"But what about—"

She shook her head as if she knew what he was about to say, but didn't want to hear. "I don't think it will be as difficult as you think. All we need do is find a young, attractive woman who has no family in the vicinity. We don't need any irate fathers asking interfering questions should any problems arise."

Evan snapped his fingers. "As easy as that, eh? And where do you propose we find this fatherless young woman? I know every eligible female in Bangor and Boston. The ones who don't have fathers are equipped with broods of priggish brothers who can ask equally interfering questions. Are you expecting to import new blood for me?"

A tap sounded at the door. Olympia raised her forefinger to her lips for silence, then called out, "Yes, who is it?"

"It's Poppy, milady."

"Come in, Mrs. Popham."

The door opened. The housekeeper stepped into the room. "Beggin' your pardon, milady, but Molly Deacon is downstairs in the kitchen. Have you decided what room you'd like her to work in?"

Olympia seemed taken aback. "I'd let it slip my mind that the girl was even coming to work this morning. No, I haven't decided where to put her, Mrs. Popham. Keep her in the kitchen and I'll be down in a few minutes. I'm sure I'll find someplace suitable for her."

And when the housekeeper had gone, Olympia Thatcher lost herself in a sudden private thought that erased the lines of concern from her brow. "Molly Deacon. My orphan dressmaker." She leaned back in her chair and graced her brother with a rare smile. "Molly Deacon. Of course."

By two o'clock that same afternoon Molly had made her first trip to Godfrey's One Price Store. She had entered the establishment with a note of credit from Olympia and had left with a gross of black-cock feathers, twelve yards of dyed black Italian lace, seven yards of green alpaca luster, eight yards of violet grenadine, and enough buckram, wire piping, bonnet glue, parchment, longcloth, and boning to fill her modest sewing room. She had taken Olympia's measurements that morning and had already cut out the lining for a skirt, but before she cut out the alpaca luster, she wanted to steam the creases out of it. The fabric had wrinkled unmercifully in shipping.

She heard the trill of feminine laughter as she opened the door to the kitchen. When she stepped into the room, she discovered one of the downstairs maidservants with her head bowed and hand masking her nose and mouth, apparently reacting to some tidbit the gentleman with whom she was conversing had just offered her. The maid's eyes flashed upward at the sound of creaking hinges, and when she saw Molly standing there, she muttered something to the man, curtsied hastily, and hurried past Molly out the door.

Evan Thatcher turned a half circle on the heel of his Alberts and regarded Molly. "Do you always have such an effect on people?"

Molly looked over her shoulder at the portal. "I apologize if I've intruded. I didn't realize you were using the kitchen. I can come back if you like," she offered, feeling more embarrassed than the girl who had fled the room.

"No, you obviously have work to do." He nodded at the yards of fabric in her arms. "You can proceed. I promise not to make a pest of myself."

She set the alpaca on the table, then filled the tea-kettle with water and set it on the stove to boil. Evan slid a chair out from the table and sat down to watch her.

"Where has my sister decided to put you?"

Molly clasped her hands at her waist and angled her body so she could reply to Evan's question without leaving the security of the stove. "On the third floor, in the room in the northeast corner. The one with the view of the stables."

"And the stench as well. Good God, we'll have to see about getting you a room with a view of the river. And some sun! Would you like that?"

She caught a glimpse of the shiny leather toes and mother-of-pearl buttons on his half boots. The buttons made her think of his painted shirt studs, and she felt her palms grow cold despite her nearness to the stove. "The room I have is fine, thank you."

"Dear girl, if you can call that room fine, I doubt you know the meaning of the word. 'Fine' is Oriental carpeting and Venetian drapes, not barren broom closets overlooking the stables. I'll speak to Olympia about re-locating you immediately."

She shook her head. "Fine" wasn't Oriental carpeting. "Fine" was red flannel and wet wool and deep laughter. "I, uh, I like where I am. It's far enough away from the dining room that I don't hear the noise from the carpenters."

"Ah, yes, the carpenters. There hasn't been a day go by when our house hasn't been overrun with carpenters. Olympia, you know. She rather reminds me of Thomas Jefferson with this constant redecorating. Do you realize there are some rooms in this house that I've lost completely? They just seem to have up and disappeared. Pity. I'd grown rather fond of some of them."

He smoothed the folds of his neckcloth. Manicured nails brushed the solid gold claw of his tie pin, and Molly wondered if those hands could fit around the helve of an axe as easily as Pierce's. "How many rooms are in the house?" she asked politely, wishing the water would boil and Evan would leave.

"There used to be fifty-seven. I don't know how many there are now. Though I imagine there are still sufficient numbers for someone to lose his way."

Molly smiled to herself, for on her way down from the third floor, she had indeed lost her way. If it hadn't been for the carpenters in the dining room, she might still be wandering the corridors.

"I don't expect your hovering over that water will make it boil any faster."

"I expect not." She glanced at the teakettle.

He frowned, unaccustomed to such cool disinterest. "Olympia tells me you're newly arrived in the city."

"Since last week."

"And you're an orphan."

She felt especially guilt-ridden about that lie, disloyal

to the memory of her parents. "It's not something I enjoy talking about."

"I can well understand that, my dear. My own mother passed away when Olympia and I were quite young. It still pains us to discuss it. I can't imagine how painful it must have been for you to have lost both your parents at such a young age."

Molly nodded silently.

"Sad they didn't live. If they could see you today, think how proud they would be of your accomplishments and your beauty."

She could feel blood rushing to her cheeks. Evan seemed enchanted by her blush and laughed aloud, but she found the sound oddly lacking. It contained none of the warmth of Pierce's laughter.

"You blush like a schoolgirl, Miss Deacon. It quite becomes you, though. You give a rogue ample reason to renounce his roving ways."

His game unnerved her. "I'm a dressmaker, sir. You should be addressing your pretty words to ladies of gentler birth."

"I own half of Bangor, Miss Deacon. I address my words to whomever I please, and at the moment, it pleases me to address them to you."

She shifted away from him to stare at the teakettle once more. "Yessir." She heard his chair scrape the floor as he rose.

"I'm sure we'll be seeing much more of each other, my dear. I have a particular empathy for people who have lost members of their family. We share a bond of grief that knits us into a rather unique family of our own, don't we? Tragic that you never had brothers or sisters. They can be a great comfort. At least, I assume you never discovered any brothers or sisters hidden somewhere in your past."

"No. None."

"That's sad." He realigned his chair against the table before crossing to the door. With his back to her she could not see the delight that played across his features. "Very sad."

At quarter of six that evening Molly trudged up the front hall stairs of 47 Hancock Street. It had been a long, active day and she was exhausted. She loosened the ties of her bonnet as she walked. When she crossed the threshold of her room, she set her carpetbag against the wall and eyed her bed with blatant longing. She would like to collapse onto the mattress and not get up till morning, but she had work to begin and knew she couldn't squander her time sleeping.

She yawned and stretched and with a slow pace made her way to the bureau. She gave herself a once-over in the mirror, and as she started to remove her bonnet, she looked down.

Her hand suddenly stilled on the pouf of calico on her head.

Sitting on the top of the bureau, next to her hairbrush, was Pierce's glass pencil. There was no note accompanying it, only a lopsided bow fashioned from bailing twine that signified its status as a gift.

"I can't accept this," she said to herself, but when she lifted it into her hand, she knew she couldn't refuse his gift twice without hurting his feelings. She touched the cool glass to her lips and smiled as the bailing twine curled against her cheek, tickling her. Still holding the pencil to her face, she crossed to the bed and removed her bonnet. She was preparing to set it on the bedpost when she stopped and gazed at the lemon-shaped cannonball. Pausing, she tossed her bonnet onto the bed, then with tentative fingers slid her palm around the wood, cupping it as if it were the curve of Pierce Blackledge's bicep, cradling it as if it were the back of his neck. She set the propelling pencil down and after a while pressed her cheek to the wood, letting it remain there a long, long time.

Pierce passed up supper with the family that night in favor of an evening with the boys in the Devil's Half Acre. Ten o'clock found him quaffing a round of ale in one of the more civilized grogshops on the waterfront.

"To bachelorhood," toasted one of his friends, kissing his mug to the eight other mugs at the table. "May it remain healthy and prosper long among us."

"Hear, hear." Gulps. Swallows. But no one noticed Pierce's lack of enthusiasm for the toaster's choice of sentiment. There was a lone snort. "No more bachelorhood for me. My Peg told me last week that if I didn't marry her before fall, she'd leave me high and dry for Heber McMahon. Said I'd kept her waitin' long enough."

Grumbles of shock. Heads shaking.

"Hell, how long's it been, Liam? Couldn't be more than seven or eight years."

"Nine."

"Nine? Hell, I've kept my Kathleen waitin' for goin' on twelve now."

Another voice. "Aren't you afraid some man'll sweep Kathleen off her feet while you're up north?"

"You wouldn't ask that if you'd ever seen his Kathleen."

Laughter. More gulping.

"So what're you gonna do if you get hitched, Liam? Peg won't let you make the trip up north, will she?"

"That's for hellfire sure. She'll wanna keep me tethered right to the bedpost probably." Hoots. Whistles. "Course you can't fault her taste. She's anxious to sample what the girls at Fanny's have been making such a fuss about all these years." Bawdy laughter. "I'll wager when she wakes up the mornin' after, she'll be tickled as a cat with two tails."

"Or as disappointed as a dog without one!" Uproarious laughter.

Pierce took a swig of ale and called for another round. Among his friends marriage was considered an institution to be avoided until a man reached his late thirties. He felt as if he were betraying a trust by harboring such strong feelings for Molly. And here he was only twenty-two. He'd be the butt of everyone's laughter if he told them he couldn't wait the customary nine or twelve years to marry Molly. He wanted her now. He wanted her yesterday. "So if you'll be stayin' in town, Liam, what'll you be doin' besides pleasurin' your lady? I've been next door to you at Fanny's. You don't take that long."

Liam grinned. "I was thinkin' of goin' into business with Peg's brother. Give the Blackledge name some competition. He put me on a crew already. Workin' up the Thatcher place. We're supposed to be remodeling the dinin' room, but I think what we're really doin' is demolishing it. The way that Olympia watches our every hammer stroke, you'd think she suspected we were gonna steal somethin'. Jeesuz, who'd want to? The place is a mausoleum. Isn't that right, Dooley?"

Dooley belched in agreement.

"Hell, the only thing worth stealing in the whole house is that new dressmaker of hers. She got lost today on her way down from the third floor and ended up in the dinin' room. Said she had to find the kitchen so she could heat up some water. Damn, she was heatin' me up just standin' there. She's some fair piece of workmanship. My Peg had looked like that, I'd-a married her long ago."

Pierce cradled his mug in his hands and quietly ground his teeth together as his friends pumped Liam for more information about the new dressmaker.

"Well, she's of a height that makes a man feel like a big strappin' bruiser." He marked a place in the air where the top of her head might reach. "'Bout yea tall. Jeesuz but I like my women small."

"So what are you doin' marrying Peg? She's half a head taller than you."

"Peg likes her men small. I'm just bein' obligin'. But this Molly—Molly's her name by the way—she's got real dark brown hair and eyes that're big as silver dollars. And gray. I've never seen such gray eyes."

"They're blue," Dooley corrected.

"Like hell. They're gray. I was the one who was talkin' face to face with her. What could you see of her hidin' behind that four-by-eight like you were?"

"Saw enough to know her eyes are blue."

"Forget about her eyes," a voice interrupted. "What else about her?"

Liam sidled an irritated look at Dooley Duffy. "Well, she's got this dimple on one side of her face that starts about here"—he touched his finger to his cheekbone and traced an imaginary line to his jaw—"and ends about here. Right side of her face I think it was."

"Left side," Dooley muttered.

Liam slammed his fists on the table. "How the bloody hell would you know? Were you the one givin' the directions?"

"Hold up, hold up," someone shouted. "Hey, Liam, is this Molly lookin' for some handsome young Irishman to teach her the pleasures of being a woman? If she is, tell her I'm available. I cut my teeth on Irish dressmakers."

Pierce shot the man an ugly look.

"Not Irish," said Liam. "She's English. One of the kitchen maids told me."

"English?" The volume of Pierce's voice produced immediate silence around the table. Eight sets of eyes stared at him. "She told you she's English?"

"Just got through tellin' you. She didn't tell *me*. She told the kitchen maid. And what're you gettin' so haired up about anyway? What's it matter to you whether she's English or Irish?"

Pierce tilted his chair back on two legs. She'd lied. She lied to get the job, and she hadn't mentioned a word about it. She hadn't impressed Olympia with her stitchery. She'd impressed her with the fact that she wasn't Irish. No wonder she'd gotten hired! How could she lie about something as important as bein' Irish? It was her heritage. It was who she was. Jeesuz, what else had she lied about?

"So how do we get an introduction to this Molly?"

"Where does she live?"

"What's her last name?"

Liam raised his hands for quiet. "I don't know where she lives or what her last name is, but I sure as hell can tell you one thing. It's common talk that one of the maids at Thatcher's had to leave 'cause she's up a stump and isn't married. I'm not one to spread gossip, but the way I hear it, Evan Thatcher spent an awful lot of time around that maid. Wouldn't surprise me if he consoles himself by taking an interest in the new English dressmaker. And if he does, the rest of you won't stand a snowball's chance in hell of sidlin' up to her. I hear the man can be some persuasive where the ladies are concerned—"

Pierce gripped his mug as if it were Thatcher's neck. The tinware buckled beneath his fingers, leaving it permanently dented.

"—and once he sees those gray eyes of hers—"

Dooley shook his head. "They're blue."

Liam raised himself off his chair. "Gray."

"Blue." Dooley blinked stupidly as he watched his mug fly out of his hands—to be replaced by Liam's fist.

"What color is this?" Liam threatened.

And for the remainder of the evening the most civilized grogshop on the waterfront became decidedly uncivilized.

* * *

With his long lumberman's stride, Pierce made quick work of the walk home. When he opened the kitchen door, he was carrying a full head of steam. He'd never known any Irishman to deny his nationality. It angered him that the woman he intended to marry should hold that dubious honor. What was she thinking of? He damn well intended to find out. It was a little before midnight, but it wasn't too late for him to have words with Miss Molly Deacon, *English* dressmaker.

He stormed through the kitchen and down the hall. A rectangle of light slanted into the hall from the parlor, and Pierce stepped into its lumination as he crossed to the room. At the threshold he stopped and leaned a shoulder against the door frame to observe the sight at the opposite end of the room.

Molly sat angled into a corner of the sofa. Her hands lay motionless atop a nest of black lace, and her head hung forward onto her chest. He wondered how long she'd been asleep. Thinking to yank her to her feet, he strode across the floor to the sofa, his body seething with self-righteous anger. "Molly."

But she didn't stir.

He reached his hands out for her shoulders, stopping himself when he realized he could break something if he squeezed her too hard. And she looked so peaceful. Awkwardness and guilt made him withdraw his hands. He hunkered down on one knee and for long minutes simply stared at her. He didn't know what there was about her that could defuse his anger, but he knew when he was around her there was a part of him that rode high as a cloud. Funny thing for a woman to do to a man, and to think that no one had told him about it before. Maybe no one had ever felt this way before. He smiled to himself. Maybe he was the first.

He bent his head to look up into her face, and he saw again the hint of sadness that pulled her lips and brow into distortion. "Why are you sad, Molly?" he asked quietly, but there came no answer other than the hushed softness of her breathing. This look of hers not only confounded him; it caused a tide of protective emotion to well within him. It seemed unfair to him that she should be so dispirited when her effect on him was so much the opposite. "You just give me some time, Molly Deacon. I'll find out what the problem is."

With gentleness he didn't know he possessed, he began inching the lace out of her hands and into his own. Her fingers rose and fell with the motion, but to Pierce's credit, he didn't wake her. Curious as to what she was making, he uncrumpled the lace and held it up, but he couldn't figure out what in hell the thing was much less where you'd wear it. Women and their clothes. Give 'em an inch of bare skin and they'd find some new way to cover it up.

He folded the lace and set it aside, then hauled himself to his feet. "Come on, sweetheart. Up you go." He scooped her into his arms. He expected the sudden movement to jolt her awake, but as he hugged her against his chest, she surprised him by mumbling something in her sleep and nestling her head against the bulk of his arm. He stood motionless. She seemed to weigh no more than the lace she had been stitching, and he realized that Liam McGinnis had been right tonight. She did make a man feel like a strappin' bruiser. It was a feeling he liked.

The cadence of her breathing hadn't altered, indicating to Pierce that she probably wasn't going to wake up. "So you sleep as hard as you work, do you?" And then he grinned at his words, because he did the same thing.

He touched his lips to the part in her hair and on a whisper of breath said her name in a way that he had never said a woman's name before. Her hair snagged in the stubble of his beard, so he lifted his mouth and pressed a gentle kiss on the slope of her brow. Her face was warm as the inside of his shirt and twice as soft, and he held his eyes closed as he grew full and hard in response. "Oh, Molly," he breathed, wanting her so badly he ached. His hand began to tremble. Slowly he carried her up the stairs to her room. He swore he wouldn't take advantage of her while she was asleep. He swore that when he kissed her she would be wide awake and willing. But as he held her over her bed, he fell prey to the primitive urgings of darkness, to the stronger urgings of his flesh, and he dipped his head to the face he could not see.

He found her cheek, the corner of her mouth, then lips so smooth they seemed an impossible part of her face. Blackness enveloped him. Silence thrummed in his ears. He brushed his lips across the curve of her mouth. Softly he kissed her, then harder, and more deeply, until he thought the fire within him would ignite his lungs. His chest heaved. His lips throbbed. He was grasping her so tightly that he heard her groan, felt her stir against him, and he knew he must leave.

She awoke with a sudden gasp of breath and slatted an eye into darkness, but sleep was heavy upon her, so she began to drift off again as quickly as she had awakened. She felt the firmness of her bed pillow beneath her cheek and in the distance heard the floorboard creak outside Pierce's room. She had stayed up to thank him for the pencil, but... *He's home*, she thought, and in the next instant was fast asleep.

Chapter Eight

When Pierce ambled down to the kitchen the next morning, he was greeted by two surprises: Molly and smoke. A thick haze filled the room and the air reeked with the fumes of pancake batter meeting a too-hot skillet. He waved his hand before him to clear the air, then looked toward the stove where Molly stood with Duncan's favorite spatula poised in her hand like a flyswatter. He'd expected her to be at Thatcher's. It took him a moment to find his voice when he discovered she wasn't.

"I thought you'd be at work. You playin' hooky already?"

She rubbed her stinging eyes with the heel of her

palm and coughed into her shoulder. "I work at home on Tuesdays and Thursdays."

Considering his feelings for her, he didn't know if her being home was a good idea or not. Squinting into the smoke, he walked across the room and threw open the window. With a discreet hand he began fanning smoke into the morning air. "Is that breakfast you're cookin'?" He left the window open and sauntered back toward the stove.

"It's supposed to be, but the stove is too hot and I can't remember what Duncan said to do to cool it down. There are so many dampers I . . . Oh, drat!"

He stood behind her shoulder as she finished flipping the pancake. His eyes lingered on the part in her hair before looking down at the stove. Crowded into the skillet were a mangled wedge, a splotch, and a shape for which no name had yet been invented. "Pancakes, huh?" All three pieces were spider black and hard as pennies. "Look good." He walked around to the side of the stove and adjusted the check damper, but he concluded it was too late to save his breakfast.

"I ruined them."

"Ruined 'em? Hell, you didn't ruin 'em. They're just a little . . . tanned."

"Tanned? They're burned. I ruined them."

He saw four tiny wrinkles worry the space between her brows. She dragged the back of her hand across her eyes, and Pierce couldn't guess whether she was reacting to the sting of the smoke or crying. She shoveled the contents of the skillet onto a plate, then gave both plate and pancakes a woeful stare.

"I wasted that whole bowl of batter. All that flour and milk . . . and the eggs. Oh, Pierce, all those eggs I wasted. Do you know how many people I could have fed with those eggs?"

He knew of at least one, but she didn't need to hear that right now because she looked as if she was about to bawl. "Are you gonna let this spoil your whole day?"

The idea of so much waste seemed to smother her. "Yes." She realized if this had happened to her in Ireland, it would have spoiled her whole year.

"C'mon, Molly. Everyone burns pancakes at least once in his life. It's like an eleventh commandment. 'Thou shalt burn breakfast on Tuesdays and Thursdays when Da's not home.'"

But she couldn't laugh. Not about this. "No. I should know better than to do something like this. I should have asked for help. How could I waste so much milk and flour when people have starved for want of them?"

Her voice vibrated with self-reproach, and he wondered if this, then, was the cause of her sadness. *What happened to you in Ireland, Molly?* he thought. *Jeesuz-God, what have you lived through?* And his heart went out to the girl who had learned that to waste a morsel of food or a moment of time was to suffer self-recrimination without solace. He stepped around the stove and took the plate from her, then cupped his hand around her chin, forcing her to look up at him. He realized then that her eyes were neither Liam's gray nor Dooley's blue. They were both, and they looked so fragile this morning that he thought they might shatter. "Listen to me, Molly. You gotta be a little kinder to yourself. You gotta laugh more and not worry so much about burnt pancakes. Hell, life's too short to cry over pancakes."

"I wasn't crying."

"Well, whatever you were doin'. Look at these things." He thrust the plate before her face. "It takes talent to burn pancakes as well as this. Why, some people can go through life and never reach the level of perfection you achieved with these buggers."

"Please stop, Pierce. This isn't funny."

"Are you sure you're not crying?"

"I'm not crying!" But she said it with such vehemence that he decided to pursue the point.

"And what if you were crying? Would that be so terrible?"

She eased his hand from her face and turned away from him. "Crying is for children. I'm not a child anymore." She hadn't been a child since the night they'd found her father in Berryhill's reflecting pond.

Confounded by her withdrawal, Pierce caressed her with his eyes. "Is laughing only for children too?"

Silence. Then, "I'm sorry about your breakfast, Pierce. Can I pour you some tea instead?"

Defeated, he blew an exasperated stream of air between his lips. "Yah. Tea's fine."

She joined him at the table after she set the spider in the sink. "I'll have Duncan give me another lesson in how to operate the stove before I attempt anything else." She waved her hand through the dissipating haze. "Do you suppose the smoke will ever clear?"

Pierce scanned the room with a critical eye. "Get a good west wind blowin' through here and the place might be inhabitable again by noon."

She watched him over the rim of her teacup. She'd dreamed about him last night. Her lips still felt raw from the impassioned kiss he'd given her in that dream. "I waited up for you last night, but I think I fell asleep before you got home. I don't even remember walking up to bed."

"You didn't. I carried you up."

"You carried me up?" It took her breath away.

"Yah. Didn't figure you could manage the front stairs in your sleep."

She stared at his red flannel shirt. He'd held her against it last night and she hadn't even known. Perhaps the touch of the flannel against her cheek had prompted the indecent dream she'd had about him.

"Any particular reason you waited up for me last night?" he asked.

"I wanted to thank you for the pencil. I'm going to use it today to make some sketches for Olympia. But I won't keep it, Pierce. I'll only borrow it. So anytime you want it back, just tell me."

His eyebrows bunched at the root of his nose. It irritated him that she couldn't accept his gift without attaching all kinds of stipulations to it. "When an Irishman gives a woman a gift, it's for keeps."

"But there might come a time when—"

"There won't!" he bellowed, silencing her. "Jeesuz-God, what've I got to do before you'll let me be nice to you? I've never met a female like you. Course, maybe that's because we haven't had too many *Englishwomen* stayin' at forty-seven Hancock Street."

Her eyes flickered with nervous emotion. He couldn't

have found out. He just couldn't. "What do you mean, Englishwomen?"

He pushed away from the table and braced his calf across his knee. "Couple've friends of mine are workin' up the Thatcher place. They told me last night that Olympia hired a new English dressmaker. Kind've coincidental that she'd hire two dressmakers at the same time. One English, one Irish, and both named Molly. Why'd you lie to her?"

All the scheming she had done, all the precautions she had taken. For nothing. If only he hadn't gone into town last night. "I didn't exactly lie. I mean, I *am* a dressmaker. I'm just not English. The housekeeper wasn't going to let me in the door if I was Irish, so I had to become English. That's not lying, it's just modifying the truth a little."

"It's lying."

"It was necessary."

"And you had the nerve to take Communion on Sunday!"

"Well, so did you, and if I had a vocabulary like yours, I wouldn't dare show my face in church!"

"Cussin's not a sin when everyone does it, but denyin' bein' Irish. Jeesuz, that's a sin in itself. Was getting that job more important to you than bein' who you are?"

"I'm good at what I do, Pierce, and being Irish doesn't have any bearing on it one way or the other. My nationality doesn't dictate the way I cut cloth or stitch hems. I can sew just as well English as I can Irish, and Olympia Thatcher's gowns won't suffer because of it. I'm not cheating anyone by claiming I'm English."

"No one except yourself. You think any Irishman's

gonna be interested in courting you when he finds out you prefer bein' a dressmaker to bein' Irish?"

"I wasn't aware that I was looking for an Irishman to court me."

He felt as if she'd just slapped his face, and he responded in kind. "Yah? Well, you won't have to worry about it when word gets around. Irishmen marry their own. They don't marry Englishwomen!"

"And who said I wanted to get married?"

"Well, why the hell did you come here in the first place if not to get married?"

"I came her to—" And then she stopped herself. She came here to be a dressmaker first and a wife second. She could just imagine what enlightening thoughts Pierce would have to deliver on that circumstance. "You know why I came here."

"I know why you *say* you came, but maybe you lied about that too. You seem a helluva lot more attracted to the idea of workin' for Olympia Thatcher than you do to the idea of becomin' someone's wife."

He had targeted the truth so well it took her breath away. She could not tell the Blackledge men that the primary reason Michael Deacon's daughter had come to Bangor was to use them as a means to an end. "I told you before, I want to *be* someone before I get married."

"You've already become an Englishwoman. Who else do you wanna be?"

"You just don't understand."

"I guess the hell not, but maybe that's because I was brought up thinkin' that if I couldn't gain somethin' by honest means, it wasn't worth gainin' at all. But what do I know? Hell, Irish wood butchers probably don't know half as much as English dressmakers. They don't know how to work themselves to death. They don't know how to keep themselves from laughin'. And they certainly don't know how to lie as well!"

"You're just a bastion of virtue, aren't you? However did you allow yourself to sit down to tea with me?" She snatched her cup and saucer off the table and marched to the sink.

"Is that all you're gonna say? That I'm a bastion of virtue?"

She poured hot water into the dishpan.

"Dammit, Molly, I'm talking to you!"

"You're not talking, you're yelling! And I have no intention of carrying on a discussion with a man who doesn't know the difference between the two!"

She heard the rasp of wood against wood, then the sound of angry footsteps crossing the floor. "When the smoke clears, shut the window." He slammed the kitchen door behind him. She looked askance to see if the door frame was still vibrating.

She shoved her teacup into the hot dishwater. She heard the outside door bang shut and Pierce's boots thump on the dooryard stairs. "Probably going down to the river to knock someone off a log," she grumbled. She rubbed her wrist across her nose and sniffed. "What does he know about anything? Raised in this beautiful house with all he ever wanted to eat. What does he know about burying babies or parents?"

She began scrubbing the teacup with a vengeance. "Sensitive? I thought him sensitive? And funny? Huh!" She threw the charred pancakes into the garbage bucket, the dirty plate into the dishpan. "He's mean is what he is. Mean and . . . and narrow-minded." She plunged the dishes into the rinse water. "Criticize me for receiving Communion, will he? Who made him pope?"

She whipped a towel off the drying rack. "Doesn't think any Irishman will want to court me when the word gets out, does he?" She stopped in her tracks. *When the word gets out?* Was he going to let the word out? Good Lord, had he told his friends already that the new English dressmaker was actually a desperate Irish dressmaker who was lying through her teeth? What if he had? No, he couldn't! If the truth spread through the Thatcher household, Olympia would fire her, and if Olympia Thatcher told her friends about the deception, Molly would never find another job in the city of Bangor.

She had to find Pierce. She had to discover what he'd divulged about her to his friends. And if he hadn't told them the truth yet, she had to plead with him not to. Her whole future depended on whether he could keep a secret or not. She hoped she wasn't too late.

She finished cleaning the kitchen as if she were running a race. She thrust the dry dishes into the cupboard and tossed the dishwater out the window. She sprinted back to the sink to wipe the area dry and was just lifting the bib of her apron over her head when she heard the outside door open. She gave a sigh of relief that he'd come back. At least now she didn't have to go out looking for him. She rushed across the floor and threw open the interior door.

"Pierce, I'm so glad you came back. I was just heading out to talk . . ." The end of the sentence hung unsaid between them. He looked like he'd been caught in a rainstorm, but—her eyes darted beyond him—the sun was shining. He pushed wet hair off his brow and wiped down his face with his hands. Oily droplets fattened the ends of his hair and beaded his earlobes. Water collected at his elbows and splashed to the floor like pearls cut loose from a necklace.

And he wasn't smiling.

"For heaven's sakes, Pierce, what happened to you?"

In answer he clenched his fists and advanced toward her. She retreated before his long, angry strides.

"You did that on purpose, didn't you?" he seethed.

"Did what on purpose?"

"Don't try that innocent routine with me, Molly. It won't work."

His shoulders appeared to swell to twice their normal size. His eyes were fearsome. "Innocent routine? I don't know what you're talking about, but I certainly wish you'd stop because you're scaring me!"

He advanced. She retreated. She backed into the chair at the head of the table, then angled her way around it, putting the width of the table between them.

"That was a pretty damned despizable thing to do."

"*What* was?"

From the opposite side of the table he stalked her. When she moved left, he shadowed her right. When she moved right, he shadowed her left.

"Are you denyin' you knew I was out there when you chucked that water out the window?"

Her feet slid to an abrupt halt. She flattened her hand on her chest as if to say "Me?" then peered toward the open window where she had disposed the morning's dishwater. *Oh dear.* "That water was supposed to go on the asters."

"It missed."

She tried to imagine what his expression had been when the cataract of dirty dishwater hit him full in the face. The vision was so absurd that instead of apologizing, she did something that he hadn't been able to get her to do since she'd arrived.

She laughed.

And not a dainty laugh. It was a high-pitched giggle that teared her eyes, strained the back joints of her jaw, and rang around the rafters. Pierce felt a rush of anger burst in his head.

"So you can't laugh at the damn pancakes you incinerated but you can laugh at me, huh?"

She pressed her fingertips into her aching joints to soothe them. She covered her mouth. She bowed her head so she wouldn't have to look at Pierce's elbows shedding dishwater over the floor, but the more she tried to suppress her laughter, the more it came flooding out. She made a waving motion with her hands in an attempt to beg forgiveness for her behavior, but Pierce was in no mood to be forgiving. He seized a kitchen chair. Off it flew to his right.

Molly's laughter faded when she saw his murderous expression. "You told me I had to laugh more."

He grabbed a second chair. Off it flew to his left.

"Oh, I see," she said as she backed toward the wall. "I can only laugh at things *you* think are funny."

He gripped the edge of the table and glared at her. "Throwing water out the window at me isn't funny, but I'll show you something that is." He gritted his teeth.

With a maniacal growl he upended the table. Molly raced for the open window. Pierce vaulted over the table and charged after her. She lunged for the windowsill. He was at her heels. She gave one stalwart swipe with her hand to fend him off, but his arms were suddenly everywhere. Around her waist. Behind her knees.

"Don't you touch me, you—"

He swung her off her feet and upward. She discovered just how wide his shoulder was when she landed atop it. She also discovered that Pierce's one shoulder impaired her breathing far more than all thirty-seven ribs of whalebone in her stays.

"If you . . . *mmmph* . . ." She scissored her feet but he bundled skirt, petticoats, and flailing legs together like thatching and banded an arm about them. "You . . . you . . ." She wrenched her body to the right and drove her elbow into the nape of his neck.

He muttered a string of words that would have necessitated her blessing herself had she known what they meant. She followed up her assault by swinging her forearm in the direction of Pierce's skull. He caught her hand in his fist and held it tight as he ate up the distance to the back hall.

"If you don't put me down, *this instant*—"

"Save it," he spat. He headed out the back door. With her free hand Molly clutched the wooden frame, hugging it with fingers and palm. Pierce kept walking. Molly's arm stretched, then strained. Her fingers whitened, uncurled, and slid helplessly across the jamb.

"Where are you taking me?" The sight of the ground bouncing to the rhythm of Pierce's strides made her dizzy. She could feel the play of contracting muscles as he strode across the backyard and began to navigate the downhill slope. "You're yanking my arm out of its socket!" But he didn't loosen his grip, no matter how much she struggled.

At the edge of the river Pierce stopped. He released Molly's hand. She snatched it from around his neck, and when she felt him relax his hold on her legs, she kicked free of his constraint.

Or so she thought.

He flipped her off his shoulder and caught her in his arms. In the same motion he swung her toward the river and, to Molly's horror, hurled her into the air. She windmilled her arms in free flight, wailing, "I can't—" *Splat.*

"See how *you* like it," he yelled to the fountain of spray that marked her entry into the water. She disappeared beneath concentric rings of waves. Feeling momentarily avenged, he stretched out on the ground, yanked up a blade of grass to stick between his teeth, and leaned back on his elbows. He lent a passing glance to the spot where he expected her head to bob up.

From behind him a dog barked a deep, enthusiastic bark and ran down the hill after him, dropping a chunk of wood on the ground by his hand. He gave the animal's head a rough caress, picked up the chunk of wood, and flung it upriver. "Go get it, Bear." He grinned as he watched the dog chase after the whirling object, then angled his head to check the water again.

The surface was smooth and unrippled. He frowned. He had expected at least a little thrashing. He jacked himself up to a sitting position. Bear stampeded back toward him and spat the retrieved wood out at his feet.

Pierce strained sideways to see over the dog. "Does it seem to you like she should've come up by now?" He draped an arm around Bear's neck, bent his knee, and shored his forearm against it. He brushed his knuckles along his jaw and worried the grass protruding from the corner of his mouth. "You suppose she knows how to swim?"

The river remained calm.

Pierce sprang to his feet. "Jeesuz." He spat out the blade of grass, hit the riverbank at a dead run, and made a diving leap into the cold Penobscot.

Five minutes later Molly was crouched on hands and knees, her head bent forward, snorting and coughing water from her nose and mouth. Her hair had come loose and was matted into thick crisscrossing strands across her face. With an unsteady hand she shifted wet clumps behind each ear, and when her knees began to shake she eased herself flat, resting her head in the bend of her arm. Her nostrils burned all the way to her eyebrows. She closed her eyes and pinched the bridge of her nose. The sound of heavy breathing close to her face made her inch her eyes back open.

Bear was nudging a slimy chunk of wood toward her nose.

Molly groaned. She turned her head in the opposite direction.

Pierce was sitting Indian style on the grass. He held one of his boots in the air, then turned it upside down. A flood of water poured onto the ground. He set the boot upright beside its mate and regarded it with disgust. "Too much water can ruin a man's boots." He drilled a look at Molly. She'd just scared the bejesus out of him.

He felt relief that she was all right, but more than relief, he felt anger. "Why the hell didn't you *tell* me you can't swim?"

She returned his angry look. Her cheeks puffed up with unspoken epithets. "You . . . you almost drowned me!"

"Drowned you? I probably just wrecked a good pair of boots tryin' to *save* you!"

"Save me?" She raised herself onto her forearm. "How dare you take credit for saving me when it was you who threw me into that water knowing full well I couldn't swim?"

"I knew you couldn't cook pancakes. I didn't know you couldn't swim."

"You didn't know? What do you think I was screaming out at you when I hit the water?"

"How the hell should I know? If you wanted to tell me you couldn't swim, you should've told me on the way down the hill."

"I would have if I'd known you were planning to dump me in the river!"

Bear deposited his chunk of wood in an obvious spot by Molly's throwing hand. She recoiled at the look of the thing. "*Why* does he keep shoving this piece of wood at me?"

Pierce removed one of his wet socks. "He's a Newfoundland retriever. He wants you to throw it."

She obliged.

Pierce threw his arm up to deflect the wood away from his head. "Not at me, dammit!" It bounced off his wrist and fell to the ground. He hurled it into the river, and when he looked back at Molly she saw something so dangerous in his eyes that she boosted herself onto her knees to run, but he got to her first. He dragged her backward against him, imprisoning her between his legs. He hugged her against his chest and trapped her head in the vise of his hand. His face was inches above hers. He looked from her eyes to her mouth, and she saw no humor in his expression as he parted his lips and lowered his face.

His hand was cold against her cheek, but his mouth was hot and angry. "Show me how an Englishwoman kisses," he said in a harsh whisper, a whisper that frightened as well as excited her. She was acutely aware of the powerful yoke of his arms, the steady beat of his heart. She felt the rough texture of his unshaven flesh chafing her face, and she lifted a hand, wanting to touch him, but she was soundly manacled in his embrace. She felt the slow movement of his lips across hers, and to her inexperienced mind there seemed something primitive about his mouth—its warmth, its pressure—something that touched the root of her sensuality and burned her like flame. His was a kiss that was raw and undisciplined and aroused in her emotions that left her breathless. She felt herself smothered by the enormous bulk of his arms and shoulders, by his mouth, by something that was fierce . . . and magnificent.

"So that's how an Englishwoman kisses." She heard him whispering the words down her chin and along the line of her jaw. She had never felt such goodness in her life, wrapped in this man's arms with his breath grazing the underside of her jaw. And for an unbidden moment she thought that perhaps this feeling of goodness would far surpass any satisfaction she could derive from achieving her dream. To awaken every morning in his splendid arms with his mouth raining kisses upon her. Perhaps it was more important to be loved than to be an English dressmaker. She felt as if Pierce Blackledge was forbidden fruit. She wondered if she had bitten too deeply to set him aside. She wondered if she wanted to.

"Pierce, someone might see us."

He kissed her eyelids shut. "I don't care." He pressed fluttery kisses down her nose and with his cold hand smoothed strands of wet hair from her forehead. "I couldn't wait any longer to do that. Here I am rough-housin' with you and I almost kill you. Jeesuz, Molly, do you know what I felt like when I dragged you outta that water. If I'd let anything happen to you—" He didn't finish his sentence. He wove his fingers through the hair at the back of her neck and kissed her deeply, greedily.

She wiggled her left hand out from where it was pinned between her hip and his leg. He felt the hesitant touch of her fingertips on his temple, then the coolness of her palm as she fixed her hand against the angle of his cheek. He lifted his face. She touched her thumb to the center of his lips.

"You scared me."

"Jeesuz, sweetheart, I scared myself."

His endearment was so wondrously unexpected that it filled the secret places in her heart with quiet joy. A smile elevated her lips. "No one has ever called me sweetheart."

"Never?"

She shook her head. "Never." But it gladdened her that he was the first.

"I'm sorry I threw you in the river."

"I'm sorry I hit you with the dishwater."

"It was worth it to see you laugh, sweetheart." He kissed the tip of her thumb, then drew it slowly into his mouth.

"I don't do it easily, Pierce. I wish I did, but . . ."

"You'll learn," he whispered around her thumb. "I'll teach you."

And it seemed to her as she lay in his arms that he would teach her much more. She felt the sucking motion on her thumb—the gentle bite of his teeth, the warmth of his mouth, the sensuous strokes of his tongue—and she felt herself warming to his need and opening to his desire.

"Bangor Tigers don't get married, Molly. They don't even start thinkin' about it till after they're thirty." She removed the tip of her thumb from his mouth and trailed it across his lower lip as he talked. "But havin' you here is like . . . it's like havin' my future dangled in front of me and not bein' able to get at it. Do you know what I'm sayin'?"

The only thing she knew at the moment was that the dream she'd had about him last night didn't do him justice. "You have beautiful lips," she said, seemingly in a daze.

He shook his head and nibbled at her thumb again. "You're not listening to me."

"Yes I am," she objected, and then her eyes climbed to his and she realized that he was right. She hadn't heard one word he said. She gave him a sheepish smile and touched the depression at the corner of his mouth. "I'm listening with my eyes."

"Is that what Englishwomen do?"

Her voice was breathy. "That's what Irishwomen do." And thinking his heart might burst he crushed her against him and rocked her in his arms. He pressed his cheek to the top of her head.

"I'm glad Conor's a priest, Molly. If you'd had to marry him instead of me, I don't know——" He felt her stiffen against him and he stopped what he was doing, realizing what he had let slip. He loosened his arms around her. She braced a hand against his chest and levered herself away from him. A hundred emotions warred within her eyes.

"Marry you? Pierce . . . you don't even know me. How can you think of——"

"I'm falling in love with you." He said it softly, simply—a statement of his intentions and his desire, and she knew that this was all wrong.

It was happening much too quickly. She'd only worked at Thatcher's one day, not enough time to accomplish anything she'd set out to do. It was too soon to be thinking about a husband, but how could she ignore the warmth of emotion Pierce inspired in her? She wanted to touch him, to kiss him, to be held in the safety of his arms, but could she give up her dream for him? *Oh, Pierce, why are you doing this to me? Why now?*

"It's too soon," she whispered, not wanting to hurt him.

"Why?"

"It just is. I *need* to chase this vision I have, Pierce. I want to chase it."

He brushed his knuckles down the length of her

cheek. "And I want you, so where does that leave me? Why are you so obsessed with this dream, Molly? Is it the same reason why I see such sadness in your eyes sometimes? No, don't look away from me." He leveled his thumb on the delicate curve where her brow blended into her cheekbone. "Tell me, sweetheart. I wanna know."

I want to, Pierce. Oh, I want to. But it's such a private thing. "It's not something I can share with you, Pierce. It's not something I can share with anyone."

"So you want to be the best damn dressmaker in the state of Maine for no reason at all."

"You've forced your way into my heart," she said quietly. "Would you force your way into my soul as well?"

"I would. And I will, but I guess I have to be patient, don't I?" He bowed his forehead against the slant of her brow and sighed. "But I can't promise to be too patient, Molly. I want you too much to be patient for too long."

She smiled as he kissed the tangled part in her hair. She could feel fairy dust tingling in her veins. She had depended on no one but herself for so many years that it seemed strange to be thinking about sharing thoughts and laughter. She had ignored the loneliness of the past five years, but being with Pierce made her realize how much she had missed. He said he was falling in love with her. His attention made her feel desirable; his love made her feel blessed. She wanted to be loved. Despite her fears and priorities she wanted to learn again how to share, and laugh, and love. *Give me time, my love. Give me time.* She heard Pierce chuckling.

"I'll probably be the only Bangor Tiger in history

who's gonna willingly involve himself with an imposter English dressmaker."

His words triggered the same fear she'd experienced earlier. Had he told anyone the truth? "Pierce, I know you don't understand why I told Olympia what I did, but . . . when you were with your friends last night, did you tell them who I really was?"

"Nope."

"You didn't?"

He laughed at the relief in her voice. "I wanted to hear your version of the story first. Thought I owed you that much."

"And now that you've heard my version?"

He eased himself away from her and regarded her long and hard. "I'm damn mad about what you did and I'll probably regret doin' this, but I'll keep your secret for you. Hell, I can't stay cross at you any longer than I can stay cross at Da."

"Oh, thank you!" She threw her arms around his neck, practically knocking him over, but he laughed at her enthusiasm and returned the favor, working his hands up and down her corseted spine. He wondered what she'd feel like beneath her chemise. And he knew if he continued in this fashion, he would do something for which they'd both be sorry.

"You need to get into some dry clothes, Molly. C'mon. We'd better head back to the house."

They untangled their limbs and Pierce gave her a boost upward. He sat for a moment, waiting for his desire to ebb, for his wet trousers would reveal more of his condition than he would like to display. He spied Bear at the edge of the river, then watched Molly gather up a handful of hem and wring a puddle of river water onto the ground. Her face mirrored concern when she noticed that one of her feet was bare.

"My shoe." She rotated in a full circle, her eyes searching the ground. "It can't be gone. It can't." She raced to the lip of the banking. Panic crept into her eyes as she squinted at the flotsam drifting on the current. She ran downriver, her head darting back and forth, her gaze never leaving the water.

Pierce came up behind her. "You lose your shoe?"

She almost seemed too distracted to answer him. "Was it on my foot when you dragged me out of the water?"

"Hell, Molly, I was too worried about the rest've you to notice your feet."

A thickness rose high in her throat. She pressed her teeth into her bottom lip to keep it from quivering.

"So I ruined a pair've boots and you lost a shoe," said Pierce. He squeezed her shoulder. "Could've been a lot worse."

"No. No, it couldn't!" Her voice struck such a high note that it made Pierce flinch. She broke away from him and crowded closer to the riverbank. She hugged her arms to herself as tears welled in her eyes. "It was made of kid," she choked out. "Do you know how many skirts I had to sew, how many hems I had to stitch before I could afford to buy a pair of kid shoes?"

"Molly—"

"I worked for five years before I had enough money. And within a space of . . . of two minutes you ruined everything I worked so hard for. All because you were trying to be funny!" She knuckled away the teardrops that were spilling onto her cheeks. "Why couldn't you have been funny with someone else? It's gone. My shoe is gone!"

He had never known anyone to make such a fuss about a shoe, but he had already apologized for tossing her in the river and it nettled him that she was berating him all over again. He didn't mind accepting some of the blame, but hell, he didn't think he deserved all of it. "I told you I'm sorry."

She desperately scanned the water, unable to accept the loss, unable to accept his words of consolation. He had no idea what the loss of a shoe meant to someone who had spent most of her life without any. And as she stood there, wet and shivering, she felt as if she were reliving every disappointment that had ever touched her life. She was dying a hundred tiny deaths. Despair drained through her body, leaving in its wake the sour taste of bitterness and resentment. Pierce came to stand beside her.

"We'll get you a new pair of shoes. Somethin' more rugged that'll stay on your feet better."

"I don't want something rugged." She peeked down at the one slipper whose satin ribbons still bound it to her foot. "I wanted these." They were only five weeks old and they'd made her feel so enchanted.

"Well, you can't have those. One of them's gone. Jeesuz-God, Molly, you could've lost your life, but all I hear you raisin' a ruction about is your shoe. You're not bein' very reasonable about this. People have lost shoes before without makin' such a fuss, but from the way you're actin', you'd think this was the first pair of shoes you ever owned."

"It is!" she sobbed, pivoting round to face him. Her eyes were red with her tears, her voice shook with emotion, and she suddenly wanted him to know how wrong he was when he called her unreasonable. "You can't know what it's like having nothing. You've always had a warm house to live in and fine clothes to wear. You can't know what it's like to wear rags around your feet in the winter because your father is too poor to buy you shoes. Do you know how my mother died? My Da never told your father because he was too ashamed. She was delivering laundry to someone in the village one night and the cold ate right through the rags on her feet. They had to cut off her toes, then her feet, and then she died. She wasn't strong enough to fight off the awful things that happened to her body when they took her feet." She scattered tears across her cheeks with her fingertips. "My Da convinced himself that she died because the village doctor didn't know what he was doing. But I know the real reason she died. She died because she didn't have shoes."

She looked toward the water again. Pierce stood silently, not knowing how to respond. "I'm sorry, Molly. I had no idea."

She laughed, but it wasn't a pretty sound. "Of course not. My Da was a proud man. He wouldn't have told his friend Duncan the truth. Little matter that Duncan might have said, 'Pack up your family, Michael, and join us in America.' No. My Da was too proud. If we were going to die, we were going to die on our own. And die we did."

"You don't have to go on with this, Molly."

"But you wanted to know," she said, unable to stop

the words from spewing forth. "You wanted to know why I'm the way I am. Why I can't laugh over burnt pancakes. You saw the scar on the bottom of my foot. I told you I got it while digging in the fields, but I didn't tell you what I was digging up."

"Stop, sweetheart." He reached out for her arm but she thrust his hand away.

"I was digging for grubs."

"Molly—"

"When the potatoes were gone and we had nothing left to eat, we ate grubs. And we thought ourselves lucky—lucky because at least we weren't starving." She looked into his face. There was horror in his eyes, but it didn't surprise her. How could any man love a woman who had groveled as low as she? His disgust saddened her as much as his attention had given her joy. And it hurt. Sweet Jesus, it hurt. "Are you happy now?" she cried at him. "You know all the secrets now, but you look like you wish I hadn't told you. Oh, what does it matter?" She yanked her lone slipper off her foot and in hopeless frustration flung it high into the air. It whirligigged into the river. "What does anything matter?"

She saw Bear plunge into the water after the shoe. "Leave it alone!" she screamed at him, for it seemed he would dig it out of the river as she had once dug vermin out of the fields, and she thought she would choke on the humiliation. "Leave it alone!"

"C'mon, sweetheart, don't—"

"Don't call me that!" she cried. "It was better when you didn't call me anything. It was better when you just left me alone." In her bare feet she fled across the flat and up the hill. Pierce took two running steps after her, then stopped. She wouldn't listen to him now. She wouldn't listen to anyone.

Snorting like a horse, Bear scrambled onto the bank and coughed up Molly's shoe at Pierce's feet. Pierce hunkered on one knee. He lifted the shoe into his palm. It was smaller than his outstretched hand, and the opening was so tiny he wouldn't be able to squeeze his hand inside. He knew now what she had lived through and why he had seen such sadness in her eyes. "Oh, Molly," he breathed. And though he could not know, as he stared at her kid slipper, his eyes reflected the same threads of sadness he had seen in hers.

Chapter Nine

Olympia invaded Molly's third-floor sewing room a week later with her newly arrived issue of *Godey's Lady's Book*. She paced the length of the room as she read aloud from page nine. "'A blue bonnet is only suitable to a fair or bright red complexion. A violet bonnet is always unsuitable to every complexion.'" She rolled up the magazine and stood before the dress form that bore the results of Molly's first week of work—a morning gown of violet grenadine. "I assume if violet bonnets are uncomplimentary to every complexion, so too are violet morning gowns. Need I remind you what color this gown is?"

Molly sat on a low stool surrounded by yards of

oyster-white gros de Suisse onto which she was sewing black twisted silk in a trailing-stem design. She answered Olympia without looking up at her. "There should be enough green in the ruching around your throat to offset the violet. My apologies to Mr. Godey, but I think it will make a handsome combination." She removed a pin from the twisted silk and stuck it into the emery cushion of her needle case. When she looked up, she found Olympia circling the dress form.

Molly was pleased with the finished product. The sleeves had fullness at the elbow but were skintight above and below. The bodice was tight to the shape and long-waisted. Bias folds of the grenadine descended from the sloping shoulders and formed a V to the deep point of the waist. Green cord edged the bias folds. She had completed the gown in less than a week, but she'd avoided Pierce during that time, so she'd had few distractions to impede her work.

Olympia lifted one of the bias folds with a fingertip and nodded her approval at Molly's tiny, almost invisible stitches. "Nice," she said before turning her attention to the ruching at the throat. "Double-hemmed."

"I always double-hem frills."

Olympia stepped back to study the gown from a distance. She tilted her head left, then right. "I like it."

Molly felt the tenseness that was cramping her neck muscles melt away with the woman's commendation. It seemed she would have her job for at least another week, which would mean another dollar saved toward her dress shop.

"Apparently you weren't exaggerating when you

claimed to work quickly," said Olympia, turning toward her. "But I wonder at the mood you've fallen into. Are you always this withdrawn when you're sewing?"

Molly's voice faltered. "Withdrawn?" Given the way she felt after her set-to with Pierce last week, she thought she'd been putting on quite a merry facade.

"My dear Miss Deacon, you have been moping about this room as if someone had told you the world was going to end this Tuesday." She paused, eyes unwavering. "Perhaps you're homesick. Leaving one's home can often be a traumatic undertaking for a young person, especially when they're leaving loved ones behind."

"I left no loved ones behind."

"None? There was no young man who was anxious to make such a pretty girl his wife? No suitor who vowed to follow you to America?"

"There was a young man once." She was staring at the fabric draped over her lap and did not see the dark look that crept into Olympia's eyes. "But he exchanged vows with someone else."

"How dreadful for you." Relief softened the line of Olympia's mouth. "Did this happen recently?"

Molly shook her head. "No. It was a long time ago."

"And there has been no one since?"

She thought of Pierce, of the kiss they had shared by the river. She remembered the moment when she had thought there could be no greater joy than to be loved by this man, but that had been before she'd realized how juvenile and unfeeling he'd been to throw her in the river—before she'd discovered that he'd lost her shoe. Perhaps they both did work with their hands; perhaps they both had lost their mothers; but that didn't make them anything alike on the inside. She never would have put him in such jeopardy just to be funny. And that was the major difference between them. Pierce Blackledge had yet to learn that life was too serious to laugh about. He would learn one day, but he would learn without her. And though he might not be of a mind to carry a grudge, she had no such reservation. She was full-blooded Irish and could carry a grudge into eternity. She would never forgive him for losing her shoe. Never.

"There has been no young man in my life since, nor will there be for a long time to come," she answered. "I came to this country to be a dressmaker, and I have precious little time to spare for anything *but* my dressmaking."

Olympia lifted her brows at the determination in Molly's voice. "Indeed, Miss Deacon. How fortunate for me that I hired so dedicated a seamstress." She removed a dainty gold watch from a hidden pocket in the waistband of her overskirt. Ten minutes past eleven. She was to meet Evan in five minutes. "Tell me, my dear, do you fashion men's clothing as well as women's?"

"I do, but I prefer designing for women. Men's clothing doesn't allow for as much creativity."

Olympia snugged her timepiece back into her waistband. "The reason I ask is that Evan has been complaining vehemently about his tailor here in the city. The man can be extraordinarily Philistine. His workmanship is shoddy, he never completes anything on time, and his manners are positively coarse. I realize it's not customary for anyone other than a female member of a man's family to sew his trousers and shirts, but I'd like to make an exception to that practice. I would like to offer you the opportunity to sew my brother's garments as well as mine, Miss Deacon. His tailor could provide you with his measurements, and I could make it quite lucrative for you if you agreed."

Molly thought of the endless number of shirts, trousers, and jerkins she had made while in Lord Berryhill's employ. It was tedious and uninteresting work, and not something that she wanted to undertake again. "I'm sorry, milady, but I'd prefer doing what I'm—"

"I'd pay you two additional dollars a week." Molly's eyes grew so wide that Olympia thought they might chase her nose off her face.

"Two dollars extra? Three dollars a week?"

Olympia nodded. Molly went through a series of quick calculations. *Three dollars a week, twelve dollars a month. In six months I'd have . . . God Lord, I'd be rich! I wouldn't have to wait another year to rent my dress shop.* "For three dollars a week I don't think I can refuse you."

"Good. Evan will be delighted to hear it. And one more thing. Now that you have secondary responsibilities, I think you should plan to work here on Tuesdays and Thursdays as well. Would you have a problem with that?"

"Tuesdays and Thursdays are fine," she said. That would mean sixteen more hours away from Hancock Street. Sixteen hours when she wouldn't have to worry about running into Pierce, and risk further humiliation. Besides, for three dollars a week she would be willing to work seven days a week and give up sleeping.

"You're a reasonable young woman, Miss Deacon. It surprises me how easy it is to conduct business with you." She lifted a sleeve of the grenadine morning dress and waved it at Molly. "I'd like to wear this to my meeting of the Union Female Education Society tomorrow morning. Can you have it pressed by then? Good. And don't be surprised if Evan comes to fetch you later on. He's quite particular about the kinds of fabric he'll wear. He's always insisted on selecting his own cloth."

"He's going to 'fetch me,' milady?"

"Yes. He'll probably want to take you to J.W. Hill's with him. He knows what he likes, Miss Deacon, but he has absolutely no idea how much to buy. I believe you can assist in that area."

"But..." She remembered what Pierce had said about Evan's getting babies on his maids. "I'm sure if your brother tells me what he likes, he can trust me to choose the correct materials. A man as busy as Mr. Evan doesn't want to waste his time in a dry-goods store. If you can provide me with a driver, I can—"

"Was I unclear, Miss Deacon? My brother prefers to make his own selections." She walked to the door and turned before leaving. "He'll be by to fetch you later."

Evan Thatcher was decanting Madeira into long-stemmed crystal when Olympia found him in the library several minutes later. "You're late," he chided her. "Detained by your dressmaker?"

"Only momentarily." She accepted the glass he extended to her. "What did you discover?"

"She seems to be who she says she is. No relatives that anyone knows of. Rents a room on Hancock Street. And you?"

"No suitors."

"Excellent. I assume you were successful?"

"Indeed I was. We now share the same dressmaker."

There sounded the clink of fine crystal as brother and sister touched glasses.

"So she's exactly what we're looking for," said Evan.

"Exactly." Olympia reached out her hand to him. He pressed her palm to the lean contour of his cheek and held it there for a long time after that.

Later that night Pierce wandered into the kitchen. Duncan was seated at the table, a sack of dried pea beans between his feet and a copper bowl balanced on his lap. His right hand was suspended before him and from between his fingers a cataract of white beans rained onto the pyramid of beans already in the bowl. Pierce crossed the floor, swung a chair out from the table, turned it in the opposite direction, and straddled it. He folded his forearms across the stayrail, then cushioned his chin against their support. Neither man spoke. The only sounds disturbing the silence were the chink of beans hitting and sliding against each other and an occasional *plink!* when Duncan tossed a dud into a bowl on the table. The victor in these bouts of silence was always the man who could keep his thoughts to himself the longest. For twenty-two years the victor had been Duncan, and Pierce saw no reason to upset his father's winning streak now.

"She in bed?"

"Eayh."

Duncan sailed a pebble toward the waste bowl, but it bounced off the rim and skidded across the table. Pierce tweezered it with his fingers and shot it back toward the bowl. It landed on the floor.

"Coulda done that myself."

"Sorry."

Silence.

"You look lower'n whale dung, boy."

"Yah. She say anything about me this week?"

"Nope. But I've contributed a few words a my own. Where you been keepin' yourself? Haven't shown up for supper all week."

"Been eatin' at the Silver Dollar. How're things goin' for her up the Thatcher place?"

Duncan scooped up another handful of beans and began sifting through them. "Fair. They have her workin' five days a week now. Gonna be makin' clothes for Evan s'well as Olympia."

"She's gonna be makin' Thatcher's clothes? Jeesuz-God Almighty, I warned her about him. I told her what he is. And I told her to stay away from him."

Duncan shrugged. "S'pose she heard you?"

"Oh, she heard me all right. She's probably just tryin' to get even with me for—" Pierce stopped. He'd been too ashamed to tell his father what he'd done to her. He'd been too ashamed to tell anyone. Hell, he didn't even have the courage to look her in the face anymore. Oh, sure, he woke up when she did in the morning. He even knew how many steps she took to cross the landing. Nineteen to the head of the stairs. Nine to his room. He'd hurt her and embarrassed her, and he didn't know

what to say that would gain her forgiveness. He wished
he knew. It plagued him that she was angry with him.
He didn't like avoiding her, and avoiding Da, and eating
every night at the Silver Dollar. The food there was fit
to make a rabbit cry. He dwelled on that thought for a
moment, realizing that years ago Molly would have
been thankful for the food he criticized. Guilt washed
over him anew. "Damn, damn, damn." He bowed his
head against his forearms and withdrew into tormented
silence.

Duncan made an impassive facial movement that
stretched his brow as well as his ears. "Told me Evan
took her to J.W. Hill's this afternoon. Said they bought
some French lawn. Guess that's the kind a lawn you
don't have to take the sickle to. Anyway, 'fore they left
Hill's, Evan, he buys her a box a dancin' Jim Crows.
Never heard tell a such a thing."

Pierce looked up, misery rampant in his eyes. "He
bought her gingerbread?"

"Eayh."

"And did she keep it?"

"Didn't ask."

Pierce raked his fingers through his unruly mane of
hair. "I'm losin' her, Da. I'm losin' her before I even
have her. How can I compete with the likes of Evan
Thatcher? He takes her to J.W. Hill's in his carriage." *I
drag her to the river over my shoulder.* "He buys her
confections." *I lose her shoe.* "Jeesuz." Demoralized
and defeated, he shook his head.

Duncan pulled on the string that closed the mouth of
the bean sack. With copper bowl in hand he walked to
the sink. "Bad thing 'bout words," he said as he dip-

pered water over the beans, "is once they're out, they're out. No takin' 'em back." He set the bowl of soaking beans on the cool surface of the cookstove, where it would remain till morning. He walked back to the table. "Good thing about words is you can always say new ones that'll help righten the ones you balled up the first time."

Pierce crooked his mouth to the side. "You ever do somethin' you were sorry for, Da? I mean, somethin' that a wart bean might've had enough brains not to do?"

"Eayh."

"No kiddin'?"

"Yup. The way I figure it, ridin' a log down a sluice, now that's easy. But always sayin' the right thing to womenfolk, that's darn near to impossible. I'm goin' upstairs to hit the felt. Douse the light 'fore you come to bed. And maybe next week you'll stop lightin' outta here like salts through a goose. Don't see how you can stomach that bilge at the Silver Dollar anyway. Stuff is fit to make a rabbit cry. G'night."

Pierce nodded his head, and when his father had gone, he made his way into his workshop. He lit the oil lamp that hung over his workbench, then pulled out a drawer in his tool cabinet, removing something small and black from its depths. He straddled his stool. Placing Molly's solitary shoe on his bench, he stared down at it.

What if Thatcher had designs on her? What if he lured her with clever words and confections, then took advantage of her like he had that maid Liam had talked about? Thatcher wouldn't care what she'd lived through. Thatcher wouldn't care about the sadness in her eyes. He'd want to use her, not love and protect her. "Dammit, Molly, I'm not gonna let him do that to you."

He lifted the shoe into his hand and smoothed the satin ribbon ties between his fingers. He wasn't gonna knuckle under to Evan Thatcher. What Da had said made sense. Maybe he could righten up what he'd done wrong. He tapped the heel of her shoe against his chin and smiled.

And while he was at it, maybe he'd just go ahead and sharpen his axe.

During the last week of May, while Molly was dusting the front room, she removed Sara Blackledge's miniature from the mantel and cupped it in the palm of her hand. Sara still had the same plain face and thin lips as before, but for some reason, Molly didn't think she looked so unattractive as she had in April. Maybe the lighting was better now. She turned round to hold it toward the window and found Pierce observing her from the doorway.

"Man by the name of Jeremiah Pearson Hardy painted that picture of Ma some twenty-four, twenty-five years ago. Before I was born." He stood there angled against the door frame, hands in his pockets, wood shavings tumbling down the front of his trousers. He'd just carried a stack of short planks into his workshop and was heading back out to the buckboard for more. He made no move toward her, but continued talking. "Da paid him five dollars for that miniature, includin' the frame. These days it'd probably cost fifty dollars for the same picture, without the frame. Man has made quite a name for himself in these parts. I've heard tell that people pay as much as two hundred dollars to have full-length portraits done."

Turning away from him Molly gave the tiny oval frame a quick swipe with her dust rag, then set the picture carefully back on the mantel. Pierce lowered his gaze to the hem of her gown. Her feet were bare and he could see that her heels were a soft blushing pink, as if they were embarrassed about being discovered without stockings. They looked smooth as a baby's bottom. It tormented him to see, but not touch.

"You still mad at me?" he asked.

She continued dusting as if he weren't there.

"Da tells me you're sewin' for Thatcher now too. Kind've unusual for a woman to be sewin' for a man she's not married to, isn't it?"

She removed another curio from the mantel and applied her dust rag to it. Pierce's eyes traveled the length of her gown to the fringe of her broadcloth shawl. The pale fringe hid from view the back of her gown, but he could see two glass buttons beneath the sway of silken cord, and he warmed with need . . . and desire. His eyes crept upward, to the place where that solitary mole graced her neck—to the flesh that he knew to be soft as an overripe peach. The pace of his breathing quickened.

"He took you to J.W. Hill's in his carriage, didn't he? Even bought you comfits."

"That's none of your business."

"The hell it isn't. He'll probably try to take you someplace other than the dry goods store sometime soon and that'll mean he's up to no good. That ever happens, you get outta the carriage and walk home."

Molly directed her reply to the mantel. "This from a man who thinks it's polite to drown his father's house-guests and lose their belongings."

Coming up behind her, Pierce circled his hands about her waist and pulled her against him. She wiggled her shoulders to break contact with him but his body was too big to elude. Bending his head he nuzzled her hair away from her ear and murmured against her neck, "Are you never gonna forgive me?"

She closed her eyes, forgetting to breathe, but then she felt the wool of the carpet against her bare feet and she remembered all the differences that existed between them. She grew stiff as a bandbox within his embrace.

"I can't get any work done with you clinging to my spine," she said in irritation. She felt the powerful flex of his muscles against her back and for a heartbeat she wished the incident by the river had never happened, that she would be happy to hear him whisper the word "Sweetheart" against her earlobe. But what she heard was Duncan's voice yelling from the kitchen, "Pierce! That our buckboard I see takin' off down the street without you?"

She heard an "Aw hell" against her neck then the sound of his footsteps charging across the room. Leaning against the mantel, she cradled her palm behind her neck, feeling the place he had nuzzled, and didn't see the wood shavings that were tumbling one upon the other down the back of her skirt.

* * *

"I'm sorry, Mrs. Popham. I didn't hear you. What did you say?"

The housekeeper stood in the doorway of Molly's sewing room the following Tuesday shaking her head. "I knew the minute you walked in this mornin' that you were ailin'. Feverish eyes. Lackadaisical. You've been staring at that sleeve ever since I got here and you haven't hardly batted an eyelash. You should be home in bed."

Despite her anger with Pierce, Molly had been unable to fall asleep these past few nights until she'd heard him climb the stairs to bed. Why she found it necessary to lie awake and count the man's footsteps she didn't know, but it was becoming habit. Last night he'd gone out and hadn't returned till some ungodly hour. Hence, her lackadaisical mood today. She pushed the sleeve aside and trained her attention on the housekeeper. "I didn't sleep very well last night is all. Now, what were you saying about Mr. Evan?"

Mrs. Popham's chest puffed up like a pigeon's. "Gory, girl, haven't you heard any of the commotion outside? Mr. Evan's phaeton carriage just arrived from Philadelphia and they're all down there in the stableyard admirin' it. He sent me upstairs with an invitation for you to come down and see it too. It's some eye-catcher. Well, come on, girl. Don't pay to keep these rich folks waiting."

"Maybe you should go on without me, Mrs. Popham. I have so much work to do." She nodded to the disarray on her worktable.

"Work? Since when is starin' work? 'Less of course

you're really plannin' to set your needle to that sleeve
sometime today. Me, I think you should be home in
bed. But that's your business. I'll give your regrets to
Mr. Evan."

Molly pulled the unfinished sleeve toward her once
again and gave it a listless stare. She had squandered the
entire morning sewing three small plaits at the point of
the elbow. By this time she should have had the lining
attached, the raw edges stitched, and the finished
sleeves sewn into the armholes of the bodice. But what
did she have done? Three small plaits at the point of one
elbow.

Disgusted with herself, she slapped the open sleeve
onto the table and spread the lining atop it. She stuck a
few pins at critical points to hold everything together,
then took up needle, sewing silk, and sleeve and began
to pace around the perimeter of the room. As she
walked, she ran the two pieces of fabric together with
tiny, meticulous stitches, her fingers keeping time with
her footfalls. When she heard the echo of voices from
the stableyard below, she paused before the window and
drew the curtain aside.

Like ants around a sugarloaf they swarmed about the
new carriage, and there, amid carpenters, maids, and
stablehands, stood Evan, waxing eloquent, Molly surmised, on Philadelphia carriages. It was a handsome
thing, with its slatted sides painted a glossy black and
its front and back paneled seats upholstered in blood-red
leather. Brass lanterns perched on either side of the front
seat, and as she watched, the May wind buffeted the
carriage whip in its socket, curling the leather thong like
a lizard's tongue.

She shifted her gaze, identifying individual faces among the onlookers—the Irish carpenter named Liam, the bashful one known as Dooley. She spied Mrs. Popham laboring through the crush of bodies, and when the woman reached Evan, she saw Evan bend his ear close to listen to her. He frowned, then nodded, then angled his head toward the third-story sewing room.

Molly stood unbreathing as he found her face in the window. Only now did it occur to her that the master of the house might be displeased about having his wishes defied. But his expression held only indulgence as he beckoned her down with a wave of his arm.

Molly hesitated, then to indicate her preoccupation, held her sewing high against the glass, pointing to it with one hand and shaking her head. Evan waved his arm at her more vigorously, but she shrugged and smiled, and then someone was firing a question at him and he turned back into the crowd, losing himself amid their curiosity and praise.

Molly stepped back from the window. She raised the unfinished sleeve to eye level, gave it a pathetic look, then wandered back to the stool by her worktable.

She passed the knuckle of her forefinger over her lips, retracing the places that Pierce had once kissed. In memory she felt a breathy sensation form at her breastbone and spiral to the pit of her stomach, and she realized that anger was a poor substitute for the feel of Pierce's mouth upon her lips. Bitterness was a poor substitute for laughter.

You're forgetting your dream, an inner voice chided. *There is no room in your life for distractions.*

"I'm not forgetting my dream," she said to the empty room in defense of her thoughts. "I'm not." And to prove her point she stabbed her needle into the lining again and tried not to think of the footsteps she'd heard shuffling across the landing at three o'clock this morning.

During the second week of June, on a night when Molly had to work late at the Thatchers', Pierce wandered down to the waterfront to join his friends at the Silver Dollar.

"Never seen you lookin' so down in the mouth, Liam. Somethin' wrong?"

Liam McGinnis shook his head over his mug of ale. "Nothin's wrong."

"Not what you told me," Dooley slurred.

"I was a damn fool for tellin' you anything."

Dooley nodded drunkenly. "Yup."

"Only one reason why a man looks so glum," a companion offered. "Creature problems."

Dooley nodded again. "Yup."

The table jumped beneath the blast of Liam's hand. "Why don't you blat all my goddamn business to the whole goddamn grogshop?"

Dooley shook his head. "None've my affair."

Pierce proposed a toast. "To Liam McGinnis, the best damn chopper who ever laid a face-notch. May he lay his bride with half as much skill. To the wedding!"

"The wedding!" chorused eight male voices. Clinking mugs. Lusty slurps.

"Not gonna be any wedding," Liam grumbled. "Peg, she decided that maybe she fancied Heber McMahon more'n me anyway. Gonna have their banns announced in church come Sunday."

"No."

"She'd do that to you after you spend nine long years gettin' yourself in the mood to marry her?"

"Women."

"Disgustin'."

"Not gonna let it bother me," Liam declared as he gulped down a swig of ale. "There's plenty more where she came from."

But Pierce thought Liam looked pretty damned miserable for a man who wasn't going to let it bother him. Probably as miserable as he'd feel if Molly up and married someone else, he realized.

"Forget Peg," another counseled. "What about that English dressmaker at Thatcher's? Why not set your sights on her?"

Pierce drilled an ugly look at the man. Liam shrugged. "Hell, you can't hardly get near her. When she's at work, Thatcher jumps around her like a cooper around a barrel."

Pierce's expression grew suddenly uglier. "What do you mean by that?"

"Hell, Pierce, she lives with you. Doesn't she ever tell you what's goin' on up there? Thatcher's always in her sewin' room watchin' her work. And when they're not there, they're goin' to Hill's and Godfrey's to buy more fancy shirt material. She lives to be a hundred and fifty she won't have enough time to make all the stuff Thatcher's expectin' her to make for him. That right, Dooley?"

Dooley nodded his agreement.

"From what I hear, he's been spendin' so much time

up there with her, you'd think he was sewin' his new duds himself. You mark my words, 'fore the year is out he'll have Molly Deacon up a stump just like that little kitchen maid he was fiddlin' with."

A chair crashed to the floor. Liam gave a shout as Pierce lifted him one-handed into the air. "The hell you say. I ever hear you talk like that again, your mouth'll be wearin' my fist. You understand?"

Liam landed with a painful thud. "Jeesuz, Pierce, what's it matter to you? Unless you're interested in her yourself. That it? You gonna hang up your boots and stay home with the little woman?"

Pierce set his chair aright and straddled it. "I'm not gonna hang up my boots." But he realized he was wasting too much time. If he couldn't persuade Molly to forgive him soon, he'd be leaving the field wide open for Thatcher. And if Thatcher ever laid a hand on her . . . His fist clenched.

"So I haven't heard that she's turnin' cartwheels over you," Liam said. "I haven't even heard her mention your name in passin'. In fact, if you were to ask me, I'd say that Thatcher has things pretty much sewn up. Stitchin' a man's clothes for 'im is the same's turnin' cartwheels over 'im."

"She's not turnin' any damn cartwheels over Thatcher," spat Pierce.

"No? Then what the hell would you call it?"

Dooley belched. "Handstands." He saw fists on either side of his face—and then he saw nothing at all.

Molly was fast abed when Pierce came home that night. When she heard the sound of furniture crashing to the floor in the kitchen, however, she didn't remain there long. Mid the blare of Duncan's snores, she jumped into her petticoat and picked her way down the stairs by the light of a single candle sconce.

She found him on the floor in the kitchen, lying as peacefully as if he were floating downriver on his back. One boot was on, one boot off, a kitchen chair was upended beside him, and against his breast he cradled his pole-axe with both hands. He opened one eye to look up into Molly's candlelit face. "I got one boot off. But this other one"—he wiggled his foot to indicate the culprit—"I think it's schtuck. And you see that chair? For shome reason it just dumped me flat on my arse."

Molly shook her head in disgust. She made a detour around him to light the oil-lamp over the kitchen table. Pierce threw a forearm across his eyes to block the sudden intrusion of brightness. "Jeesuz, is it mornin' already?"

"Shhh! You'll wake your father."

So he cupped his hand around his mouth and said in a loud whisper, "Is it mornin' already?"

She let out an exasperated sigh and with hands on hips, looked him up and down. "I don't suppose you can get up?"

One knee rose. Up came his head. He took a deep breath. Down went the knee, followed by his head. "Nope."

"Well I don't think I can carry you up the front stairs, so it looks like you'll be spending the rest of the night down here."

"S'allright. Won't be the first time. Da tells me shome-times that life woulda been a whole lot eashier if I'd a shtayed puny."

"Da was probably right."

"Need a pillow. Where's my boot?" He flung out his right hand in search of the boot that was lying a yard away from his left ear. She rolled her eyes at him then bent down to retrieve the fallen boot. When she stood up, she felt a hand wrap itself around her ankle.

"Pierce!"

"Found it."

He tugged on her ankle, dragging her closer to him. She hopped toward him in pursuit of her foot. "Don't like havin' you mad at me, Molly." He lifted her bare foot and snugged it beneath his chin like a stuffed toy. "You think if I'd a known all that stuff you told me by the river that day that I'd still've thrown you in? Didn't wanna hurt you. How come you won't believe me, Molly?"

And because the sight of him cradling her foot re-minded her of the day when he had warmed her toes in his workshop, she began to relent. She fanned her toes beneath his chin and felt the scrape of his beard against her flesh. "Have you had your fill of my foot yet?"

"Unh-uh." He elevated her foot and pressed his mouth to the rising arch of her instep. Molly made a sudden hop to keep her balance. She closed her eyes as a churning warmth settled in the pit of her stomach and spread downward. The boot in her hand grew suddenly heavy. She felt the unhurried slide of his palm up the back of her calf, higher, higher, until the pressure of his hand was warming the bend of her knee, just below the fringe of her drawers. The boot slipped from Molly's fingers. Pierce felt the thud close by his ear and a quiver of discomfort as his delicate balance of body fluids threatened imminent upheaval. With a hand gone clammy, he retraced the long curve of her leg back to her ankle. The sole of her foot seemed so cool and dry against his lips that he flattened it across his forehead. "You think I might bother you to get the Jamaica Ginger in the pantry?"

Molly's eyelids fluttered open. His complexion rivaled his eyes for the deeper shade of green. "Oh no."

"Oh yes."

"Oh dear." She sped across the room for the pain-killer, returning to lift his head and hold the bottle to his lips. "Should I get the basin?"

He made a face as he swallowed the medicine. "Don't know." He motioned her to stopper the bottle and set it aside. "Could use a pillow though."

She considered running upstairs for the pillow off his bed, but instead she sat down on the floor, curled her legs to the side, and lifted his head onto her lap. With her left hand she gently smoothed hair from his brow. "How's this?"

He nodded his head almost imperceptibly, eyes closed, complexion still bordering between apple and olive green. She'd never held a man's head in her lap before, but it made her poignantly aware of how much she had missed Pierce Blackledge.

Minutes passed. His complexion drained to a calmer hue. Her hand continued stroking and soothing.

"Your hand's cool," he breathed. Reaching up he held it flat against the clammy warmth of his forehead. "Your mother ever hold your head when you were little?"

"Sometimes." She watched his lips, suddenly wanting to touch them with her own.

"When I was little, if I was ever sick, Da would feed me chicken shoup. Damn but I drank a lot've chicken shoup as a kid. Never told Da, but what I really wanted was shomeone to hold my head. Used to think it woulda been nice havin' my Ma alive back then. Shomeone who had cool palms and a soft voice. Cool palms are nice when you're feelin' poorly." He moved her hand from his forehead to his cheek. "Used to hang around with Liam and Dooley back then. Used to brag about the things we were gonna have when we grew up. Dooley, he wanted to have a shtable full've ponies and Liam wanted to own a hundred million acres of prime timber. Me, I told 'em I wanted to own my own sawmill cause I was afraid they'd laugh at me if I told 'em what I really wanted."

"And what was that?" she asked softly, a catch in her throat.

"I wanted to have a woman hold my head when I got sick. A woman with a soft voice . . . and cool palms. Shomeone who could do the things that I wish Ma'd had a chance to do."

He brought her hand to his mouth, and when she felt his lips touch the hollow of her palm, she whispered, "Oh, Pierce." She touched her nose to his cheek, knowing then that this man would always have a place in her heart.

* * *

"If you have a moment, I'd like to show you something, Molly."

She sat up so straight on her sewing stool that Evan heard her backbone crack. He laughed at her startled expression. "Forgive me for frightening you. I didn't think I was being all that quiet coming down the hall. You didn't hear my footsteps?"

"No," she said, breathless. "No, I didn't." His footsteps were lighter than Pierce's. There was no creaky floorboard in the hall to warn of his approach. And she had been too preoccupied to think about footsteps in the hall.

"Olympia mentioned that you brooked no nonsense where your needlework was concerned, but it's difficult for me to believe that you could find a piece of cotton cloth so intriguing."

She held up an edge of the material. "It's mous delaine." And she hadn't been thinking about the cloth in her lap. She'd been thinking about black wool, and red flannel.

"Whatever, I want you to come with me. I've something to show you." He escorted her down the hall and into another room. "So what do you think of it?"

She squinted at the brightness. She was standing in the third-floor turret of the mansion—in a room that admitted sunlight through a hundred squares of window glass; in a room with a view of the river; in a room that was appointed with every convenience a seamstress could wish for. Long tables. Dress forms.

Comfortable chairs. And bolt upon bolt of fine imported fabric.

She spun round in a dazed circle, missing nothing, unsure what to make of it. "Have you hired another dressmaker?"

He laughed aloud at her question. "My dear Molly, you are either very gullible or very forgetful. I told you several weeks ago that I'd speak to Olympia about relocating you. So this is it." He indicated their surroundings with a sweeping gesture. "Your new sewing room."

"Mine?" Her eyes flew from the cloth to the dress forms to the banks of windows. She had never been in so cheery a room. The possibility of working here five days a week amid all this sunshine brought a smile to her lips. "Truly?"

"Truly. No more sunless mornings. No more stench from the stableyard. Look around, girl. Don't stand there spinning on one foot."

"It's so lovely." From a single spot at the front of the room she could see far downriver to where the Penobscot Bridge spanned the river to Brewer, and far upriver where long ranges of sawmills hugged the banks of the Penobscot. Evan wended his way to her side. He pointed to the scullers who were steering a raft of logs to one of the sawmills.

"You'll never find the view boring. There are days when the river vies with Exchange Street for the greater thoroughfare of traffic."

She pressed close to the window, her eyes trained on the rivermen who piloted the raft. Their only navigational tools seemed to be their balance, quickness, and long oars. She imagined Pierce on one of those rafts, his muscles straining against the pull of the current, his naked arms moist with perspiration.

"These rivermen are like cowboys," said Evan. "They ride their logs as if they were riding bucking broncs, and they use their calked boots like spurs. The flavor of the West right here on the Penobscot. Did you know that most of the men on the river and in the woods work for me?"

Molly turned her head. "For you?"

"Somewhat indirectly, I suppose. The majority of them are employed by the Penobscot Boom Corporation, and since I'm the primary stockholder in that company, I can probably make the claim that they work for me."

Molly wondered if Pierce worked for the Penobscot Boom Corporation. She doubted it, knowing how he felt about Evan. *But what if he doesn't know who owns the company?* Wouldn't that be a rude awakening to discover he swung an axe for the man whose chest he'd like to bury that axe in.

"Are you smiling at a private jest or can you share whatever is causing you so much amusement?"

She turned away from the window, color staining her cheeks. "It's not a jest. I . . . I was smiling with delight. Your generosity is overwhelming. It leaves me quite at a loss for words."

"I'll have the carpenters remove all your materials from the northeast room and transfer them here for you." He watched her cross the room to the worktable.

She passed a hand over the material stacked on the

table. "Thank you. I'm sure I'll be able to stitch beautiful shirts for you in this room."

"I hope you will get as much enjoyment out of this room as I've derived from your company," he said as he made his way to the door. "And think of it, Molly. This is only the beginning."

Her hand froze on the cloth. Of course, Molly thought. If the rumors about him were true, he would want to exact payment for his kindness. The dread that suddenly knotted her stomach told her that whatever the price, it would be too high. She hadn't seen him wear his painted shirt studs recently. She wondered if he had retired them in favor of having Jeremiah Pearson Hardy paint him a new crop. She imagined a miniature of her own face encased in gold and thrust into his shirt somewhere below his chin. The knots in her stomach twisted into an agonizing pain, and in that moment, she knew fear.

Chapter Ten

The aroma of freshly sawn pine hung on the wind as Molly trudged up the backyard stairs that evening. She walked through the hall and into the kitchen and nearly dropped her carpetbag when the door from the front hall burst open and Pierce came rushing through. He skidded to a halt when he saw her and backpedaled a step, as if afraid of her. He couldn't remember much about the scene in the kitchen last night, but he remembered enough to know that Molly had held his head and spoken soft words to him, and a woman doesn't do that if she hates you. "Evenin'," he said, pressing his hands together as if unsure what to do with them, then folding his arms across his chest.

"Good evening," she responded shyly, happy to be speaking to him again, but feeling awkward about doing so. "You must be going somewhere," for he was wearing a shoestring tie that sat at a crooked angle to his shirt studs and a black frock jacket that was buttoned all the way to his lapels to disguise the fact that he wore no waistcoat. His jacket sleeves ended three inches above his wrists, allowing his cuffs to stick out like legs wearing high-water trousers. Even his hair was parted on the side and slicked down with macassar oil.

"Am," he said. "Goin' to the Bangor House for supper."

She looked impressed. "My goodness, so fancy."

"Can afford to be fancy when it's a special occasion."

"What's the occasion?"

He wedged his forefinger between his neck and collar and gave it a wiggle. "Can't tell you yet. You gotta change into your other ones and come with me."

"Change into . . . You mean tonight? Right now?"

"Yah, tonight. Yah, right now."

"I—I can't, Pierce. Not tonight."

He looked like she'd just doused him with river water. "You can't?"

"Evan is coming by for me in less than a half hour."

He scowled. "*Thatcher* is coming here? For you?"

"You have no cause to shout."

"No cause? Jeesuz-God, the man hovers over you eight hours a day, he's startin' to pay social calls on you, and you tell me I have no cause to shout?"

Her eyes darkened to an angry gray. "I don't know who you've been talking to, but Evan *doesn't* hover over me, and he's *not* coming here tonight to pay me a

social call. He happens to have made an appointment
with Mr. Hill for a private showing of some fabric that
just arrived from England."

"It's gonna be dark pretty soon, for crissakes. You're
gonna be out in the dark with that snake!"

"I'm going to be in the dry-goods store, which will
hardly be dark if Mr. Hill expects to make a sale."

"Yah? Well, you think the sun's gonna come up to
light your way home?"

She pinched her eyes shut and threw her head back in
frustration. "His carriage has lanterns! And you, Pierce
Blackledge, have the most suspicious—"

"How come he couldn't take you there this afternoon?"

"Because the shipment only arrived this—"

"And I suppose he'll buy comfits for you again tonight?"

"That's not the reason he—"

"And what does he do for you that I couldn't do?"

Her eyes flashed fire. "*He* lets me finish a sentence
once in a while. And if I stand here listening to you any
longer, I won't be ready when he comes."

"Oh, yah?" He watched her troop past him to the hall
door. "I'll warn you now. If he tries anything with you,
don't expect to come cryin' to me." She stalked down
the hall. "You'll be sorry you didn't listen to me." Up
the stairs. "I liked you better when you were Irish!" He
slammed his fist into the palm of his hand. He'd geared
himself up tonight for the Bangor House, forgiveness,
and a marriage proposal. But it seemed he was too late.
Damn Evan Thatcher.

By the time Molly and Evan left J.W. Hill's that evening, daylight had diminished to silver shadows. "I'm sorry you didn't see anything that appealed to your eye," Molly said as he assisted her into his phaeton carriage.

"But I did see something that appealed to my eye," he countered. "The problem is I'm under the impression it won't be purchased cheaply."

There were undercurrents and hidden meanings in his reply that made her skin prickle beneath her chemise. She guessed he wasn't talking so much about English cloth as he was about English dressmakers, so as he untied the reins from the hitching rail, Molly squeezed herself into the corner of the seat and tried to look calm and confident, no easy task as she remembered all Pierce's warnings.

"Have you seen much of the city since you've been here?" Evan asked as he took his place beside her.

"A little," she said, realizing her blunder when, instead of heading for Hancock Street, Evan directed his team toward the opposite compass point. "Where . . . where are we going?"

"I'm taking you for a spin around the city. Surely you can't object to a little sightseeing."

"But it's nearly dark."

"The carriage has lanterns."

Serves me right, she thought as she sank lower in her seat. "Lanterns. How convenient."

A city of rivers, Bangor was of necessity a city of bridges. There was the stately covered bridge that spanned the Penobscot above its headwaters—the one that Molly could see from her sewing room. There were the bridges at Franklin, Central, and State streets that traversed Kenduskeag Stream like the tines of a devil's fork. And there was the old covered bridge that angled across the Kenduskeag at a bend in its course, linking the outer fringes of civilization to the wilderness beyond.

It was across this last bridge that Evan Thatcher escorted Molly in his phaeton carriage.

She eyed the dark places where wooden beams arched above her, and she felt like covering her ears to dull the overpowering echo of horse hooves on wooden planking. But she was too paralyzed with apprehension to move. If anything untoward happened, she would have no one to blame but herself. Just this once why couldn't she have listened to Pierce? "Aren't you afraid that someone important might look upon this ride of ours with serious disfavor?" She had waited till they were through the bridge to pose the question.

Evan laughed. "I wasn't aware there was anyone's opinion more important than my own. And certainly not in Bangor. You worry overmuch, Molly."

She'd thought that Pierce worried too much too, but now she wondered if his anxiety hadn't been justified. What if Evan tried to force himself on her? She would have two choices. She could fight him off and lose her job, or she could submit to his advances and end up like the kitchen maid everyone was talking about. *Oh, dear*.

The road that bordered Kenduskeag Stream was in far worse condition than any other road in Bangor, but the Thatcher bays held their heads high in their check reins as they high-stepped through the mud. Half a mile down the road, on a flat of land by the banks of the stream, a skeleton of a building rose tall and straight in the air. Hoping to prevent Evan from taking her farther away from the city, Molly pointed toward it.

"Do you know what that building is going to be?"

"Indeed I do, but I'm scandalized to think you don't. You have led an extremely sheltered existence since arriving in Bangor. We'll have to see what we can do about changing that." Tugging on the reins of the lead horse, he urged the bays down the short drive to the building. He stopped in the foreground and made a grand gesture toward the framework.

"You are looking at the future site of Thatcher's Foundry and Manufactory—a three-story complex that will utilize some of this nation's most advanced machinery to produce more of this nation's most advanced machinery."

Molly scanned the length of the framework. It seemed to cover an area larger than the three-acre potato field they'd rented in Ireland. "It's big," she conceded.

"Big? It's gigantic! I plan to make this the largest and most productive complex in Bangor." He angled his body around and pointed a gloved finger at the east wall of the structure. "That's where the boilers will go, in the basement. Two of them. They'll be used to power the steam engine which will be the heart of the entire operation. Steam-driven belts, Molly. Think of it."

From the corner of her eye she regarded him. She thought it incongruous that a man in a moleskin hat and knitted gloves should be talking so passionately about boilers and steam engines. She would expect such conversation from Pierce but not from Evan. It seemed a rather odd obsession for a man of his elegant tastes to have, but then she admitted that it was probably no more uncommon than her obsession with dressmaking or Pierce's with wood butchering. And as long as it was keeping his mind and hands occupied, she shouldn't complain.

"I'll be hiring upwards of seventy men who'll be manufacturing light tools, steam engines, shingle and clapboard machines, boilers. I might even have them make a few small fire engines for river steamboats. Seems to me there are enough boiler explosions on steamboats to warrant it. This venture will be the biggest success Bangor has ever witnessed. I can smell it."

Molly thought perhaps she should clap, but didn't. "How will you find upward of seventy men to hire?"

"Offer higher wages than the competition is paying. Advertise."

"What about people who are newly arrived in the city?"

"You mean immigrants?" He shook his head. "No Irish. I won't have them. They're all troublemakers."

She felt a pang of unease that the Irish were so poorly received in this other Bangor. But his comment reinforced her attitude about the lie she'd told concerning her nationality. She would accomplish nothing as an Irishwoman. Best to be English in a city that despised the Irish.

"It's getting late, Evan. You really should be taking me back to the house." She heard the fobs on his watch chain jingle as he consulted his timepiece.

"It's not even eight-thirty yet."

"Yes, but the men will probably be wondering what

happened to me." *If you allow me to arrive home safely this time, Lord, I'll never go riding with Evan after work again. Never.*

"Do the men with whom you reside have some special interest in you, Molly?" Darkness masked the unease that played across his features.

She surmised it wouldn't bode well if she told him about Pierce. He might feel compelled to ask how an Englishwoman could tolerate the affections of a trouble-making Irishman, and his questions might not end there. "Their interest in me is much the same as that of a man who wants to make sure that his dog is inside before he closes up the house for the night. And the occupants of the Blackledge house retire early."

Evan laughed at the analogy. "Do remind me to tell Olympia how you are thought of at the Blackledge house." There was relief in his voice that Molly was not even aware of. "So you think I should be getting you back. I suppose I can't refuse. But first there's something I have to do."

Her throat constricted so violently that she saw spots dance before her eyes. "No," she wheezed, turning her face away from him. She felt the phaeton dip, but not toward her. Away from her. Safe for the moment, she inched her head around.

"No? You don't want the side lanterns lit?"

"The side lanterns," she said, feeling suddenly ridiculous. "By all means, light them."

Having spent an hour skipping stones on the Penobscot, Pierce finally tired of the sport and climbed the banking back toward the house. "Pickin' out material, are they? I can clear a swamp in faster time than it's takin' them to pick out their goddamn English cloth. Jeesuz-God, they could've been to England and back by now."

Reaching the crest of the bank, he saw a carriage pull up before the house and a glow of apricot light bathe the printed calico of Molly's bonnet. Stopping where he was, he watched Evan Thatcher alight from the vehicle. "Finally decided to bring her home, did you?" he said in an undertone. "She damn well better not have any tales to tell me." But as he saw Molly alight from the phaeton, he realized that he didn't like the idea of Evan Thatcher's being anywhere near Molly much less walking her to the front door. What if Thatcher tried to kiss her? "That happens, fella, she'll be the last woman you ever put a lip lock on."

With fists clenched in anger, he stole around the clotheslines to the west side of the house. He flattened himself against the clapboards and poked his head around the side of the porch.

The carriage lantern fed light into darkness, backlighting the two who strolled the path to the house. Side by side they walked, close, but not touching, heads bent almost shyly. Pierce could hear the blend of their voices in seemingly lyric measure, but not the pattern of their words. He wondered when Thatcher would make his move. He readied his fist in preparation.

Their voices grew louder as they neared the front stairs. Pierce inched closer to the porch. He heard a trill of unrestrained laughter from Evan, and then he heard something else.

Panting.

He pivoted his head to the side and searched the ground. He saw a shadow, a flash of iridescent eyes, and then he felt his head slamming against the house as 150 pounds of Newfoundland retriever made a doormat of his chest and a peppermint stick of his face.

"Oh . . . Jeez-uz . . . get . . ." He threw his forearm to fend the dog off. "G'down."

Bear answered him with a bark that dried the licks off his face.

"Nooo you . . . get your tongue outta my . . ." He ducked his head, clamped his hands around the dog's muzzle, and wrestled him to the ground. "Shh! I can't frig around with you tonight. I'll let you go but you gotta promise to get outta here."

Pierce let go.

Bear resumed barking.

Cursing, Pierce lunged for the dog's muzzle again. Bear avoided the hand and grabbed a mouth full of red flannel sleeve. Pierce heard footsteps running back down the path toward the carriage. He glanced in that direction. "Dammit, dog. Let go."

He wriggled his arm. Bear dug his hind paws into the ground and pulled Pierce flat onto his back. Pierce pulled back on his elbow as the retriever made to drag him away like a bone. Twisting his body around, he tensed his muscles, and with a mighty wrench of his arm, ripped his sleeve free.

Bear barked.

"Oh, hell." From the front of the house there came a glow of apricot light. Pierce cradled his arm against his neck, then turned away from the nose that was making wet tattoos all over his face. He felt the dog drop a heavy object onto his chest and grimaced when it bumped into his chin on its backward roll. It was damp and disgusting.

The glow brightened as someone carried the carriage lantern near. Pierce grabbed the lump off his chest. In the glare of the advancing light he sidled a look at the thing in his hand. It was a wooden cylinder that might have been a pestle or a belaying pin. As the light came to hover above him, he shielded his left hand over his eyes and through the spaces between his fingers squinted into the faces of the man and woman who peered down at him. He smiled as he hefted the cylinder in the air. "Evenin'. I don't suppose this belongs to either one of you?"

"I have never . . . ever . . . in my *entire* life . . . been so humiliated!" Once through the outside door, Molly seized it with two hands and swung it back on its hinges. Pierce blocked it with his shoulder and crossed the threshold behind her.

"Will you slow down long enough to listen to me?"

She charged into the kitchen. He charged after her, stopping short when the kitchen door slammed in his face. He bared his teeth. He looked down at his logger's boots. Da would annihilate him if he set foot inside the house with his boots on—but—Da wasn't home.

He flung the door open and stormed inside.

The room was darker than a vat of blackstrap molasses. "Molly." He heard movement by the pantry and looked in that direction.

"Of all the ignorant, simpleminded, *pin*headed

pranks," came her voice. "This time you have truly demonstrated the stuff you're made of."

Pierce struck out toward the stove to find a match. "I don't see what in the name of Godfrey Moses you're getting so riled up about. Those grass stains on Thatcher's coat didn't look all that bad to me."

Molly whipped off her bonnet and shawl. "How could you tell in the dark?"

Pierce found a match and headed across the floor with it. "Hey, Thatcher was the one who broke the lantern into a million pieces. When he asked me what I was doin' with a pestle, I thought maybe he wanted a look at it himself. When I pitched it to him, he was supposed to catch it in his hand, not deflect it off the lantern glass."

"It was a natural reaction."

"For an idiot, maybe."

Molly threw her shawl and bonnet onto a wall peg. Pierce fumbled with the lantern that hung over the kitchen table. The room filled with light.

"What do you intend to do about his top hat? It was made of genuine moleskin."

"Wasn't my fault Bear ran off with it."

"Oh? What were you hoping the animal would do when you pointed him at Evan and yelled, 'Sic 'im!'"

"Well, I sure as hell didn't think he'd knock Thatcher down like that. Maybe in the dark Bear thought that top hat was some long-lost relative."

Molly rolled her eyes. "I've probably just lost my job. All because of some stupid pestle!"

Pierce grew silent. "Might've been a belaying pin."

"Why were you spying on me?"

"I wasn't spying."

"Why were you eavesdropping?"

He hunched his shoulders and hooked his thumbs around the leather ends of his suspenders. "I wasn't eavesdropping. I couldn't hear a thing either one of you were saying. Aw, hell. You wanna know why I was out there? I'll tell you why I was out there." He made a fist, striking a pose with it in the air. "I was watchin' to see if he tried anything with you, because if he did, I was gonna give him *this* between the face and eyes. And while we're tossin' out questions, maybe you'd like to tell me why in the hell you were gone so long."

She planted her hands on her hips and fixed him with a defiant glare. "Not that it's any business of yours, but it was a large shipment of cloth."

"Oh, yah?"

"Yah!"

"So did you buy any?"

Something changed in her face. Something that hinted of her earlier apprehension, and Pierce was too perceptive not to notice. "No. Evan couldn't find anything to his liking."

"Nothing except you, you mean."

Her eyes shifted nervously. "That's not true," but she could feel her cheeks growing hot and didn't dare subject herself to any more of Pierce's green-eyed scrutiny. He was too close to the truth and she didn't want to admit that he'd been right. With a nonchalance she didn't feel she started to walk around him, but he caught her around the arm, stopping her.

"Did you come right home when you were through at Hill's?"

She looked from his face to his hand. "For a man who may be the cause of my losing my job, you're supposing to ask a lot of questions that you have no right to ask and I have no intention of answering!"

"He took you someplace, didn't he?" His question was accompanied by a tightening of his fingers around her upper arm.

"Let go of me, Pierce."

"Where did he take you?"

"You have no right to—"

"I have *every* right," he ground out. He seized her beneath her arms and she let out a startled sound as he plucked her high into the air. Her legs kicked out into nothingness and then she felt the solid bulk of his chest and the warmth of his mouth on her lips as he kissed her. Her feet were so far off the floor that her toes tilted with his shins. He braced his arm across the width of her back, crushing her to him, imprinting her breast with the pebble hardness of his shirt buttons. She felt his anger in the rigid muscles of his body, his lust in the hard insistence of his mouth.

He lifted his mouth away from hers. He was out of breath, his voice low and throaty as it whispered across her countenance. "Can you get it through your head that I don't want to fight with you?" He sampled her bottom lip with his teeth and she felt the skin he was tasting fill with blood and throb with forbidden pulses. She could feel the warm air from his nostrils fall softly upon her flesh; the strong and steady beat of his heart as it vibrated against her own. She felt safe and protected within the powerful gird of his arms, weightless and light-headed. And as his mouth continued to play over hers, she suffered a sweet ache in places that were hidden deep within her—places that were dark, and hot, and, of a sudden, slick with desire.

He rotated a half step to lean his tailbone against the table, then snugged her between his parted legs, flattening her gown with the pressure of his thighs. Molly felt the heat of his palm upon her cheek. His fingers touched her ear. His thumb stroked her temple. She smelled the fragrance of pine on his fingertips, so fresh and clean as it mingled with his own scent. "I wanted you to come to the Bangor House with me tonight because there's something I wanted to tell you." He worked his thumb into her balled fist, elongating her fingers, and lifted the heel of her palm to his lips. Where his mouth pleasured her skin a sensation bloomed that raised the down on her arm all the way to her shoulder. His lips moved higher, to the underside of her wrist, where a feathering of pale blue veined her flesh. She felt the pulse that beat there strengthen as the tip of his tongue christened the steady vibration. She inhaled a quick breath and held it quivering in her throat while Pierce's mouth skimmed across her wrist, slow and unhurried.

"I wanted to tell you that I love you, Molly." He lifted her other hand to his mouth and with soft kisses unbent each of her curled fingers. "Jeesuz, I love you more than I think I can stand." He kissed the warmth of her palm, then, blinded by his own need, lifted her against him again.

Her hightop boots brushed the front of his boots, the wool of his trousers, dancing upward, flattening his trousers against his shins. When their noses were tip to tip, Molly threw her arms about his neck and clung tightly. Moisture bound their cheeks one to the other and Molly felt the play of Pierce's tongue through their joined flesh, hard strokes up and down. She bent her cheek away from his and touched the corner of his mouth with her lips.

"About what you told me that day by the river, I know it must've bothered you tellin' me. I mean, if I'd been in your shoes, I don't think I would've wanted anyone to know those things. But I'm glad you told me. Makes me realize that I've had a pretty easy time've it growin' up. I know there's nothin' I can do to change what happened to you, but I can promise that I'll never let anything like that happen to you again. I swear it."

"Oh, Pierce," she whispered, voicing for the first time what she had been too stubborn to admit to herself, "I love you."

Smiling, he kissed her, and the touch that grazed her lips became as firm as the sinew that sculpted his young body. With a gentle thrust of his tongue he parted her lips while with its sensitive tip he probed the dark satin of her flesh. A tightness formed in Molly's breast as Pierce found the root of her tongue and stroked upward, arresting her senses with the taste of him. Their tongues embraced in a ballet of motion—touching, twining, bending in unison to the music that hummed in their blood. Pierce's heart became a hammer. His mouth grew hot. His hunger for her flowed like a current through his body, burning into his loins, inciting him to devour her.

Impatience began to rule the hands that held her. He inched her skirt upward, above her ankles, her calves, her knees. He found the whitework hem of her chemise and slid his hand beneath, conforming his palm to the back of her thigh. Her drawers were split from knee to knee to an inverted U, the open seam divorcing them enough from men's trousers to make them decent to the eye. His fore- and middle fingers chanced upon her bare thigh between that split in her lingerie. Four fingers parted the muslin and caressed the limb from back to front, climbing ever upward. He spanned his hand across the curve of her buttocks and shocked himself with the feel of her, for she was as firm and round as a pair of burl bowls.

So intimate was his touch that Molly felt herself begin to tremble. Pierce pressed his hand hard against her, trying to still her against his body. She tensed her arms around his neck and whispered into his mouth, "We mustn't do this. Not yet, my love. It's too soon. Much too soon." She felt the rhythm of his breathing alter and drew her lips away from him. Joy and passion mingled in his eyes. Joy and passion . . . and the physical pain of desire. He tried to smile, but couldn't.

"I didn't know that loving you would hurt so much, sweetheart." But he understood her objection and respected it. He couldn't treat her like one of the common wenches he'd known. He wanted more from Molly Deacon than a minute's pleasure behind the wood-chip pile.

Drawing in a deep breath, he lowered her to her feet

but kept her snug within the vise of his legs. She leaned into his body and there, between his thighs, felt the heat of his emotion and the immediacy of his desire. "Tell me again," she said, smiling into his eyes.

With one hand he cupped her neck from front to back. Resting his thumb on the soft hang of her earlobe, he slowly stroked upward along the outer curve of her ear, and downward along its silken underside. There was something so provocative in his touch that Molly's coloring heightened to an incredible hue. He smiled as he relaxed his thumb in the hidden angle beneath her lobe, idling there with patient restraint.

"I love you, sweetheart. I love you, and I want you to be my wife." He tilted her face upward with the pressure of his thumb, and then she felt his lips upon her brow, just at her hairline, lingering there on the sweet scent of his breath. He cradled her against him, shading her face with the breadth of his shoulders. He traced her hairline with the curve of his mouth, and when he reached the center of her brow—where her hair formed its part—she felt his lips bow into a smile as he teased her.

"You should be outlawed. No one should be allowed to taste this good."

Molly closed her eyes as his lips sketched a vertical path down the center of her forehead, pausing at the slight depression between her brows. He held her like that for a moment, breathing quietly, the tip of his nose touching her forehead. "Well, do you think you have the courage to marry a common wood butcher?"

She braced her hand against his chest. "I do, if you have the courage to marry an English dressmaker."

He was smiling again. She could feel the play of his facial muscles as his mouth followed the contour of her eyebrow to its outer edge. "It won't always be easy. There'll be lean times as well as good."

"But we can leaven the lean times with laughter, Pierce. I'll be able to live through anything as long as I can hear the sound of your laughter."

He eased her hand beneath the webbing of his suspenders. She felt the fullness of his chest against her palm. A stout layer of wool separated her hand from his flesh, but Molly felt his body heat radiating through the cloth as if no barrier lay between them. His heartbeat was even and strong underneath her fingertips and seemed to duplicate the rhythm of her own. He nuzzled the outside corner of her eye.

"We'll have to fill the house with children."

"Lots."

"It'll probably require practice every day."

"Day?"

"I love you." He whispered the words across her closed eyelid. He trailed a kiss down the slope of her nose, then followed her cheek upward to a rise of flesh as flowing and soft as cream.

And Molly knew such joy that she felt a knot of emotion well in her throat. She stirred at the lingering touch of his lips on her temple. She felt the glide of his suspender against her knuckles as she slid her hand down the length of his chest. And when her palm rode the

hard slant of his rib, Pierce cupped her head within the
long curve of his hands and kissed her.

"I'll make you happy," he said against her lips.

"You already have." She placed her hands on the
clean, sloping planes beneath his cheekbones, wanting
him, loving him. "You already have."

Chapter Eleven

They told no one of their exchange that night. Their feelings were so new, so fragile, that they guarded them with silence—sharing their secret as preciously as they shared their love. In the days that followed they learned to cherish those fleeting moments when they could brush fingertips in passing, when Pierce could press a kiss on the back of her neck without anyone seeing, when Molly could mouth the words "I love you" across the supper table. There was excitement in their secrecy, exhilaration in their touch. It seemed unimportant when they would marry, only that they loved, and loved deeply.

Molly was glad for the secrecy. It gave her time to

prepare herself for what would happen when Evan and Olympia discovered she was engaged to an Irishman. Perhaps it wouldn't matter to them, but she rather thought it would. And since finding another dressmaking position was not something she liked to think about, she shelved the thought in the back of her mind and decided to let it take care of itself. She didn't want potential problems spoiling her present joy. She didn't want to ruin their moments together by fretting about prejudices and jobs and obsessions. There was scant time in her day as it was to touch his face, to taste his lips. Soon there would come a day when she would have to discuss all these details that would affect their future life together, but for now it was simply enough to love.

Pierce was glad for the secrecy. It gave him time to prepare himself for the razzing he knew his friends would give him when they discovered he was going to get married ten years before the norm. But maybe the razzing wouldn't last too long when they learned that he intended to get married without quitting the woods. Fact was, he'd be kind of a trailblazer in the area. He could hold his head up to his cronies and boast that *his* Molly loved him too much to put foolish female restrictions on him. He, unlike his other friends, would reap the benefits of a wife *and* the woods. Course, he'd have to discuss his plans with Molly, but for the present he didn't want to spoil their joy with talk of leaving. He had till the middle of October before that would happen. Plenty of time to resolve the details of their future life together, plenty of time to get married. But for now, it was simply enough to love.

* * *

During that August of 1845 the clang of Old Settler Engine No. 5's fire bell became a familiar sound. It rang out its alarm as it raced to extinguish the flames consuming the stove foundry on Central Street, the saw and hardware business of Michael Schwartz, the furniture company on Broad, and the stove and blacksmith shop on Harlow Street. On the night of August 31, while Molly was whipping rosewater into a pan of homemade cold cream, she sniffed something acrid and scorched. Thinking she was again running the stove too hot, she adjusted the check damper and removed her pan from the surface of the cookstove, eyeing the black leviathan with intense dislike. She had yet to master its intricacies. It made her impatient with herself.

As she set the pan on the kitchen table, she heard the whapping sounds of Pierce's lathe fade to silence and then a rash of oaths so hideously profane that Molly raced to the back hall. She ran into his workshop, expecting the worst.

Pierce looked up from his carpenter's bench. In his hand he held a finely turned length of wood that he looked angry enough to hurl across the room. Molly was so relieved to find all his limbs and digits still attached, she expelled a rush of air and backed against the edge of the door. "I thought you'd hurt yourself."

"Only thing I hurt was this." He elevated the wood. "Ruined it. The last piece of curly maple I own. So much for Conor's traytop table." He threw the wood onto his workbench and shook his head at the waste.

"You ruined it? How did you ruin it?" She walked toward him, wading through a carpet of wood shavings as curly and blond as shorn cherub locks. She picked up the table leg he had cast onto his workbench and rotated it like a spit. "What's wrong with it?"

"What's wrong with it? I'll show you what's wrong with it." He removed it from her hands, reached for a second table leg, and placed them side by side on the bench before her. He thwacked the disputed wood with the backs of his fingers. "That's what's wrong with it."

Molly looked from one to the other. "Pierce, they're identical."

"Identical? Look at this." He pointed to each carved segment of the good leg. "Three buttons, a spool, and a vase. Now look at this one. *Two* buttons, a spool, and a vase. It's unsymmetrical. Lopsided. It's ruined." He combed his fingers through his hair and held his hand on the crown of his head as if trying to prevent it from falling off. His one concession to the hot weather was that he'd stripped off his flannel shirt and now wore his woolen long johns as outerwear, along with his trousers and suspenders. Molly glanced at him and saw that moisture darkened the wool in long stains from his underarms to his waist. She looked away, too hot to be dwelling on something that could only make her hotter.

"How do you suppose you miscounted?" she asked.

"Not concentrating." He watched her as she rounded the corner of the bench. The uppermost buttons of her gown were unfastened, the material folded under in a deep V, and down her throat there crept plump beads of perspiration.

"What were you concentrating on?" she teased, as sure of his response as she was of his love.

His eyes lingered on the pinpricks of moisture cling-

ing to her brow. To her temple. He watched water droplets floating over the rise of her collarbone, and he
thought to catch one of those droplets on a fingertip and
press it to his tongue. "You know damn well what I was
thinkin' about," he said, circling his hands round her
waist and lifting her high onto his workbench. Arms
stiff, he braced them like a wishbone on either side of
her and smiled as her feet dangled playfully against his
legs. "I was thinkin' about"—and then he stopped, mis-
chief in his eyes. "I was thinkin' that it's pretty late for
you to be burnin' pancakes in the kitchen."

She pulled a face at him. "I wasn't burning pancakes.
I was making cold cream."

"Still smells like you burned it. Why does an English
dressmaker need cold cream anyway?"

She presented her cheek to him as evidence. "It
makes my skin soft."

He trailed his thumb in a path from her cheekbone to
her jaw. "Mmm. It works. Make lots." And then his
voice grew hushed, seductive. "Anyplace else where
you use it that you'd like to show me?"

She kissed the thumb he held to her lips. "You know
there is, my love."

And her words were like to drive him mad. The two
of them would have to set a date for the wedding, he
thought. They would have to do it soon. With the same
thumb that bore the stamp of her kiss, he smoothed
loose strands of hair behind her ear. "I almost forgot. I
have a surprise for you. Close your eyes."

"The last surprise I had was when your Da told me
my husband-to-be was a priest. Is this surprise going to
be anything like that?" She watched him cross the room

to a cabinet and pull out a drawer. He looked back at
her.

"Your eyes aren't closed yet."

"All right, all right." Reluctantly she obeyed. She
wiggled her toes in anticipation as she heard Pierce
wending his way back to her.

"You can open your eyes now."

Set within the palm of each of his hands was a black
kid slipper with low heels and satin bows and streamers
of ribbons rioting earthward.

"My shoes." She lifted one of the slippers from his
hands. "You found the shoe I lost in the river."

"Kind've. I had the cobbler make you a new pair."

"But they look exactly like my other ones." She took
up the second slipper, turning both shoes upside-down
and sideways as she inspected them. "Oh, Pierce,
they're lovely."

And he could tell by the way she said his name that
he had done the right thing. Molly hiked up her skirt
and slid the shoes onto her feet while Pierce eyed the
slender ankles that peeped beneath the hem of her petticoat. With the ribbons tied across her feet, Molly sat up
straight and swiveled her feet to right, then left, admir-
ing the fit of the slippers. "They're perfect. But how did
you know what size to tell the cobbler if both my shoes
sank?"

"Bear retrieved the one you catapulted into the river.
The cobbler cut the pattern from that." He continued to
eye her ankles. He'd swear they were smaller than his
wrists.

She preened over her slippers again before smiling
into his face. Seeing the appreciation in her eyes made

Pierce realize that he liked the person Molly Deacon had become. He liked her a lot.

"Thank you, Pierce. I think this is the most thoughtful thing anyone has ever done for me."

Pierce rotated his palms around the balls of her shoulders. "I'm glad," he whispered against the crown of her head. He kissed her hair. "Enjoy them." And because his hands were nearly trembling with want, he said, "I suppose we gotta tell people pretty soon about this engagement've ours. You won't walk out on me like Liam McGinnis's Peg walked out on him, will you?"

"I know Liam McGinnis. He's one of the carpenters at Thatcher's. He's probably even the one who feeds you all your information about Evan, isn't he?"

Pierce shrugged his innocence.

"Your spies are everywhere. But he's looked so gloomy lately, Pierce. I'd heard talk that his lady jilted him. It's true, then?"

"Every word. They were gonna get married this fall, but Peg decided she'd rather have another." Pierce removed a freshly laundered handkerchief from his pocket. "He's some broken up about it."

"The poor man. Of course he is. Some women have hearts of stone. How long had they been engaged?"

"Nine years."

Her expression suffered a reversal from sympathy to incredulity. "Nine years? She devoted nine years of her life to the man and he still couldn't find the wherewithal to marry her? Good Lord, the poor woman must be a saint. No wonder she decided to marry someone else. She should have done that eight years ago."

Pierce cupped one of his hands around the back of Molly's neck and with the other sponged the pinpricks of moisture from her brow. "Nine years isn't that long, sweetheart. Some've my friends have been courtin' the same women for goin' on twelve."

"That's ridiculous."

"That's what it's about bein' a Bangor Tiger." He traced the corner of his handkerchief down the slope of her nose, then crossed to her temple.

"Bangor Tiger or not, I'd not allow any man to do that to me."

Pierce's voice softened as he caught her gaze and held it. "You won't have to." He slid the square of linen from her temple to the underside of her jaw. "You're so hot." And the timbre of his voice made her hotter. She felt the soothing friction of muslin down her throat, the iron control of the hand at the nape of her neck. A moment's coolness skimmed her flesh in the wake of the passing linen, and she shivered as he slid the cloth beneath the opening of her collar.

The cotton of her gown lifted with the intrusion of his fingers. His thumb lingered against her nakedness, and his breathing slowed as he guided the cloth downward. He drew her closer. He felt the batiste of her chemise soft against his fingers, and with his thumb he touched the yielding swell of her woman's flesh. He dipped his thumb lower and made a sweeping arc across the full-ness of her breast, repeating the motion once, twice, softly, sensuously, until she closed her eyes and leaned into the pressure of his hand. He rested the flat of his thumb in the hollow between her breasts and suffered an urge to replace his thumb with his mouth. "You shouldn't have the stove fired up when the weather's this hot," he said in a low voice.

He withdrew his hand from her bodice and elevated it to her throat, abutting his thumbs over the U-shaped depression in her collarbone. With the tips of his thumbs he stroked upward to the curve of flesh beneath her chin. "Poor Liam. I imagine it's a hard thing to lose the woman you love. He was gonna stay on at Thatcher's with Peg's brother, but now he'll be goin' back up north. Swampin' out a stand've pine is a good way to forget about creature problems if you have any. Your skin's so soft, Molly." He felt a rippling motion under his thumbs as she swallowed, and he sensed that the color that rode high on her cheekbones was a result of more than just temperature and humidity.

"Olympia will be losing all her carpenters. She won't be pleased about that."

"Don't image so. Jeesuz but it's hot." He crumpled his handkerchief and mopped his own brow with it, then with a lazy hand began unfastening the buttons of his underwear.

Her eyes clung to him. She knew it would be a terrible sacrifice for him to give up his wood butchering. But he had told her that Bangor Tigers quit the woods when they got married, and he wasn't being shy about the fact that he definitely wanted to get married. His friends would all be going back up north and he would remain alone with her in Bangor. She surmised it would be an occasion of great sadness for him to be left behind, and it endeared him all the more to her. "What will you do when you quit the woods?" she asked.

He exposed a long strip of chest between the parted

wool of his underwear and slid his handkerchief deep
inside, separating the damp wool from his flesh. She
watched the bulge of his hand as he wiped perspiration
from his chest, and she felt a warm sensation throb behind her eyes as she realized he was swabbing his flesh
with the same linen he'd used to wipe her brow.

"What'll I do when I quit?" He looked ten years into
the future and recalled what she had said about her
dressmaking. "Oh, I just might become the best damn
cabinetmaker in all of Bangor, maybe in the whole state
of Maine." The handkerchief was damp and wrinkled
when he finished mopping his chest. He shook it out
and hung it over his vertical vise to dry.

Molly scanned the room. "There's no stove in here,
Pierce. We'll have to buy you a stove else you'll freeze
in the winter."

He stepped close to her again and touched his mouth
to her temple. "Well, I'm not freezin' now and it's a
hundred and ten in here, so can we talk about somethin'
other than stoves?"

She traced the shell of his ear with her fingertips.
"What do you suggest we talk about, my love?"

He grazed her lips with his mouth. "I suggest we not
talk at all."

Her lips parted at the touch of his. She felt the glide
of his tongue across her teeth, then the gentle pull of his
fingers as he unlooped her bodice buttons, one by one
by one.

They spoke no words. The warmth of her lips spoke
for her; the play of his fingers spoke for him. He kissed
her long and hard while his fingers roved, and then she
felt the ribbons of her chemise giving way and the

stroke of his baby finger on the underside of her breast. Soon one finger became four and it seemed to Molly that her breast was growing as full and hard as that of a wet nurse. Suddenly thirsty, she slid her tongue into his mouth while her body ached for him to suckle the places he touched with his fingertips.

Deep within her something contracted and grew soft. Deep within Pierce something expanded and grew hard.

His mouth left hers, moving ever downward, over her chin, her throat, then lower—idling at the place where moisture ribboned her naked breastbone. She clasped her hands to his head, holding him close, then felt the tip of his tongue . . . there . . . against her flesh, blending the cool wetness of his mouth with the hot wetness of her body.

"I love you so much," she murmured against the thickness of his hair. She heard the ring of Engine No. 5's fire bell almost within the same instant and, sidling a lazy glance toward the window, saw a pillar of flame shooting upward from the Devil's Half Acre—a fire so hot that it seemed to melt the very darkness that it touched. "Oh, my God." She leaned away from Pierce and snapped his head toward the window.

Passion drained from his face. "Jeesuz." He ran toward the window while Molly fumbled with her bodice buttons. "Looks like it might be one of the boardin' houses or grogshops on the waterfront," he said. Molly joined him at the window. For long seconds they stared at the awesome spectacle. The glow from the fire bathed one side of Pierce's face with its eerie light. "Wind's blowin' this way." And Molly saw his features stiffen as she followed the progression of his thoughts. "Maybe I

should go down there and see if they could use some
help with the fire buckets."

"Be careful," she said, touching his hand.

He pulled her hard against him and kissed her lips.
She felt his fingers at the curve of her throat. "How
could I not be careful when I've you to come home to?
Tell Da where I've gone."

Not even stopping to grab his red flannel shirt, he
left.

Molly and Duncan sat on the porch for hours that
night, kept company by the rhythmic creak of the bench
swing's support chains and the hurried footfalls of the
curious. The waterfront blazed like a funeral pyre, bil-
lowing thick clouds of smoke and spewing cinders like
snowflakes. Molly caught one in the hollow of her
hand.

"Time summer ends, Bangor'll be nothin' but chimneys and cellars," Duncan reflected, mesmerized by the
sight. "Never seen anythin' like this. Kinda reminds
me of the old growth a yellow birch we used to find in
the swamp. Trees had long curly streamers a dead bark
hangin' down 'em, and after dark, someone'd take a
match to that bark. Flames'ud shoot up the trunk and
out to the branches like St. Elmo's fire. Wouldn't last
more'n half a minute but it was better'n fireworks."

"Do you miss the woods?"

"Some. I miss Sara more." He opened his fist. Nes-
tled within the shadow of his palm was a tiny oval of
brass. Molly smiled in affection.

"How long have you been sitting here with Sara's
miniature hidden in your hand?"

"Since we come out. The way I figure it, the house

goes up in smoke, I can replace the whatnots, but I'd be hard put to have Jeremiah Pearson Hardy paint another picture of my Sara. He's good, but he ain't that good." He squinted at the portrait and chuckled. "Funny thing 'bout this picture. Pierce, when he was a young'un, he'd sneak it off the mantel and hide it in his room. Used to find it under his pillow sometimes and the frame'ud be all sticky from where he'd held it so tight in his hands. Hard for a boy when the only motherin' he gets is from a two-inch painting. But I never heard a peep a complaint outta him. Maybe he didn't miss Sara s'much I thought he did. Your eyes stingin' from the smoke, Molly?"

She rubbed at her eyes and nodded, but far worse than the sting in her eyes was the sting in her heart.

It was after midnight when the corona of orange light that hovered over the waterfront bled itself of color. It drained into such blackness that Molly didn't realize Pierce had returned until she heard his footsteps on the front stairs.

"That you?" asked Duncan.

The shadow stopped at the top of the stairs, blending into the darker shape of the support beam. "Yah. It's me."

"Decided they could use another pair a hands, did they?"

"Yah. But it wasn't enough, Da. It just wasn't enough. Conor was there. He wanted me to ask you to come over to the rectory for the night. They're bringin' some've the survivors over there, and he said he could use your help. I'll be inside cleanin' up." His steps seemed weighted as he crossed to the door, his pace slow and spiritless. Duncan dragged his heels to check the motion of the swing.

"Boy needs some doctorin'. You think you can handle him while I head on out to the rectory?" He stood up and walked to the stairs. Molly followed him.

"Is he hurt? It's so dark, how could you tell?"

"There's some hurts you don't need to see to know they're there. Take good care of 'im."

She found him sitting at the kitchen table, head bent, face blackened with soot. He didn't even seem to notice when she entered the room. She filled a basin with soapy water, grabbed a washrag, then took a seat beside him.

"Pierce?" she asked softly. "Are you hurt?"

He looked up as if shocked by her presence. His eyes were red-rimmed and glassy and he lifted a hand to rub them. "Eyes sting a little." His hands were as black as his face and left dark smudges over his eyelids when he finished rubbing. A tuft of hair above his brow was singed and crinkled and bore a stench that surpassed smoky wool for foulness.

"You burned your hair," she said, wanting to touch the foreshortened lock.

He tested the hair with the tips of his fingers. "Yah, I guess I did." He gave the basin and washrag an absent stare.

"Do you want me to lather your face for you?"

Pierce blinked several times before applying the heels of his palms to his stinging eyes. "I can do it. Just a little slow tonight." He soaked the rag and after wringing it out lifted it to his cheek. With a listless up-down motion he began rubbing the soot from his flesh. "It was

Cavannaugh's roomin' house that caught fire. Started in the kitchen and shot up to the third floor like nothin' you've ever seen they tell me. There were fellers on the upper floors who never knew what happened. Some've 'em asleep. Some drunk. Jeesuz, those were the lucky ones."

He held the washrag to his jaw as if reliving the memory, then dipped it back into the water. "I've seen cant-dog men crushed to death by a peak log skiddin' off a loadin' sled. I've seen men disappear tryin' to break a jam. I've seen a tree split and fly backward and take a man's head clear off. That's what bein' a chopper's all about. But this fire tonight. Jeesuz, they were so helpless." He contemplated the basin of smuttied water. "They were screamin' at us from the third floor. Grown men screamin'. And there wasn't a thing we could do about it except watch. Some've 'em tried jumpin'." His silence bespoke the outcome of that endeavor. He lifted his rag again, making slow swipes with it all over his face. Molly's heart went out to him as he only succeeded in smearing the soot from one side of his face to the other.

"Was Cavannaugh's the only thing that burned down?"

"Yah. We kept the buildin's on either side of it wetted down. Never passed so many buckets've water in my life." He hung the rag over the rim of the basin, then held his hands before his face to examine his palms. "You wouldn't expect anyone who uses his hands as much as me to get blisters, would you?" But blisters he had—whole ranges of them on the upper ridges of his palms—strung together like the beads of a rosary and each one a hard pocket of blood. "Helped with the pumpin' too. Got my hands pinched in the damn mechanism."

"You could use some clean water," Molly announced when she saw what his efforts had done to his hands. She returned from the sink with a fresh basin of water and a clean square of flannel. "Put your hands in and let them soak for a while. I don't know what else we can do for blood blisters."

Pierce shook his head. "Give 'em awhile and nature'll take care of 'em."

For endless minutes she sat with him, allowing the water to salve his flesh and her companionship to salve his spirit. And while Molly sat, partaking in the silence and the scattered conversation, she learned much about those hurts you didn't need to see to know they were there.

She patted his hands dry with the flannel, and because his blisters looked so angry, she went to fetch some liniment, but returned empty-handed. "We're all out. But I can pick some up tomorrow in town."

And then she noticed the pan of cold cream she had left to cool on the table. "I think I just found something that will work just as well as liniment."

She set the pan in front of her, opened Pierce's hand, and scooped a finger's worth of the cream into his palm. With her fingertips she worked the balm into the depression that shaped his palm, then smoothed it outward toward the rise of flesh below his thumb.

His skin reddened with the friction of her touch, growing warm and supple beneath the gloss of cream. She massaged the coarse surface of Pierce's thumb,

moving from there to his index finger, using quick upward strokes, then elongating the flesh downward. She
made a glistening sheath of each of his fingers and with
a delicacy of motion spread the excess along his ridge of
blisters. Halfway across his hand her quick circular
strokes became semicircles, then arcs, and she paused
as she realized that this was not just any hand. This was
Pierce's hand—a hand that could hurl an axe with
deadly precision. A hand that could wield the power of
ten men.

She resumed her ministrations more slowly now, conscious of how the gentle abrasion of his flesh caused her
own to tingle. And when the cold cream was dispersed,
she gave his hand a final rub, smoothing her fingers
upward from the base of his palm, gliding to a stop
when the contours of their flesh locked—the heel of her
palm filling the hollow of his, the fleshy part of his
palm filling the hollow of hers.

Her fingers settled atop the divisions between his. He
spread his fingers wide, and when he did, she let hers
drift. Downward they slid, slowly, sensuously, filling
the spaces between each of his fingers. She felt his
muscles stiffen, then watched as his fingers curled over
the top of her hand, folding her gently within his grasp.

She looked into his face and saw that the eyes so
given to devil-may-care gleams were soft with moisture.
"Thank you," he whispered, and she knew at that moment that no one had ever loved as she loved, nor ever
would again.

"Turn your chair around, my love. I think some more
soap and water will help the cause immensely."

She wrestled his suspenders over his shoulders, then

worked the sleeves of his long johns down his arms. When his chest lay bare, she rinsed out the washrag, then began bathing his skin with it, cleansing him of the stench of smoke and the horror of the night's memory. She spoke gently, of everything and nothing. He listened, saying little, his eyes following the movement of her hands over his body.

"That's better," she said as she dried his chest and arms. "I think you're ready for bed now." She kissed his forehead and urged him upward.

He was slow getting up, but when he finally gained his feet, he swayed off balance and threw a hand out to the table to steady himself. He bowed his head and closed his eyes, then felt an incredible softness grazing his ribs.

Molly's hands.

He set his own hands atop hers and looked down into her face, loving her, needing her. And then he was tracing her hairline with his mouth, warming her in places he had yet to touch. He kissed her eyelid shut, then turned her face with his hand and slanted his mouth hard across her lips. And at that moment, pinned against him, warmed by his body and his mouth, she knew that some emotions burned hotter than fire.

Reaching upward she cupped her hands around the back of his neck, craving the pressure of his mouth, craving his goodness and his love. She could smell the cream on his fingers as he held her face, could taste the warm length of his tongue as it stroked the interior of her cheek, softly, slowly. There was much they hadn't said that needed saying, but for now there were no words, only the lingering touch of tongues swaying and twining, blending his desire and her affection. She worried he would taste fear on her lips, but she worried more that he would stop kissing her, so she wound her fingers in the thickness of his hair, holding his face to hers, kissing him without shame, without constraint. And thinking that his desire would eat him alive, Pierce swept her up into his great naked arms and in a voice low and hoarse whispered against her throat, "Tonight we'll need only one bed."

His room was stifling—too hot to be burdened with the added heat from a candle sconce. So when they loved, they loved in darkness.

Together they stood beside the bed. With two fingers Pierce withdrew her hair needle from where it secured her hair to the crown of her head, and in the next instant the heavy mass was spilling over his hands, twisting and turning upon itself like a living thing. He imagined her neck was too spare to support the weight of that unraveling mass of hair, but she didn't strain with the burden as it fell onto her back. He lost his hands in its richness for a time—until his fingers brushed that soft skin at the nape of her neck, making him crave more.

He searched out her bodice buttons, but the cream on his hands made him clumsy with the tiny beads of glass so Molly eased his hands away from her and unfastened in a trice what he had been struggling with.

He saw movement within shadow then. Shoulders twisting. Arms stretching. Sleeves flapping into nothingness. He heard the glide of cloth against flesh, cloth against cloth, and then he saw a paler shadow—one of soft white batiste and ivory skin. "Oh, Molly."

She felt his fingertips skimming the flesh of her bare

arms, and then he shaped his hands around the back of her skull and pulled her up to meet the hard force of his waiting mouth. His desire raged with that kiss. He proved with that kiss that he was hard, and male, and wanted her. And she responded in kind, opening herself to the rhythms of his body, preparing herself in wondrous manner to receive him.

She felt his hand at her bodice, loosing the ribbons of her chemise, parting it wide. She felt his fingers roving the flesh he could not see and could feel pleasure surge through his body when the peak of her breast hardened against his palm. His touch made her head light, her knees weak. He moved his hand slightly so that her nipple brushed his chest and she groaned at the soft scratch of his hair against her. She clung to him as he coaxed the chemise down her arms, but when he would have eased his lips away from hers she strained upward with him, loath to sever the connection of their mouths. So once again he scooped her into his arms and when next he lay her down, it was atop his bed.

Cradling her arms to herself, she watched as he stood by the side of the bed to unbutton the front closure of his trousers. She remembered the shadow hidden within that closure and felt her mouth go dry. He sat down on the edge of the bed to remove his boots.

"I'm scared, Pierce," she said in an undertone as his boots thudded to the floor. "I'm afraid I might disappoint you."

He stood up and she could see the pale gleam of his flesh as he slid his trousers and long johns down his legs. Naked and splendid, he sat himself on the bed again and turned to her. "C'mere, woman."

A moment's hesitation bespoke her fear, but she made her way to him on hands and knees, and when she was close, he girded his forearm behind her back and held her soft against his side. "How could you ever disappoint me?" He formed his palm to the shape of her breast and whispered into the warm hollow of her throat, "I love you." He worked his way up her throat, trailing kisses from the curve of her ear to her temple, and then he drew the lobe of her ear into the slick warmth of his mouth and she thought that never again would she catch her breath.

She felt the smoothness of cream on his flesh as he slid his hand down her ribs to her waist. With his mouth he sought her lips; with his hand he sought the drawstrings that bound her drawers. She circled her arms around his neck, wanting him closer, wanting him as a woman wants a man, in the quiet of this room, in the intimate shadows of darkness. And as their tongues glided and stroked as a prelude to more earthy play, he made a cup of his palm and cradled it high between her legs. Where he touched her, she felt a wondrously liquid pulse begin to throb like a heartbeat, and she christened his palm and fingers with her desire, shuddering when she felt him press his thumb to a place of raw and naked sensation.

Her breathing raced. She gasped his name into his mouth, and he responded by easing himself onto his back and taking her with him. Her hair fell forward, cloaking their faces with a darkness that smelled of lemon balm. Her hair rained upon him, teasing, taunting. He broke their kiss, then with his hands fixed at her shoulders, angled her chest above his face. Balancing her weight in his hands, he lowered her slowly, steadily, and she felt a sudden wetness where his tongue reached up to stroke the full hang of her breast.

She let out a soft cry of surprise, of pleasure. He circled the dark tip of her breast once, twice, then she felt the warmth of his mouth enveloping her fully— drawing, distending, stroking—and she strained against him, aching for him to taste more.

"I love you," she said between sieges of breathless-ness and flashes of thirst.

Pierce needed no other words to fan his passion. He rolled over with her, rid her of her drawers, and pinned her beneath him. He could see little, but he could sense her awe as she guided her hands over the arms he had braced on either side of her head. And she realized that she had been right about his bicep. It filled her hand from her fingertips to the heel of her palm . . . and then some.

"Do you trust me?" he asked, kissing her eyelids.

"Yes."

"But I might hurt you."

"Joy and pain," she whispered against his mouth. "They mingle and become one. But the joy is what we'll remember. Kiss me, Pierce. Please kiss me."

Of a sudden she felt a phallic thrust against her thigh, a probing, then a gentle push against her maidenhead. Her breathing quickened.

"I'm hurting you."

"No, my love. No, you're not."

A straining of membrane. A thinning. Pierce could taste the fear on her lips. He pumped, and her head buzzed with the pain of it. *Joy and pain*, she thought.

Joy and pain as he cushioned himself within her, gently now, allowing her to warm to the newness of a man's flesh.

And warm she did—to the fullness and power of him, to his muscled arms and rugged back, to the touch of his lips and the gentleness of his hands, to the goodness in his heart and the miracle of his laughter. Always his laughter.

She smiled against his cheek and he knew then that the worst of her pain had passed. He strained upward, hips and pelvis beginning to pump with a slow rhythm. She quickened to the intensity of his thrusts. Her fingertips tingled. She closed her eyes and saw sparks of light flashing behind her lids. Thirsty. She was so thirsty. And now the pulsebeats were everywhere, binding her inexorably to the pattern and flow of his lovemaking, to the thrusts of his body. Sliding. Stroking. Faster. Harder.

Her breath caught high in her throat, then higher . . . higher, until she could no longer contain it. It escaped in a frenzied sound of joy and pain—a sound that Pierce cut off with his mouth as he shuddered with his release, filling her with his seed. Stroking. Stroking. Then breathlessness, and quiet. Still above her he kissed the sweat from her brow, her temple, then gave her mouth an exhausted kiss, and she noticed that his lips, which had been so hot with his lovemaking, were suddenly cool.

The night air carried with it the lingering smells of smoke, the lingering sounds of love. They slept, and loved, and grew refreshed. Pierce discovered a warm place for his fingers and a warmer place for his mouth.

He filled the hollows of her flesh with feathery kisses, with the sweat of his passion, with his own flesh.

"I've used you all up," he murmured against her hair.

"Mmm." In the darkness she sketched the extraordinary pattern of sinew that defined his chest. A shapely pillow of flesh here, hard as bone, lifting to the powerful rhythm of his heart.

"I love you." His voice accompanied his hand to her cheek.

She kissed the balls of his fingers while her own encountered mystery upon mystery. Ridges. Knots of muscle. All whipcord lean and flexing.

"What've you found?" he asked when her hand stopped moving.

A gentle stroke of her knuckles and Pierce thought he would leap out of his skin. "Enough," he laughed, reaching for the errant hand, but it played tag with him in the darkness, discovering another place of wonder, and then another, until soon what had seemed enough, wasn't.

"*There,*" he rasped, folding his fingers around her hand. "Sweet mother, there."

Anyone passing beneath the second-floor window of 47 Hancock Street a short time later might have thought Pierce's outcry was one of pain.

. . . It wasn't.

Chapter Twelve

She awoke to a moist warmth caressing the inner curve of her ear. "It's seven o'clock." His voice touched her. "I thought you were the one who liked to get up early?"

She groaned as his lips left her ear and journeyed lower. "It's Saturday."

"Never stopped you from getting up early before."

"I can't move," she complained, her limbs feeling heavy and sated. "My body won't work this morning."

"We'll see about that." He bent his head and drew into his mouth that soft, plum-colored part of her that kindled pulsebeats in her loins.

She startled, laughing in disbelief. "You can't be serious about wanting—"

But he was.

And they did.

By 7:15 her chest resembled a Flemish tapestry, so pink was it from the meshing and friction of their flesh. "You look like a rainbow," he said as he touched a thin blue vein that trailed like a stem to the dark tip of her breast. She held his hand to her for a moment before lifting it to her mouth and gracing each of his knuckles with a kiss.

"Your father could come home at any minute, so please tuck this hand away before it causes any more distractions." She posed it at his side before crawling to the foot of the bed and fishing her chemise off the floor. She looked back at him as he lazed against his pillow, fingers linked behind his head, his face framed by iron-sculpted arms, every tendon throbbing with an axeman's might. And she thought what joy it would be waking up in those arms every morning to the feel of his lips on her ear. Anticipation made her giddy as she slid her chemise over her head. "So when do you propose to make an honest woman of me?" Hands, wrists, then arms poked through her lacy armholes.

She heard him laugh. "Anytime you want. But while we're talkin' about honesty, maybe you'd like to tell me whether I'll be marrying an English dressmaker or an Irish dressmaker."

Her chemise seemed to thud onto her shoulders. Molly brushed wisps of hair from her eyes. "Would it matter that much to you?"

"Hell, yes, it would matter to me. It's kind've amusing that you've been able to fool everyone at the Thatcher place all these months, but when we get married, I'd like people to know that it's a nice Irish-Catholic girl I'm marryin'. I don't want all that deceit hangin' over our heads, Molly. It was fine for a while, but I think it's run its course."

She smoothed her chemise over her thighs. The motion was a slow, disheartened one. "I'd been putting off thinking about what would happen when Evan and Olympia discovered I was going to marry an Irishman. I know the English and the Irish don't mingle in this city, much less marry each other, so I know they would ask me lots of incriminating questions. Of course, there's always the possibility that they'd decide to keep me on in spite of—"

"Keep you on when they discover you've been lying to them for four months? Think again, sweetheart. Rich folk don't like to be made to look the fool. When they learn they've taken in with open arms one've the despised foreigners, how do you think they're gonna feel?"

Molly bowed her head. "Not very happy."

"Like fools," reiterated Pierce.

She sat back on her heels and sighed. "Where else can I find a position that pays three dollars a week, Pierce? I could have my dress shop in just a few more months if I continued to earn wages like that. But I guess it's not meant to be, is it? Not if I'm going to become Mrs. Pierce Blackledge. Well . . . all I can hope is that Olympia doesn't poison my name with all the other wealthy ladies of Bangor. If I'm lucky, maybe I can find someone who'll offer a position to a talented dressmaker recently turned Irish."

"I don't see why you're so concerned about findin'

another job, Molly. You'll be quitting after we're married anyway, so it seems like a lot've fuss about nothin'."

"Quitting?" A flag of warning popped up in her head. She stared at him with incredulous gray eyes. "What do you mean, quitting?"

"I plan on takin' good care of you, sweetheart. No need for you to have to sew other people's clothes to earn money. I don't earn much, but I'll be earnin' enough to provide for the two've us."

Silence. Then, in a low voice, she said, "But I don't want to quit."

He seemed to grow confused. He brought his arms down quickly. "Correct me if I'm wrong, but it's the husband who earns the money, and the wife who keeps the house, cooks the meals, and cares for the kids. That's the way folks around here do it, and it seems to work out pretty well. Man provides a home for a woman and she does what she can to make it comfortable for 'im. You got a problem with that?"

"No . . . but . . . my dressmaking is my dream, Pierce. My life."

Silence. "I thought I was your life," murmured Pierce.

"You are, but—" Words eluded her. His features tightened with her silence.

"What you mean is I'm a *part* of your life, but not the part that's as important as your dressmaking."

"I didn't say that."

"You didn't have to."

More silence.

"You know how much it means to me to open my

own dress shop, Pierce. It's the only thing I had to live for after my Da died, the only thing that kept me going day after day. It's the only reason I came to this place!"

His body grew deathly still. "I thought you came to this place to marry Conor."

Her eyes widened in horror at what she had let slip. *Oh, Lord.* "I—"

"You must've been real pleased to learn that Conor was a priest. No way he could interfere with your plans. Right? Too bad I had to come along and spoil them."

"You didn't spoil them," she said, making a supplicating gesture with her hands. "I love you. I want to marry you, but—"

"But you don't love me enough to forget this stupid obsession of yours."

"It's not a stupid obsession!"

"No? What would you call it when a woman is so preoccupied with something that she's willin' to overlook all the rules that everyone lives by? Wives don't earn money by sewin' clothes and openin' dress shops. Jeesuz-God, you don't have to have the sense of a wart bean to know that. It's not done, Molly. It's just not done. Wives stay at home where they belong—where God intended 'em to be!"

"That's unreasonable!"

"The hell it is! I'm not gonna have people talkin' about me behind my back sayin' that I earn so little money that my wife has to open a goddamn dress shop to help pay the bills. Jeesuz, woman, don't you think I have any pride? When I take a wife, *I'll* pay for her needs." He slapped an open hand to his chest. "*I'll* buy the food that'll put meals on the table. *I'll* buy the mate-

rial that'll put the clothes on her back. No wife of mine
is gonna make me into a laughingstock."

She had thought it would be so easy to have her
dream and Pierce, but perhaps she had only wanted it to
be easy. He was asking her to make a choice that she
didn't want to make—a choice she couldn't make. Why
did men have to concern themselves so much with foolish pride? Why couldn't they content themselves with
simple dreams and attainable notions? "If you loved me,
Pierce, you'd understand what I'm asking. You'd let me
do this one thing without worrying about your being
made to look the laughingstock."

"A man can't serve two masters," he said after a
space. "It's the same for a woman. You can't have it
both ways, Molly. I don't want you to be my wife only
fifty percent of the time. I want you a hundred percent
of the time. I wanna be able to carry you up to bed
without your sewin' rope stitches in things while I'm
doin' it. I don't wanna share you with merchants and
customers and people like Evan Thatcher. I want you all
to myself, and if that's bein' selfish and unreasonable,
then I guess that's what I am. There's only gonna be one
person wearin' the trousers and makin' the money in our
family, Molly. And by God, it's gonna be me."

"So you're asking me to make a choice."

"I guess I am."

She looked away from him, eyes filling with tears.
She'd thought it charming when he'd told her a month
ago that he hadn't realized love would hurt so much.
Now she was experiencing it for herself. How could she
make such a decision? The man she loved or her dream?
It was like trying to decide which she'd rather keep, her

right foot or her left. But in the end she knew which one would have precedence. She would choose the one that gave her greater joy. The one that made her laugh . . . and made her cry. The one that would sustain her through the days when her hands would be feeble and her eyesight weak—when she could no longer gauge the cut of a cloth or fashion a stitch. Without looking she said, "You know which one I have to choose."

"No, I don't know. But I know which one I *hope* you choose." And when she finally looked up at him, he knew that she hadn't failed him. He flashed her a relieved smile. "Shall I speak to Conor about announcin' the banns?"

She nodded.

Then, thinking to ease the tension of the moment, he said, "Gotta see what we can do about makin' an honest woman of you before I head up north for the winter."

She was so sure she had misheard him that she cocked her head and asked, "Before you what?"

"Before I head up north for the winter. But that won't happen till mid-October so we have a good six, maybe seven weeks to spend together. And if Conor announces the banns for the first time tomorrow, we can get married in three weeks. That would give us four weeks to continue what we started last night." He grinned his delight at that thought before he noticed that Molly wasn't sharing his enthusiasm. "How come you're lookin' at me so funny?"

"You told me that Bangor Tigers quit the woods when they get married."

"Yah, most've 'em do, but—"

"You told me they quit the woods because it's too

hard on the women with the men being gone seven months of the year."

"Yah, that's true, but—"

"Do you think I'm that different from other women?"

"Well . . . no, but—"

"Then why did I just hear you say that you'll be going up north come mid-October?"

"Jeesuz, God! Lemme slip a word in sideways, will ya?" But the look on her face made him nervous. It wasn't exactly how he'd expected her to react. "I probably should've discussed this with you before, but I didn't want it to spoil anything. I guess I've been thinkin' that it'd be kind've nice to do both—to get married to you and to keep my job with the company. I know it's hard on most women, but you're not most women, Molly. You've got more spunk than most, and you've got Da to keep you company while I'm away. Fact is, I was hopin' that you'd love me enough so that you wouldn't fuss about my wantin' to continue wood butcherin'. I've got a good ten, fifteen years left in me yet."

His words smacked her roundly, causing blotches of scarlet to marble her complexion. "So I'm supposed to condone your wood butchering while you condemn my dressmaking. That seems fair, doesn't it?"

"C'mon, Molly. You don't have to get sarcastic."

"Sarcastic? You're right. I shouldn't get sarcastic." She threw her hand toward the commode. "I should grab that ewer and break it over that wooden head of yours! Who am I supposed to make my home comfortable for for seven months of the year? Who's going to be carrying me up the stairs to bed for seven months of the year? That *is* why you wanted me to yourself for a hundred percent of the time, isn't it. You *dare* ask me to choose between you or my dressmaking when you're planning to spend no more than five months of the year with me? For the next ten or fifteen years?" Her voice was so loud that he flinched. "Why should you care if people laugh at you for having a wife who sews other people's clothes? You're not planning to stay around long enough to hear them! What am I supposed to do while you're gone, Pierce? Is it more important to you that I pine over you rather than do something worthwhile with my time—like open a dress shop?"

"Dammit, Molly, we've already been through that."

"Well, we're going to go through it again."

"The hell we are! You're tryin' to tell me that your dressmakin's as important as my wood butcherin' and it's not holdin' water. My wood butcherin' is my life, for crissakes."

"And what do you think my dressmaking is?"

"Your dressmakin' isn't gonna put food on the table! It's not as important as what a man does, dammit."

Her eyes spat fire. "Not important! Why, you narrow-minded, *pig*headed Irishman! You . . . you . . . ohhh! To think that I'd been willing to give up *everything* for you. Did you think you could enter into this marriage without making any sacrifices at all? You get the job, the girl, and you even get the girl to give up what she's been working toward for a quarter of her life. Doesn't that make you even a little embarrassed?"

"No, it doesn't! That's just the way things are, and if you'd get your nose outta that goddamn stitchery of yours, you'd know what I was talkin' about. A man's work is his life."

"And I'm supposed to love you enough not to interfere with your life's work, but you don't have to love me enough *not* to interfere with mine. Is that right? How supremely just of you."

"Will you stop twistin' things around?"

But she was too angry now to stop. "Tell me, what would you say if I told you you had to give up your cabinetmaking?"

"I'd tell you to go to hell. That's how I'm gonna make my livin' when I quit the woods. And if you're gonna tell me that my cabinetmakin' is the same as your dressmakin', you're full' ve owl urine!"

"*I'm* full of . . . ! We both have to draw up plans for our work. We both use other materials to make our designs. We both sell our products to other people. How is it different?"

"It just is, dammit."

"But how?"

"Stop harpin' at it, Molly!"

"You can't tell me how it's different because it's not different at all! It's the same thing. Your work means as much to you as mine does to me, but you expect me to make all the concessions and smile prettily when you troop off to the woods. Well, I won't do it. If you run off to the woods, Pierce Blackledge, don't expect me to stay at home cooking meals and keeping house for a husband who isn't there. If you continue your wood butchering, *I* continue my dressmaking."

"As what? An Englishwoman or an Irishwoman? Jeesuz, at least the work I do is honest work. I don't have to lie to make a dollar. I don't have to deny who I am to get anyone to hire me."

"You'll never let me forget that, will you?"

"Lemme tell you what I'm not gonna let you forget." He thrust his finger at her. "I'm not gonna let you forget that you're gonna be one miserable creature if you keep up this charade of yours. And I'm through keepin' my mouth shut about it. Now anyone asks me, I tell 'em Molly Deacon's Irish."

She slatted her eyes at him. "I'd expect that of you."

"Good, because that's what you're gonna get."

And because she was hurt and confused and disappointed, she lashed out at him mindlessly. "You could have left me alone when I came here, but no, you couldn't, could you? You had to try to win me like some prize in an axe-throwing contest. Well, I wish I'd never *heard* the name Pierce Blackledge. I wish I'd never fallen in love with you. I hope you *do* go up north, and I hope you never come back!"

He riveted a look at her that sent a chill up her spine, but she could not see how her words had torn into his heart, hurting him as no other words had. "All right. If that's what you want." He threw his legs over the side of the bed and snatched his trousers off the floor. "Maybe I was too hasty askin' you to marry me in the first place. You don't belong on Hancock Street with the Irish. You belong up on State Street with Evan Thatcher and the rest've his kind." In went one leg. Then the other. He stood and, with his back facing her, buttoned his fly front.

"And if you don't know what his kind is, let me be specific. It's the fancy, phony, piss-cutter type who'd rather cross to the other side of the street than brush against an Irishman on the sidewalk. It's the type who show how decent they are by sewin' fancy nightgowns for the city's orphans but who'd slam a door in the face of any Irishman who climbed their front stairs askin' for honest work."

Angry tears burned her eyes as she watched him eat up the distance to the door. Before he crossed the threshold, he turned. "I spent so much time worryin' that Thatcher'd take advantage of you. Hell, I don't know what I was worried about. I should've seen it from the beginnin'. You two deserve each other. And if you're lucky, maybe he won't mind that you've been slightly sullied by a common wood butcher."

He left her then to herself . . . and her tears.

She hid in her room, unable to stop the tears, wanting to break a leg off her nightstand so she could use it to knock the lemon-shaped cannonball off her bedpost and send it flying. Her hand ached to do the same thing to Pierce's head. "It's all right for *him* to do exactly as he wants, but not all right for me. No. I have to give up everything for a man who's not even going to be here to appreciate it." She looked at herself in the mirror, and, seeing the puffy rings beneath her eyes, began crying again.

She heard Pierce downstairs as he stormed from room to room, banging furniture and slamming doors. She shot a hostile look at the floor. "Throwing Evan Thatcher in my face when I don't even like him. That's how much you know." She pounded her foot on the floor in angry frustration, then not wanting to listen to any more of Pierce Blackledge's idiotic clatter, she grabbed her bonnet and shawl and sought out noise of a less distracting nature.

The waterfront still stank from the smoke of last night's fire, as Molly imagined it would for days to come. There was one consolation with the smoke, however. Molly wasn't the only one sporting red eyes. She found a seat for herself on a bundle of cedar shingles piled on the steamboat landing and from there watched men begin to tear down the charred remains of Cavannaugh's.

Pierce could have been hurt in that fire, she thought. He might have been killed as he fought the flames that killed those other men. And that gave her pause. There were wives who would probably never see their husbands again because of that fire—wives who would be willing to give up anything to spend five more months with the men they'd lost. She bowed her head, feeling suddenly selfish. If Pierce had been killed, she would have looked at those five months he was offering her as a precious gift. They *would* have been a precious gift, considering the alternative—the emptiness those other women were now left with. Perhaps five months a year was not so stingy a thing for a wood butcher to want to share with the woman he loved.

I shouldn't have said that I hoped he'd go up north and never come back. She'd be devastated if that ever happened. So why had she said such ugly things to him? And why had he said such ugly things to her? Why was it so easy to hurt the person you loved most in the world?

Morning blended into afternoon. Cavannaugh's came

down in a black and steaming heap, and still Molly sat, so weighted with regret that she could hardly lift her head. She was sorry that they had tried to settle their differences with harsh words rather than soft ones. Sorry that they hadn't tried to work out some kind of compromise to their dilemma. But he'd been so hot to have her make choices and she'd been so hot to return the favor that neither one of them had taken time to look farther than the tips of their noses. But things were growing clearer for her now, and she almost smiled with the solution she worked out.

What if she went up north with him? She could find a room in a boardinghouse close to the place where he'd be working. Then at least they could see each other on Sundays. She could take orders for gowns here in Bangor and do all the work while she was away. And the money she would earn would help pay for her board. It was possible! She knew it was. They could get married, he could keep his job, she could keep hers, and they would still be able to see each other during those seven months when he was away. Why hadn't she thought of it sooner? Pierce would agree to it. Pierce, who had his mother's disposition and could never stay angry long. Of course he would agree to it!

It was late afternoon when she headed back to the house, her heart suddenly so light that she feared it might float away.

"He's what?"

Duncan drew on his pipe. "Gone. He was packin' up his gear when I come home early afternoon. Said he knew the company was short a timber cruiser to survey the East Branch the Penobscot, so Pierce, he thought he'd volunteer. Prob'ly cruise from now till the end a the month, then crawl back to civilization long enough to find out where he's s'posed to build the base camp this year. Don't know why he volunteered for the extra duty. Was tight's a clam about it when I asked 'im. You wouldn't know anything 'bout it, would you?"

A vibration high in her throat prevented her from speaking. Stunned and sick inside, she sank onto the sofa beside Duncan, and when the initial shock wore off, all she could mutter was, "He'll be back."

"I suspect so. Come April or May. Depends on when the ice goes out."

"No. Sooner than that. He has to come back." *He loves me. He's going to marry me. I didn't mean what I said about hoping he would leave.*

"Could be sooner, but it could be later too. I've seen the ice go out in June couple a times in my life."

But what if he doesn't come back? He'll never know I found a solution to the problem. I have to tell him. "How can I find him, Duncan? Is there someplace I can go? Someplace I can write?"

He contemplated the blue smoke that swirled about his head. "Wish I could help you, girl, but there ain't a postman in all a Maine who could follow a cruiser round the East Branch to deliver a letter. Awful big place the East Branch. Might's well be China."

She walked back to his workshop, half expecting to find him there—Pierce, who could never hold a grudge, who could never stay angry long.

The floor was swept clean of wood shavings. Flannel

sheeting covered his workbench. There was stillness here . . . and an emptiness that wrenched at her soul.

"He'll be back," she whispered. "He wouldn't leave me."

But he didn't come back. Not that night, nor the next day, nor the day after that.

She realized then that he was indeed angry. He was indeed gone.

She also realized something else. She could be carrying with her more than just the heartache of Pierce's abandonment. She could be carrying his child.

On Thursday of that same week Olympia Thatcher entered the third-floor sewing room to find Molly staring out the window. "Evan tells me you've been doing a lot of that this week."

Molly spun round at the sound of the woman's voice. "Excuse me?"

"Staring out the window. You've been doing a lot of it."

"Have I?" And when she marked the three naked dress forms that stood about the room, she knew Olympia spoke the truth. "Yes, I suppose I have."

"I'd heard of the mercurial temperaments of creative people, but I'd never experienced it before. Perhaps you're in one of your dormant stages. I hope this means I can expect a flurry of activity from you next week. I'm anxious to see what you're going to do with the blue peau de soie."

Molly crossed to her worktable and dug the fabric out for Olympia's perusal.

"Yes, that's it. Now where are those sketches you were working on?"

She spread out a half-dozen drawings on the table before looking back to the window.

Even after her father died she had never felt so hopeless, so lost. What would she do if she discovered she was pregnant? She wouldn't be able to stay in Bangor. No. She couldn't subject Duncan to such disgrace. She would have to leave. *And go where?* she asked herself. Pregnant, alone, and Irish, who would want her? And as her anxiety increased, so did her resentment of the man who had shared in the pleasure of their lovemaking while escaping all its consequences.

It was easy for her to forget that she had told him to leave. It was easy for her to forget everything except that Pierce Blackledge had deserted her knowing full well she could be pregnant. For the next nine months he would be with his friends doing his "men's things" while she, desperate and disgraced, would slowly bloat with his seed. In her mind no epithet was lurid enough to do him justice. He had left her without a word, without any way of contacting him. He had done to her what he had accused Evan Thatcher of doing to other women, and she hated him for it. If she was pregnant, she would end up no better off than she'd been in Ireland. All these months of hard work would be lost. She would once again be poor, with two mouths to feed instead of one, living God knows where, doing God knows what. She would bring into the world a bastard baby who would share none of the praise she had hoped to earn as a dressmaker, but all the indignities that would be heaped upon the illegitimate child of an Irish immigrant.

So she thought of Pierce Blackledge; she thought of the mingling of joy and pain; and she tasted the bitterness of love as it mutated to loathing.

"I think this one," said Olympia, separating one sketch from the rest. "Perhaps with some marabout feathers on the bonnet. Which reminds me. I'm going to be wearing the green alpaca luster to the ribbon-cutting ceremony at the manufactory this Saturday. I don't believe I mentioned it, but the last time I wore it, I received so many compliments from a female acquaintance in Boston that I thought she might strip the dress from my back. She's going to be in attendance on Saturday and has expressed an interest in meeting you."

"Meeting me?"

"I believe she has a notion to enlist your services, not that I'm anxious to share you, but she is a friend. So I think it would suit everyone's purpose if you attended the ceremony with Evan and myself. Actually, you might find it rather enjoyable. Everyone will be there. The mayor, the members of the Common Council and their wives, several luminaries from Boston."

"But . . ." How could she be expected to attend ribbon-cutting ceremonies when her life was falling apart. "I can't. My work—"

"Your work has consisted this week of staring out the window. We'll be by for you at noon."

"But I don't know any of those people. I don't belong there."

Olympia brushed a speck of dust off Molly's table and blew it off her fingertip. "You will."

The phaeton carriage arrived promptly at noon on Saturday. Evan apologized as he helped Molly onto the front seat. "Olympia was feeling rather under the weather today, so I fear you're stuck with my homely face instead of her lovely one. I've nonetheless been given strict instructions to introduce you to everyone. Olympia said to make this a very special occasion for you." And as they struck out down the street, Molly wondered why Olympia Thatcher should feel obliged to say something like that.

Thatcher's Foundry and Manufactory stretched like a many-tentacled beast alongside the waters of the Kenduskeag. It sported great black smokestacks, stovepipe vents, hundreds of windows, rain barrels atop the roof, a glossy coat of barn-red paint, and enough colored banners to rig a clipper ship. Evan delivered a brief speech before cutting the ceremonial ribbon and opening the doors to his select group of guests. "The furnaces are in the basement," he announced to those who filed past him. "The machine shop on the first floor will handle the heavy iron work. We'll make lighter tools on the second floor, and the third and fourth floors will house the patterns for machine castings and parts."

The boilers and steam engine were located in a building on the far side of the complex, and it was here that Evan whisked Molly. She was bewildered by his enthusiasm for the ugly behemoths, still thinking it a rather odd foible that a man so given to luxury would find so much appeal in pressure gauges and release valves. He spent a good part of the afternoon explaining the intricacies of the system to the Boston luminaries in attendance, but ever chivalrous, he always made sure that Molly was being entertained by someone. Molly found his friends to be elegant and gracious and not at all as she had anticipated. They were people of breeding who put her at her ease despite the fact that she was a lowly dressmaker who was garbed in merino wool on a day when wool was unfashionably hot.

By the time Evan delivered his last treatise, Molly felt she could state the purpose for every shaft, pulley, belt, and overhead pipe in the room. She hadn't met Olympia's Boston friend, the one who had wanted to enlist her services, but she considered the afternoon a success. At least she had done something other than worry about her life for a few hours.

"Everyone today found you most engaging, Molly." Evan insisted on taking the scenic route home, so they had crossed the Kenduskeag downstream and were following a meandering carriage path back to Bangor on the opposite bank. In a wooded overlook above the stream he suddenly drew rein and dropped his whip into its socket. "Yes, indeed. They were quite impressed with my beautiful English orphan. So impressed, in fact, that I received several inquiries about when I proposed to announce my intentions." He saw the look on her face and laughed. "You look surprised. Don't tell me that everyone at the ceremony could read my intentions except you?"

"Your intentions? Evan, I really don't know what you're talking about."

"You don't? My dear Molly, why do you suppose you've been sewing my shirts all these weeks?"

She recalled her conversation with Olympia. "Because your tailor has the manners of a Philistine."

He laughed again. "I do find your innocence refreshing. No, Molly, you're sewing my shirts because I could think of no better way to learn more about you. And I must admit that I'm delighted with what I've found."

"Really, Evan," she said, not liking the bend of the conversation, "I don't think this is at all proper."

"*Why* are you so concerned with propriety?"

"Why are you so unconcerned with the lack of it? It doesn't frighten you what people will say? It certainly frightens me."

"Why?"

"Because people can misunderstand situations and start vicious rumors," she said, thinking of what they would say about her if it happened that she was indeed pregnant.

"Yes. I'm well acquainted with vicious rumors." He grew pensive for a moment, and Molly suddenly came to wonder if all the vile intimations Pierce had made about him were true. After all, she had never seen him act in an ungentlemanly manner toward any of the women in his house, and he'd certainly never been anything but kind and courteous to her. Perhaps he was not so much the rogue as people thought. The women on his shirt studs could very well be cousins, not lovers. And she suffered a pang of guilt to think that for the past weeks her suspicions about the man—suspicions rooted in conjecture—had colored her feelings for him. Colored them with a dark, negative light. She'd been so blind about so many things and so many people. "But from now on, Molly, you let me worry about the rumors," she heard him say. "I assure you that none will arise from this liaison of ours."

"Liaison?"

"I hired you as my personal tailor for a reason. I

never do anything without a specific purpose in mind, and it's been my purpose all along to ask you to become my wife. Will you, Molly? Will you marry me?"

She was so stunned that when she opened her mouth, nothing came out.

Evan circled an arm about her shoulders, laughter trilling in his throat. "I'm in shock. You really weren't expecting this, were you?"

"Of . . . of course I wasn't expecting it."

"This is amazingly ironic. I must be losing my touch. For years women in whom I've shown no interest at all have expected proposals of marriage from me. And now the one woman who has stolen my heart tells me she was oblivious of my feelings. You've had your nose buried in one too many of Olympia's satin flounces. You don't know what's happening around you. I want to pamper you, Molly. I want to buy you the most expensive gowns, take you on the most extravagant trips, throw the most grandiose parties. I want you to be the most envied woman in existence. All you need say is yes."

What he was saying was so bizarre, so unbelievable, that she actually chuckled with the absurdity of it all. "Evan, there are ladies of breeding in Bangor who would scratch my eyes out if I ever presumed to wed the city's most eligible bachelor. I'm a *dress*maker, not a society lady. Why ever would you even consider a . . . a liaison with me when you can have your pick of any of the city's finest ladies?"

"They bore me. Mealymouthed and weepy. I have no desire to share my name with a woman who will do little but slobber over it."

"I'm being serious, Evan, and you're making light of me."

"No, Molly, *I'm* the one being serious. I want to marry you."

She shook her head, still unable to fathom his words. Marrying Evan Thatcher would be akin to marrying Lord Berryhill. It wasn't something a poor Irish girl would ever think of aspiring to. "I could never fit into your world, Evan. I . . . I wouldn't know how to act at a grandiose party, or what I was supposed to do on an extravagant trip. People expect you to marry a grand lady. I'm not a grand lady and I never will be."

"Nonsense. What makes a lady grand? You don't slouch. You don't swill your food, do you? You're not boisterous or frowsy. In essence, my dear, you have all the makings of a grand lady. And you won't have to make the transformation alone. Olympia and I will be there to help."

Marry Evan? she thought. Impossible. She didn't love Evan. But he was being serious about the proposal —of that she was sure. And then he said something that changed everything.

"Is there something in this life that you've wanted more than anything else, Molly? Something for which you were willing to give up everything?"

Pierce, she thought. She'd been willing to give up everything for him, and he'd repaid her by abandoning her. She'd been so foolish to think that anything in this life ever changed. She'd forgotten the lesson she'd learned in Ireland—that everything you held dear was eventually wrenched away from you. She should have listened to the voices in her head. Love was a trap. It lured you with wondrous feeling and excitement. It snared you, used you, then left you with emptiness and pain. She should have known better. She should have remained loyal to the dream she had imagined for herself. Not long ago the pursuit of that dream had been reason enough for her to give up everything. "I'd always had a dream about renting a dress shop," she said in a low voice.

"Nothing more than that?"

"Given my beginnings it would be quite extraordinary if I ever accomplished it."

"Done," he said, which prompted her to lend him a strange look. "Marry me, Molly. I'll not only rent you a dress shop, I'll buy you a whole city block of stores. I'll buy you fabric and hire women to sew for you. Marry me, and you'll have that dream of yours."

"You'd buy me a dress shop?"

"And more."

She shook her head and pressed her fingers to her brow. Pierce had asked her to make a choice between a husband and a dream. Now Evan was offering her both.

But I don't love Evan, she reminded herself.

You loved Pierce and look where that got you, said her inner voice. *He left you, betrayed you. You tried love, and now you know the truth. Love is for children. And you're not a child anymore. Love will bring you nothing but heartache . . . and bastard babies.*

What if I'm pregnant? she argued. *How can I deceive Evan like that?*

Life is full of deceptions. You can marry Evan and have security, or you can walk the streets with your bastard. Do you want your baby to end up like your

*brothers? Dead from sickness and starvation? That's
what will happen if you have no husband to support
you. The man is offering you what you've always
wanted—no restrictions, no qualifications. You were
stupid to fall in love with Pierce. Don't be stupid again.
Marry Evan quickly and he'll never know if the baby is
his or Pierce's. Your child deserves that much from you.
Marry him, Molly. Marry him, marry him, marry him.*

And she thought, *Marry him? I have no other choice
but to marry him.*

She bowed her head as she spoke. "I feel like I should
say something wonderfully clever or romantic," she
began. "I'm flattered, Evan. I think every woman
dreams of becoming wife to a man like you. But few of
us are ever asked. And even fewer of us have the chance
to say . . . yes."

Her reply was so subtle that he almost missed it. "Did
you just do me the honor of saying yes?" When she
nodded, he smiled and drew her close. "Ah, Molly,
you've made me a happy man. We'll be married within
a month. A spectacular affair at the house."

"House? But I'd always thought to marry in a . . . a
church."

"Is there a church in town that you attend? I suppose
we could always have the ceremony there. Which
church is it?"

"Saint—" She bit back the words. The Irish attended
the Catholic church, not the English. If she told him
what church she attended, she would be as good as ad-
mitting she was one of the hated foreigners. She
couldn't tell him. He wouldn't marry her if he knew the
truth about her nationality, and it seemed urgent to her

now that he marry her, that he give her baby a name and some semblance of a life. But to give up the Church? She couldn't. It was who she was, what she was. It was as much a part of her as being Irish. But if she didn't give it up, if she didn't marry Evan, what then? Her choices were few. She could suffer her hell after death, or she could suffer it here on earth with her baby. *I can't give it up, but I have to. I have to. Forgive me, Lord. Forgive me for what I'm about to do.* "It's not important what church I attend," she said quietly. "A wedding at the house will be fine."

It never occurred to her that this man who would be her husband had not spoken of love—nor even tried to kiss her.

Chapter Thirteen

"This what you want?" asked Duncan when she told him of her intended nuptials.

"It's what I want," she said. *It's what I have to want*.

"I'd kinda hoped you'n Pierce might eventually get together."

Molly's faced masked the hurt she had suffered at Pierce's hands. "We're too different, Duncan. We want different things, have different values. Evan and I are . . . we're much more suited to each other. You'll see. I'll make him happy."

"Never had any doubt 'bout that. I s'pose this means you'll be wantin' to talk to Conor 'bout setting a weddin' date and having the banns announced." When she didn't answer him immediately, he looked askance at her. "Molly?"

She fiddled self-consciously with the fingers of her gloves. "I can't talk to Conor. I—uh, I can't be married in the church."

And when she didn't continue, he nodded. "I see. This what you meant when you said you and Thatcher are suited to each other?"

She lowered her eyes. "You don't approve, do you?"

"Didn't say that. It's yourself you gotta please, not Duncan Blackledge. You might wanna remember one thing, though. Once you miss the first buttonhole, you'll never get anything to button up right. You gonna give yourself time to think about this?"

"I have till October third. Evan doesn't believe in long engagements."

"October third. What day's that?"

"A Wednesday."

"'Monday for wealth, Tuesday for health, Wednesday the best day of all.' I got married on a Wednesday. Sara, she was superstitious."

"I hope Evan and I can be as happy as you and Sara were."

He nodded but made no comment. Molly stood up. There was one more thing she had to tell Duncan, but she dreaded having to do it. "I want you to know that I appreciate everything you've done for me since I appeared on your front porch, Duncan—taking me in, feeding me, befriending me."

"You gonna be addin' a 'but' here someplace?"

She tucked in her lips. "The truth is that Evan thar asked me to move into the mansion right away so he and

Olympia can start grooming me for the wedding. He says I'll find the next month less trying if I allow him and Olympia to spoil me a little. So I said yes. Someone's coming by this evening to pick up my things."

Duncan nodded. "Can't blame you for wantin' to be spoiled."

"I guess I should go upstairs and pack."

"Eayh."

She took slow steps into the hallway. She was marrying the city's wealthiest man and would finally have her dream realized. She would have security and a father for her baby. So why didn't she feel happy? Why was it so hard to smile?

Moving into the newness and glitter of the Thatcher mansion helped banish most thoughts of Pierce Blackledge from her mind. She slept on Scottish linen and sat on rococo side chairs with carved crests and ice-blue satin de Bruges upholstery. Her bed was four-postered, its velvet counterpane embroidered with flowers and arabesques on its satin underside. On the third finger of her left hand she wore a diamond that was as big as a pillbox. Yet in the gilded halls of the Thatcher mansion, she heard no laughter.

She learned of grandness and riches. She learned the proper use of finger bowls and sterling and bellpulls. She memorized the names of each piece of furniture and learned to identify each Thatcher relative whose portrait graced the foyer. She learned of menus and servants, of literature and letters, of forms of address and addresses of importance. She studied books on etiquette and books on art, and cried uncontrollably one day when Olympia demonstrated how to pour tea—for lying atop the silver tray, as big and glossy as the finial on her bedpost, was a solitary lemon.

Throughout that month the *Bangor Daily Whig and Courier* buzzed with the news of the upcoming wedding:

> The editor of this paper would like to extend his congratulations to Mr. Evan Thatcher and Miss Molly Deacon, of this city, on the announcement of their engagement. We have learned that the wedding will take place at the Thatcher home on Wednesday, October 3rd. Gifts will be on display throughout that day for the perusal of the wedding guests. A reception will be held immediately following the ceremony in the dining room of the Bangor House. The menu is said to include Roast Duckling with Orange Sauce. . . .

> Miss Olympia Thatcher and Miss Molly Deacon are spending three days at the famed Tremont Hotel in Boston while Miss Deacon is fitted for her wedding gown and trousseau. Sources close to the bride-to-be inform us that the bridal gown will be fashioned from pale blue figured silk brocade, silk blonde lace, and seed pearls. While in Boston the Misses Thatcher and Deacon will be the guests of honor at a soiree hosted by Mr. and Mrs. William Rhys Endicott, longtime friends of the Thatcher family.

> A tea honoring Miss Molly Deacon was hosted yesterday by Mrs. Enoch Pond at that lady's home. The centerpiece was an arrange-

ment of white flat-top and purple asters. Attending the gathering were the Mesdames Sayward, Bryant, Godfrey...

Mr. Evan Thatcher has commissioned well-known Bangor artist Jeremiah Pearson Hardy, to paint a full-length portrait in oil of his fiancée, Miss Molly Deacon. It is reported that this will be Mr. Thatcher's wedding gift to his bride. For the sitting Miss Deacon will wear a robe of royal-blue velvet with a low corsage fitting close to the shape. The tight sleeves are trimmed down the side with fancy silk buttons and finished with a cuff. The skirt is ornamented with a deep border of fur. At her throat she will wear a blue square-cut diamond encrusted with brilliants, a family heirloom that matches Miss Deacon's engagement ring.

Mr. Evan Thatcher and Miss Molly Deacon will attend the Second Cotillion Party at the Bangor House on Thursday next. Dancing will commence at 7 o'clock P.M. Carriages will be provided by Mr. Woodard.

And buried within the depths of the paper, in an obscure section that few people had the time or inclination to read, there appeared the first reports of a blight that was sweeping across Ireland, turning healthy potato stalks into rotting plants that were "black as your shoe and burned to clay."

* * *

In the early evening of October 2, in a smoke-filled barroom in Grindstone, Maine, Pierce Blackledge looked up from the advertising page of an outdated *Whig and Courier* to find Liam McGinnis and Dooley Duffy making their way toward his table. And for the first time in a month, Pierce smiled. With the toe of his boot he propelled two chairs away from the table to greet them. "Si'down, si'down. Jeesuz, I haven't seen a friendly face for a month. Barkeep! A round of ale for my friends here."

"Who'd you do your cruisin' with?" asked Liam as he seated himself.

"Feller by the name've O'Shaunessy."

"And didn't he have a friendly face?"

Pierce shook his head. "These cruisers are odd birds. I've tramped through more mud and brush, climbed through more windfalls, forded more streams, and slept in more pole beds than one man should ever have to. And the black flies near 'bout drove me mad. But I never heard a word've complaint outta O'Shaunessy. Man's gotta be some kind've God-cursed pervert to enjoy the life of a cruiser. No more for me. From now on I'll stick to wood butcherin'." Besides, the long hours in the woods and the quiet had given him too much time to think about Molly. He was supposed to be forgetting about her, not remembering that night a month ago in graphic detail and realizing how much he missed her.

The barkeep served the ale. Pierce shoved the newspaper toward Dooley, who gave it a casual once-over as he nursed his ale.

"So how come you left town in such an all-fire hurry anyway?" Liam inquired.

Pierce ran his forefinger around the rim of his mug. "City heat was gettin' to me. Needed to get away to where it was cooler. So what's new back home?"

"There's a few very nice old dun fish for sale by A. K. Norris," Dooley quoted from the front page of the paper.

Liam rolled his eyes. "Guess the big news is about my Peg."

"What? She decide not to marry Heber McMahon after all?"

"Nope. She married him all right. Word has it she's already in the family way. My Peg and Heber McMahon. Jeesuz, he probably got a baby on her the first time they did it. He would a had to to have her breedin' this quick. What're you lookin' so queer about, Blackledge? *I'm* the one should be feelin' queer, not you."

During the past month he had thought about the possible consequences of their lovemaking once, maybe twice. But he hadn't worried the issue. Hell, how many times had he done it with Fanny Bright, and she'd never gotten pregnant.

Had she?

But Fanny's experienced. She knows how to avoid such things. Molly's not. You could've gotten her pregnant that Friday night as easily as Heber got Peg pregnant. And Heber might've only done it once. How many times did you do it?

He'd lost count after three. *Jeesuz.* He drained his mug and ordered another round.

"Maybe I'm lookin' queer 'cause I haven't had anything decent to drink for a month. So . . . what else is happenin' in Bangor? Olympia sorry to see you and Dooley leave?" *Tell me about Molly, Liam. Has she been sick? Has she been pale? Don't make me ask you plain out.*

Dooley read from page three. "Says here that the town of Augusta decided against grantin' licenses for retailin' ardent spirits even for mechanical or medical purposes. That's the way they're gonna be about it, piss on 'em."

"Hell, Dooley, you've never even been to Augusta."

"Nope. And if they stop servin' ardent spirits, I don't plan to neither."

"What about Olympia?" Pierce cut in.

Liam snorted. "What about her? She's got to be the most ornery creature I've ever had the misfortune to work for. Nag, nag, nag. You should've heard her all last month when she realized we were all gonna be headin' back to the woods and leavin' her with no one to finish the dinin' room 'cept Peg's brother and one gawmy apprentice. 'I'll never hire another Irishman as long as I live,' says she. 'You're too noisy, you're too slow, and where'm I gonna find another carpenter to finish up the mess you made before the third of October?'"

"Yah, yah. A woman can be a damn pain to try and please," agreed Pierce. But since it appeared that Liam wasn't going to volunteer any information, he swallowed his pride and asked in as nonchalant a manner as he could muster, "You, uh, you see much of Molly lately?"

"Yah, I've seen her. She's been kinda in and out. Had

a lot've teas and parties to attend this last month. And then she was in Boston for those few days with Olympia. Thatcher was s'posed to go with 'em, but he got called outta town on business at the last minute. Molly, I think she was kinda upset 'bout that."

Pierce was obviously puzzled. "What's she doin' going to Boston with Olympia? And what's all this about teas and parties?"

"Didn't anyone tell you?"

"Hey, Liam, it's in this paper too," interrupted Dooley, quoting from page four. "'The editor of this paper would like to extend his congratulations to Mr. Evan Thatcher and Miss Molly Deacon of this city on the announcement of their engagement. We have learned that—'"

"Gimme that." Pierce grabbed the paper off the table. He scanned the newsprint till he found the article in question. "'...the wedding will take place at the Thatcher home on Wednesday, October third.'" He looked up from the paper. "Jeesuz-God, that's tomorrow! She getting married tomorrow! Why's she doin' it? She doesn't love Thatcher."

Liam shrugged. "Maybe she loves his money." He was instantly sorry, for the look that Pierce shot him was frightening.

"What're you sayin', Liam? Are you tellin' me you think Molly'ud marry a man for his bank account? Is that what you're sayin'?"

Dooley nodded agreement.

Liam shook his head. "No, Pierce, I wasn't sayin' anythin' like—"

Up came Pierce off his chair, inch by angry inch.

"And furthermore, you've been sittin' in that chair carryin' on about *your* Peg and *your* problems when you could've been tellin' me somethin' important!"

Dooley nodded agreement.

Liam leaned far back in his chair, trying to escape the increasing volume of Pierce's voice.

"I could be halfway to Bangor by now! Hadn't been for Dooley, I'd probably still be listenin' to you crab about diddlysquat. I oughta spread your face all over Christ's Kingdom!"

Dooley nodded agreement.

Liam tilted his chair away from the table—but it wasn't far enough.

"When he comes to," said Pierce, rubbing his fist, "you tell him I borrowed his horse to ride into Bangor. You see an ugly redhead named O'Shaunessy, tell 'im I had to get myself to a tooth carpenter. I'll be back soon's I can. With a wife by God."

When he'd gone, Dooley leaned across the table and with a satisfied smile on his face toasted Liam's lifeless form.

Pierce rode through the night keeping a slow but steady pace over terrain lit by a thin crescent of moon. By the time he reached Medway, his ears ached from the cold and his fingers were numb, but he pushed Liam's nag forward. He knew Molly was pregnant. Why else would she marry Thatcher in such a hurry?

Maybe because that's exactly what you implied she should do, an inner voice reminded him.

All right, so maybe he'd been wrong to throw that at her. Even so, he didn't think she'd actually go out and do it. Since when had a creature ever done anything a man had wanted her to do?

Maybe since you ran out and left her stranded. What else was she supposed to do?

She could've written, he told himself. He would've gone home and married her if she'd told him about her condition.

Where did you expect her to address the letter? A knothole in some pine tree?

This gave him pause, for indeed, he had made himself as inaccessible as a man could get. Outside Pattagumpus he came to the painful realization that if Molly married Thatcher, he would have no one to blame but himself. Outside Mattawamkeag, sixty-two miles from Bangor, Liam's nag broke his leg.

"Lemme in! Lemme in before I break the goddamn door down!"

The portal to the Thatcher mansion flew open. A fresh-faced young maid in a crisply starched apron feigned courage as she confronted Pierce Blackledge.

"I wanna see her," he demanded, shoulders heaving with exhaustion. "I wanna see Molly." He crossed the threshold, and when the maid tried to block his way, he clamped his hands around her upper arms and moved her aside like a chess piece on a game board. "Where is she?"

"It's eleven-thirty at night," the maid squealed. "Are you mad?"

He searched the foyer. Potted palms, ferns, and tall vases of roses festooned the room. Garlands of pink clover blossoms hung in swags from the railing of the circular staircase and spiraled down the newel post.

"I must ask you to leave, sir. Mrs. Thatcher has already retired for the evening and Mr. Thatcher is expected back at any moment. If you were hoping to extend your congratulations to Mrs. Thatcher, perhaps you would care to leave your calling card. I'll make sure she receives it."

His body went rigid. His eyes traveled to the doors on the second floor. "Mrs. Thatcher. She really did it then. She married him."

"At four o'clock this afternoon. And a lovely wedding it was. But truly, sir, I must insist that you leave."

He stared at those doors and wondered which one she was behind, which one Evan Thatcher would enter tonight and not leave till morning. He felt a constriction in his chest that worked its way up to his throat and for a moment he couldn't breathe.

"Please, sir, if you don't leave I'll have to—"

But he turned toward the door even as she spoke, his spiked boots clicking on the marble floor as he headed out the way he'd come in. The maid hurried after him.

"If you have no calling card, perhaps you'd at least tell me your name. If Mrs. Thatcher asks, I'll have to tell her something."

On the opposite side of the threshold he hesitated, then turned. "If Mrs. Thatcher asks, tell her—" and as the fragrance of roses and clover blossoms wafted through the air, he realized the futility of more words. "Never mind. Don't tell her anything. It's not important anymore."

* * *

For her wedding night Molly would sleep on bedding of ivory satin rather than the Scotch linen she was accustomed to. She would wear a pale pink lawn night rail rather than her normal muslin chemise. And into her bed she would welcome a man who had never kissed her, but whose right it was to share an act of intimacy with her that she had shared with none but Pierce. The thought of it twisted her stomach into tight, grinding knots as she sat at her vanity. How could she do with Evan the same things she had done with Pierce? She didn't love Evan. With Pierce the union of their flesh had been an act of beauty and joy; with Evan it would be an embarrassment, a gross indignity that she would have to endure to guard her secret. Perhaps she could close her eyes tonight and pretend that Evan was Pierce, but the thought turned suddenly sour. If Pierce had truly loved her, he would have come back a month ago. If he'd cared anything for her, he wouldn't have left her the way he did. No. She would make love tonight with the man who deserved her love—with Evan Thatcher.

She still had no idea if she had conceived on that night a month ago. Her menses had always been erratic, so there was no way of knowing if her lack of flow in September was part of her normal cycle or if it meant something else. Whichever the case, she had made her decision and she vowed to be a dutiful wife to this man who was her husband. She would submit to him and strive to be a source of pride to him, for unknowingly, he had rescued her from the circumstances that threatened her existence. And for that, she would always be thankful.

Evan and Olympia had remained at the reception longer than she this evening, Olympia insisting that Molly return home early to prepare herself for her wedding night. So while the twins continued to entertain the elite of Bangor and Boston, Molly had ridden home alone, bathed in silence, and wondered if perhaps a wedding night should be more festive than this. She worried what would happen if Evan discovered she wasn't a virgin. She'd given little thought to that notion the day he'd proposed, but now that the time was upon her, she was terrified. He had kept a tight rein on his emotions throughout the month and had favored her with only an occasional peck on her forehead. She'd been grateful that he had been attuned enough to her emotional state to leave her alone, but she doubted he would be so solicitous tonight. She was his wife. He reigned over her body as surely as he reigned over his own. And realizing that, she knew fear. If he discovered her deception, it would be disastrous—disastrous for her *and* her baby. She couldn't let that happen, but how to prevent it?

Don't let him find out, Lord. I know I have no right to ask, but please, don't let Evan find out I'm not a virgin.

And as she crawled into bed that night, cold and afraid, all she could think was, *Damn you, Pierce Blackledge. It should be you I'm spending my wedding night with. It should be you.*

It was well past midnight when she heard the front door open and the echo of two sets of footsteps across the marble foyer. Up the staircase they climbed, dignified and unhurried. Two sets of footsteps, pausing outside her bedroom door. Molly riveted her attention on the crystal doorknob and felt an all-consuming dread wash over her as she saw it turn. With a creak of hinges the door opened inward. Evan stepped quietly into the room and in the chamber's candlelight found his bride staring at him.

"You're awake! Good. I was so long at the reception I was afraid you might have fallen asleep without me."

She watched him close the door and stride across the room toward her. His black tailcoat and pantaloons looked as fresh as they had that afternoon, but he had loosened his neckcloth so that the pointed ends dangled down his shirtfront and onto his waistcoat, a white satin affair with a cobwebby pattern stamped onto it. He sat down on the edge of the bed and began to unbutton his waistcoat.

"In the event that I hadn't mentioned it before, you looked especially lovely today, Molly. I was quite proud. I think you'll do the Thatcher name proud."

"I hope to," she said, sincere in her statement.

When his waistcoat lay open, he reached up and began removing the onyx studs from his shirt. Molly caught sight of a bit of flesh and felt the knots in her stomach coil tighter.

"I didn't notice that you were too upset today about that Blackledge fellow's not attending the wedding."

Molly averted her eyes. She had fought to invite Duncan to the wedding, but to no avail.

"I'm sure Olympia explained to you that his presence would have been quite a strain on our other guests. The Irish simply do not attend social gatherings of this caliber. But I somehow knew you wouldn't make a fuss."

He lifted her hand to his mouth and kissed her knuckles. "I choose my women with care."

She felt his lingering gaze on the bodice of her night rail and she blushed in response. Though high-necked and long-sleeved, the gown had a dozen scallop-shaped windows cut into the bodice, allowing a husband a peek at all that had previously been forbidden to him. Evan's eyes roved the cut-outs, from pale flesh to dusky shadow. He released her hand and slowly lifted his eyes to her face.

"The gown is breathtaking. Is that one of the ones you had made in Boston?"

She nodded.

"Good. Good. But it probably pales in comparison to anything you might design yourself, eh? So just to prove that I'm a man of my word, next week I shall take you on a tour of the buildings in the city that might be suitable for your use as a dress shop. I must tell you that Olympia isn't in favor of the idea. She says it would be more dignified to be drawn and quartered than to manage a dress shop, but you just leave my sister to me."

"I don't want to cause friction between you and . . ."

"Nonsense. Olympia always gives in to me. So you determine how many seamstresses you need and we'll set about hiring them. You realize of course that you won't be able to frequent the store. That would be a bit too familiar on your part. But you can draw your designs here, then send them to the store to be sewn. Will that suit you?"

Neglecting the overseeing of her shop was not exactly what she had in mind, but it was more than Pierce had offered her. Yes. She could be happy with that.

"That's generous of you, Evan."

"Is it?" He looked pleased as he got to his feet. "Well then, I'm glad to be generous. And now, my dear, you've had an exhausting day and must be tired, so I'll leave you to your sleep." He leaned over and kissed her forehead.

"You're leaving?" There was elated disbelief in her voice that she could not disguise.

"I don't really think it's necessary for me to stay. Do you?"

"Well, I . . ." She nearly shook with relief.

He pressed his finger to his lips for silence and shook his head. "It's late, Molly. We'll discuss this later. Good night now."

She managed to utter a "Good night" before he left the room. She heard his footsteps joined by another as he proceeded down the hall, and in a few moments she heard the door to his bedchamber creak open and click shut.

She stared at her doorknob in confusion, half expecting it to turn again and Evan to reappear, but within the house all was silent. And then she remembered her entreaty and realized that in His own way, God had answered her prayer. Evan had not found out she wasn't a virgin. But why hadn't he wanted to bed her? What had she done wrong?

She slipped out of bed to douse the candles and halfway across the room stopped cold. Those two sets of footsteps. They had faded at the same time, which meant that they had both entered Evan's room. Evan might not be spending his wedding night with her, but neither was he spending it alone.

She remembered Pierce's warnings about her husband—warnings that she had come to accept as vicious rumors—and she wondered again about their truth. Why would a new husband want to avoid his bride on their wedding night? Why indeed, unless his tastes ran to livelier fare. But to bring a woman home with him on their wedding night! To sleep under the same roof with his wife!

Her cheeks burned with the humiliation, and she wondered who, in this marriage of hers, had deceived whom.

"You warmin' up yet, boy?" Duncan piled another blanket onto Pierce's shoulders, then peered into the basin of water where he was soaking his feet. "Seems to me you coulda rented a horse somewheres near Mattawamkeag 'stead a walkin' far's you did."

"Only had two bits on me, Da. Can't rent a horse for two bits."

"Maybe not. But your feet are some messed up."

"Probably what my face'll look like when Liam finds out what happened to his nag."

Duncan dragged a rocker close to the stove beside Pierce. He lit his pipe as he sat down.

"You go to the weddin', Da?"

Duncan shook his head. "Girl wasn't married in the church. Couldn't attend a Protestant service where one a the participants is Catholic and should be married otherwise. You know that, boy."

And Pierce realized then that if she hadn't married in the church, she couldn't have told Thatcher the truth. She would remain an Englishwoman now, in an Englishman's mansion, and would bear an English child—and it was all his fault. She would give Evan Thatcher's name to *his* child, and he wouldn't be able to do anything about it. He was the one who had deserted her. How could he expect any concessions from her when he was the one who had run? How she must hate him. God, how he hated himself.

They were quiet for a time, listening to the pop of hemlock in the firebox, smelling the aromatic blend of Duncan's tobacco. Pierce bowed his head, and the pale green of his eyes darkened with his torment. "Had a real knockdown argument with Molly the night of Cavannaugh's fire. Stupid fight. I expected her to give up her dressmakin'. She expected me to give up wood butcherin'. I told her I needed more time in the woods. Well, I've got time now, haven't I, Da? All the time I'll ever need. And Thatcher's up there at this very minute probably showin' her—" His voice broke and he threw his head back, clenching his teeth against the pain of his thoughts. "It should be *me*, Da," his voice rasped. "Jeesuz, it should be me."

"Should," Duncan agreed. He rose from his chair and hunkered by the basin of water at Pierce's feet. "Water's cooled off. Better be fetchin' some more." He trekked out to the wellhouse, and while he was gone, Pierce dug something out of the pocket of his shirt—something he should have returned to Molly long ago but had kept for himself instead. He rubbed it against the unstubbled angle of his cheek, then gathered it into his fist, crumpling it mercilessly.

When Duncan reentered the kitchen with his bucket

of water, he found Pierce standing over the stove's fire-box. "You addin' more wood to the fire?"

Glassy-eyed and dispirited, Pierce nodded, while in the flames there burned a spray of whitework flowers embroidered on a froth of linen and lace that bore the initials MD.

Chapter Fourteen

During the week of October 21, the following announcement appeared in the *Whig and Courier*:

"Mrs. Evan Thatcher has been appointed a trustee of the Bangor Female Orphan Asylum. The next Board meeting, set for November 3rd, will be held at the Thatcher residence. Included on the agenda will be the cutting and sewing of nightgowns for the Asylum's nine occupants...."

On the morning of November 3, between sips of tea and bits of pastry and gossip, the ladies of the Bangor Female Orphan Asylum fulfilled their Christian duty to the city's homeless children. Nine gowns of varying sizes were cut from a bolt of plain cambric donated by

Mr. Rufus Dwinel, and each lady worked on a separate gown, individualizing it with the stitch that was her specialty. Molly sat next to Emmaline Pinkham, who was embroidering the border of her bed gown with a flower design using a crewel stitch and point de pois. Molly was making horizontal runnings through the bodice of hers in preparation for four rows of puffings. She listened to the conversation between Lydia Hathorn and Mary Alice Marley as she fashioned her stitches.

"She's five months along, and I told her she would have to give up one or the other—her baby or her job."

"That seems terribly callous, Lydia."

"Hmph. You haven't been forced to hire any of these Bridgets. I'll not have her baby in my house. Just the time when I'd need her most she'd be off tending the baby. Do a good turn by one of these Europeans, and they repay you by multiplying like rabbits."

Molly's fingers slowed over her work. Two weeks ago she had resumed her monthly courses, which eliminated any possibility that she could be pregnant. She had felt relief, but the relief had been coupled with a kind of draining introspection of what she had done, and why she had done it. She had married Evan Thatcher out of fear, out of disillusionment, out of desperation. And she had married him because through him, she could attain the one dream of hers that had not yet been shattered. She had not employed any feminine wile to snare him. On the contrary, it was *he* who had pursued, *he* who had cajoled. She wondered now at the cajoling that had contained not one word of love. She'd been unaware that desperation could so deafen one's ears.

She did not love Evan as she'd loved Pierce. She did

not desire him as she'd desired Pierce, but she had not thought to treat her marriage vows lightly. Be they pronounced man and wife by a priest or a judge, she felt bound by the words. In the eyes of God she was not married, but in the eyes of the state and in her own eyes, she was. She had promised herself to be dutiful, but how could she be dutiful to a husband who seemed to have taken a vow of indifference? The only time he had spent alone with her in the past four weeks was to show her his proposed location for her dress shop. The rest of the time he'd been conducting business meetings or running down to the manufactory to baby-sit his steam engine or conversing with Olympia about something.

Thoughts of Olympia made her want to grind her teeth. The Thatcher house was large enough to accommodate fifty residents comfortably, so why did Olympia always make a habit of appearing in the very room that Evan was occupying? And why did he always seem so delighted to see her? Perhaps there was a bond that ran more deeply in twins than in ordinary siblings, but Molly found it distressing. Even at their wedding he had danced more with his sister than with his wife. She was beginning to think that he might have enjoyed marrying Olympia if she had been someone other than his sister. Perhaps Olympia would know whose footsteps accompanied Evan into his room at night. Perhaps Olympia would know why her brother showed no interest in consummating the vows he had recited a month ago. Had he married her for no other reason than to ignore and humiliate her? For that's exactly what he was doing. Whereas Pierce's betrayal had left her feeling bereft, this kind of betrayal left her feeling as though there was something terribly unnatural in the Thatcher mansion— something unwholesome and unclean.

Through the haze of her thoughts, she heard Lydia's voice again. "So she's writing to some relatives in Boston to see if they can board the baby. If they can't, out she goes. Shall I send her to you, Mary Alice? You seem so concerned about her welfare. Perhaps you'd like to take the two of them under your maternal wing."

"Well, I would but . . . Nathaniel says we have sufficient help at the moment."

"There. You see? You're perfectly willing to criticize me, but you're quite unwilling to do anything about the problem yourself. Oh, honestly, someone pass her a handkerchief before she drenches her sewing silk. I didn't say anything so scathing that you have to cry about it, Mary Alice."

Molly handed Mary Alice a clean hanky, but what she really wanted to do with it was stuff it down Lydia's throat.

"I've heard if you hire these Bridgets as nursemaids, they'll make every effort to steal your baby from its cradle and carry it off to a priest to be baptized."

"And declare themselves the godmother! It's something all of us must concern ourselves with, ladies. These Irish immigrants are intellectually inferior and morally degenerative and they are corrupting society as we know it."

Molly separated her running threads and yanked on one as she glared at Lydia Hathorn. How dare they say such things about the Irish, she thought. How dare they!

The cambric bunched like ribbon candy, then flattened out as she ripped the thread clear out of the gown.

"Who knows what diseases they're bringing into our homes with them," Lydia continued. "Most of them are fresh out of steerage passage, where they've lived in Lord only knows what kind of filth."

"And now with the blight, who knows how many more of them will show up at out doorsteps? Something should be done."

"Blight?" Molly puzzled. "What blight?"

A dozen ladies eyed Molly, then tittered knowingly as they eyed each other. "I can't imagine how you've been occupying yourself this past month, my dear." Lydia winked at her companions. "The *Courier* has been publishing reports about the devastation every other day. It seems the potato crop in Ireland was thriving one day and rotting the next. They say there's not a healthy stalk left in the whole country, and the stench alone is enough to send people packing. So they're boarding ships by the thousands and coming here. I believe it could be compared to an infestation of vermin. Only, these vermin expect a fair wage once they get over here."

"They should stay in Ireland, blight or no blight."

"Yes, I think it's terrible what they're doing to our city."

"My goodness, Molly, you're as bad as Mary Alice," scolded Lydia. "No need to look so maudlin, dear. They're only Irish. And if you ask me, any people who don't have sense enough to plant something other than potatoes to feed themselves deserve to starve."

"How can you say—" Molly buckled her lip before her tongue ran away with her, and she recalled what

Pierce had told her about never finding happiness if she continued to deny who she was and where she came from. A Thatcher would have no reason to argue with Lydia. She realized the woman was saying nothing worse than what she herself might contend. But for Molly to make those contentions was one thing. She was Irish and had every right to point out the flaws of her countrymen. Listening to Lydia Hathorn do the same thing was something else entirely. "I'm sure you don't mean that, Lydia."

A giddy sound from Mary Alice drew everyone's attention. "The baby just kicked," she said, pressing her hand to her side. "It's the first time I've felt it. Oo, there it is again." So while discourse reverted to Mary Alice's impending motherhood, Molly thought about Pierce, hating him for being so right, hating him for leaving her. With a mechanical motion she rethreaded her needle and began to repair the damage she'd caused to the bed gown. The shrill chirp of female voices in the background made her teeth ache.

"The first one is always the worst."

"I had a much harder time with my third."

"I think they're all equally bad. What men expect us to endure for the sheer pleasure of their flesh is unconscionable."

"And speaking of unconscionable, my George suggested the other night that we do . . . you know . . . with the candle sconce lit."

"No!"

"I told him I would do my wifely duty by him, but if he wanted to practice unnatural acts, there were other places in the city he could visit."

And unbidden into Molly's mind came the memory of that Friday night when she and Pierce had touched in darkness, and loved in light. There had been nothing unnatural in their union. It had been wondrous, and good, and if these women could call it unconscionable, they knew nothing of desire. They knew nothing of love.

"I tell you, the morals of this younger generation of men is appalling. Asa and I have been married thirty-seven years, and he has yet to see me without my chemise."

"Evan Thatcher belongs to the younger generation. Do you think we could convince Molly to tell us how he feels about candle sconces?"

"Or chemises?" Giggles. Tsking.

Startled by the comment, Molly lost aim with her needle and drove it deep into her thumb beneath the cambric. Catching a painful breath, she dropped her stitchery and grabbed her thumb with her other hand. For a moment the flesh seemed unblemished, but then a scarlet pearldrop welled to the surface, and suddenly there seemed no end to the blood.

"You'd best take care of that, dear," advised Lydia. "We wouldn't want to stain your lovely bedgown, would we?"

Molly hastened her work aside and stood up. "I'm sorry, ladies. Married life has apparently rendered me butterfingered. I'll clean this up and return shortly. Please, continue working." She was glad she'd punctured her thumb. She wanted to leave, and she didn't want to come back.

Lydia made sure she was out of sight before she ad-

dressed her companions. "The poor lamb looks fright-
ful. That man probably doesn't give her a minute's
rest."

"Well, I don't have any sympathy for her. She must
have heard the rumors about Evan before she married
him. All of us did. He must be an animal. Did you
notice the dark circles under her eyes?"

"I cringe at Nathaniel's insistence that we do it twice
a month. I can't imagine how dreadful it must be to
indulge more often," said Mary Alice. "Do you think
perhaps someone should have warned her?"

In the kitchen Molly held her hand under the water-
spout while Mrs. Popham worked the pump. "Watch out
for your cuffs," the housekeeper cautioned. "You don't
want to splash water all over them. Don't see how you
managed to stick yourself. It's not like you."

"Simple stupidity, Mrs. Popham."

"Here, let me get you something clean to wipe your
hand on." So while Mrs. Popham removed a dry linen
from the sideboard chest, Molly stood with her hand
dripping into the sink. "You need some salve to put on
that?" the woman asked.

"No, thank you. I think I'll survive." She looked over
her shoulder at the sound of footsteps to find Olympia
standing just inside the door.

"I hear there's been an injury. I came to check on the
patient."

Molly dried her hand, then pressed the linen to her
thumb for a while longer. "It's nothing. No need to concern yourself."

Olympia crossed to the sink. "Evan would want me to
concern myself."

"Would he? Well, I suppose you would know more about Evan than I would."

Olympia lifted her brows in surprise at Molly's tone. "Perhaps you should leave us, Mrs. Popham."

"Yes, milady." The housekeeper curtsied and left. Olympia tapped her finger against the sink.

"I've always made it a policy never to air out differences in front of the help. I thought I'd made that clear over the past few weeks. Do remember in the future. Harmony is essential. Appearances are everything. You're a Thatcher now. You should know that. Now, why don't you tell me why you seem so snappish? I'd been about to congratulate you on your effortless entry into the inner circle of society. The ladies seem quite comfortable with you."

"They're comfortable because I bear the name Thatcher. And the only reason they're here is because *you* invited them. Emmaline Pinkham told me that after she was accepted into the inner circle she waited two long years before they would consent to a meeting at her house. You ask them once, as a favor to your sister-in-law, and here they are. It seems they, like your brother, can refuse you nothing."

Olympia's hazel eyes grew nut hard. "If it's complaint I hear in your voice, might I remind you that in eight short weeks we have plucked you from servitude and surrounded you in elegance? You selfish creature. You have clothespresses full of new gowns, coffins of jewels, a husband who thinks enough of you to cater to your whim of wanting to continue to play at your dressmaking. What more do you want?" Her voice was frosty as she studied Molly's face.

I want to be the old Molly. I want to be Irish again, and Catholic. I want to lay those creatures in the parlor flat on their crinolines for what they said about my heritage. I want to take back the words I said to Pierce. The ones I didn't mean. The ones that sent him away.

"I think," continued Olympia, "that a little soul-searching might be in order. You've come farther than any English dressmaker in recent history. I suggest you learn to appreciate what my brother has done for you. And I won't have you subjecting him to your sour moods. Is that understood?"

Molly met Olympia's gaze. "There's little chance of that. Your brother occasions to see me only rarely, but you already know that, don't you?"

Olympia's flesh tightened over her cheekbones. "I trust you'll be in better humor before we leave for the musicale tonight. If not, perhaps you should remain indisposed until your mood improves. I have a luncheon engagement. On my way out I'll do you the courtesy of telling your guests that you'll be back to entertain them presently." She left the room without another word.

Molly removed the linen from her hand and pressed her thumb to her lips. She supposed she had to return to the parlor. She was a Thatcher now. It was expected.

By midafternoon the ladies were gone, the house blissfully quiet. Molly wandered through the dining room, wondering if the floor would ever be in one piece again, the wainscoting attached. The last of the carpenters had departed on Monday with the charge that if Olympia thought she could do a better job on the dining room with her hands tied behind her back, she was welcome to try. The two men had trooped out the door and, much to Olympia's horror and surprise, had left her with a room full of wood shavings and a mouth full of empty threats. "If I ever allow another Irishman inside this house," she raved, "shoot me!"

Molly roamed the first floor, strolling through winding corridors and poking her head into rooms she hadn't known existed. There was a solarium in the far southwest corner of the house, and a lovely water closet that she found off some little-used hall. The water closet was much smaller than the one adjoining her own bedchamber, but it didn't contain the six-foot-long copper bathtub that was the primary feature of hers.

She discovered a new route to the entrance foyer and, after scrutinizing the sober faces of Evan's gilt-framed forebears, wandered down another corridor, this one more familiar. She passed the library, then, thinking that since she was down here anyway she should finish some correspondence, she backtracked several steps and entered the room. She still had several "at home" cards to send out to inform guests of the days and hours when she would be available to receive them for tea. If Olympia discovered she hadn't finished her cards yet—that she'd been sketching designs instead—she knew she would be in for the lecture of her life.

She lit the oil lamp on the desk, and as she removed her cards from her writing box, she glanced toward the gun and munitions case and found her carpetbag shoved into the space at its side. So that's where she'd left it! She hadn't seen it in so long that she'd given it up for lost.

Ignoring her correspondence for the moment, she retrieved the bag and carried it back to the desk with her.

She couldn't even remember what she'd been working on when she'd set it aside. Into the depths of the bag went her hand. Out came a length of printed calico, a tape measure, three belt ribbons, a broken marabout feather, and at the very bottom—

She grew quiet as she curled her fingers around the shaft of cobalt-blue glass. Pierce's propelling pencil. For an instant she relived the joy she'd felt on that evening when she had come home from work and found it beribboned with bailing twine on her bureau. And she remembered what he'd said the following day: "When an Irishman gives a woman a gift, it's for keeps." He had given her the gift of his love. She wondered if that had been for keeps. Did he still love her? He was the one who'd run away, but she was the one who had married another man. How would she feel if he had married another woman?

The answer to that was clear. She would be crushed. She would despise him. And she couldn't expect him to react any differently. Pierce Blackledge probably hated her now, but he couldn't hate her any more than she hated herself. Evan Thatcher would see to the fulfillment of her dream, but it seemed a hollow victory for her. Oh, yes, she still derived pleasure from creating new designs, and it was thrilling to have other women fashion in cloth what she had imagined on parchment. But her satisfaction wasn't as great as she had anticipated. She missed Pierce's leaning over her shoulder and teasing her with: "Someone's actually gonna wear that? In public?" She missed his asking her opinion about things that would matter to no one but the two of them: "You're a woman. Which do you prefer—spindles or S scrolls? . . . What's this on the bottom of your foot, Molly? I'm not makin' fun of it. You should see some've *my* scars. . . . Your mother ever hold your head when you were little, Molly?"

Oh, Pierce. She touched the glass shaft to her lips as she had that evening so long ago. She had no painted miniature of his face to remember him by. This was all she had left of him—a length of lead and glass that could neither feel her sadness nor see her tears.

A noise in the hall disturbed her mentations. Evan's voice. Reflexively she dried her eyes and rubbed a hand across her cheeks. The door opened and Evan entered, speaking to the housekeeper.

"If you could have those ready by six-thirty, I'd appreciate it, Mrs. Popham. The musicale is at seven, and I was thinking of wearing them tonight. They should go well with my peacock-blue brocade, don't you think? Yes, I thought so too." He started when he saw Molly sitting at the desk. "I didn't expect to find you in here, Molly. I rather thought you'd be doing whatever females do to prepare themselves for an evening out."

She eyed him coolly. "I expect if you'd known I was in here, you wouldn't have come in yourself."

"Why ever would you think that?" He crossed to the bookshelf and scanned several titles before removing a slender volume. "I hear you suffered an injury today for the cause of the Female Orphan Asylum."

She did not have to speculate long about how he'd come by that knowledge. "You must have spoken with Olympia."

"Indeed I did. We had lunch together at the Penobscot Exchange. I should take you there sometime, Molly.

Mr. Woodard has done a remarkable job of renovating the old coffeehouse. It's quite a delightful place now."

Molly placed the pencil close by the inkpots at the front of the desk, then rose from her chair and walked toward her husband. "So Olympia enjoys downtown lunches while I'm banished to the parlor to entertain the visiting hens."

"Hens?" Evan laughed aloud, then closed his book so he could devote his attention to his wife. "I thought you would enjoy entertaining your new friends."

"They're Olympia's friends, not mine. But I imagine she already told you about that too."

"She did mention you were rather out of sorts today. Anything I can do to cheer you up? Bitters? Tea? A posset perhaps? Shall I summon Mrs. Popham?" He started for the bellpull, but Molly's voice stopped him.

"I don't need bitters, Evan. I don't need a posset. What I need is . . . to talk. Can we sit down?" She walked to the sofa and seated herself. Seemingly reluctant to sit beside her, Evan paced to the desk and reclined against it.

"Very well, talk. I'm listening."

There was no way to broach the subject except directly. "Why did you marry me, Evan? Not for companionship; you prefer Olympia for that. Certainly not to beget heirs. If that had been your reason, you certainly would have—" Her voice faded, leaving the words unspoken. "So you see, I'm curious about why the wealthiest man in Bangor was so bent on marrying a woman he obviously has so little interest in. And please don't tell me that every eligible female in Bangor and Boston was either too mealymouthed or too weepy. I might have believed that once, but not anymore."

"I rather thought any woman would enjoy marriage if she were exposed to all its social trappings and none of its earthier side. I'd thought to spare you, my dear, but apparently the trappings aren't enough to pacify you. I've sorely misjudged you, Molly. So you want to know why I married you. A fair enough question. I married you because it was convenient to marry you."

She shook her head. "What does that mean, it was convenient?"

"You're extraordinarily attractive, pleasant, and, unlike the elite of Bangor and Boston, you have few friends and no family. Though it seems harsh to admit, I must confess that was your strongest selling point."

"That I had no family? But . . . but why?"

"You can well imagine the results should a Boston heiress divulge to her family that her new husband had yet to consummate their marriage vows. Grandfathers wanting grandsons. Brothers wanting nephews. Much too risky for my taste. I realize it's rather sad, Molly, but you have no one to tell of this happenstance . . . except me."

She felt as if her head and hands had come detached and were floating about the room. She remembered his words from their wedding night, how he'd boasted that he always chose his women with care. All the questions made sense now: "You never found any brothers and sisters in your past, Molly? . . . There was no young man who wanted to make such a pretty girl his wife, Molly?" She paled to think how well he had chosen her. "Why did you bother getting married at all?" she choked out at him.

"It was time that I should be married. It was becoming critical that I achieve the kind of respectability that marriage brings. And to quote something that you've probably heard before, you were in the right place at the right time, where my intentions were concerned."

"So I'm a . . . a showpiece for you, is that it? And what happens when you meet a woman with whom you truly fall in love? What then? Are you thinking to cast me aside like a jackstraw?"

"Why, Molly, I thought you might have guessed by now. I'm already in love, my dear."

His face became an image that doubled, then tripled before her eyes. "You're already . . ." Her breath soughed through her lips. "Then why in the name of God didn't you marry her?"

"Why?" He laughed then. A cold, hard, convulsive laugh. "Do you think if there had been any possibility of marrying this other person that I would have consented to marry an English dressmaker?" He laughed again, driving the words more cruelly into her mind. If she lived a hundred years, she could hate no one man more than she hated Evan Thatcher at this moment.

"I won't let you do this." Her voice shook, but she steeled herself against her tears.

"Oh, come, Molly, what do you suppose you can do?" Laughter still rang in his voice.

"I can have this sham of a marriage annulled."

Her words checked his laughter. His eyes hardened with the look of Olympia's. His expression suddenly became a frightening thing to behold. "Should you ever feel compelled to do something so foolish, it would go very badly for you, my dear. Very badly indeed."

She leaned back in the sofa as if that would allow her to escape the ominous look on Evan's face. This man was a stranger to her. This man with his manicured nails and frilled shirt was not the Evan Thatcher who had asked for her hand in marriage. "What can you possibly do to me?" she said, feigning courage.

He glanced behind him and snatched something into his hand. Molly didn't see what it was until he grabbed it by its tip, holding it over the floor like a dart over its target. "The question you should be asking, my dear, is what *can't* I do to you?"

"My pencil. Don't . . . !"

It dropped like a plumb bob, shattering into a spray of glass chips when it hit the hardwood floor. Molly clapped her hands over her mouth as she watched jagged fragments spin across the floor in every direction. She bit down on her lip while tears sprang into her eyes.

"I can take away as easily as I can give, Molly. I trust you'll remember that should you entertain further thoughts about annulment." The flintiness drained from his eyes as quickly as it had appeared. He straightened his neckcloth blithely, as if he'd just finished afternoon tea with her. "I'll send Mrs. Popham by to clean this up." He flicked a fragment away with the toe of his Alberts, then pushed off from the desk and strode across the floor, stopping casually before he reached the portal. "I expect you'll enjoy the musicale tonight. Olympia will be wearing green. Perhaps you can keep that in mind when you dress. Appearances, my dear," he said, aping his sister. "Appearances are everything." He closed the door behind him.

Numbed, Molly walked to the desk. Gathering her skirt about her legs, she knelt down in a safe place, then with a slow, tender hand began picking glass chips off the floor. *What have I done, Pierce?* she thought in horror. *My God, what have I done?*

Chapter Fifteen

A wolf howled.

Pierce knuckled his eyes, trying to rid them of the sting of the omnipresent bunkhouse smoke. He lay on a bed of lumpy cotton batting underlaid with fir and hemlock boughs, one among twelve men who shared a common resting place. They slept spoon fashion, snoring and wheezing, oblivious to the ripe fragrance of steaming socks, moldering woolens, and wet leather boots. The cookfire had burned low, allowing the hole in the roof above it to act more as an inlet for cold air than an outlet for smoke. To counteract the dropping temperature the men huddled closer beneath the twenty-foot spread that covered them. Pierce could feel Dooley

Duffy breathing down his neck and Liam McGinnis burrowing into his lap. It made him feel like a slab of meat between two pieces of rye bread.

The forest crackled with bitter cold. Once again he heard the howl of the wolf. It was a sad sound. A lonely sound. And he suddenly felt as one with the animal who roamed the snowscape, for in the weeks since October, he had come to learn much about sadness and loneliness. He cursed when Dooley drove his knee into his tailbone.

"Dammit, Dooley." He reached around back to reposition the sleeping man's knee and vowed that if one more pointed appendage was thrust into his body, the whole ram pasture would hear his displeasure. Not that an outburst from him would surprise anyone. The whole crew had been complaining about his moods since October. But it wasn't his fault. Hell, he couldn't help it if the jokes they told weren't funny. *But you used to think they were funny,* he reminded himself. And so what if he didn't feel like sittin' around the cookfire spitting tobacco juice into it. Maybe he'd lost his taste for tobacco. Why couldn't they all just leave him alone to brood in silence? They were nagging him worse than a wife.

He grew pensive at that thought. He wondered what Molly and Evan were doing right now, and he ground his teeth as jealousy and pain riffled through him. He was twenty-three years old. Decisions came quickly and easily to him, but no one had warned him that the consequences of one wrong decision could have so great an impact on his life. He had never looked ahead to the end of his life before. It had seemed so far away. But lately he could see each separate day and feel the emptiness that would accompany an existence without Molly. As men do, he'd somehow thought his days on earth would be too short. Now he realized they would be much too long.

Needing to switch sides, he yelled out, "Flop!" As one, eleven sleeping men turned over, still retaining their spoon shapes. Through the haze in the room Pierce saw the hay wire that crisscrossed the bunkhouse sagging with the weight of drying clothes, and as he settled onto his left side, he caught a whiff of something indescribably foul.

He remembered a time when it had been lemon balm that filled his head, teased his senses—when he had smelled it in Molly's hair and tasted it on the back of her neck. Sniffing beneath the covers he discovered that Dooley's shoulder reeked of the same foul stuff the teamsters rubbed onto the oxen when they went lame. And as he craned his neck in quest of purer air, his conscience taunted him. *This is what you wanted instead of Molly. Enjoy it.*

Logs were hauled from stump to landing on eight-foot-wide yarding sleds pulled by teams of three-yoke oxen, hitched tandem. The ideal road over which these oxen could pull their loads was one with a gradual descent, without level stretches or cuts. Unfortunately, conditions were not always ideal and steep downhills could not be avoided.

So it was with the winter camp outside Grindstone. In the southwest quadrant of the cut, the terrain from stumpage to stream formed a hill some six hundred feet long. With ice or snow on the ground, a twenty-five-ton load of saw logs would gather too much momentum for a team to control, so special precautions had to be taken. The camp boss stationed road monkeys at critical spots to clean up ruts and spread gravel or hay in the runner tracks. Brindle chains were wrapped around sled runners to serve as brakes. And at particularly steep pitches, hay sheds were constructed—solid roofed structures like covered bridges to keep the road bare of snow. Hauling season usually began in January, but in the southwest quadrant the camp boss decided to begin early. It was easier to keep a hill cleared of two feet of snow than to keep it cleared of six.

Such was the reason why on the morning of Friday, November 24, Pierce was applying a coat of tar to the canvas that covered the roof of the hay shed he'd constructed. It was twenty-six feet long and twelve feet high and made of timber so green he could probably bend it ninety degrees wi...out breaking it. The shed shielded from the elements a dip in the road that could be neither bridged nor filled. The camp boss assigned Dooley to road-monkey duty this day, and since he was posted near the hay shed, he was also given the responsib ility of keeping the tar buckets hot for Pierce. He kept three buckets going at once, with about a five-minute turnaround period, for the tar didn't have to be exposed to the fifteen-degree temperature very long before it became impossible to spread. During the course of the morning he literally wore a rut in the snow. Pierce felt no sympathy. He figured anyone who wore ox liniment to bed deserved such punishment.

"I'm ready for that next bucket," Pierce yelled. "The

stuff in this is about froze. And you'd better put your arse behind it." He looked toward the crest of the hill. "Looks to me like they're about ready to bring a load down."

And so they were—six thousand feet of thirty-foot logs. Poised at the summit were three yoke of oxen hitched to a short, heavy yarding sled. On the bunk of the sled, stacked some six feet high, were the butt ends of the timber. The tips dragged on the ground to act as a further deterrent against momentum. Three binding chains secured the logs to the bunk, and around the bunk and load the teamster threw a two-inch-thick manila rope which he wound around a tree stump. When the team descended the incline, a man called a snubber would pay out the rope by small degrees, providing slack where appropriate and tightening up when the load needed to be slowed.

Dooley finished spreading hay on the stretch of road fronting the hay shed before trekking back for the hot tar bucket. At the top of the hill the teamster climbed aboard his load. With copious squirts of tobacco juice and spates of profanity, he signaled his drivers to apply their goad sticks. Pricked by a half inch of pointed steel at the end of a four-foot length of hickory, the oxen snorted and moaned and leaned into their yokes. The sled lunged forward, runners creaking and chains rattling. The snubber shortened the slack on the rope. And Dooley returned with the tar bucket.

Pierce trained an eye on the six long-horned oxen, their sides heaving with the strain. "New teamster looks like he can keep a fair hand on his team. But I'll tell you one thing, by Jeesuz. If those bovines smell anything like you did last night, I'm gonna be outta here before they get within a hundred feet of me. You know what that liniment smells like?"

"Yup." Dooley hung the tar bucket on the swivel hook of his cant dog and hoisted it up to Pierce on the roof.

"So do you wanna walk around smellin' like ox dung?"

"Does ox dung smell better'n the horse manure the bullwhackers put in that liniment I was usin'?"

Pierce shook his head. He lifted the bucket off the cant dog's iron hook and hung the empty one in its stead.

Fifty feet from the top of the hill the off-ox confirmed the species' penchant for stubbornness by going down to his knees. The teamster swore, the bullwhackers goaded, and the snubber tightened up on the rope again to prevent the load from careening down the hill.

Cussing most hideously, the bullwhacker drove his goad stick into the beast's ear. The ox practically leapt off his knees and with uncommon swiftness pitched headlong down the hill, dragging the rest of the team behind him.

Or so it seemed.

After an initial forward spurt, the bovines crossed over in their chains, entangled themselves in their traces, and fell like dominoes. The yarding sled skidded behind them, but the snubber's line held the load in check.

Pierce squinted at the fallen oxen. "Jeesuz-God." Dooley looked up the hill at the commotion just as the manila rope snapped. Weakened and frayed from use, it broke where it chafed the corner of the sled and lashed the air like a whip. The load shifted, catapulting the teamster over the heads of the oxen. He landed on his stomach and slid three rods downhill on his face. The logs, poised on a downward angle, broke one binding chain, and then another. The peak log flew out like a thrown javelin and sluiced down the incline out of control. Behind it, twenty tons of green timber followed suit.

The whole scenario took no more than fifteen seconds, but in that time Dooley watched the falling timber fragment six oxen and one teamster into indistinguishable shapes and parts. The earth rumbled. The air boomed. And like an avalanche the logs roared downward.

Dooley's mouth hung open. His feet refused to move. Fear and horror weighted his limbs.

"Run!" Pierce screamed, ready to take a flying leap off the roof, but Dooley simply stood there, his cant dog levered against his shoulder like an honor guard's flag.

The logs rushed down. Three hundred feet away. Caroming off ledges and snowbanks at breakneck speed. "Dooley!"

Two hundred feet away. Fear twisted Pierce's insides. He dropped to his stomach by the edge of the roof and reached for the end of Dooley's cant dog. "Damn you, Dooley! I'm not ready for hell yet. Grab hold!" And with death a hundred feet away, Dooley did.

His cant dog was a stout wooden shaft, five feet long and thick as a man's arm, used as a lever to lift and turn lumber. When Dooley saw Pierce reaching for it, he boosted it higher. Pierce locked his fingers around the iron ring that bound the swivel hook to the shaft and with a nod of his head signaled Dooley to climb.

Dooley was short but agile. With a stand of thirty-foot logs crashing down toward him, he was also damn quick. He grabbed the cant dog high as he could and swung his feet off the ground. Pierce slid forward with the sudden weight. He wishboned his legs to retain his balance and heard a rattle and clatter as he sent the tar bucket spinning. He clung to the iron ring, muscles screaming.

Fifty feet away. The roar was deafening. Dooley found Pierce's wrist, then his elbow. Pierce released the cant dog. He felt a burning pain in his right leg as if someone had set it afire. Without seeing, he knew where the hot tar had spilled. He inched himself backward, boot toes and knees scraping the canvas roof, drawing Dooley closer to the edge of the roof.

Twenty feet away. Dooley looped his arm around Pierce's neck. A grunt. A yell. Then he was swinging his leg over the lip of the roof. Another yell and up went his other leg. Beneath him the peak log shot through the opening of the hay shed at an angle. It plowed through the side of the structure like a runaway train and kept right on going. Behind it the rest of the load kept pace. Two thirty-foot logs hit the shed at fifty miles an hour and sheared the support beams off at ground level. The roof shook as the logs gained speed on the downward pitch. Dooley clung to Pierce's back as another onslaught hit the shed on a horizontal roll, disintegrating the base like a hand sweeping through a stack of building blocks. The roof collapsed. Onto the rolling logs it fell, a twenty-six-foot raft riding to hell. Pain knifed through Pierce. There was no air in his lungs. Scenery became a blur. His fingers felt like they were being ground to the bone.

The raft veered to the right. A curve at the bottom of the hill awaited them. The first log hit the curve. The tip skated along the high banking. The butt end slammed into a big spruce on the opposite side of the road. And there it stopped. Dead in the road ahead.

Three logs hit that piece of lumber before Pierce and Dooley. The way was jammed up like a dam, but instead of crashing into the waiting timber, the raft veered high onto the banking and skidded over the top... where it greeted an old elm head-on. For the second time in as many minutes the two Irishmen got the wind knocked out of them, while in the road twenty tons of lumber rumbled into silence.

Dooley rolled off Pierce's back and into the snow. The roof lay in three large sections around them, remarkably undamaged for what it had just been through.

"Pierce? You all right?"

A clump of snow moved, then lifted. One green eye peered through a mask of white, then a nose. He shook his head, ridding it of its cap of snow, and let out a groan. Looking down at the width of roof that still supported him, he flashed a cocky smile. "Is that some roof I built or is that some roof I built?"

"We were lucky."

Pierce tried to roll over, but his right leg wouldn't budge. "Damn tar has me glued in place. Probably rip six layers of skin off when I try to get up. Don't suppose you have your axe on you."

"Nope. Left it up there when I was choppin' wood to keep your damn tar heated." Shouts echoed out to them from somewhere up the road. Dooley shambled to his feet and dug the snow out of his neck and sleeves. "I think we're bein' rescued. I'll see what I can do about an axe."

Pierce blotted the scrapes on his chin with the back of his hand. His fingers, where he'd been clinging to the edge of the roof, were cut open and bleeding. He shook his left leg, realizing that Dooley had been right. They'd been lucky to escape with only a few cuts and bruises. It was then he heard the sound. He looked up.

Loggers called it a widow-maker—a dead, loose branch caught in the upper limbs of a tree. The logs' impact with the elm had jarred it free, and with the speed of a lightning bolt, it was falling straight at him.

There had grown a custom in America that in the winter following their wedding a bridal couple should give a dinner party or formal ball to entertain all those people who had attended their wedding and presented them with gifts. At this soiree it was appropriate for the new bride to wear her wedding gown, minus the veil, to emphasize her new status. When the bride found herself in the family way, she would pack the dress away forever, along with memories of her innocence and youth.

On Saturday, November 25, at an hour when she used to take her weekly bath at Duncan's, Molly roved the length of the Thatcher parlor in the pale blue figured silk brocade gown in which she'd been married. Her starched petticoats rustled as she drifted from guest to guest, nodding, smiling, making blithe comment about things of little consequence.

"Has Mr. Hardy finished your wedding portrait yet, dear? I don't see it hanging up anywhere."

"He should have it finished by Christmas, Mrs. Hathorn. You'll have to come by to see it then."

"Your hair looks positively spectacular like that, Molly. And so simple. Of course it's the hair net that makes the look. Tell me, dear, are all those gemstones real? But of course, your Evan isn't one to stand for anything artificial, is he?"

"No. No, he's not," Molly said mechanically, moving on.

"It's called a daguerreotype and . . . Molly, there you are. Come over here so I can show you." Mary Alice held up a slender, velvet-lined box that contained what looked like a rectangular mirror. When she angled it away from the light, an image of Mary Alice herself appeared on the surface. "Isn't it amazing? They say it's going to be quite the rage. After the baby is born, Nathaniel and I are planning to have a family photo taken. You and Evan should have yours done, Molly. With Olympia, of course. I wouldn't want to forget Olympia."

"Yes. Evan would be upset if you forgot Olympia. Excuse me, will you?"

Mary Alice watched her leave. "I said something to upset her. Did you see the look on her face? Maybe I should apologize. Oh, dear." Someone handed her a handkerchief.

Molly scanned the room. She caught sight of Evan and a comely female by the fireplace, their heads locked in sober discussion. She wondered if this was the woman he was in love with. She couldn't recall the creature's name, but she did know the woman was married. And over the past month Molly had concluded that Evan's lover had to be married. What other obstacle could have stood in the way of his marrying her? Certainly not class. He could have wed a maid as easily as he'd wed a seamstress. So the woman had to be rich and she had to already have a husband. But the question remained, who was she?

"Madam." Molly jumped at the steward's voice. "Would you care for champagne?"

She removed a crystal goblet from the tray. "Thank you." She took a sip and eyed her guests over the rim of the glass. The majority of the women in the room were married, so it could be any one of them. Emmaline Pinkham? Mary Alice? The woman whose name she couldn't remember? She turned slowly on her heel, watching Evan, waiting for him to betray himself with a covert look, a covert touch.

But he was clever. Ever since their talk he'd been on his guard. She'd only heard the two sets of footsteps once in the past weeks, and when they passed her room she had crept to her door and turned the knob. She wanted to see the woman whose illicit pleasure she was paying for with her life. But when she'd pulled back on the door, the hinges whined so loudly that she didn't dare open it farther. Spying on Evan and his lover was one thing. Having Evan *discover* she was spying on him was something she didn't want to chance. After their discussion, she feared what he might do. So she decided she would simply have to be more clever than he. The next day she'd asked Mrs. Popham to see that the hinges on her bedroom door were oiled. Yes, she could be clever as well.

Sipping more champagne, she turned a half circle. Near the parlor door she found Olympia, a covey of men standing around her, looking to all the world as if she were a great English queen holding court. Molly's eyes grew long and narrow. Olympia Thatcher wasn't fooling her for one minute. The woman knew exactly what was going on in this house with her brother. She was probably the one who had helped select Molly as the unlikely bride. What Molly couldn't understand was how Olympia still could look her in the eye without so much as a twitch of guilt. Had she no conscience? Was she so ruled by her brother's wishes that she could condone adultery and deception and threats? Olympia might have a handsome facade, but beneath the jewels and the satins and the perfume Molly knew there was another Olympia Thatcher—one who was just as ugly and just as treacherous as the being who lived inside her twin brother.

She downed the last of the champagne and, deciding she liked the taste, looked around for the steward to provide her with another glass. She regarded the male guests in the parlor, all garbed in black tailcoats, then once again perused the females. *Which one of you is sleeping with this man who calls himself my husband?* But she realized that even if she knew, what good would it do? Who could she tell? The woman's husband?

She shook her head, negating the choice. What man would believe the accusations of an upstart dressmaker about his wife? No, it would definitely not go well for her if she did that.

I could tell Pierce, she thought, but that, too, seemed impossible. He wouldn't even be back in Bangor till next year. And besides, Pierce hated her. He wouldn't care about her tale of woe. She had gotten herself into this situation with lies of her own making and knew she deserved no sympathy, but there was a part of her that regretted having to spend a lifetime being punished for something she had done neither cruelly nor maliciously.

But what if Pierce listened to you? What if he tried to help? A spark of hope brightened her outlook, but only for an instant. The sight of her propelling pencil smashing to the floor had stamped itself too indelibly on her mind to even think about such a thing. Evan Thatcher was too rich and powerful to cross. She didn't know what his methods might be, but they could work as easily on Pierce as they could on her. She imagined Pierce throwing his axe with Evan as his target. He'd threatened as much at one time, hadn't he? She could also imagine Evan reaching for his father's Forsyth sporting gun in the munitions case and explaining to the authorities later: "The Irishman went berserk. He tried to attack me with his axe. It was clearly self-defense." No, no, she couldn't tell Pierce. She wouldn't be able to live with herself if anything happened to him because of her. And if she shared her misery with him, she knew he would suffer the consequences of knowing. Evan would see to that. *I love you too much for that, my love. I can better live with your absence and your not knowing than I could live with your death. You mustn't learn the truth, Pierce. I must never tell you.*

Her eyes strayed to Mary Alice's rounded belly, and with a gentle hand she pressed her fingers to the deep V at the waist of her own gown. She wished now that Pierce's seed had taken root. It would have been a part of him that she could have cherished for the rest of her life—dearer than a painted miniature, less fragile than a glass propelling pencil. They could have shared a child, and love, and laughter—if only she hadn't thrown it all away.

Her vision starred with tears. She turned abruptly, desperately wanting another drink, and she knew where she could find all the champagne she would ever want. The kitchen. As she passed by Olympia, she heard her sister-in-law's voice chiming clearly: "So that's why we'll be dining tonight in the ballroom rather than the dining room. I loathe the way the carpenters left the room. It's so imperfect. I hate stepping foot inside it. But, I ask you gentlemen, where can you find quality help these days when all that the marketplace offers us is Irishmen and more of them?"

Crystal goblet in hand, Molly left the room without ever hearing the gentlemen's reply.

She had never seen the kitchen in such a flutter as it was tonight. Cook was wielding her butcher knife like a machete and the kitchen help were bustling about like wild hens. Dinner would be served in forty-five minutes, but you would never guess it from the confusion. She heard the maddening clink of silver and china as she stood inside the door searching for the champagne, and when she spotted it, she moved through the preoccupied mass of humanity as if she were invisible. At one end of the kitchen table three maids were spooning fresh fruit into crystal bowls, and though their conversation was hushed, Molly heard their every word as she passed them.

"Widow Quimby told my mum they'll probably have to take his leg off below the knee."

"I don't know why they want to go into the woods in the first place. Trees falling on top of them and whatnot. No thank you."

"Wasn't he the man who came banging at the door the night of the wedding? The handsome Irishman. What did you say his name was?"

"Blackledge. Pierce Blackledge."

The sound of splintering crystal halted activity. Two dozen pairs of eyes riveted on Molly, whose hand was suspended in the air as if she still held her champagne glass. With her face gone white, she whirled round to the maids, grabbing the girl who had spoken by her wrist.

"What did you hear? Tell me what you heard!" Her voice was high and shrieky. There was terror in her eyes as she gripped the girl's arm with near bone-shattering strength.

"They brought him back from the woods this afternoon," the maid cried out, frightened and in pain. "There was a terrible accident yesterday. One man died and poor Mr. Blackledge was crushed under a log. That's all I know, but if you were to ask Mrs. Quimby—"

Molly was out the door before the girl could utter another word. *Not Pierce, Lord. Please not Pierce. Let him be all right. I didn't mean what I said about hoping he'd never come back. He doesn't deserve to be pun-*

ished. It's all my fault, not his. Let him be whole and well. Don't let him die. Please, don't let him die.

She didn't remember running up to her room for her cloak or traipsing through the snow to the livery. But she could feel her wet slippers sticking to the soles of her feet as she searched the stable.

"Hello!"

A young boy stumbled out from the tack room, his mouth falling open when he saw the mistress of the house.

"Are you the only one here?"

"Yes'm. The men are out tendin' the guests' vehicles."

"What's your name, boy?"

"Caleb, ma'am."

"Have you ever driven a sleigh, Caleb?"

"No, ma'am."

"Hitch the team. You're about to learn."

When Duncan opened his front door twenty minutes later, he found Molly with her arm supporting a young boy whose eyes were big as harvest moons. "Is he going to be all right? I want to see him, Duncan. Please, let me see him."

Duncan moved aside and motioned her up the stairs. "He's in his room. Guess you know your own way up."

She found him propped up on pillows in his bed. His eyes were blackened, his chin was bruised, both hands were bandaged, and beneath the covers his legs were inert lumps. But when he saw her standing in the doorway, the pain that was etched on his face became surprise, then something she could not read but didn't think she could bear.

"Molly?" She stood there in a satin cloak with sable trim, jewels sprinkling her hair net and a blue diamond that was big as a walnut on her finger. Her finery made the room where he'd first made love to her seem shabby in comparison. And he knew with finality that she was lost to him forever. She had a husband who was laying the world at her feet. What woman could not help falling in love with such a man? "Does Thatcher know you're here?" he said in a quiet voice.

She shook her head and walked slowly into the room, unable to avoid looking at the outline of Pierce's legs. "I heard about . . ." She bobbed her head toward his legs, unable to say the words. "I'm . . . I'm so sorry." His eyes. She'd forgotten how green they were.

"Yah. So am I." And because he didn't know what to say that could make amends for what he had done to her, he lay there and commented on things that were meaningless and safe. "I imagine you could hear me yellin' all the way from Grindstone. You should've heard me on the trip down. Liam must've dragged that litter they rigged for me over every bump in the road. And I let him know about it."

She stared at his face, memorizing the shape of his mouth, remembering the warm taste of it against her lips. She would memorize it now, for she would probably never have another chance. That thought tore at her, and within her she wept for the children she would never bear, for the life they could have shared, for the leg that Pierce would never walk on again. Fear and sorrow, regret and heartache—they blended so freely that she could no longer distinguish one from the other. She blinked away tears and dashed moisture from the corners of her eyes. And still Pierce talked, as if they had never loved, as if there had been nothing more between them than verbal niceties. *He does hate me*, she thought. *He truly does*.

"You interested in how I did all this?" Before she could say yes or no, he rotated his bandaged hands in the air. "These were a result of my clingin' to the edge of a roof while it was skidding down a few tons of rollin' logs." He indicated his right leg. "This one got a few layers of flesh ripped off it when I tried to yank it outta the tar that had it glued to the roof." Left leg. "This one escaped a direct hit from the branch that was fallin' outta the tree, but the branch bounced and caught my shin at a queer angle. Broke the bone midway between my foot and knee."

She frowned, for she had not heard him use the words "crushed" or "amputated" at all. "Your leg is broken? Not . . . not anything worse?"

Pierce rubbed his left thigh, preferring to look at his counterpane rather than Molly. It was less painful that way. "Yah. Broke the bone midway between my foot and knee," he repeated stupidly. Sentences were not easy to construct in her presence. None of the words he had reserved for her were suitable anymore.

"It's only broken," she repeated, and she felt such joyful relief that she thought her knees might give way beneath her. She set her hand on the finial of his footboard to steady herself. "I'd heard much worse." And even if he did hate her, she was glad that he would walk on two good legs again. *Thank you, Lord. Thank you.* Pierce pointed to the scrapes on his chin.

"These happened when the roof flew over the bank

and slammed into that old elm. But I can't make anyone around here believe that I was stuck to a roof that was sliding down tons of rolling logs."

She would like to have laughed, but couldn't. "And your two black eyes. How did you acquire those?"

He grinned crookedly in spite of himself. "From Liam. He didn't appreciate the names I called him all the way down from Grindstone."

They exchanged tentative glances. She thought that he looked older, more somber—a vestige of his hatred. He thought she looked younger, more beautiful—a vestige of her newfound love. They averted their eyes and tried not to look as uncomfortable as they felt, but it was impossible. The steeple clock took that moment to ring out the first of its chimes, and Molly breathed gratefully.

"I hadn't realized it was so late. They'll be wondering where I am. Dinner is supposed to be served promptly at nine."

Pierce regarded the flounce of brocade that was visible beneath the sable hem of her cloak. He nodded in approval. "Thatcher dresses you well."

She followed Pierce's gaze to the bottom of her gown, and in a voice barely audible said, "It's my wedding gown."

"Your wedding gown?" He strove for a note of glibness in the midst of his desolation. "Well, don't stand there all covered up. Take your cloak off. Lemme see what this dress looks like."

She shrugged, loathing herself for coming here, for dredging up the memories of everything they had shared. "It's just a dress."

"I missed the wedding. I'd like to be able to say that I at least saw the dress."

With great reluctance she unhooked the frog at her throat, swung the cloak off her shoulders, and draped it over her arm. "You see, it's nothing extraordinary."

The gown was cut so low off her shoulders that Pierce wondered how she could raise her arms. Like the upper border of a Valentine heart, the bodice dipped toward the center of her breasts. A single layer of blond lace veiled her flesh from her neck to her bodice, and he remembered well the feel of that flesh as it had lain beneath his hand. The V waist was long and stiffly boned and cinched more tightly than most axemen cinched their boots. The sight of that waist filled him with longing.

"Turn all the way around," he said, bobbing his head to imitate the required motion. And so she did, slowly, self-consciously. Her hair was turned under and caught in that jeweled net, but he wanted nothing more than to bare her neck and find that solitary mole of hers with his mouth. He focused on her waist once again and watched as she swung her cloak back over her shoulders. He knew without a doubt that she wasn't pregnant. He had lost everything, and now even this.

Head bent, she fastened the frog at her throat. "Is he good to you, Molly?" she heard him ask in a strained voice. "Does he treat you well?"

If only she could tell him the truth. "He's good to me." She drew her hood over her hair.

"Are you happy?"

She touched his face with her eyes. There was only one thing she could say that would insure Pierce's never discovering the truth, and she hated herself for having to say it. But it was necessary. It was the only way she could protect him from Evan's treachery. "Evan has given me everything a woman could ever want—a home, security, social standing. He's even given me the dress shop I dreamed of owning. How could I not be happy?"

He nodded in resignation. He deserved that, but it still hurt to hear her say the words. "I'm glad you are. You look like you're happy. You look like you're in love."

Her eyes filled with tears she couldn't blink away. "They'll be wondering where I am, Pierce. I can't stay any longer." She walked to the door, turning when he called after her. Through the blur of her tears, she saw him straining to smile.

"You've done well as an Englishwoman, Molly."

Yes, she thought as she crossed the landing to the stairs. *I've lied and been dealt lies in return. I have a husband who sleeps with his lover under my roof and a sister-in-law who thinks it's all quite normal. I've lost my identity, my religion, and the only man I'll ever love. Oh, yes, Pierce, I've done well as an Englishwoman.*

Stony-faced and ominous, Olympia waited at the back door of the mansion. She pulled the door open even before Molly reached for the handle. "We have a parlor full of guests waiting to eat a dinner given in honor of the new Thatcher bride. But the new Thatcher bride is nowhere to be found. Would you mind telling me where you've been?"

Molly threw her hood back as she entered the tiny passageway. This entrance was so rarely used that she wondered how Olympia had known to wait for her here. "I was performing my Christian duty—attending a sick friend."

"Every friend you have is in our upstairs parlor."

"Every friend *you* have is in the parlor. My friends would be more comfortable in the kitchen."

Olympia's unpainted lips grew taut, but she didn't respond to Molly's sarcasm. "You're here now, so don't stand there like a ninny. My friends or yours, they still must eat." She preceded Molly through the maze of corridors leading to the parlor, and at various intervals made comment over her shoulder.

"If you had to attend a sick friend, you might have had the courtesy to wait till after dinner was served."

"I thought he might be dying, and I didn't know if he would have the courtesy to wait till we finished supping."

"He?"

It galled her even having to speak to this woman. "The son of the man I used to rent the room from."

"Oh, yes. The Irishman. And was he? Dying, I mean."

"No. He only broke his leg."

Olympia didn't speak again until they had passed the library. "What will your friend do while his leg is mending?"

She softened at the thought of Pierce's lying in bed, counting cracks in the ceiling for two months. "When he's able to get about, he'll probably do some woodworking in his shop."

"Woodworking? He's a carpenter?"

"For five months of the year he's a carpenter." And if

I had been less selfish about those five months, I'd be his wife right now instead of a figurehead for Evan Thatcher.

Olympia slowed her steps as they entered the marble foyer. "Tell me, has your friend seen a doctor?"

"Someone at the logging camp set his leg in splints, and I suppose that will suffice until the bone has healed."

"I have a physician friend in Boston who is an absolute genius with broken bones. Perhaps we should send for him before the river freezes over. He might see that your friend doesn't limp for the rest of his life. Yes, that would be a good turn, wouldn't it? I'll see to it tomorrow."

Confused, Molly stared at her sister-in-law. "Why are you doing this, Olympia? Remember, he's Irish."

Olympia snapped her fan open as she turned toward the parlor. "If you don't mention it to the physician, neither will I."

On the day before Christmas, Molly stood on Duncan's front porch like one of the Magi. In her hand she carried a handwoven basket filled with presents that she'd wrapped in silver tissue and red satin ribbons. But her packages seemed less festive than her eyes, which sparkled with some secret expectation. She shuffled her feet with the cold and had to rap on the door a second time before she saw movement behind the glass oval. The portal opened, releasing into the frosty December air a fragrant bouquet of tobacco and apple pie smells.

"Molly!" Duncan greeted her. "Come in, come in. Cold's-a clam digger's hands out there."

She scooted over the threshold and shivered in her pelisse. "I can't stay. I just wanted to stop by to deliver this." She extended the basket to him. "Merry Christmas."

She could tell he was stunned by the way his pipe was sliding off his bottom lip, but he made no movement to take the basket. All he seemed capable of doing was staring at it. "I . . . I don't know what to say, Molly. Wasn't expectin' anything like this from you."

"Say 'Merry Christmas to you too, Molly,' and take it out of my hands. It's getting heavy."

He lunged to catch it by its underside and laughed as he set it on the floor. "Don't think I've ever seen this many presents in one place in my life. This was real nice of you, girl, but I'm a mite embarrassed to take this from you and not give you somethin' in return."

"I don't want anything in return, Duncan. This is my way of saying thank you for everything you did for me this past year. For remaining my friend despite everything I did."

"Didn't need to give me a basket a presents to thank me, Molly. Didn't do anything more for you that your Da woulda done for my boys."

Her eyes strayed to the stairs. "How is Pierce doing?"

"Doin' fine. Gettin' around some. He's tinkerin' out back. You wanna see him?"

"I can't. I mean, Caleb is waiting in the sleigh and he'll freeze to the seat if I'm not quick. But I'm pleased about Pierce. Sounds like he has made quite a remarkable recovery."

"Eayh. Funny thing 'bout that too. Feller come up from Boston and says he's the doctor for the Penobscot

Boom Corporation and wants to have a look-see at Pierce's leg. So he takes off the splint, shakes his head a few times, and decides to redo the whole God-blessed thing. Didn't take long. Waved a few pointy things front a the boy's nose, watched him faint dead away, and triced him up like new. Nice feller. But I never knew the P.B.C. to send out any company doctor to check on laid-up choppers."

"That's strange, isn't it?" she said, hating to admit to herself that she was grateful for Olympia's intervention. She hesitated. "Would you and Pierce be my guests for Christmas dinner tomorrow?"

"Like to, Molly, but Conor's expectin' us for dinner at the rectory. It's his birthday, ya know."

"Well, bring Conor along too. The table is big enough." Though she paled at the thought of facing Conor, since she hadn't attended mass for the past four months.

Duncan tapped the mouthpiece of his pipe against his bottom lip. "Truth of the matter is, Conor invited a houseful a parishioners to join us, and I'm the one s'posed to do the cookin'."

"Oh." She lowered her eyes, her disappointment apparent. Duncan swallowed around a lump of guilt.

"Why don't you 'n' your husband join the whole've us at the rectory? There's always room for two more."

Molly flashed him a brilliant smile. "We couldn't, Duncan. Really. We're expecting a whole houseful of guests ourselves. Looks like we'll have to plan something for another time, when neither of us is so busy."

"Eayh. Looks that way, don't it? Well, a Merry Christmas to you, Molly. I'll tell Pierce you said hello."

"Give him my . . . my best," she said on her way out the door. But what she wanted to say was—*Give him my love*.

At noon on Christmas day Molly sat in her appointed chair at the far end of the thirty-foot dining room table. The house smelled of roast fowl and apricot tarts, and the disorder of the room was disguised beneath evergreen boughs, pinecones, and holly berries. For this occasion she wore a black velvet morning gown with a white lace bertha and black lace mittens. Around her neck she wore Evan's Christmas gift to her—a diamond choker set with polished jet beads. Above the mantel hung her full-length portrait by Jeremiah Pearson Hardy, six feet high in its gold-leafed frame and weighing more than she did. The eyes of the painted Molly were perhaps more blue than gray and in their downward cast beheld all that her namesake could call her own. The silver flatware with its hand-painted porcelain handles. The Limoges china. The silver wine cups. The tree of crystal baskets individually filled with pistachios and olives, brandied peaches, cherries, and Portugal plums. The half-dozen branches of candles whose flames danced in the table's highly polished mahogany surface.

From a decanter of leaded crystal she poured herself a cup of wine. Evan was spending Christmas in Boston with a business associate who was said to be the linchpin in some new venture. Olympia was in New York with friends. Molly heeded the sixteen empty chairs flanking each side of the table, then raised her wine cup and toasted her portrait. "Merry Christmas," she said.

For a moment she thought about the girl she'd been in Ireland, and she realized how very far she'd come. *But*

have I? she asked herself. At least that girl in Ireland
had had a dream. What did she have now?

She brought the cup to her lips and stared at those
empty chairs as if transfixed.

She had everything . . . and nothing.

Chapter Sixteen

Molly sat down at the breakfast table on the morning of December 28 thinking that something was afoot. Olympia was humming, and Olympia never hummed. "You're in uncommonly good humor this morning," Molly commented.

"I *am* in good humor this morning," Olympia agreed as she lifted a tea strainer off her cup. "I'm finally going to have this ungodly mess we call the dining room cleaned up. In one month's time you won't recognize the room. The floor will be finished, the wainscoting will be attached and painted, and your portrait will have a pleasant setting over which to prevail."

"You must have hired carpenters while you were in New York."

"I hired *a* carpenter, but not in New York."

Molly placed the sterling strainer across her teacup and reached for the teapot.

"He lives right here in Bangor. I hired your friend Mr. Blackledge."

Molly's hand froze on the teapot's handle. "You mean Duncan?"

"I mean Pierce. And if you don't take your hand off that handle you're going to have quite a welt to show for it. You'll have to wear mittens at the tea this afternoon to cover it up."

Molly snatched her hand away and brought it to her mouth, applying her tongue to the center of her reddened palm. Pierce, here? No! He would be too close to the truth here. And how could she avoid him if he were in the same house? She would be close enough to touch him, but could never touch. Near enough to hear his voice, but never hear him whisper her name against her ear. She ached at the thought. Now she understood why Olympia had taken such an interest in Pierce's injury. Olympia needed a carpenter, and with some professional doctoring, Pierce would be available. It seemed neither of the Thatchers did anything without a specific purpose in mind. "He's still recovering from his accident, Olympia. How can he come to work for you if he's hobbling on one leg?"

Magnanimous this morning, Olympia poured for her. "He's getting around well enough to complete the projects I need him for. I stopped at his house yesterday evening and made all the necessary arrangements. And while he's here, he'll be staying in one of the downstairs rooms which I'm making available for him for overnight accommodations."

"You what?"

"It will be much easier for him if he doesn't have to travel back and forth. Besides, if he doesn't have to leave, maybe he'll work longer hours."

"He's going to live here?" She might have laughed at the irony if she'd been able to find anything humorous about the situation. But there was nothing humorous about living in the same house with the man you love and never being able to speak to him of love. And she was fearful—fearful that Pierce would discover she didn't sleep with her husband, fearful he would ask her why, fearful she would tell him, fearful of the guns in the library. He couldn't come to live here. Dear lord, he couldn't. "Have you forgotten he's Irish? You said you'd never allow another Irishman to cross the threshold. You said if you ever suggested it to shoot you."

"It can't be helped. I'm desperate. He'll be here on the second, so enjoy the quiet while there's still quiet to enjoy. And if he's half as good as people claim, I might even decide to keep him on to redo the sitting room."

Unmoving, Molly stared into her teacup. Olympia had not served tea this morning. She had served a cup of quiet desperation.

Time can be too long when we're young, and too short when we're old; but when we love, time can be eternity. And so it seemed to Molly that she had listened to the hammer strikes in the dining room for endless days before deciding to intrude on Pierce. In reality, it had been one short hour.

He was sitting on a stool with his left leg stretched stiffly before him. On his foot he wore a wool sock with two toes poking through, and around his waist he wore a canvas apron that bulged with the same objects he was grasping between his teeth—nails. He wielded his hammer with the same precision with which he wielded his axe, driving a nail with two quick blows and moving on to the next one. His hands flew, his shoulders swung forward, and it seemed to Molly there was no force on earth greater than the raw power in Pierce Blackledge's right arm.

"Hello," she said from just inside the doorway.

Pierce nicked the head of a nail and ducked as it went spinning off like a ricocheting bullet. "Jeesuz."

Molly shot a glance around the room, wondering where the thing had landed.

Pierce spat the nails from his mouth into his hand. "Didn't hit you, did it?"

She stepped backward, ruffled her skirt, then shook her head. She looked back at him. "I just wanted to poke my head in to say hello." *And to see your face. I've missed you so, my love.*

He hefted the hammer in his hand, and she was reminded of that day in April when she had found him sitting on the front stairs grinding down his axe bit. Her eyes lingered on his hand. Her breast tingled in sweet memory at the feel of that hand, and she felt herself quicken shamelessly. "When—uh, when did you take the bandages off your hands?"

"Couple've weeks back. Came out good as new." He

turned one hand over so she could see. "Not a scar on 'em."

It seemed trite to be exchanging small talk with him, but if this was the only way she could see him, then so be it. "And your eyes. They're not black anymore."

"Nope. Liam didn't light into me half as hard as he could've. I think he went easy on me because I was hurt. I wouldn't've been such a softy if the tables had been turned. Anyone talked to me the way I talked to Liam, they'd have more than a couple've black eyes to reckon with."

But she knew that wasn't true. Pierce Blackledge, for all his power and might, was the gentlest of men. It was one of the reasons she loved him so much. There was completeness in a man who could give as well as take, soothe as well as shove, laugh as well as cry. She wished he didn't hate her. She admired his attempt at civility, but she knew what his true feelings were, and it was too great a burden to bear. "I suppose I should let you get on with your work," she said, reluctant to leave, but knowing she must. "If you need anything—"

"You don't have to rush off, Molly," and his eyes were suddenly so intense that she could feel their warmth burning into the back of her skull. The look both confounded and frightened her, and she wondered for a moment if this was his way of punishing her for marrying another man.

"I do have to rush off," she said as she fiddled with her fingers behind her back. "Someone from my dress shop is coming by to look at my latest sketches, and then I have to meet with Mr. Hill about ordering more fabric. Besides, Olympia will serve my head for supper if I keep you from your work."

He gestured her near with his forefinger, and when she stood but an arm's length from him, he cupped his hands around his mouth. "Olympia can go sit on a whore's egg."

She took two steps back from him and favored him with a curious look. "If you don't care a pin for Olympia's directives, why did you agree to come to work for her?"

And Pierce thought that if Molly could ask such a question, she was indeed blind to the feelings he still fostered for her. She was blind and in love with her husband. Disguising his disappointment behind activity, he reached into the pocket of his apron for a fresh supply of nails. "Actually, it got kind've cold workin' out back without any heat, so when the lady offered me work, I couldn't refuse. Figured your place had to be warmer than mine. But with these damn high ceilings, I think the only things keepin' warm are the chandeliers."

Molly followed his gaze to the one hanging above them. "Olympia refuses to install parlor stoves. She says they're ugly."

"She should take a good look around her. The whole damn place is ugly."

"Pierce—"

"I know, I know. It's your house now too. I should be more reverent. But I see you've already added some class to the place." He nodded toward her portrait. "Pretty." It was the first thing he had noticed when he walked into the room this morning, and if she had hand-picked a way to torture him, she could have thought of no better ploy. "But it's not a true likeness. He left out your dimple."

She touched her hand to her cheek. She'd forgotten about her dimple, how it deepened when she smiled. "I wasn't smiling enough for my dimple to show through."

"Yah, I noticed. Funny how you wouldn't be smilin' considerin' how happy you are." He saw her lips part, but no words were forthcoming. He bowed his head.

She worried that he could see the truth in her face, in her eyes. She should have exercised more patient restraint when she'd heard him this morning, but she couldn't deny herself this one pleasure. There had been so little to be joyful about since September. Seeing him, if only for a few minutes, would fill so many voids. "If I remember correctly, your mother wasn't smiling when Mr. Hardy painted her picture either."

He nodded, not understanding himself. There was a part of him that wanted Molly to be happy, but there was another part of him that wanted her to admit that she had made a mistake. That she was just as miserable as he was.

Molly heard the nails in his hand jingle like coins as he lined them up in his palm, and she knew that he wanted to return to work. He wanted her to leave. But she would give her right hand for a few more minutes with him. "What color are you going to paint the wainscoting?" she asked suddenly.

Pierce regarded the carved panel of pumpkin pine he had just nailed to the wall. "I'm told it's to be a lightened shade of soldier blue. Similar to the color Hardy made your eyes in the portrait. But he was wrong about that too. He didn't add enough gray. If I were your husband, I wouldn't pay the man till he got it right."

And Molly thought that if Pierce were her husband, Jeremiah Pearson Hardy would have captured much more in her portrait than a hollow-eyed woman in royal-blue velvet. He would have captured joy and love and laughter. She stared at the floor, thinking she was about to choke on her emotions, but then she saw him wiggle the toes that were poking out of his sock and she smiled. "You've made amazing progress with your leg. That doctor undoubtedly knew what he was doing."

"Yah, I guess . . ." He threw her a suspicious look. "How did you know about the doctor?"

"Duncan," she said quickly. "Duncan told me. You know, the day before Christmas."

"Oh, yah. Anyway, I'm supposed to head down to Boston the last week in March so the doc can check on things. Said he could probably take these cussid splints off then if the leg was healed right. And the Penobscot Boom Corporation is footin' the whole bill for me and Da to make the trip. Never known the company to be so generous. Must've come under new management or somethin'."

"Or something," Molly agreed, knowing that the "something" was Olympia's need for a carpenter to finish the dining room. "How are you managing the ice and snow on one leg?"

"Cautiously. But I've had some help. Made myself some a these." He reached down beside the stool for his crutches, but only found his hammer. He searched the other side of the stool, then craned his neck to look over his shoulder. "There they are."

The stool on which he sat was low, splay-legged, and so sturdy that it could support a 500-pound man as easily as it could a 210-pound man. Weight distribution was critical for balance, however, and it was the very thing Pierce forgot about as he leaned backward to retrieve his crutches.

"Made these outta some scrap hick—" Up popped the stool's front legs. Down went the back ones. Pierce's arms flapped. The nails in his hands flew up, then clattered down, rolling beneath Molly's feet as she dashed forward, catching Pierce by his arm, his head, and a knee beneath his shoulder. The stool locked in place. Pierce let out a relieved breath as Molly clutched his head to her breast.

"Are you all right?"

He responded by wrapping his right arm around her waist and holding her like he had wanted to hold her that night so long ago, when she had found him half naked in the kitchen after his Saturday bath. He flattened his hand against the stiffness of her corset, and when she made no move to release him, he worked his hand upward along her spine, then across her shoulder blade to her side. Still his hand did not stop, and still she did not release him. His fingers inched along the front of her gown until they found the upward thrust of her breast, and he suffered a pang of pure desire as he felt the tight bud of her nipple pressing against his palm. "Jeesuz, Molly," he whispered, wanting her right here, right now. He lifted his eyes to hers, but he didn't see desire. He saw fear.

With her free hand Molly placed two fingers across his lips. She peered down the length of the room. Had

anyone heard the commotion? If Evan caught them . . .
"Someone might be coming, Pierce." But the tremor in
her voice was no ordinary tremor. It augured something
that ran far deeper than nervousness. It warned him that
there was something wrong here, and he was going to
find out what.

With a mammoth effort she heaved him upright, but
when she would have let him go, he caught her hand
and cradled it between the two of his, smoothing his
thumb across her knuckles. "What's wrong? Why are
you so scared?"

"I'm not scared. I . . . Oh, it was madness for me to
come down here." She tried to pull back on her hand,
but he brought it to his mouth instead. She felt the softness of his lips trailing kisses down her fingers, and in
that instant she knew joy and torment in equal measure.
If he had to live in this house, it would be far better for
him to hate her. She had to protect him from Evan. She
had to. "Stop it, Pierce," she begged, looking over her
shoulder once again, and her plea was so urgent that he
let her go.

"Jeesuz, Molly, will you tell me what's—"

"I won't bother you again," she said breathlessly, and
she didn't walk from the room. She ran.

Pierce raked his fingers through his hair as he stared
at the place where she'd been standing. And all he could
think was that perhaps she wasn't lost to him. Perhaps
there was hope after all.

Scooting his stool across the floor, he picked up his
crutches and made his way to the portrait that hung
above the fireplace. "I had you first," he said to the eyes
that were too blue to be Molly Deacon's. "And I'll have

you last. And neither you, nor Thatcher, nor God Himself is gonna stop me."

One week passed. Then two. She avoided seeing him, but the sound of his labors echoed throughout the mansion like a heartbeat—his heartbeat. She heard his name spoken on Olympia's lips. She heard the color of his eyes extolled by the kitchen maid, the width of his shoulders adulated by the upstairs maid. She lay in her bed at night wondering if he was asleep, if he was thinking of her. She wondered if his flesh was warm beneath the covers, if she could find the pockmark on his collarbone with her mouth . . . in the darkness. She touched a place on her body that he had once touched, and she thought it strange that her own hand did not evoke the same sensations. She lived in those weeks that he was there without really living. She wanted and desired, but most of all, she knew fear.

Midway through the fourth week, on a night when snow was falling as gently as down, Molly held a candle above the parquetry that was stacked in the dining room. Three dozen more tiles to lay, the wainscoting to paint, then Pierce would be gone. She wanted to insert the parquetry herself so he would have an excuse to leave; she needed to hide the parquetry so he would have an excuse to stay. She wanted him to remain; she needed him to go. If Olympia said Pierce could stay until the leaves fell from the trees, Molly would want a great defoliating wind to blow through Bangor the next day, but she would tie every stem to every branch so no leaf would ever fall. Her mind became the battleground for her warring emotions, and in one of her saner moments, she decided that other people probably lived with these same emotions . . . prior to going insane.

"Are you sure Olympia specified that *I* should be the one to show you where those things might be?" Molly shot the key into the door lock and rattled it from side to side.

"Your sister-in-law said I could probably find some pails in the old stone building out behind the cedar hedges. Since *those* are cedar hedges and *this* is a stone building, I assume this is the place."

"But why me?" It was so dangerous being with him, and she had done so well in her efforts to avoid him. She gave the key another rattle.

"I don't think she trusts keys to anyone outside the family. She's probably afraid someone'll be overwhelmed by greed and want to steal something behind those locked doors. She's appointed you as my guardian, it seems."

Since back and forth wasn't working, Molly tried jerking the key up and down. "I don't know why she didn't tell you to send someone downtown to buy you a couple of pails to mix your paint in. It's not as if she doesn't have the money."

Pierce had to grapple for a reply to that one. "Maybe that's why she has so much money. She doesn't squander it on new pails when there are old pails to be found and used."

"I can't believe there weren't any pails in the house that you could use." She pushed the key up. Then down. Right. Then left. Right left right left right.

"There weren't. Do you have that door open yet?"

"Mmmnh!" she dropped her hand. "It's stuck."

"Outta the way. Lemme try." He grabbed the key. "You're right. It's stuck." Pierce hobbled backward a couple of steps, bored the ends of his two crutches into the hard-packed snow, concentrated his weight on his arms and shoulders, and swung the heel of his right boot up and into the door.

It popped open like a blown shutter.

"There. Not stuck anymore. Ladies first."

Molly stepped inside and sniffed. "Smells like a tomb in here." She pinched her hood closer beneath her chin.

"How many tombs have you been inside?"

"It smells like I *imagine* the inside of a tomb would smell."

"You should say what you mean, Mrs. Thatcher." He gave her a look she could not read.

The room had no order. From the rafters there hung a winter sleigh, three horse harnesses, a child's wooden wagon, and an array of spindle-back chairs in dire need of spindles. Cranberry barrels and coffee bins were stacked, furniture was piled, and dirt coated every visible surface. "Olympia can't know what this place looks like," Molly hypothesized as she strolled around a spinning wheel. "She would have had it redecorated long before this." She opened the glass front of a corner cupboard and perused the interior. A delftware posset pot missing one of its handles. A Bristol glass cruet set with one of the stoppers missing. A pair of porcelain figurines—a man in knee breeches and a frock coat offering flowers to a woman wearing a stomacher and paniers. But these two appeared flawless. She picked up the woman. Finding nothing awry, she looked at the man.

320 Mary Mayer Holmes

And then she saw it. A tiny chip no bigger than the head of a pin broken away from one of the flowers in the bouquet he held. Turning the figurine upside down she saw the word "Chelsea" painted on the bottom. She returned it to the cupboard. The chip was so insignificant. Banishment to the stone outbuilding seemed an unjust fate for Chelsea porcelain marred by so tiny a flaw. Lord Berryhill had displayed his collection of Chelsea porcelain in the grandest rooms of the manor house. She paused in her examination because of the clamor from the side of the room where Pierce had headed.

"Pierce?"

The only response was a crash that shook the floorboards, a whooshing and splintering of glass, and a delayed thudding as of furniture vying to occupy the same space.

"Pierce? Are you all right?"

One last breakable fell to the floor and broke. Silence again.

"If you can hear me, don't move," Molly shouted across the room as she began leaping over the objects strewn in her way. "You might have reinjured your leg." She yanked up her skirt and petticoats and ran across the room. Behind a settle bench she saw his feet. His crutches lay abandoned on the floor. "Ohhh."

She found him faceup on a feather tick. And he wasn't moving.

"Say something, Pierce. Tell me you're all right." She crawled to him on her hands and knees, all the while thinking, *Thank God he landed on something soft*. She grabbed his shoulders, shaking him gently, and when he groaned, she stopped shaking him and pressed her palms to his cheeks. "Does it hurt? Show me where."

He took her hand as if it were the last movement he would ever make. He slid it down his chest, over his ribs, past his hip, then flattened it against the inside of his thigh.

"Here? This is where it hurts?"

He groaned weakly in response. With a gentle hand Molly rubbed the contour of his thigh, while through his slatted eyes Pierce watched her expression change from concern to horror as she realized just what it was he claimed was hurting him. Her hand flew up. "Pierce Blackledge, you—"

His arm was suddenly around her back, his hand behind her head. He pulled her onto his chest and with that powerful right hand of his, forced her mouth against his own. The taste of her bolstered his greed for her, fueled the desire that had smoldered within him for five agonizing months. But her lips were unyielding. He felt her fists on his shoulders, pushing herself away.

"Ssstop!" She struggled upward. He banded both his arms around her back, trapping her. She squirmed in his arms. "You didn't need to find any pail at all, did you? Olympia didn't tell you to have me take you out here, did she?"

"Wrong on both counts." He rolled over with her in his arms and poised his face only inches above hers. "I definitely needed something to mix my paint in, so Olympia told me to have someone take me out here to see what I could find. I chose you." High on her cheekbone he found a place lush with softness. He caressed it with his lips. "You've been avoiding me. Why?"

"You know why," she panted, turning her face away.

"No, I don't know why. But suppose you tell me. And while you're at it, tell me what's in that house that you're so afraid of."

"I'm not afraid."

"You're lying!" And she saw such fierceness in his eyes that it frightened her. "Do you think me a complete fool? Do you think I don't have eyes in my head? That I don't have ears? Maids talk, Molly, and I don't hear them tittering about Mr. Evan and his bride. Why did you marry him? Why?"

"Because you left me!" she screamed at him. "I could have been pregnant! But you didn't stop to think of that before you ran away, did you? No. It was easy for you to run, but what was I supposed to do if I'd found myself in a family way? I couldn't run off to the woods like you did. And you didn't even think enough of me to tell me where I could reach you. What did you expect me to do?"

"I didn't expect you to marry Thatcher!"

"And what was I to do with your bastard?"

"Jeesuz, Molly, I made a mistake! A stupid mistake! Do you want to know if I'm sorry? Yes, I'm sorry. I've never been more sorry in my life. Hell, I'm used to settlin' things with my fists, but I couldn't very well do that with you, could I? So I ran. I thought I'd be happy goin' back to the woods, but I wasn't. You wanna know why? Because the thought of you in Thatcher's arms was eating me alive. It's still eating me alive. Jeesuz, some nights I lay in my bed and I think of you upstairs with him and I want to kill him with my bare hands."

His words were an agony for her to hear. To know

that he still cared for her only made her situation seem more hopeless, for Evan loomed ever large, ready to threaten her and everything she held dear. She shook her head as if to warn him. "Don't say these things, Pierce."

"But I want to say them. I have to say them. Sometimes you don't see the value of somethin' till you've lost it, Molly, and I wish to God I'd learned that before I said those things that drove you into Thatcher's arms. You were mine. I could've had you. If I hadn't been so stupid, maybe it'd be my bed you'd be crawlin' into tonight instead of his. You'd be my wife, not his. Do you love him?"

Her throat tightened at the look in his face. She ached to tell him the truth, but couldn't. "You're so heavy, Pierce."

"Do you love him?" he repeated, enunciating each word separately.

"I—"

"Answer me!"

"Yes, I love him!" she cried out, the image of her splintered pencil still alive and quivering in her mind. She knew her words would hurt him mercilessly, but she also knew that these were the only words that could protect him. "He's my husband and I love him."

"You're lying."

"Am I?" she said, gazing hard into his green eyes. "Do you think a common wood butcher could give me a tenth of the things that Evan Thatcher has given me? Love isn't all kissing and pawing. Love is jewels and clothes and recognition by the finest people in society. So don't tell me that I'm lying. I'm Molly Thatcher,

Pierce. I'm envied and pampered, and I might not have loved my husband when I married him, but I love him now. And if you think I could ever leave him to run away with you, then you'd better think again. Only a fool would give up what I have. And the last time I played the fool was the night I allowed you to make love to me. Now get off me before I yell loud enough to bring the stablehands raining down on your head."

She saw blood rise to stain his cheeks. He stared at her as if he'd never seen her before, and she felt sick inside as he rolled wordlessly off her. She knew then that if he hadn't hated her before, he did now. She crawled across the ticking, and as she struggled to her feet she looked back at Pierce. The face she loved was turned away from her. His forearm was flung across his brow. She had hurt him deliberately and could only wonder if one day he would understand why. She left the stone house then, but she knew that she had left a vital part of herself within its cold confines. And as she trudged back to the mansion, she felt the January wind whip around her, echoing through the hollow vessel that was her heart.

She heard the footsteps that night. The creak of risers. The deflection of wood. She felt each step as if it were weighing on her chest, crushing her. But tonight she would know. Tonight she would see with her own eyes the woman whose love had forced Evan Thatcher to seek respectability—the woman who boasted Evan's lust and Olympia's sanction. She would see her face, and then she would plan her revenge.

Past her room she heard them walk. She threw off her

covers and on cat's feet crept to her door. A quarter inch at a time she turned the knob, and when it would turn no more, she drew it back. The hinges were well oiled and made no sound. Slowly, noiselessly, she rotated the knob to its original position and released it. She stepped into the opening and, bending her head around the door frame, peered down the hall.

A pale nimbus of light backlit the two figures. They stopped at Evan's door, and when they turned, Molly saw the candle sconce in her husband's hand, and in its lumination, the face of the person who preceded Evan into his room. When the hall was dark once again, Molly remained at her door, staring numbly into blackness, for the person who entered Evan's room was not a woman at all.

It was a man.

Evan Thatcher was a sodomite.

Molly ignored the knocks at her door as she had been ignoring them all day, but Olympia was persistent.

"I made your excuses to the ladies of the Union Female Education Society, but I will not be embarrassed like that again. Do you hear? And you haven't eaten all day. Mrs. Popham is here with some food, and if you don't open the door, I'll have Mr. Blackledge remove the hinges and open it that way. It's your choice."

Through the darkness Molly regarded the locked door. She didn't want Pierce to see her like this. She didn't want him to know about . . . And she felt the brackishness well in her throat again as the memory of what she had seen last night played before her eyes. She felt so . . . so defiled. They had made such a mockery of her, and she had never even suspected the truth. Oh, God! How they must have delighted in her naiveté.

"Very well, Molly. I'm sending Mrs. Popham downstairs to—"

"No!" She didn't want Pierce involved in any of this. It was too ugly to share with anyone, even the man she loved. She wouldn't feel relief telling him; she would feel only shame. "I'm coming." Dragging herself out of her chair, she crossed to the door and turned the key.

Olympia heard the click and turned the knob. The door swung open into cold and blackness. "Are you trying to conserve camphene?" she asked, frowning. She motioned Mrs. Popham into the room. "Don't fall over anything. Do you see the table? Never mind, just set the tray on the bed, and for God sakes light the lamp."

Curled in the security of her rococo side chair, Molly squinted against the lamp's brightness. She covered her eyes.

"You can leave us now, Mrs. Popham. Thank you." Olympia seated herself across from Molly. "And now suppose you tell me what all this nonsense is about."

Molly uncovered eyes that looked black as knotholes, and when she trained those eyes on Olympia, she saw a tiny crack appear in the ice of the woman's reserve. "I know," Molly said in an undertone.

Olympia met her gaze before dropping her eyes. "How long have you known?"

"Since last night. I saw the two of them going into Evan's room."

Olympia nodded. "I told him he had to be more discreet now that he was married. He did well for a while, but . . ." She shook her head. "But there are certain urges that no amount of wealth or power can control."

"You knew," Molly accused her. "You knew what he is, yet you allowed him to lure me into this marriage knowing full well I'd be nothing more to him than an excuse to disguise his perversion. Did it ever occur to you that I might want affection in a marriage? And children? Did you ever stop to think of me for one minute, Olympia?". She pressed her palm to the center of her brow as if to stop her head from aching. "To think that you groomed me to become one of you. Groomed me to become one of the favored elite who know the price of everything and the value of nothing. I *wanted* to become one of you. But I could never match you for lying and deceit. How could you condone what he is?"

"Condone?" Olympia drilled a harsh look at her. "I don't condone what he is. But he's my brother. What would you have me do with him? It's easy for you to judge, isn't it? You don't love him as I love him. Why do you suppose I never married? Who would protect Evan if I married? Who would take care of him?"

"He *threatened* me," Molly raged.

"Did he?" Olympia's hazel eyes looked suddenly sad. "He never would have carried it out, you know. He's a gentle man, Molly. My father thought him a weak man. He always said that Evan and I were misplaced in each other's skin. I should have been the boy and Evan the girl. I had the strength and Evan the tenderness. It should have been the other way round. I wish to God it had been. When I learned of his . . . his rather uncommon preference I vowed that he should never be harmed by it. It hasn't been easy creating an alter image for him. His secret has taken manipulation on my part to maintain."

"His shirt studs," Molly said in a whisper.

"Who but a rogue would wear a portrait gallery of females on his shirt? Clever, don't you think?"

Molly nodded, remembering what a libertine she had thought him for possessing such shirt studs. A ruse. All a ruse. "But there were rumors about him that he had dalliances with your maids, that he fathered hosts of bastard children."

Olympia shook her head. "Evan developed a knack for being seen with the wrong people at precisely the right time. It wasn't hard to discern which of our domestics were of loose character. He merely had to be seen frequenting the space around them, and when they found themselves in the family way, rumors would fly. It was quite effortless, actually. But then things began disintegrating on another front. His society ladies were becoming insistent that he choose a wife amongst them, and of course, that would have been quite impossible."

"So that's when you decided to make use of your dressmaker."

"Indeed. It was rather convenient that you happened upon the scene at that time. You were perfect—young and pretty, an English orphan. You were nearly too good to be true."

Molly laughed then—an almost hysterical laugh that engendered revulsion and irony and a touch of madness. "Oh, Olympia, I *was* too good to be true. We've deceived each other, you and I. I wanted to work for you so desperately that I lied to you. I'm not an orphan. I had a mother and father and five brothers who died before they reached the age of two. And I'm not English. I'm one of the hated foreigners, Olympia. I'm Irish."

Olympia's face remained impassive. "So, we are both guilty of duplicity. I've never had an Irishwoman in my house, Molly. I had thought them to be largely uncivilized. I see now that I was wrong. I'm sorry for the distress we've caused you, but you do understand it was necessary. We had to maintain appearances." She stood up and paced to the unlit fireplace, rubbing her hands against the cold. "I should see about installing parlor stoves in the second-floor bedchambers, but they're so ugly. I hate the thought of spoiling these lovely rooms for the sake of warmth."

And Molly realized she had found the person who had banished the Chelsea figurines to the stone outbuilding because of their flaw.

She turned to face Molly. "Have you ever been in love?"

Molly felt her heart wrench with the love she nurtured for Pierce Blackledge. "Yes. I've been in love."

"Then you know what it's like to want to protect someone from harm. I have made Evan my whole life. He's my greatest blessing and my greatest curse. He has his dalliance with this other man, but I have his heart, and without it, I would be nothing. Can you understand?"

It annoyed Molly to have any sympathy for this woman, but yes, she understood. For indeed, Pierce was her whole life. Without his affection and laughter she felt the same emptiness that Olympia was speaking of. Oh, yes, she understood very well. "I understand," she said, "But how do you expect me to feel, Olympia? What do you expect me to do?"

Olympia ran a finger over Molly's standing embroidery frame. She seemed distant and preoccupied, as if she hadn't heard the question. "I'd thought this would be the perfect solution to the problem. I thought if we provided you with everything you could ever want that you would see fit to overlook the unusual circumstances. It could be your little secret as it were. But I gather you'll want to leave now, won't you? Your sense of decency has been offended. We've never allowed any hint of scandal to taint the Thatcher name. Divorce is out of the question. I'll have to consider the options, Molly. I'll have to think what's best for Evan and what will be easiest for you, then we'll see. Will you give me a few days to decide what to do?"

"Yes, I'll give you a few days," she said quietly, for she realized now that she had little to fear from Evan Thatcher. Olympia was the twin whose word reigned supreme, and Olympia, it seemed, was willing to make amends. Yes, if there was a graceful way out of this, she would give the woman a few days.

"You should light a fire, you know. It must be all of forty degrees in here." Straightening her already erect spine, Olympia walked to the door and placed her hand on the knob. "Evan and I will be attending Mr. Thoreau's presentation at the Lyceum tonight. I don't imagine you'd care to join us."

Molly shook her head. "I don't imagine I would."

"I'm sorry, Molly. Truly I am."

The odor filtered into the room when Olympia opened the door. It remained even after she left. Paint. A lightened shade of soldier blue, Molly remembered. Like the eyes in the portrait. And she thought, *This nightmare is going to end, Pierce. We can be together.*

And she knew joy.

In his dream he was chopping down an old elm with strokes that echoed throughout the forest. He awoke with a start to find the sound still echoing in his head. But it wasn't axe strokes on elm. It was knuckles on oak. Someone was knocking on his door.

"What?" Pierce barked at the intruder. The response was softer, faster raps. "Jeesuz-God." He threw his hand onto his night table, found a matchbox, and slatted his eyes so he'd be spared the brightness of the candle flame. He leaned on one elbow as he collected his wits, and in a voice gravelly with sleep demanded, "Who's there?"

The knocking stopped long enough for him to hear an indistinguishable female voice reply, "Me." *Me*, he thought as he tossed his covers off and grabbed one of his crutches. Who the hell was *me*? The little blond kitchen maid who kept nosin' around the dining room while he worked, or the redhead who brought him a bed warmer full of hot coals every night? Tired and disgruntled, he jerked open the door to his bedchamber to find Molly, nightgowned and hollow eyed, with tears streaming down her cheeks.

"Would you hold me, Pierce? I need someone to hold me." And before he could react, she had her arms wrapped so tightly around his waist that his eyes widened with the pressure.

"Molly? What——" With his free arm he hugged her to

his chest. He poked his head into the hall to see if anyone had followed her, then jockeying her back with him, closed the door and locked it. "What's the matter, Molly? Why are you crying?"

He hopped backward to support his shoulders against the door, and when his footing was sure, eased his crutch from beneath his armpit and leaned it against the wall. She buried her face against his chest, bathing his long johns with her tears, pouring out her anguish in great racking sobs that even his powerful lumberman's arms could not quell.

"Shh. I'm here, Molly. I won't let you go." And despite the words they had exchanged in the outbuilding, he could not deny her himself. Her hair was unbound and teased his fingers with memories of a hot August night. Her nightgown was a heavy flannel thing, but beneath its many folds he could feel the fullness of her breasts pressing against him. He slid his hands down the length of her back, then up again, down and up, warming her, loving her. And after long minutes he felt her shoulders still and her breathing calm. He shaped his palms around her head and with a gentle motion angled her face back so he could see her.

Her sad, haunted eyes stared back at him. Pierce went rigid. "Has he hurt you? I'll—"

She rocked her head from side to side in denial. "No. It's just that I've been so miserable. I didn't mean any of those things I said yesterday. I was lying. I don't love Evan. I only said I did because I thought he might hurt you if he discovered how you felt about me. I've been so frightened. I'm sorry, Pierce. I'm sorry for lying to you, and for marrying Evan, and can you ever forgive me for all those awful things I said?" This outburst precipitated a fresh spate of tears that dampened Molly's cheeks and Pierce's long johns with equal favor.

"C'mon, sweetheart. Help me over to the bed. Sounds to me like we're in for a long night."

And when she had him settled on the edge of the bed, she knelt between his parted legs, banded her arms around his hips, and rested the side of her face against his lap. Her hair surrounded her like a dark curtain, hiding her from him, but he gathered it away from her face, away from her neck, coiling it around his hand as if this one link would forever bind them to each other. "Now tell me," he said softly.

And so she did, in spurts and sobs, with guilt and self-reproach. "You were right, Pierce. About everything. You told me I could never be happy denying who I am and where I came from. I've denied my heritage. I've denied my faith. And I haven't been happy. I've been miserable. You told me I'd fit right in with Evan's highbrow friends, but I didn't. I didn't fit in at all. I despised them for the horrible things they said about the Irish, and I despised myself for not having the courage to dispute what they were saying."

With his thumb Pierce found the flowing curve beneath her earlobe and stroked gently, rediscovering the secret places he had found last summer. She closed her eyes at his touch, feeling unworthy of his goodness.

"When you left me last year and Evan proposed, I thought that even if I'd lost you I could still have the one thing that really mattered to me. My dress shop— the one thing that could never be taken away from me because it would be filled with things that *I* created.

Well, I have my dress shop, Pierce, but . . . but it's not how I thought it would be. Oh, I can look at something and think, 'Isn't that lovely,' but the satisfaction comes not from my thinking it, but from your saying it. The satisfaction comes when you're there beside me, sharing in the joy of what I'm doing. Do you know how I spent Christmas? I spent Christmas in my dining room with thirty-three empty chairs. Evan gave me a necklace that could be pawned to feed half of Ireland, but I didn't get any pleasure out of staring at it by myself. Oh, Pierce, I was so wrong. The things I thought were so important weren't important at all. And all the things I didn't think mattered turned out to be the only things that matter—who I am, what I believe in, who I love."

She squeezed his hips more fiercely as his fingers dipped low on her neck, replacing the flannel of her night rail for warmth. "When Olympia told me you'd be living here for a month, I died a thousand little deaths. I could look at you, but I couldn't touch you. And I wanted to touch you. I wanted to touch you all over and tell you how much I love you. That I never stopped loving you."

His hands were suddenly rubbing her arms, then fastening themselves around her elbows, coaxing her to her feet. "Let me look at you, Molly. I've been cheated of your face for so long." And when she stood before him, he lifted her hands to his mouth and graced each of her palms with a kiss. "Tell me of your husband," he said, pressing her hands to either side of his neck, warming them with his flesh.

Molly bowed her head in shame of what she must tell him. But they would have no life together until they spoke of these things. She would allow no more lies or secrets to drive wedges between them. "He doesn't love me, Pierce. He married me because he needed a wife for appearances. He . . . he told me he loved someone else after we were married, and when I asked him why he hadn't married her, he said because it would have been impossible. I thought the woman probably had a husband already, but I was wrong. I'd hear two sets of footsteps entering Evan's room sometimes, and last night I looked. He has a lover, Pierce. But it's not a woman. It's a man. Evan is a . . . a sodomite."

Beneath her fingers she felt the muscles in his neck tighten. His eyes in the candlelight darkened with unnamed emotion. "No. He's a womanizer. Everyone knows he's a womanizer. He can't be a—"

"But he is. You thought he was a womanizer because that's what he wanted you to think. Olympia told me as much this evening."

"She knew?" Molly could feel the pulse in his neck throbbing against the side of her hand, racing with his anger. "Why the hell did she let you marry him if she knew? Why did—"

She hushed his words with a touch of her mouth, a kiss so soft that he hardly felt it. "I've wanted to do that for so long," she whispered. "I've missed you so much. I've wanted you so much."

But Pierce wanted to wrap his hands around Olympia Thatcher's neck. "He's a sodomite," he rasped, and the thought made his flesh crawl. "Has he ever touched you, Molly? Has he?"

She shook her head, loving him for his concern. "There has never been anyone but you. There will never be anyone but you." And he smothered her against him, unable to talk but able to have her nearness soothe the wounds of his spirit. For a long time they said nothing, but then Pierce found his voice.

"You can get an annulment if the marriage was never consummated. You can marry me, Molly."

Her reply drifted into his mouth on an excited breath. "Soon, my love. Soon. Olympia has promised to see about ending this charade."

"Olympia?"

She nodded. "She wields the power in the Thatcher family, Pierce. Evan might appear to, but it's Olympia who makes the decisions."

"And what makes you think she's going to help you?"

"Because she doesn't want to hurt either me or Evan. She thought a marriage like this could work, and now that she knows it can't, I think she'll find a graceful way of ending it. I don't think it was ever her intention to humiliate me, Pierce. In fact, locked within that cool exterior of hers, I think there's a very loving woman. She just never learned to show it. I feel sorry for her."

"You feel sorry for her after what she did to you? After what they both did to you?"

She hugged her hands close to his face and probed his eyes with her own. "She's devoted her whole life to Evan. She loves him very deeply. Not in the same physical way I love you, but I can understand when she speaks of wanting to protect him. I feel sorry because she's never had anyone like you who could teach her to smile"—she kissed his forehead—"and laugh"—the tip of his nose—"and love"—his mouth.

He guided her fingers to the top button of his long johns. "Unfasten it," he urged. And when she had, he said, "And the next one." So she opened that too, and the next, and the next. Opened every button till there were no buttons left.

She stood slightly back from him and smiled into his face. "When we marry, which would you prefer to wed? An Englishwoman or an Irishwoman?" And as she spoke, she slid her hands beneath the red wool of his underwear, parting the material and drawing it back over his great wide shoulders.

"I don't care," he said, his eyes never leaving her face. "I know what life's like with you, and I know what it's like without you. And I want you any way I can get you. I don't care whether you're English, Irish, or nothin' at all. And you can have a thousand dress shops if that's what'll make you happy. But I'll never be happy, Molly. Not unless you're there to share your life with me."

And she smiled to think what deviant paths they had taken to arrive at the same conclusion. She eased his sleeves down his arms, over biceps and elbows and forearms. She grabbed hold of his cuffs, then held fast to the material as he plucked one hand then the other from its woolen confinement. For a moment she merely looked at him, then touched a shy hand to his naked shoulder. "I'd forgotten how very beautiful you are."

Delighted by her flattery, he sat purposefully still, allowing her to reacquaint herself with his body. Her fingertips played across his shoulder and down his arm, lingering on the stark definition of sinew that shaped his flesh. And when she felt a quick tightening of muscle beneath her fingers, she lifted his arm upward and angled his forearm over his bicep. "Flex it for me," she asked shyly, thinking he might refuse her, but it pleased him that she could be aroused by something so commonplace to him, so flex it he did.

It swelled like a bellows, straining his flesh, highlighting a pattern of muscle and veins that invited the touch of a woman's hand. She circled her fingers around its hardness and found that her fingertips would not meet around the circumference. Her blood raced at the unexpected thrill. She felt comfort in his power, warmth in his might, awed that this beautiful man could desire her as she desired him.

Her fingers strayed downward—a hesitant passage over the thatch of hair beneath his arm, then down his long, smooth flank. "Do all axemen possess your beauty?" she asked, her eyes growing hot at his physical appeal. And in answer he guided her hand lower still, over the coarse furring of hair that darkened his flesh to a fragile place that was suddenly hard as his bicep. Bracing his forearm behind her neck, he drew her near to his face.

"Make love to me," he whispered against her cheek, urgency in his voice. "Now. Tonight."

She felt a gentle tug on the ribbon at her throat, a finger down her breastbone to the second, a caress down the flat dish of her stomach to the third. Fabric parted, palms glided, and then her night rail was at her feet. She shivered as the January air skimmed her flesh, but warmth soon replaced coolness as Pierce spanned her naked back with his palms. She felt blessed by those hands as they took quiet measure of her spine, blessed by the fingers whose touch was light as the fall of hair that grazed her back.

Seated as he was, they could almost see eye to eye,

but Pierce dipped his head when she would have kissed him and kissed instead a place beneath her arm where her rib pressed against her flesh. She bowed her head as his mouth continued its play. Her heart slowed a beat when he parted her buttocks with the side of his hand. And suddenly she was no longer cold.

He turned her with his hands, striving to make her more accessible to his mouth. She felt the cold touch of his nose and the warm pressure of his lips as he traced her rib from side to front. She could see little of his face below the rise of her breast, but she sensed his pleasure when she brushed his countenance with its softness. He soon forgot her rib. She felt blood humming in her ears as he graced the full underside of her breast with light touches and warm breaths. She made a sound of pleasure and clasped her hands around his upper arms, loving the feel of hardened sinew that filled her palms. He spoke his love with his mouth. With supreme patience he contented her with the gentlest of touches, plying her, readying her, and when he drew the fullness of her nipple into his mouth, she arched against him, wanting to give of herself that they could be one.

He slid his forearms beneath her arms and pressed his wrists to her shoulder blades. With a fluid motion he gathered her hair into each hand, then pulled steadily downward on it. He forced her head back with the gesture, and as her chin lifted, he scattered kisses ever upward, over the soft rise of her bosom to the shallow dip in her throat. His mouth lingered there while his tongue savored the fineness of her flesh, and she felt the cadence of his breathing grow faster as he kissed the high curve of her neck and strained upward to find her mouth.

"I love you," she said before the probing warmth of his tongue slid between her lips. His touch spoke much of yearning—a yearning of the flesh, of the mind, of the spirit. Her arms, when she glided them about his neck, all soft and supple in their nakedness, told him that she was his, now, forever. She hugged him within the warm circle of those arms, a tender complement to his strength, and as he kissed her, she felt what was soft within her grow softer and flow like tears, preparing a frictionless sheath to welcome the arching length of him. As he flattened his hand high on her shoulders, holding her hard against him, he visited upon her lips the passion that was near choking him. He was full and hard and swollen. He ached and throbbed and wanted release for his passion and his love.

"Enough." His mouth was hot against hers. "It's time."

Their love knew no awkwardness, no shame, so as he lay on his back in deference to his leg, she saw with clarity the role she must play. She sat him gently, legs bent and calves flanking his hips, and into the warm space carved within her she drew him. He could feel her tightness surrounding him, and it gave him joy that she was so, that she had acted as wife to no other but him. Her face grew bright that they conformed with such physical ease, and as she spread her fingers over the hard muscles of his chest, she bent forward and against the scar on his collarbone whispered, "Perhaps this is the way it will always be between Deacons and Black-ledges."

Their joining purged her thoughts of Evan Thatcher. The glide and thrust of their bodies reaffirmed for her the inexorable bond that existed between a man and a woman, and she delighted in its purity. They strove in unison, growing breathless with their exertion, the long curve of his hands spanning her waist, her hair sweeping forward to cloak him with darkness. She felt within her the pulsing and rise of sensation, and then the pulses were floating outward, warming her, setting fire to her, wrapping her in the consuming web of passion spent.

She lay against him later, her breath whispering across him, raising gooseflesh beneath the dark coils of hair on his chest.

"I haven't been to mass since last August," she confessed after a while, their lovemaking bringing to bear upon her mind all that she needed to correct before she could marry Pierce.

"You'd best talk to Conor about that."

"I'm afraid to, Pierce. I'm afraid when I tell him everything I've done, he'll confirm what I already know—that I'm going to hell."

"I don't think so, sweetheart. But he'll probably tell both've us what we already know—that we better get married and damn quick. Come home with me tonight, Molly. I don't want you stayin' in this place any longer."

But she had already made her mind up about that. "No. I told Olympia I'd allow her a few days to work out a solution, and I'll remain here long enough to hear her out."

"You don't owe her any kind of loyalty."

"I know, but I gave her my word. And when an Irishwoman gives her word, it's for keeps. Nothing will happen to me, Pierce. I'll listen to what she has to say and then I'll come to you."

"I'll be through my work here tomorrow. I won't see you after that. When will you come?"

"Soon, my love."

And responding to that, he pulled her onto his chest and kissed her mouth. "It'll never be soon enough."

Chapter Seventeen

Olympia came to see her late the following afternoon.

"I believe I've arrived upon a viable solution, but you might object, so sit down and allow me to explain." And ever practical, Olympia Thatcher described to her sister-in-law how they might all save face in light of the circumstances.

"A grand tour," she said. "Evan and I celebrate our twenty-eighth birthdays on February fourteenth, so we could purport to use that as an excuse for leaving. You could make the journey with us as far as Boston, then go your separate way. Evan and I would travel five or six months abroad, and when we returned, it would be without you. We would tell our friends that while in

Europe, you found yourself with child and died giving premature birth. Evan could return to Bangor a respected widower and you, my dear, could live wherever you wanted to once again as Molly Deacon. There are discreet solicitors in Philadelphia who would grant you an annulment to your marriage, and we, in turn, would see that you are well provided for, in return for your cooperation, of course."

Molly was incredulous. "You want me to leave Bangor?" *Leave Pierce?* "But this is my home now. I . . . I can't leave." *I won't leave Pierce.*

"It's the only way. If you expect your marriage to be dissolved, you can't expect to remain in the same city with Evan. He still has a reputation to protect, appearances to maintain."

"I don't care what he has to protect! I won't leave Bangor. Think of some other solution."

"There *is* no other solution."

Molly's expression became inflexible. She would not allow her happiness to be snatched away now that she felt it within her grasp. "I'll bend, Olympia, but I refuse to bend as much as you're asking. There are solicitors right here in the city who could grant me an annulment, and I'm sure the *Whig and Courier* would be greedy for the details."

"You could do that," said Olympia. "But you won't."

"And what makes you so sure of that?"

Olympia probed her face. "Because you're a decent person. Because if you're Irish you've lived through hurt, and I think you remember those hurts too well to deliberately want to cause pain to someone else. And you would be causing pain. Evan's life would be ruined.

My life would be ruined, and not just for a few months as yours was. The damage would be permanent. And I don't think you have that much vindictiveness in you. Think about what I've said, Molly. You'll see the wisdom of my solution."

So Molly thought. For the rest of the afternoon and through supper she thought, then long into the evening. And still the conclusion was the same.

I won't leave Pierce.

Olympia's solution was no solution at all. Evan would emerge from this unscathed while she would be banished to some strange city. No. She wouldn't agree to it. *She* was the one who'd been wronged. *She* was the one who had been made to look the fool, who had been humiliated. Why should she be the only one to make reparations? It wasn't fair. She couldn't leave Pierce, and Pierce wouldn't leave Bangor. His work was here. His friends were here. Duncan was here! She wouldn't allow these things to be taken from her ever again. She would stand firm, and if Olympia couldn't provide some kind of compromise, she would have to take action herself. She did, after all, have the upper hand in the matter. It was Evan's life that would be ruined by the annulment, not hers.

And that gave her pause.

One word from her and she could deprive Evan Thatcher of the very things she had fought to preserve in her own life—dignity, reputation. His friends would shun him. His business associates would sever their dealings with him. He would be ruined, and he and Olympia would spend the rest of their lives in this mansion, growing old and unhappy together.

She could do that to Evan Thatcher. She had the power. But did she want to?

Yes, she wanted to.

But could she do it?

She sighed with indecision and walked to her bedroom window. A frigid silence hung in the night air. Snow blanketed the lower rooftops of the mansion and in the moonlight it looked crusted over like stale white bread. She touched her palm to the cold pane of glass, and as she did so, she heard in the distance the familiar clang of Old Settler Engine No. 5's fire bell. She searched the night sky for evidence of flames, but there was none of the spectacle that she had witnessed this past summer when Cavannaugh's burned. The sky remained dark.

Can you do that to Evan? she asked herself again. And then she recalled something she had found easy to forget. She had married Evan primarily because she had thought herself pregnant. She could have refused his offer, but he was her only salvation at the time. She had taken advantage of him as blatantly as he'd taken advantage of her, so how could she condemn him without condemning herself as well? She couldn't. She had to accept responsibility in the matter. She couldn't blame everything on Evan as she'd been so willing to do. In trying to protect herself from the stigma of unwed motherhood, she had made a grave mistake. Ruining Evan's life would not correct that mistake; it would merely place her in the same category as the people in Bangor who knew the price of everything and the value of nothing. She would be stooping to their level—without compassion, without equitableness. And Molly suddenly realized that Olympia was right. She was too decent to do that to another person—maybe because of her own experiences, maybe because she was Irish... maybe because she was in love.

As the sound of the fire bell faded into the night, she pressed her forehead to the glass. So what was she to do now?

Long stretches of time passed as she stood at the window, fantasizing, thinking, drifting. She wondered whose house had gone up in flames tonight, whose life had been destroyed. What person had stood in a snow-covered street watching all his earthly possessions consumed by fire? It was so cold outside—as cold tonight as it had been hot in August. And she thought again of the fire at Cavannaugh's, of the men who had lost their lives, and she remembered the relief she'd felt that Pierce had escaped harm. Pierce. Her love. Her life. And she knew then that if she recited a litany of everything she held dear, she could lose all of it and still thrive—so long as Pierce stood beside her. They would manage to survive because they loved, and in their love there was strength.

So perhaps she could leave Bangor, if Pierce would leave with her. They could survive in Boston or Philadelphia as easily as they could survive in Bangor. And maybe Duncan would want to come with them. Pierce could open a furniture shop and become the best damned cabinetmaker in Boston, maybe in the whole state of Massachusetts. She could open another dress shop, bigger than the one in Bangor, better. Pierce would be leaving his friends behind, but they could make new friends, mutual friends, Irish friends. And the ones from Bangor would always have a place to visit. If she agreed to Olympia's plan, she would really be giving up very little. She would be forfeiting a place of residence, but in return she could be Catholic again, and Irish, and Pierce's wife, and viewed in that light, the exchange was more than fair. It was the perfect solution!

But will Pierce agree?

She remembered what had happened the last time they'd discussed his occupation, and she felt a sudden dread as to what his reaction might be. But she wasn't going to let that deter her. She suspected that this time they would both be more reasonable about the whole thing. She wanted to tell him. She wanted to tell him right now.

As she was going for her cloak, she heard the shouts in the foyer. A babel of male voices. The shrillness of Olympia's scream. She raced out the door and down the landing to the head of the stairs. When she saw the men, she wondered what the crew of the city's fire company was doing in her foyer, but then she saw the stretcher . . . and she knew.

"He was at the manufactory, ma'am," the chief called up to Molly as she hurried down the stairs. "Steam pipe burst. I sent someone for the doc. You want us to carry him to his room? Stand aside there. Let Mrs. Thatcher through."

She smelled it before she saw it—the putrid stench of burned flesh. She walked through the path the firemen made for her and felt an expectant silence close around her as she looked down at Evan.

"My God." She covered her mouth and looked away.

"I tried to warn your husband before about those boilers, Mrs. Thatcher. They get too hot and they can burst their pipes easy as they do on the side-wheelers. All this equipment is so new yet. But you know how he felt about that machinery in the manufactory."

Molly looked back at the stretcher. The handsome face of her husband no longer resembled the face of anyone human. She thought she would retch. "Was anyone else hurt?"

"No, ma'am. The foreman was in the room with him, but he wasn't standing under that pipe like your husband was when it burst. Foreman was the one who sent someone to fetch us."

Olympia was standing as still as a pillar of salt at the foot of the stretcher, her hands crossed over her mouth, her eyes fixed unblinkingly on her twin.

"We'd best move him upstairs," Molly whispered, swallowing the bile that was burning its way up her throat. "Please. This way." And as she led them up to the second floor, she didn't notice that Olympia remained behind, staring at the floor as if Evan were still lying at her feet.

"It could be much worse," Dr. Bledsoe informed them three hours later. "The rest of his body could have been burned as badly as his face and hands, but he was spared that. When he comes to, he'll be in terrible pain, so I left you something for him on his nightstand. Your husband will probably require a lot of it in the next few weeks, Mrs. Thatcher. Bring the bottle to the apothecary to have it filled as often as you need. And you'd better get in a supply of bandages. He'll need his dressings changed every day for a while. When we're done here, I'll take both you ladies upstairs to show you how it should be done."

The parlor was cold despite the fire blazing in the hearth. Molly rubbed her hands together as she watched Bangor's only physician pace before her chair. Across from her Olympia sat with her spine erect and her eyes downcast.

"Will he recover?" Molly asked.

"Burns are strange phenomena, Mrs. Thatcher. Sometimes the body recovers quite rapidly. Other times the burns seem to invite a host of separate illnesses into the body. I can't predict which way it will be with your husband. But he's a healthy young man. If anyone has a good chance of survival, he does."

"What you're saying is that if he doesn't die, he'll probably recover."

"I wouldn't have stated it in quite those terms, but yes, I suppose that's what I'm saying. And one more thing: you realize that his eyes were affected. It's too soon to tell how much harm was done, but I should warn you, the damage might be permanent. He could be blind. I'm going to look in on him before I leave now. If you ladies would meet me upstairs in a few minutes, I'll show you what I'd like you to do for Mr. Thatcher. If you'll excuse me."

Molly watched him leave, but rather than follow him immediately she sat for a moment, still stunned, still dazed. When she'd heard the fire bell earlier, she'd never dreamed that the life being destroyed was Evan's. She willed herself to her feet and walked to the side of Olympia's chair.

"Are you coming?" But her sister-in-law didn't

move. Molly placed her hand on the woman's arm. "Olympia?"

"I can't look at him, Molly. He wouldn't want me to see him like this. You go. When the doctor shows you what to do, tell him you're taking instructions for the two of us."

"But—"

She gripped Molly's hand with bone-crushing fierceness. "I can't go up there. Do you understand? I . . . I can't."

Molly flinched with pain. There was a strangeness in Olympia's voice that frightened her—a strangeness that cautioned her to tread lightly. "All right, darling. All right." She patted the woman's hand and let out her breath when she felt her grip loosen. "Perhaps you can see him later."

"You'll take good care of him, won't you? Promise me, Molly. Promise me you will."

No! Molly thought. *I have my own life to think about, my own happiness.* But when she saw the pitiable look on Olympia's face again—the look of a woman who loved too much—it touched that part of Molly that was likewise woman, that likewise loved. And she knew she couldn't leave. "I'll take very good care of him."

She released Molly's hand and gazed toward the fire. "There. You see? I knew you would. You might not love Evan like I do, but I knew you wouldn't leave him. You're a decent person, Molly. I knew I could depend on you."

Molly thought of her hopes, her dreams, her love, and realized that Evan's life had not been the only life destroyed tonight. "Yes," she said wistfully. "You can depend on me."

She was bone weary when she finally returned to her room that night. She left Evan's door open so she could listen for him and left instructions that it was not to be closed. He might need her, and if he did, Dr. Bledsoe said it was important to respond quickly. And she'd given her word to Olympia.

Her word to Olympia.

Mrs. Popham appeared at her door, a bundle of clothing in her arms. "I'm awful sorry about Mr. Evan, missus. Terrible thing to happen. Terrible. You have anyplace special you want me to put these clothes of his? They're all damp so they'll need to be dried out."

Molly looked up from where she stood at the fireplace. "Set them there on the table, Mrs. Popham. I'll take care of them."

"Anything I can get you before I head for home?" the housekeeper asked.

"Not tonight, Mrs. Popham. Thank you."

And when the woman had gone, Molly walked to the table and separated the clothing with a listless hand. The stink of burned flesh still filled her nostrils, but as she shook out Evan's frock coat a more familiar scent touched her senses and she bowed her head and held the garment to her breast, for the smell evoked memories of a time, it seemed, she would never recapture, of lost dreams and lost love. It evoked memories of gentle hands and cold toes and incredible warmth.

She smelled wet wool.

* * *

One week passed. Then two. Evan's twenty-eighth birthday came and went that month, unobserved.

Olympia held a private celebration in her room, kept company by the fire, her brother's whimpering, and the voices that had begun living in her head.

Olympia looked up. When she saw Molly dressed for outdoors, her eyes mirrored her panic. "You told me you wouldn't leave! You promised! No, you can't go. I . . . I won't let you go." As she clutched at the black wool of Molly's cloak, Molly caught her hand and cradled it within her own.

"Listen to me, darling. Evan is asleep. Do you hear the quiet? He's not in any pain right now."

Olympia cocked her ear. "The pain is gone?"

"For now. While he's asleep. So you can be happy for him. You can also do something else for him. Why don't you get out of your nightclothes and comb your hair, and we can take a walk outside together."

"Leave him? No, I couldn't—"

"Not leave him, darling. Just take a walk down by the river. I haven't been out of this house since Evan's accident and neither have you. And that was over five weeks ago. I think we should try to get some fresh air in our lungs. They're skating on the river this afternoon. We could go down and watch them for a while. The paper says the ice is starting to break up north, so this could be our last chance to see the skaters till next year. I think Evan would want you to."

"Did he tell you that?" Olympia touched her hand to

the hair she hadn't washed since this ordeal began, to the nightgown she didn't have the energy to change.

"He didn't tell me that specifically. But he has asked me where you are. He wants to see you, Olympia."

She snatched her hand away from Molly. "He wants to see me? How can he see anything? He's blind."

Molly squeezed the bridge of her nose to relieve the pressure in her head. "That's not his fault."

"No, but . . . he shouldn't ask to *see* me when he knows he'll never be able to see anything ever again."

Molly sighed. "He's your brother. Are you never going to speak to him again?"

"Can he speak to me without . . . without whimpering? I . . . I can't stand it when he s-screams like that. I can't stand it when he hurts. He's going to die, isn't he? I heard them whispering that he's going to die."

"Who did you hear whispering, darling? The servants?"

Olympia looked toward her window. She outlined her lips with her fingertips. "No. Different voices. I . . . I don't know who they belong to."

Molly gave the woman a worried smile. "He's not going to die, Olympia. Dr. Bledsoe says he's going to need lots of rest and medical attention, but he's through the worst of it. He's not going to die."

"Then why does he cry?"

"Because his body hurts."

Olympia cocked her ear again. "But not now. He's sleeping now, so he doesn't hurt."

Molly nodded. She smoothed her sister-in-law's hair back from her face. "I'm going for a short walk, darling, but when I come back, we're going to take you into your water closet and give you a hot bath. We'll wash your hair and sprinkle some sweet-smelling toilet water on you, and then we'll dress you in a fresh gown and give you something to eat. And maybe by then Evan will be awake and we can both go in and see him together. Would you like that?"

"If he doesn't cry. Only if he doesn't cry."

"I'll speak to him," Molly assured her. "Now you rest. I'll be back in ten minutes."

Olympia's voice stopped her on the way to the door. "Molly? Do you hate us for what we did to you?"

She hesitated, not knowing how to describe the emotions she felt. There were days when she felt bereft, days when she felt anger. There were moments when she could choke on her despair, and moments, when she had lulled Evan to sleep, that she could cry with relief. There were days when she despised Evan's needing her so much, and days when she felt joyful at being able to help. And always... always there was Pierce, in her mind, in her heart. Some mornings she wanted to run to him, away from the stench and the sickness, but she would remind herself that she was a decent person, so she would stay. There were days when she hated everything and everyone, but today she felt as though Pierce were living inside her. Today she could hate no one. So in answer to Olympia's question she said, "No, Olympia, I don't hate you."

"I'm glad. I don't think I'd like you to hate me. I'm glad Evan married you, Molly. He did well to marry an Irishwoman."

And it seemed to Molly as she left the room that everything had come full circle.

From her bedroom window Olympia watched Molly descend the outside stairs to the street. "We shouldn't wake him up," she whispered to the window. "He'll scream if he wakes up. He'll hurt if he wakes up." She left the window and in her nightgown and bare feet made her way downstairs. There was no one there that Sunday afternoon who saw her enter the library, and no one there who, minutes later, saw her leave again.

Molly had never skated in Ireland, but the young men and women who were cutting figure eights on the bumpy Penobscot ice held her fascinated. The temperature had risen steadily since the second week in March, so much so that she could see slush spraying outward from the skaters' blades. Clouds were thick overhead today and presaged rain—she could smell it in the air. But how thankful she was to be smelling something other than the sickness in the house! She had been breathing for twenty years and never appreciated fresh air so much as she did at this very minute.

The river was wide at this point. The ice skaters glided past her—two hand-holding girls book-ended by two boys who kept their hats low on their foreheads and their hands deep in their pockets. The quartet waved to Molly as they passed, and from where she stood on the banking, she waved back, wondering for the briefest of moments if Pierce had ever learned to skate. Maybe next year she would try her luck at skating. Maybe next year.... And she didn't dare complete the thought. Next year would undoubtedly take care of itself.

She felt a raindrop slap her nose and when she looked skyward, felt another one hit her eye. She supposed it was time to go back anyway. It had taken her nearly ten minutes to walk one way. Olympia would be wondering where she was. Drawing her hood farther over her forehead, she climbed the bank and headed across the flat. She was so preoccupied with keeping her footing in the snow that she didn't even see the man who stood in the road till she was practically upon him.

He stood with his shoulders humped around his ears to ward off the chill air. The collar of his wool jacket rose with his shoulders to hide half his head, and the blackness of the wool so blended with his hair that he might have been wearing a monk's cowl. He peered at her with those green eyes of his, touching places whose secrets he had shared. She felt something in her heart wrench.

"How's Evan?" Pierce asked hoarsely.

"He has good days. He has bad days. When the ice goes out, I plan to take him to New York. Dr. Bledsoe has been wonderful, but I think there might be other doctors better equipped to handle the question of what can be done about his face and hands. Do you remember how handsome he used to be?" She focused on the house on the hill. "Olympia can't even stand to be in the same room with him anymore. Your father once talked to me about the hurt you didn't need to see to know it was there. Olympia's like that now, Pierce. Evan's wounds are on the outside, but she's carrying hers on the inside where no one can see them. She wasn't at the manufactory the night of the accident, but she's hurt just as much as Evan. Maybe she's hurt even more than Evan."

"Looks to me like you could use some doctorin'

yourself." He reached out and tilted her chin up. Forest scents clung to his bare fingertips. "You should be taking better care've yourself. How much weight have you lost? Your face doesn't look any bigger than the side of my hand. Even your dimple is sunken in. You wouldn't have to be smilin' for Jeremiah Pearson Hardy to see it now." He parted the front of her cloak and held it wide. "Look how thin you are."

She saw his gaze shift from her waist to her bodice, and she burned with the intimacy. She placed her hand over his. "Someone might be watching."

"I wouldn't count on it. I've been here almost every day for a month and I've yet to see any noses pressed to your window glass."

She allowed her hand to linger on the back of his hand before she slipped the cloak from his grasp. She bowed her head as she straightened its fall. "You've been here every day?"

He leaned heavily on his crutch and looked as if he wished he hadn't said that. "Yah, well, Da got fed up with lookin' at me all day, and I got fed up with lookin' at him, so he's been visiting Conor and I've been coming up here. Does us both some good to get out. He gets his ears exercised and I get my good leg exercised. Don't wanna be a cripple by the time this contraption gets taken off."

But she had seen the steely muscles in his calf and thighs and knew that no amount of exercise would make those muscles any harder than they already were. "You could have come to the door, Pierce. I would have been grateful for the company."

He shook his head "I don't belong in that house.

Standin' here was enough. Made me feel a little closer to you anyway. Besides, what would your husband's friends say if they saw me payin' my respects to his wife?"

"They'd have to see you first. And since none of his friends have been by to see him, my guess is you would have been fairly safe. Throw a party and your friends arrive by the carriageload. Have an accident that renders you imperfect, and your friends seem to forget where you live. Poor Evan. He's lost his eyesight, his face, and his friends. What does he have left?"

"He has you," Pierce said in a quiet voice. "He doesn't deserve you, but he has you, and I envy him for it."

Through the mist of falling rain she saw the depressions on either side of his mouth begging to be kissed. Raindrops beaded his eyelashes and cried out to be caught on her fingertips. The hair on his forehead curled with humidity and pleaded to be twined around her finger. "Sometimes I want to run away," she admitted.

"But you haven't. Sounds to me like everyone else has, but you've stayed."

"Don't ascribe any great virtues to me, Pierce."

"Only the ones I know are there. Only the ones I've come to love."

She shook her head with her helplessness. "I'd worked it all out. How we could be together, how Evan could keep his secret. I was coming to see you that night. We could have been happy. All of us."

"That was before Thatcher's accident, sweetheart. Before he really needed you. You'd never run out on anyone who needed you."

"You're presuming to know a lot more about me than I know about myself, Pierce Blackledge."

"Maybe that's because I love you more than you love yourself."

Their eyes locked. He saw her blink away raindrops —or was it tears?

"It can never be," she whispered. "Not now. Not for a long time."

He wanted to press his lips to the back of her neck one last time. He wanted to loosen her hair needles and fill his hands with her hair one last time.

She saw him blink away raindrops—or was it tears?

"I know it can never be, sweetheart. I wouldn't ask that of you."

In the center of her brow four tiny creases appeared and it seemed to Pierce they would consume her whole face. He had to leave before that pathetic look of hers made him forget all his noble intentions. "I need to be getting back, Molly. Have to pack some things for the big trip to Boston to see that doctor." He took a step toward her. She moved out of the way for him. From his six foot three inches he looked down at her. "We're gonna catch the *Bangor* outta Boston on Thursday or Friday. When you decide to take Evan to New York, if you need any help, let me know. I'll have two healthy legs to walk on by then. I can probably maneuver him around a lot better than you'd be able to. What're you smilin' at?"

"That's the second time you've called him Evan. You always referred to him as Thatcher before. The weather must be thawing more than the ice."

Her observation seemed to surprise him. He grinned. "Yah, maybe it is."

"And thank you for the offer of your help. It means a lot to me."

"Like Da would say, family will help 'cause they have to. A friend will help 'cause he wants to. So if you want me, I'll be there for you." He gave her a secret look. "Guess that's the way it'll always be between Blackledges and Deacons." He gazed skyward. "Better get back to the house, Molly. Looks like the sky's gonna open up."

He should have left her then, but he couldn't. With moisture glazing his eyes he pulled her against him and kissed her mouth. His tears fell upon her face and mingled with her own, though he would have said it was rain that bathed his cheeks, that Bangor Tigers never cried. Their kiss was a kiss of parting, of longing, of unfulfilled promises, and when he broke the connection of their mouths, he held her to him for a trembling moment, remembering how well they fit together, how well they might have loved. "I'll always love you," he said on a whisper, and then he was hobbling away from her —leaving her as if forever.

The quiet was so pervasive when Molly entered the foyer that she stopped to listen. She'd grown accustomed to the backdrop of suffering that emanated from Evan's room. To have it silenced seemed unnatural, but the silence meant he was still sleeping, and for that she was thankful. Perhaps he'd sleep until she finished bathing Olympia, but as she started to climb the staircase, she remembered she had given the household help the afternoon off. There was no one to carry the hot water up from the kitchen.

As she neared the second-floor landing, she reminded herself that it hadn't been so very long ago that she'd been the one doing the toting. It wouldn't hurt her in the least this afternoon.

From the top of the stairs she started to turn right toward Olympia's room, but as she did so, she looked in the opposite direction and noticed a peculiarity that stopped her cold.

Evan's door was closed.

She'd left it open when she'd gone out. And there'd been no one in the house to close it. . . .

. . . except Olympia.

Molly would never remember running down the corridor or throwing Evan's door open. But she would never forget the sight of Olympia sitting on the edge of the bed, swaying gently as she crooned a song that Molly remembered from childhood. In her lap lay Evan's bandaged hand. She was stroking it as if it were a wounded paw. Something else gleamed in her lap.

"Olympia?"

The woman looked up as Molly crossed the floor to her. A thin smile touched her lips. "Molly. We didn't hear you come in. But we're glad you're here. We wanted to share our surprise with you. Didn't we, Evan?"

"Give me the gun, darling. Yes, that's a good girl."

"I couldn't let him hurt anymore. I couldn't let him cry because he didn't have a face. I loved him too much for that. You understand, don't you, Molly?"

Molly cradled her sister-in-law's head to her breast.

She smoothed her hand over the red-gold hair that was splattered with flecks of blood. "Yes, darling. I understand."

"He's sleeping now. We should be quiet so we don't wake him up."

"We'll be quiet," Molly soothed. "We'll be very quiet." From the tail of her eye she saw the glistening red stump of Evan's head and she closed her eyes against her tears. "Oh, Olympia, I don't think he'll ever wake up again."

"It's none of my business, missus, but if Dr. Bledsoe says those people will take good care of Miss Olympia, I'd believe him."

"But why Portland? It's so far away."

Mrs. Popham dragged a side chair back to its proper place by the parlor window and straightened the antimacassar. "It's not that far away. Come summer there'll probably be a steamer leaving every day for Portland. World's getting smaller all the time."

"Do you suppose by summertime she might recognize me?"

The housekeeper stopped her fussing to ponder Molly's back. The floor-to-ceiling window dwarfed the girl and made her look small as a sparrow. "She might. We can hope she will."

But Molly held little hope. When Dr. Bledsoe took Olympia away on Monday, she'd already withdrawn into an uncommunicative shell, answering no one's voice but Evan's. And her eyes. Molly had never seen such eyes. Constantly shifting. Constantly tormented.

"Anything else that needs straightening in here?" Mrs. Popham asked.

Molly turned away from the window. They'd rearranged the furniture in the parlor to accommodate Evan's coffin and the mourners who came to view it. That had been yesterday. It angered Molly that the people who couldn't spare the time to visit Evan when he was sick found so much time to shed a public tear over his coffin. She eyed the room. Except for the black crepe draped over the mantel, the room was back in order. "Everything looks fine, Mrs. Popham."

"Where do you want me to bring those gentlemen when they come this afternoon? Poor Mr. Evan not even cold in his grave and you're expected to open your doors to a parade of men who want to tell you what you should do with your money. Makes you wonder where their hearts are."

"Where would Evan meet them?"

"In his study."

"Then I'll meet them in the study." The sound of pelting rain drew Molly's attention back to the window. She looked up at the fat-bellied clouds that blackened the sky. "I wish we could have buried him in the sunshine. The rain is so cold. Look at it, Mrs. Popham. I don't think it's ever going to stop."

The housekeeper joined her at the window. "I've never seen the river in such a ruction either."

Far across the flat Molly could see where the fractured river ice had jammed against itself, forming a dam from bank to bank that looked fifteen feet high in some places.

"It's this thaw that's doin' it," Mrs. Popham continued. "The ice usually gives way without any fuss a'tall. Things are just happening too fast this year for the river to do what the Lord intended it to do. Nothing's followed any kind of order this year, has it, missus?"

"No it hasn't, Mrs. Popham."

"Poor Mr. Evan getting hurt like that. Then Miss Olympia. Makes a body think about setting things right with his Maker 'cause you just never know what's going to happen."

An uncomfortable warmth prickled Molly's neck. And as she regarded the wall of ice across the Penobscot, she heard an ominous rumble that set every windowpane in the house to rattling.

Mrs. Popham nodded. "That's the ice shifting. But it sounds more like the gates of hell rumblin' open, doesn't it?"

Molly snapped her head around. Her eyes looked frightened and filled her whole face. "Yes, I suppose it does." She stepped back from the window. "Mrs. Popham, would you ask Caleb to hitch up the carriage? I'd like to go out."

The housekeeper's face registered her horror. "But . . . you shouldn't leave the house for a month. It's not fittin'. Except on the Sabbath when you'd be goin' to services."

"Sometimes there are services other than on Sunday, Mrs. Popham. And I know for a fact that one city church has a special service each day from two to three. Now, would you tell Caleb?"

The woman left the room shaking her head. Molly Thatcher hadn't attended any church since moving into the mansion. She wondered now what kind of service the girl planned on attending in the middle of a Thursday afternoon.

The pews of St. Michael's Catholic Church were deserted when a figure in black bombazine walked down the aisle to the building's lone confession box. The woman parted the curtain of the confessional and knelt before the grated window that separated her from the priest. After a moment the curtain on the other side of the grating slid back and the woman saw a man's head cast in shadow. She hesitated as she stared at his profile. It seemed appropriate to her that the man she'd thought had ruined her life by entering the priesthood would be the same man who could help her place that life in order again. Molly took a deep breath and into the ear of Conor Blackledge began—

"Bless me, Father, for I have sinned. . . ."

Molly was seated at the desk in the library the next day when Mrs. Popham appeared at the door.

"There's a caller to see you, missus."

She looked up from the piles of legal documents before her. "I'm not receiving callers today, Mrs. Popham. Please have them leave a calling card. I'll get back to them as soon as I possibly can."

The housekeeper left, returning two minutes later. "He says he doesn't have a calling card, but would a chocolate cake do?"

Molly heard his voice in the hall as she stared at the cake basket in Mrs. Popham's hands.

"I told Da that a woman with a kitchen full of cooks doesn't need a cake, but he told me when there's a death in the family, it's only neighborly to bake something for the grieving relatives no matter how many cooks they have in the kitchen."

If she'd been blessed with wings, she would have flown to him. "You can set the cake on the desk, Mrs. Popham. I'll speak to Mr. Blackledge in here."

Pierce crossed the threshold as Mrs. Popham scurried to the desk. He wore his Sunday best today—his starched muslin shirt and his black jacket with the too-short sleeves. She decided he didn't belong in dress-up clothes. Some men were simply too manly for frock coats and ruffled shirts.

He closed the door after Mrs. Popham, and when he turned, he was holding his arms open for her. She ran into his embrace, and for her, it was a homecoming. He hugged her to him, his body tall and unwavering, his arms sure and steadfast. She felt the strength of him . . . and she never wanted to let go.

"I wanted you to come home," she said, flattening her hands against the muscles in his back. "I wanted you to be here."

"I'm sorry about what's happened, sweetheart. It's been a hard week for you. C'mon, let's sit down. I've done a lot've walking today on my new leg."

"Your leg. I haven't even asked you about your leg." She stepped back from him.

Pierce leaned over and tapped his shin with his knuckles. "It's whole again. I threw my crutches into Boston Harbor after I got the splints off. I wasn't too keen on that doctor, but he sure knew what he was doin'." He threw a long arm around Molly's shoulders and ushered her to the sofa, and when they were seated, he lifted his hand to her face and with his thumb stroked the high slope of her cheek. His voice touched her senses with its gentleness. "It's all over, Molly. No more misunderstandings. No more waiting. When do we announce our good news to Da?"

"Our wedding plans? Well, we should wait a proper amount of time, I mean with Evan and Olympia and everything."

He nodded, ever understanding, and she felt blessed. "Yah, I guess you're right. What do you need? A month?"

"A month!"

"Too long?"

"Long? Pierce, I'm in mourning. I can't marry you for at least a . . . a year, maybe two."

"A year! I can't wait a year. Jeesuz-God, with the way I feel, a month is even stretchin' it."

"Well, I don't like it either, but there's little we can do about it. I love you, Pierce, but if we're going to live in this city, we're going to have to follow its rules of etiquette."

"Etiquette, hell." He sprang to his feet, scooped her off the sofa, and tossed her over his shoulder. "*I'll* show you etiquette," and across the floor he went.

"Pierce! Put me down!"

Out the library door.

"I'm not waiting for anything else to come between us."

Down the hall.

"Where are you taking me?"

"The place where I should've taken you seven months ago."

Into the foyer. Across the floor. Past the servants.

He nodded pleasantly.

They gaped.

"You can't do this!"

"Watch me."

"We *have* to wait a year."

"The hell we do."

And out the door they went.

"We should have waited, Pierce. I'm in mourning."

"I hate you in black."

A pool of black bombazine spilled onto the floor.

"But what will people say?"

"That we love each other."

A froth of petticoat landed atop the bombazine.

She touched the scar on his collarbone with a finger-tip, with her mouth. "Will it always be like this?"

He cradled her head against his chest, bent her neck, smoothed his knuckles over the silken down that glazed her nape. "Always."

She found a warm place for her hand. He filled it with flesh gone hard.

He found a warm place for his mouth. She filled it with flesh gone soft.

"Tell me again how much you love me," she whispered.

"I won't tell you," he whispered back. "I'll show you."

And so they came together on that Friday afternoon, almost eleven months to the day from the time he had first landed in her buckboard on Exchange Street. They loved in joy, touched by memories of a first smile, a stolen kiss. They loved with emotion born from absence and loss. They loved as they thought no one had ever loved before, or ever would again, this man and woman, this husband and wife—this common wood butcher and his Irish bride.

Epilogue

July 8, 1847

To the citizenry of Bangor the Thatcher mansion would forever be called the Thatcher place, but to Duncan Blackledge, it had become the Blackledge place. Molly had added touches here and there, and Pierce had added a few of his own. But the grandest addition to the house was right here in his arms, Emily Elizabeth Blackledge. Age—one day old.

He rocked her in the Boston rocker he'd brought over from the house. Every nursery needed a Boston rocker, and a grandfather with a lap for sitting and arms for hugging. Emily was too small for Duncan's lap yet, but she was just the right size for his arms, so he rocked her as he'd once rocked Conor and Pierce, before they'd outgrown his arms to become men. He thought of Michael Deacon as he held the baby against him and on a whim, parted the afghan above her face so her other grandfather could see what she looked like—just in case he was watching.

"You're a beauty, you are," he crooned to the sleeping infant. He rocked, and thought, and after a while spoke again. "You might not know this, Emily, but last year my good friend Story Jones became a grandfather for the first time. Eayh, a rugged little grandson. Be kinda nice if we could arrange somethin' 'tween you two, wouldn't it? Always said there's nothin' can bind a friendship like a betrothal in the family."

He rocked, and thought, and smiled a secret smile. "Emily Jones. Has a nice ring, don't it?"

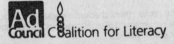